MW00533891

ASSASSIN OF REALITY

ALSO BY MARINA AND SERGEY DYACHENKO

Vita Nostra

Daughter from the Dark

ASSASSIN OF REALITY

A NOVEL

MARINA AND SERGEY DYACHENKO

Translated by Julia Meitov Hersey

HARPER Voyager
An Imprint of HarperCollins Publishers

This is a work of fiction. Names, characters, places, and incidents are products of the author's imagination or are used fictitiously and are not to be construed as real. Any resemblance to actual events, locales, organizations, or persons, living or dead, is entirely coincidental.

ASSASSIN OF REALITY. Copyright © 2023 by Sergey Dyachenko and Marina Shyrshova-Dyachenko. English translation copyright © 2023 by Julia Meitov Hersey. All rights reserved. Printed in the United States of America. No part of this book may be used or reproduced in any manner whatsoever without written permission except in the case of brief quotations embodied in critical articles and reviews. For information, address HarperCollins Publishers, 195 Broadway, New York, NY 10007.

HarperCollins books may be purchased for educational, business, or sales promotional use. For information, please email the Special Markets Department at SPsales@harpercollins.com.

Harper Voyager and design are trademarks of HarperCollins Publishers LLC.

FIRST EDITION

Library of Congress Cataloging-in-Publication Data has been applied for.

ISBN 978-0-06-322542-8

23 24 25 26 27 LBC 5 4 3 2 1

To my husband, Sergey Dyachenko,
and to our beloved daughter, Anastasia

CONTENTS

PROLOGUE

S omeday, my dear, you will be approached by a stranger. This stranger will bear no ill will toward you. He will assign you a task, ridiculous and rather unpleasant, and you will complete this task every single day. You will do that with no exceptions or excuses. Because if you miss even one day, something terrible will happen to your loved ones.

Your adviser really does not wish you ill. He will bring you to the Institute of Special Technologies, a place where only the dead get expelled. And you will become a model student, one who does not miss classes, who studies as diligently as she can—and sometimes even more diligently than that.

Eventually, the day of the final exam will arrive. You will enter a spacious hall to cease being human and become a Word of the Great Speech. You will long for this—this is your destiny.

You wanted desperately to become a Word. You studied hard, the top of your class. And yet . . .

CHAPTER ONE

Alexandra woke up a split second after her dark blue Škoda crossed the center line and drifted into the oncoming traffic. A local bus rushed straight at her, its lights blinding Alexandra. The bus howled, and the driver must have howled as well, but the mechanical roar drowned his stream of obscenities. Seeing nothing, obeying her instincts, Alexandra twisted the steering wheel to the right, then all the way to the left. Its brakes screaming, the car slid to the curb, then rolled down to the river, stopping dead a couple of feet from the concrete bridge support.

Alexandra somehow found the presence of mind to turn off the engine. She sat still for a while, listening to the creaks and groans of the car. All kinds of sirens yelled above in different voices; never before had Alexandra Koneva née Samokhina fallen asleep at the wheel.

She glanced at her watch: it was five in the morning. That meant she'd been with her husband for almost forty-eight hours, and these forty-eight hours were not spent in the throes of passion. They began like two responsible adults well aware of the value of a fair agreement. However, the longer they'd conversed, the quicker the diplomatic veneer had disappeared, melting like a layer of gold leaf—and fake gold leaf at that. First, they lost their poise, then their ostentatious benevolence.

At some point they went to different rooms to cool off and compose themselves. At the start of the second round, however, they almost immediately slipped back into a low-class, shrill, revolting squabble.

Their marriage had been doomed for quite some time. Alexandra had hoped for a civilized divorce, but even that was no longer possible. She'd given fifteen years of her life to a worthless, empty, vicious, and vindictive man, and now it was ending, abrupt and dirty.

Not bothering to wait for sunrise, she'd started the car and drove toward the city. The road calmed her down, pacified her, and gave her a strange sense of hope. After all, she wasn't even thirty-five yet, and her life was far from over. Finally relaxed after the terrible couple of days, she'd fallen asleep instantly, gripping the steering wheel and staring at the road markings as if at a hypnotist's pendulum.

Until a local bus had rushed straight at her.

"Sasha, honey, what happened? Why did you come in a cab?"

Mom stood in the doorway, a robe over her nightgown, the habitual anxious expression on her face. She worried about every little thing, and so Alexandra never told her the truth.

"I stalled on the highway and had to call emergency services. They towed my car to the mechanic. Don't worry, it's some minor issue. Go back to bed."

"How's Ivan?" Mom asked, a bit calmer now.

"Ivan says hello. He's fine. He'll take care of the cottage's new boiler."

Alexandra went into her room. By a previous agreement, her thirteen-year-old daughter, Anya, was sleeping over at a friend's house. Anya loved sleepovers; she felt cramped in their old two-room apartment, under the watchful eye of her grumpy grandmother and permanently aloof mother.

Alexandra didn't blame her.

She sat down at her desk, hung her head, and tried to compose her thoughts. Death had flown by, granting her a short panic attack that meant she hadn't had to think about much of anything, followed by forty minutes of euphoria, and now a wave of depression. She glanced at the digital photo frame on her desk, the kind that was fashionable many years ago. The frame shuffled through a handful of sentimental old photos: a young Sasha with her mom at the seaside. Sasha's high school graduation. Sasha's first assembly at the university. Sasha's wedding to Ivan Konev. Sasha holding a swaddled newborn on the hospital steps. Mom with baby Anya in her arms. And again: a young Sasha with her mom at the seaside.

The slideshow stopped. The last photo froze in the frame. Sasha and her mom, tanned and joyful, posed at the edge of the surf. The sun lit up the sea, and the red metal buoy glowed in the distance, warning the swimmers not to go beyond it . . .

Alexandra sensed someone's presence behind her back. She realized she couldn't move.

"Mom, is that you?"

There was no answer, but she knew it wasn't her mother, and it wasn't Anya. It certainly wasn't Ivan, changing his mind and coming back from the dacha. It was something different, something simple and unimaginable, like a bad dream that makes one want to hide under the blanket.

"Who is it?" she asked.

"It's me," a soft voice said behind her.

Alexandra looked back. A few steps away, in the middle of her room, stood a girl of about twenty, dressed in jeans and a light jacket, backpack straps on her shoulders. Her hair was pulled back in a ponytail, and her enormous eyes were full of terror, as if she were facing a serial killer armed with a circular saw.

Alexandra jumped up. For a few long seconds she couldn't figure out who the visitor reminded her of, and then she shuddered in comprehension of the voice's words and the uncanny valley effect of the intruder's face. The girl looked exactly like Alexandra Samokhina in her fourth year of college, and yet she didn't resemble her at all, and it was utterly incomprehensible. A sudden arrival of a young relative would be shocking and unexpected, but it wasn't insane—such things did happen every now and then, one could certainly cope with something like that.

A sudden arrival of a doppelgänger from one's own past, however—especially a strange, distorted doppelgänger—was a different matter.

Some nightmares make do without monsters and wildfires. It is when they are at their most mundane that they drive humans mad.

"Who are you!" Alexandra screamed.

The girl blinked and took a step forward, her face growing paler by the second. Alexandra shrank away from her, bumping into the corner of her desk. The girl stretched her dry lips in an apologetic smile and touched Alexandra's shoulder . . .

The world spun around.

The girl's touch became a point of entrance into a different reality, like a breach in a spaceship that lets the cosmos in. As if two cans of fresh paint had been spilled, and one spot flowed into another, swallowing it whole. The girl stepped into Alexandra's consciousness into her memory, into her existence.

Protecting her mind, Alexandra shouted:

"I want it to be a dream!"

She woke up a split second after her dark blue Škoda crossed the center line and drifted into the oncoming traffic. A local bus rushed straight at her, its lights blinding Alexandra.

CHAPTER TWO

T raffic stopped on the suburban highway. Police lights flashed and sirens howled. The bus driver had suffered minor injuries, but the dark blue Škoda had been squashed into a pancake. "Looks like she fell asleep at the wheel," the EMT said distinctly. From a distance, Sasha was able to read his lips.

Alexandra Samokhina, the woman who died on the highway today, never matriculated at the Institute of Special Technologies. She lived a life of her own, never having heard of the Great Speech, never recognizing herself as a verb in the imperative mood. Sasha stood by the side of the road, wondering if she should envy this woman or pity her.

Yesterday, January 13, a student of the Institute of Special Technologies set off to take the most important exam of her life and pass it in order to become a Word and finally *reverberate*. Instead of passing the exam, though, she now stood by the side of the road, shaking in the piercing wind, convinced for some reason that today was September 1, the official first day of school.

But of which year?

Catching a few suspicious glances directed at her, Sasha checked her reflection in a random car's side mirror: she looked perfectly ordinary, no scales or feathers, only a shocked expression on her face. But everyone at the scene looked shaken up. When accidents happen, like this one on the highway, it's hard not to consider one's own mortality. So, nothing to elicit stares or sideways glares. Still, she felt them.

The ambulance carried the bus driver away. The body covered by a piece of tarp lay by the side of the road. Grim-looking cops stood nearby, smoking. A tow truck picked up the remains of Alexandra's car. Sasha wanted to get closer but knew she could never do that: she was terrified of this woman, dead or alive.

Or, rather, not of the woman herself but of the *idea* of her—the concept of that body, the same body she also seemed to own. Which one of them was the other's projection? Were they both projections of the same being? They weren't exact duplicates, that was for sure.

The dead Alexandra had never met Farit Kozhennikov.

Sasha looked around, studying the faces of strangers, searching for a man in opaque black glasses. Onlookers climbed out of the cars stuck in the traffic jam. Someone was filming the scene with his phone; one of the bus passengers was wiping the blood off his scratched-up face. No one wore sunglasses on this cloudy early morning. *Perhaps we are the same,* she thought. *Perhaps Farit Kozhennikov never existed in this world.*

Sasha recalled the raw terror on the face of Alexandra Samokhina when she saw her doppelgänger. She felt a twinge of it herself. Because what she had just thought was a fantasy, not the nightmare she was used to. No, Farit Kozhennikov could not be canceled. He was in every shard of any text, in any draft, any sketch, any grammatical construction. "It's impossible to live in the world where you exist," Sasha said to him once. "It is impossible to live in a world where I do not exist," he replied. "Although it's hard to resign oneself to my existence, I realize that."

Back on January 13, something went wrong during the exam. That meant Sasha was being punished, and what had just happened to Alexandra Samokhina was a part of that punishment, and not even the most terrifying part. There would be something else, and that something else was getting closer by the second; in a minute or two Sasha would wake up in front of her apartment entrance, in front of her childhood bedroom door, so familiar to the minute detail, and she'd know that something had—imperceptibly and irretrievably, but wholly tangibly—changed. She would walk into the room and see Alexandra, see herself as she would be without the institute. She'd *claim* this woman and see her entire life, and the other Alexandra would desperately wish to wake up, and she'd drive into the oncoming traffic, and the howling and the screeching would commence, and everything would repeat . . .

Sasha pressed the tips of her fingers to her temples, trying to push the anxiety back in. Something slipped through the muddy stream of her panicky thoughts: a sound idea, perhaps even a solution, some help, an exit.

At the Institute of Special Technologies, Sasha was an exemplary student. She knew not only how to *claim* people and objects, but also how to unlink time loops. She searched her mind and realized she hadn't forgotten that. Which meant that all she had to do to break out of the nightmarish circle was to restructure the probabilities for Alexandra to survive.

Piece of cake, she thought wryly.

The instant rush of hope gave Sasha heart palpitations and moist palms. She walked away from the scene of the accident and placed her backpack on the wet grass. Ignoring the inevitability of stains on her pants, she kneeled down and rummaged inside. Notebooks. Philosophy notes, an English textbook. A desiccated bread roll in a plastic baggie—how old was this bread roll, where did it even come from? A wallet in an inside pocket, empty aside from a few coins and cafeteria tokens. A scratch pad with just a few lines. A pencil case.

It was enough. To manage the flow of time, Sasha only needed pencils and paper, along with all the impossible-for-regular-humans skills she'd been taught at the institute.

Another service vehicle squeezed by the stopped cars and idle onlookers; it came for the body. Shaking, Sasha stared at the sheet of paper in front of her, trying to concentrate.

She used to know how to do it—just a second ago, she was certain she could do it. But now she doesn't. There was no way out of this nightmare, then, and there was no way to change the course of events. Sasha was locked in the *Untime*. Everything would repeat over and over again: the terror of meeting a double. The reflection of the woman's fear. The noise and howling of the accident. And again. And again.

"I want it to be a dream," Sasha whispered.

Nothing happened.

The traffic jam refused to disperse, even though the damaged bus was already pushed to the side of the road and the police car was gone. Another half an hour, and the memory of the accident would remain only in the Internet news feed, and even that would be gone by noon—except for Sasha noon would never arrive, so this would always be part of reality.

"Sasha."

She twitched as if under a blow and immediately felt numb, realizing that her own personal version of hell included a meeting with Farit Kozhennikov.

"Let's go," Farit said, his voice calm and unassuming.

Where was she supposed to go? What did he want from her now?

"They told me I was going to ace the exam," Sasha whispered, refusing to look at Farit. "They told me I was the best student they had, and that I would definitely pass. They—"

She burst into tears, then forced herself to get up. She didn't want to kneel in front of him.

Winter, a long time ago. Third years of Group A sat at their desks. A cold draft blew from the window, and the radiators were so hot the air above them shimmered.

"Today is December thirteenth," their professor Nikolay Valerievich Sterkh said. "That means that exactly one month remains until the placement examination. This month will require all your strength. Unfortunately, there is no makeup date for this exam: you have exactly one chance."

Farit led Sasha to his black SUV and opened the passenger door. Through a thick mental fog, she recalled his previous car, a milky white Nissan. Whatever he was driving, Sasha always hated getting into her advisor's car.

"Today I will tell you in detail what it is like to take the placement examination," Sterkh told them. "It will help you to keep it together and be prepared for the challenge at the defining moment. On January thirteenth, at noon sharp, both groups, A and B, will enter the large assembly hall and take their seats. You will be introduced to the examination committee. You will not be nervous, will not feel anxious."

Sasha huddled on the passenger seat, trying not to think of how this ride would turn out for her. The recurring nightmare of her dying doppelgänger no longer seemed all that terrible; Sasha suspected she might desperately miss all that looped insanity.

The black SUV slid into the break-down lane to avoid the traffic jam.

"You will have three assignments," Sterkh said back in the faraway past. "The first two are standard; the third one is individual, selected for each one of you according to your future specialization. In the process of completing this assignment you will cease being a human and commence as Word; for the first time you will *reverberate*, my dears, and this should be very dear to you."

They were approaching an exit leading to a toll road. The black SUV slipped through the toll gates and sped up along the highway, smooth as butter. Yesterday was January 13; today felt like the very beginning of autumn. Even her thoughts were starting to loop.

What happened during the exam? Sasha gnawed on her lips, trying to remember the details: the assembly hall, her classmates, her professors, old wooden stairs, rows of desks. She recalled getting the assignment, sitting down at one of the desks . . .

The rest was darkness.

"No, you are not going to remember what happened then," Farit Kozhennikov finally broke the silence. "Don't even bother. You can just accept the fact that the final exam *did* happen."

"My classmates." Sasha swallowed, but the lump in her throat remained. "Did they pass?"

"Some passed, some didn't." Farit got into the far-left lane. "The usual."

"What about Kostya?"

His expression did not alter much—only the corners of his lips went up a bit. *Kostya passed, otherwise, Farit wouldn't be smirking like that,* Sasha thought. Or did he? Why couldn't Farit just answer her question and just tell her "He passed," or "He got an F."

"Remind me, what did they tell you would happen if you failed the exam?" he asked conversationally, and all thoughts of Kostya flew out of her head.

Existence that is worse than death: that's what she'd been promised, that's what they said would happen to everyone who failed the exam. That's how the faculty motivated the students.

"Yet your meeting with Alexandra and her death are not what they threatened you with," Farit said. "It's not the standard form of reckoning for failure; in fact, it's not punishment at all."

Sprawled in the driver's seat, he barely touched the steering wheel as the car flew down the highway. Trees and clouds, the sky and the road, all merged in motion, reflected in his dark glasses. Sasha tried to comprehend his words. Did that mean the reckoning was still coming?

"No," Farit said. "You need not worry—I bought you out, Sasha."

The speed made the road appear out of focus; trees and buildings flew backward as if carried away by a hurricane.

Despite—or maybe because of—his words, her worry was immense.

"Let me explain this to you in simple terms," Farit continued after a pause. "To be honest, it was much more complex, but you'll never understand otherwise. I say I bought you out, but what I mean is I changed your fate. If you think a little harder, you will figure out what I did and how I did it."

Sasha opened her mouth to say she had no mechanism to think with at the moment, just like a dead toad on the side of the road had no mechanism to fly. But that wasn't true. Because a second later she recalled the day before the final exam. Her old notes, papers, drafts smoldered in the fireplace. Farit rang the doorbell, and for the first time in her life his appearance did not scare her. She was calm, cool, and collected; she was preparing for the exam, she believed in herself, and she wanted to win.

Back then, Farit had said, "As your advisor, I am officially offering to release you from the placement exam. To release you from your tenure at the institute. Officially. Once again you will be sixteen years old. Everything that happened later would turn out to be a dream and shall be forgotten."

Any of her classmates would have given their right hand for such a chance.

"Think about it. 'It was a dream.' Say it—and you will wake up," Farit had said to her. "Back on a cot in the rented room, next to your mother, in a town by the sea. And nothing will repeat again and again. There will be no me. There will be no institute. You will be accepted at the School of Philology—if you don't fail the entrance exams." Without waiting he continued, "Well, have you decided?"

It was the most frightening temptation of her life. Her advisor took off his glasses, something he'd only done on very few special occasions, but she had trouble seeing his face through her tears.

Sobbing, she'd said, "I have decided. I want to finish the institute. Become a part of Speech. To *reverberate*. That's why tomorrow I am going to take the placement exam."

His eyes looked as if they were lit up from the inside. Sasha recoiled.

"Is that your final word?"

She shut her eyes.

"Yes."

Now the black SUV flew down the highway, leaving the scenery behind and in the past. The speed limit was quite high, but Farit was still going above it.

"Do you remember now?" Farit asked benevolently, as if in appreciation of Sasha's excellent memory.

"But . . ." A weird sensation of splitting in half and getting stuck between that winter day and this late summer one made her feel disoriented. "Back then . . . I refused your offer."

"And *she* agreed," he said slowly. "And very enthusiastically."

A fork, Sasha thought. He caught me in a fork. I chose the final exam . . . but the other me, the one who took his offer, woke up on a cot in a rented room in a town by the sea, and she was sixteen again. There was no Farit in her life. No gold coins. No Institute of Special Technologies. That girl had a nightmare, but promptly forgot all about it. She enrolled in the university of her choice. Married Ivan Konev. And then . . . and then she fell asleep at the wheel and drove into the oncoming lane.

"You made a backup copy," Sasha whispered. "Another projection of me."

"Awkwardly phrased but essentially accurate," he said with a faint smirk.

"And you killed her because I failed the exam?"

"She was killed by Newton's Second Law," he said ruefully. "The acceleration of an object as produced by a net force is directly proportional to the magnitude of the net force, in the same direction as the net force, and inversely proportional to the mass of the object."

"That's not what I meant!"

"You should always say what you mean."

This? Coming from *him*? Through gritted teeth she said, "But it was me who failed the exam! Yet she was the one who crashed into the bus!"

"Exactly. Because that woman existed only to crash into the bus," Kozhennikov said.

Sasha felt a layer of frost form on her back under her thin sweater.

"Her entire life was tied to the moment of her death, that lynchpin of the great design," Kozhennikov continued ruthlessly. "Her life was worthless, it was dull and empty, but her death . . ."

Sasha felt offended, as if someone close to her was being humiliated.

"It was a perfectly normal life!" Sasha said. "She fought to save her family . . . She didn't hurt or offend anyone. Even driving into the oncoming lane, she didn't kill anyone! Why do you speak of her like that?"

"You're right, I am biased toward her," he said after a pause, surprising Sasha to no end. "You see, she chickened out. She retreated. And then she got what she deserved. Overall, you have to agree she didn't fare too badly. It was very quick, and she didn't even have time to get scared."

"What about—me?" Sasha's voice broke mid-sentence.

He seemed genuinely confused. "What about you?"

"What do I deserve?" she said thickly. "What will happen to me?"

"You will be fine," he said lightly, but with a hint of subtext. "As long as you demonstrate enough discipline."

He'd already said that to her a few times before, during the moments of unbearable horror and grievous lamentation, always in answer to her question: Why me? What have I done to deserve this? So very cold now, Sasha made herself even smaller, trying to disappear in the depths of the massive seat.

Keeping his eyes on the road, Kozhennikov turned on the heat.

"You will have to return to the institute and correct your mistakes. I'll tell you right now that it'll be more painful than starting from scratch. Fourth year is going to be quite difficult."

He held on to the steering wheel with the tips of two fingers. Sasha had a fleeting thought, obscene yet tempting: What if she jerked the wheel all the way to the side; would Farit manage to stop her?

Would it even kill him?

"So childish, seriously," Farit murmured with reproach. "Like the first year again, temper tantrums, fantasies . . . come on."

He switched on the windshield wipers to get rid of dead gnats.

"I am nothing but a bug smashed on glass," Sasha said without thinking. "The acceleration of an object as produced by a net force is directly proportional to the magnitude of the net force—"

"Stop." He turned his head for a second. "You know perfectly well that I never ask for the impossible. It's hard, yes. But always doable. This will be no different in that regard. I rescued you from a much darker fate. And believe me, it wasn't easy."

Sasha squeezed the backpack in her lap so hard a few pencils in the inner pocket cracked.

"But why?"

"I find you fascinating."

He didn't seem to be joking. "Once again, you defied your teacher's expectations. I am curious to see what else you are capable of. And what you will accomplish. Perhaps nothing whatsoever, and then it will have been a waste playing marbles with time, space, and distorted reality."

"Marbles." Sasha heard her own voice, heavy, dull, and old. "Marbles, you call us. What about Valentin?"

"Valentin who?" Farit asked with accentuated surprise.

"My mother's husband." Sasha knew the truth from his voice, but didn't want to believe it. "The father of her baby, the little boy who was born during my second year . . ."

"Valentin, his spontaneous relationship with your mother, and their baby were only necessary to ensure that you could go to Torpa without any obstacles," Kozhennikov said. "Alexandra never enrolled in the institute, hence her mother never met Valentin, their son does not exist, and never has."

"What do you mean, he doesn't exist?" Sasha said dully. "What do you mean, he never existed?"

"He was never born in the first place," Kozhennikov said gently. "Instead, there is another child, the daughter of Alexandra Samokhina and Ivan Konev."

" 'Instead?' "

"There is also Alexandra Samokhina's mother, who never remarried," he continued patiently. "She doesn't trust men and is not interested in a relationship. You of all people should know that only ideas are absolute, while projections—projections end up differently, like shadows on cave walls."

For a few minutes Sasha said nothing, organizing fragments of the broken and reassembled reality in her head. Did she love her brother, that boy who had been the product of Valentin and her mother? Was she really attached to him? Was it worth mourning him, considering he did not die? He was never born, never conceived. And yet Sasha remembered his smell, his tiny snowsuit, his smile . . .

Sasha felt a tremendous wave of pity for her mother. No love, no marriage, no new family. Sasha felt ashamed of how jealous she was when Mom first started seeing Valentin, and how she considered her mother a traitor. And now her mother was a completely different person, with a different experience, almost certainly about to be crushed by the sudden loss of her only daughter.

"It's cannibalism," she said out loud.

"You don't say," Farit replied. "But look at it from another angle: the fallen Alexandra's daughter is nearly grown and will surely provide much-needed comfort to her grandmother. I can certainly go down the cannibalism route, but you haven't yet given me any reasons."

The engine was so quiet that it seemed as if the car stayed in place while the road rushed under its tires. Sasha did not remember roads like this one. She didn't remember cars like this either, or road signs like the ones they were passing; she spent many long years in the *Untime,* and now like a fly out of amber, she was hurled into a world that had changed significantly—and yet somehow remained tangibly the same. She didn't know what she was supposed to do with this knowledge.

Sasha took stock of herself and realized she was shocked but not crushed. Her time at the Torpa institute had left its mark—she accepted anything, even the falling sky, as yet another lesson.

"I want to see them," she said, annoyed by the pleading notes in her voice. "She's still my mom, isn't she? Even if she's gotten older? And the girl . . . she's *my* daughter, isn't she? My biological daughter?"

"Do you really think they'd be happy to see you?"

Sasha swallowed, recalling the expression of horror on Alexandra Koneva's face. She, Sasha, would be but a walking nightmare for both her aging mother and her unknown daughter.

"And what do you mean, 'biological'?" Farit spoke in the voice of a kind but weary mentor. "Are you a monkey? Perhaps genetics might appear similar, but you are an informational object, Sasha. Grammatically, these people have nothing to do with you."

"There is one thing I don't understand, then," Sasha whispered. "Who are you going to kill if I don't study hard enough?"

"You've gotten cheeky," Farit muttered, but then grinned.

The smile made Sasha's face go numb.

...

At the airport bathroom, Sasha stared into the mirror, studying her face and comparing it to the face of the fallen Alexandra Koneva. What had that other girl been thinking, getting hitched so young, and to Ivan Konev of all people? She must have been the envy of all the girls in her class—a strange thing for her to consider at this moment.

"Your flight is in an hour and a half," Farit Kozhennikov had said when he escorted her through the airport doors. "You will have to run very fast. Don't be late."

She had hurried. She ran, but the mirrors called for her, grabbed her, and glued her to their smooth surface like a gob of chewing gum. Sasha stopped at anything reflective to study her own face, trying to get reacquainted, to build a bridge between *herself-then* and *herself-now*. Eventually, though, she had no choice: only a few minutes remained until her flight. She ran again.

The problem was the mirrors showed a different reflection every time: a pale and sickly wretch in one mirror; a rosy-cheeked, confident twenty-year-old woman in the next. Back then, her professors told her that after the final exam, she would cease to be human. Sasha longed for that moment of liberation: everything human that was still left in her by the third year held her back, like a kettlebell tied to her ankle. Now she knew that failing the exam pushed her back into human form, and it was just as hard to comprehend as if a pile of minced beef flowed back into the grinder and emerged as a whole solid hunk of meat.

She passed a pay phone and slowed her steps. She could almost see herself picking up the receiver and punching in the number that hadn't changed since she was little—at least, she assumed that was true for the other Alexandra. She could taste the shock and sorrow on the line. What would she say? *Mom, it's me. Yes, the accident did happen. No, I am not lying. It's really me, don't you recognize my voice?*

Absolutely not. Not now. Later Sasha would think of something.

"My number hasn't changed," Kozhennikov had told her. "You can call if necessary. But try not to get into a disciplinary situation. Work *with* your teachers."

He'd made it sound like she had a choice.

She heard the final boarding call for the flight to Torpa.

17

. . .

Once on board the aircraft, Sasha truly lost all sense of reality.

She'd always traveled to Torpa by a train that had a one- or two-minute stop at the tiny station, always at four in the morning. And prior to this, Sasha had taken many railroad trips with her mother, and she loved those—until she met Farit Kozhennikov. Mom hated planes, and so Sasha had flown only a handful of times. Mom's anxiety always affected Sasha, and both used to listen to the sound of the engine, expecting malfunction, and watch the faces of the flight attendants for signs of worry or even panic behind their professionally welcoming guises. Any mild turbulence sent Mom into a panic attack; every time she swore she'd never again purchase a single plane ticket.

Sasha—through sympathy or empathy—had done the same.

But now, for the first time in her life, Sasha was flying alone, and for the first time she was not afraid. Farit sending her on this flight meant the plane would land safely anywhere, from Mars to the dark side of the moon. Anything Sasha had already been through and anything that still awaited her in the future made any degree of turbulence seem like child's play.

She watched the ground below, wondering if the patches of fields and curlicues of rivers had been drawn on the inner surface of her eyes. Winter, summer, Mom, people who disappeared without a trace and people who came out of nowhere; Sasha willed her thoughts into a circle like herding a flock of sheep into a corral and made herself think of what she could see, hear, and touch. The smell of the aircraft cabin, not terrible but not particularly pleasant. The light from the round window, and the outline of the wing stamped with the airline logo. A comfortable seat, a sip of tangy apple juice, a touch of plastic straw on her tongue.

"Dear passengers," the flight attendant spoke up. "The captain just activated the seatbelt sign. This means we are about to encounter some rough air. Please stay in your seats and fasten your seatbelts. Excuse me, sir, where are you going?"

A thickset man in a plaid shirt rose from his seat, reaching for the luggage compartment above his head.

"Take your seats! Fasten your seatbelts!" the flight attendant demanded, and the man mumbled something about there being no goddamn reason to shout.

Sasha was watching their squabble when the plane jolted with such force that the juice box, by then thankfully empty, flew out of Sasha's hand and landed under a different seat. The plane shook again. Preventing the suitcases from tumbling down, the man in the plaid shirt stood like Titan holding up the falling sky. The flight attendant pushed the hapless hero back into his seat and hung on to the overhead bin, trying to close it shut.

The aircraft shook like a child's toy.

A middle-aged woman across the aisle from Sasha began to pray. Her neighbor, a man in a suit and tie, squealed in fear, asking her to shut up in rather colorful language. A baby cried somewhere in the front row. A few seconds later everyone was praying, except for the screaming baby, the flight attendant struggling with the luggage compartment, and Sasha, for whom everything that was happening seemed no more than the play of light and shadow on the membrane of a soap bubble.

Then the bubble burst.

Sasha felt the weight of her body, the precipice under her seat—kilometers' worth of emptiness. And full fuel tanks right there, built into the wings. It all mattered and none of it mattered at all. Primary in her thoughts was the question of where Farit Kozhennikov was sending her, to which branch of Torpa, for her error correction assignment.

For the first time since she'd boarded, she shivered with terror, a wave of nausea leaving a metallic taste in her mouth. The flight attendant was crawling along the aisle on all fours, and the baby was choking on her own scream . . .

"Dear passengers," a voice came over the speakers, "this is your captain, Yaroslav Grigoriev, speaking. We are encountering turbulence. It is perfectly normal, it's safe, and will be over very soon. Please stay in your seats with your seatbelts fastened and remain calm."

The voice was even, deep, a tiny bit irritated, but its parental notes reached into the subconscious of each passenger. *Calm down. Enough of your temper tantrum. Stop acting like a child.*

The crying baby was the first one to hear the command in the mundane words and stopped fussing as if switched off. As red as a boiled lobster, the flight attendant made it to her seat and buckled up. One by one, the passengers fell silent; someone even cracked a joke, and someone else chuckled nervously. The aircraft tilted one more time, and then continued to glide as if along a smooth highway, the most reliable solid ground. Pleased with the good news and embarrassed by their childish fear, passengers were now pretending nothing had ever happened, and only the flight attendant kept rubbing her knee and giving the plaid-shirted man an evil look as he got up to root through his bag once again.

Sasha wanted the plane to land as quickly as possible and she also wanted the flight to go on forever; her desires intertwined in her heart and in her gut, and Sasha perceived them as hunger and thirst. Finally, the seatbelt sign went on again, and the same voice said calmly, "In a few minutes, the aircraft will be landing in Torpa airport."

True to the captain's word, the aircraft landed as softly as if the runway were lined with pillows. The passengers applauded with relief—all but Sasha, already on to her next thought. The reality clicked and switched on again, like the next slide of a vintage film strip. She was back in Torpa and today was September 1, the first day of classes. If the first block was Specialty, an unexcused absence was guaranteed.

The airport was only slightly bigger than a newspaper kiosk. There was a new sign, TORPA, and another one, straight across from it, that read, APROT. Torpa had never before had an airport, and Sasha was still unsure why one was even necessary in a tiny town lost on a map.

Yet the plane had been full, and Sasha followed the throng of passengers like a wood chip following the current.

"Taxi!" a man in an old-fashioned denim jacket called out. "Miss! A taxi!"

He correctly gauged the lost expression on Sasha's face, her anxious eyes, and the backpack clutched to her chest, and gestured toward an ancient bright-lemon-yellow car:

"Welcome to Torpa!"

"How much?"

He named the price; Sasha blinked. Farit Kozhennikov had given her an envelope stuffed with cash, an advance on her stipend, and this money was just enough for the ride. Sasha had no idea of the current prices, but all she needed to do at this point was to get to the institute as soon as possible.

Grinning, the taxi driver ushered her in. Sasha sat on a worn-out leather seat, drowning in the aroma of stale tobacco and a pine-tree air freshener. A second before the car door slammed shut, it was intercepted by another hand.

"Hold on a moment."

Sasha flinched and turned her head. A young man, dressed in a pilot's white shirt with black epaulets but no cap, stood next to the driver. His expression was full of bile, and Sasha felt fear again: someone who looked that angry could pull her out of the car by her hair, accuse her of something, and call the police . . .

"Exactly how much are you asking her for, Uncle Boris?" the pilot asked softly.

The cab driver mumbled something unintelligible.

"I am in a rush," Sasha said to the pilot, as if she owed him an explanation.

"He's robbing you," the pilot said curtly. "He's literally stealing from you. Come out, I will take you for free, I have to go into town anyway."

"Why don't you fly the hell back." The driver spat on the ground.

"Come on." The pilot kept looking at Sasha, ignoring the driver. "Where do you need to go, the institute?"

He drove a silver Mazda; his pilot's cap and a wheeled suitcase lay on the back seat.

"I guess I was on your flight," Sasha said.

"There are only two flights a week, to Torpa in the morning, back that same night. To be honest, it's a pretty dumb schedule, but I have a vested interest—my father lives here. I keep my car here in long-term parking. My father doesn't drive anyway, he's nearly blind."

"So you're leaving tonight," Sasha said.

"I am." He merged onto the highway. "I apologize for sticking my nose into someone else's business, but I hate obnoxious jerks like that. And to think of it, I've known this cabdriver since I was a little kid; he used to be a decent guy. Oh well."

"Turbulence," Sasha said softly.

"It's life," he said serenely. "It's unpleasant. But what can you do?"

"I meant today's flight."

"Oh, that." He smiled easily. "The most dangerous thing about turbulence is unsecured suitcases. It's not exactly like flying through a storm front."

Sasha would have happily listened to his voice forever, but he switched to the left lane and fell silent.

Of course he knew she was in a hurry.

"Is your name Yaroslav?" she asked, determined to make him speak again.

"Yes." He wasn't exactly chatty.

"I am Alexandra."

He nodded, as if taking her name into account. New buildings, brightly colored and nearly identical, flew by, showing off their sparkling windows and vast vertical rows of balconies.

"Torpa has changed quite a bit in the last fifteen years," Sasha said.

"Have you lived here before?" He seemed surprised. "I assume you were a child here since you remember it from so long ago."

"I've heard about it," Sasha blurted out awkwardly, then rushed to change the subject. "How did you know I needed to go to the institute?"

"You flew in on September first, you seem to be running late, and also, only students come to Torpa with this lost look in their eyes."

"The power of deduction," Sasha said, smiling bitterly.

"Did I offend you?" He glanced at her face.

"Of course not," she said, surprised at the very possibility. "How often do students end up on your flights?"

"Not often, but it happens."

The residential area finally ended, and the car drove into the historical center. Brick buildings and balustrades, weather vanes and tile roofs hadn't changed. For a second Sasha thought she was back in the past, that the final exam hadn't yet happened, and wouldn't happen for eternity . . .

The digits on the dashboard flowed mercilessly one into another; it was almost eleven.

Reality jumped again: the car drove along Sacco and Vanzetti Street, and the linden trees were still green. It was as if yesterday she and Kostya, the first years, dragged their suitcases along the same street. It *felt* like yesterday.

And there it was, the familiar facade. The plaque on the door was the same:

MINISTRY OF EDUCATION. INSTITUTE OF SPECIAL TECHNOLOGIES

Sasha realized she couldn't get out of the car: her legs felt numb.

"Are you sure you don't need any help?" Yaroslav asked softly. "It's a new town for you, after all."

"Torpa is like my motherland," Sasha admitted. "I'm sorry. I—"

At that moment, a bell rang behind the tall door of the institute, quite faint but so familiar it sent a chill down her spine. Sasha forgot what she was going to say. Her legs carried her out of the car.

"I am sorry—I am late. Thank you for all your help. I'm going to go now."

"Good luck," he said to her back, his voice soft and very much resigned. For a second, Sasha looked back and saw his eyes. They were bright green. Sasha slowed down her step; she wanted to respond. She wanted to say something nice. After all, he'd helped her, this pilot, both in the sky and on the ground.

But the bell kept ringing, and Sasha still didn't know her schedule. Only that she was already late.

Since the day Sasha entered the assembly hall for the last time, fourteen and a half years had passed in this provincial university. She now knew why the first and second years never ran into those students who had taken the final exam. A wall of time separated them, a wall even a newly formed Word couldn't break.

Fourteen and a half years for the entire world. Several months for her classmates. Less than a day for Sasha.

There was some familiarity. The equestrian statue still rose up in the middle of the vestibule, the horseman's head disappearing far above in the semidarkness of the upper floors. But the concierge booth had been fitted with a glass wall and now resembled an empty terrarium. And an electronic display replaced the scheduling board. The vestibule, the corridors, and the staircase were completely deserted: everyone was in class.

Immediately upon entering, Sasha ran over to the schedule. At first she couldn't find her way among all the rows and columns. Her classmates had moved up to their fourth year—did this mean she was a fourth year as well?

Today, year four, Group A started with the second block. Auditorium 1. That meant Portnov was teaching, and he was going to be brutal about her tardiness. On rubbery legs, her old sneakers squeaking against the glimmering floors, she approached the familiar door.

"Goldman, Yulia," someone said from behind the closed door.

"Bochkova, Anna. Biryukov, Dmitry. Kovtun, Igor."

She raised her hand to knock, then froze, as if a granite monument were running late to class and all of a sudden remembered that granite monuments could not walk away from their pedestals. The voice behind the door was unfamiliar; or rather she had heard this voice before, but it wasn't Portnov's. Someone else was conducting the roll call.

No one answered. No one said, "Here," as usual. No one's chair creaked, no one coughed, or sighed heavily. One could imagine that the unknown professor addressed an empty classroom.

Sasha pressed her ear to the door, like a first grader a second before her teacher scolds her for eavesdropping. She shuffled through their names, one after another, like prayer beads, each one familiar, terrified that the thread would break. A dropped name meant a failed exam, oblivion, fate worse than death. And she doubted they'd be given the second chance she was being given now.

Her late arrival was getting later and later with each second, and yet she lingered by the door, afraid to knock. The fear of seeing empty chairs instead of students who had failed was replaced by a different kind of fear—what happened to the ones who passed? What sort of metamorphosis awaited her classmates after the exam? Who—or perhaps, what—was she going to see inside?

The roll call stopped for a second. Sasha knew which name came next, but for some reason the professor took his time to say it, and the very thought that this name could be skipped turned Sasha's granite monument form into a melting chunk of wax. Her knees buckled.

"Kozhennikov, Konstantin," the professor said behind the door. Sasha shut her eyes as if trying to push them inside her skull. Kostya passed. Kostya survived.

"Korotkov, Andrey. Myaskovsky, Denis." The dull sound carried from behind the door. "Onishhenko, Larisa. Pavlenko, Lisa."

The next name on the list was Sasha's own. Her eyes still shut, she faintly knocked on the door, heard a curt "Come in," stepped over the threshold, and only then opened her eyes.

Not that dissimilar from a regular classroom, the auditorium looked exactly the same as Sasha remembered it. Wrought iron bars still protected the windows, and desks and chairs were arranged in two rows. People—actual human beings—sat motionlessly behind the desks. Sasha gathered up her courage and looked at her classmates. Every single one of them stared back.

Alive, human eyes. Shocked expressions. Sasha saw herself from many angles, as if, instead of one girl, a crowd of shadows stepped over the threshold, a throng of memories and threadbare images. She felt dizzy; she was being washed away by their stares, scattered in the wind like a column of smoke. Her classmates seemed to question whether she were a ghost, a product of someone's delirium, and for a second Sasha wondered the same thing herself.

The floor swayed under her feet. She lowered her eyes, unsure if she felt shy or ashamed of something, or needed to cut off their attention like cutting a wire with plate shears.

"Samokhina, Alexandra," the person behind the professor's desk said, and Sasha had no choice but to look back at him.

At first, she didn't recognize him; a moment later she inhaled sharply. For two and a half years she, along with her entire class, knew him as the physical education teacher, the athletic coach, a young, charming professional athlete. Her sweet Dima Dimych, beloved by all the girls, the object of ardent flirting, the shy idol paying attention to all and to no one in particular. At the end of her third year, during her final exam, Sasha finally saw the real essence of her gym teacher—his complex, forceful, and ominous structure. And now, his youthful face appeared dispassionate, preter-human, detached like a gas mask on a mannequin. His eyes shined like pieces of glass and his black pupils pulsed, first contracting, then spreading over the irises.

"Samokhina, Alexandra," the former gym teacher said again, this time with a hint of doubt. "You're late."

Sasha did not reply. She had no excuse. Plus she'd just become mute.

"Sit down," the gym teacher said. "Any free seat."

His words, or something else entirely, restored the firmness of the floor under Sasha's feet. Once again, her lips felt dry and her backpack heavy. Perhaps she could now take a step or even manage a word—

"Samokhina!" the professor said a tad louder. "Sit down! We're in the middle of a class!"

Swaying like a ship at sea, she advanced toward the last row. She moved between the tables, passing by Denis and Andrey, Lisa, then Kostya. She knew every single one of them like the back of her own hand, saw them out of the corner of her eye, knew them by smell. Nineteen people, including Sasha herself: Group A, together since the first day of the first year.

There was one more name after Sasha's.

Sasha looked back sharply, expecting the professor to say: "Toporko, Zhenya." But the former gym teacher was already flipping through some papers on his desk, clearly done with the roll call. *Some passed, some didn't. The usual.*

Sasha sat—or rather, collapsed—onto an empty seat by the window. Linden trees threw a rich shade onto Sacco and Vanzetti Street. Her classmates' heads turned in her direction, their eyes glued to her face. The professor held a pause, making some notes in his journal, then finally called them to order:

"Group A! Am I interrupting you?"

Reluctantly, they all turned to the whiteboard—that was new—and sat up straight, as befitted diligent students, facing the professor, their backs to Sasha. Only Kostya continued to stare; his eyes were strangely vacant, as if he couldn't quite place his former classmate.

Zhenya wasn't there because she had failed the final exam. The girl with braids, who so easily took Kostya away from Sasha that first year by simply sleeping with him on New Year's Eve. Kostya's shrewd, jealous wife. Ex-wife. It no longer mattered. They had ceased being human; who cared who screwed whom?

"Kozhennikov, do you require a special invitation?" the former gym teacher inquired sweetly.

Kostya tore his eyes away from Sasha and lowered his head, demonstrating that no, a special invitation was not necessary. It was such a human, such a "Kostya" gesture that Sasha's heart began to ache.

Everyone in this room, possibly aside from her, was a function, a part of Speech. Why, then, did Kostya's gaze make her shiver?

"So, fourth years, this semester you should expect a lot more practicum than classroom training." The former gym teacher spoke dispassionately, not like an automaton but rather like an experienced teacher who long ago ceased being emotional. The previous occupant of this room, Oleg Borisovich Portnov, had mastered the skill of exasperating students with the most mundane phrases and scaring the living daylights out of them with a single glance over his skinny frames. The former gym teacher seemed confident he would not lose his audience's attention under any circumstances, even if he fell asleep behind his desk.

He was very much awake now, though, his eyes penetrating each student.

"For the most part, we'll be working with models within each individual specialization," he said, continuing to shuffle the documents on his desk. "Today, however, is an introductory lecture for the entire class. Attention to the whiteboard, please."

He rose, a tall, muscular man, as strong and graceful as a wild cat. Sasha was used to seeing Dima Dimych in a tracksuit; today he wore conservative gray slacks and a light sports jacket that seemed almost too small for his ripped shoulders.

A shiny whiteboard replaced the old blackboard with its accompanying rag and pieces of chalk. A set of markers poked out of a magnetic cup. Sasha recalled the very first class of their first year when Portnov made Kostya draw a horizontal line on the board. That's how it all began.

She blinked. No single line this time. Not deigning to provide any explanation, the former gym teacher covered the board with signs and symbols. At first, Sasha was happy to recognize the multidimensional structure she'd learned from Portnov. But the marker kept moving over the surface, and the lines intertwined and grew more complex, infused with incomprehensible meaning.

Sasha felt the lights dimming, leaving the whiteboard brightly illuminated, and along with it the system drawn on the plane, the system pushing its way into the third dimension. Then the fourth. The fifth. Sasha felt nauseated.

"From simple to complex," the gym teacher said calmly. "Scanning, analysis, and synthesis. Grammatical parsing, if you just want a passing grade. Verification is needed for a B. Visualization—for an A. Watch this carefully, I am not going to repeat myself."

Sasha breathed deeply through her mouth. She couldn't grasp a single conceptual layer—it was too fast; on the whiteboard, the diagram drawn in blue marker grew, stretched, spread out in space and time. The intertwined symbols ripped a hole in reality and forced an opening into the world of chaos, and from that aperture—that breach—came a gust of extreme cold. Sasha wanted to pull away, and that was when, like a live, breathing creature, the diagram sensed her presence.

The diagram rushed into Sasha's head like an iron squid, its tentacles slipping into her eyes and ears, and the tangible, physiological sensation almost made Sasha scream. She felt a hostile creature enter her brain, jerking, devouring, destroying everything on its way. On the verge of losing consciousness, Sasha had but a split second to cover her eyes with both hands.

Sweat rolled down her face; her thin sweater stuck to her back. The auditorium was very quiet, as if the air was sucked out of the room and no one could breathe. Realizing she was still wearing her jacket, Sasha suddenly felt very warm. Her skin itched under her damp sweater. Her hair hurt in the vise of her scrunchie, her mouth was dry, she needed water and really needed to use the bathroom. Sasha locked herself inside her body, and that body claimed its rights. And yet, at this moment, it was the only protection from what was written on the whiteboard.

Pressing her hands to her face, Sasha cowered in her seat until the bell rang.

After Sasha washed her hands and came out of the bathroom, swaying as if in a fog, she saw them waiting for her in the hall.

It seemed like the epitome of humiliation, this mass vigil by the door to the women's toilet. All seventeen of them? Including Kostya?

"Hello," she said through gritted teeth.

Again, she saw herself through their eyes: a ghost from the past. A violation of rules and traditions, albeit cruel ones, and yet universal and obligatory. A miracle, perhaps a joyful one, yet unjust. She thought she saw them looking over her shoulder, as if they expected Zhenya Toporko to appear.

"If you want to know," Sasha said defiantly, "I'd have happily switched places with Zhenya."

Kostya ran his hand over his forehead as if trying to erase an unpleasant thought or memory. Lisa smirked. *Don't bother making excuses,* her smirk said. *We know you're special, a straight-A student, a teacher's pet. Don't expect us to be merciful.*

"Coach asked you to come back to the auditorium," Andrey Korotkov said softly. "I'd go immediately if I were you."

For a couple of seconds, Sasha vacillated between the two evils: to continue this conversation or go back to the auditorium, where a symbolic structure on the whiteboard wanted to dismember her alive. Physically, she wasn't sure she could go into the classroom. Emotionally, she was positive she couldn't stay here. She shut her eyes and shuffled back to the auditorium, bumping into walls.

Standing in the open door, her eyes still closed, she realized the diagram was gone. She peeked with one eye open and knew she was right: the whiteboard was pure white again, like an empty yard after it had snowed overnight. Sasha's backpack was lying on the floor by the window. Coach (she wasn't sure she could think of him as anything but at this point) sat behind the desk.

"What exactly is this habit of running away before you've been dismissed?"

"Bladder issues," Sasha muttered.

"That's too bad." He gestured for her to sit down in the first row. "Here."

Like a defensive army force, Sasha retreated toward the window, where she'd left her backpack. He shook his head.

"No, not there. The first row, please."

He sat behind the desk and stretched, as if his own skin were too tight. Sasha squeezed behind the desk, trying to connect this being before her with the man she remembered. Dima Dimych was one of very few positive experiences the first years were allowed to have; girls in particular enjoyed his company. Everyone believed him to be kind, a bit dim, and quite unambiguous. He seemed common, even ordinary, but loyal. A source of warmth and sympathy in the dismal realm of the institute. Sasha felt as if she had been offered a fake candy bar all those years ago, and inside the wrapper she now found not even a mundane rock, but poison.

"I remember you as a first year, practically a child," Coach continued leisurely, as if inspecting her thoughts against the light. "Not that I am particularly sentimental . . . I am not. As you know, I am outside of the human emotional sphere. However, I am familiar with the concept of empathy since empathy is necessary for working with younger students. Do you understand what I'm saying?"

Sasha nodded, avoiding his eyes.

"If I tell you that I sympathize with your plight," he said, getting to his point, "that I feel sorry for you, I would not be imitating feelings. Well, it would be more than a simple imitation. I tell you all that so I can say that I was against reinstating you at the institute."

Taken aback, she looked directly into his pupils—and immediately looked away, shuddering.

"But it has nothing to do with my feelings," he said after a pause. "This is about you. Teaching you the fourth-year program is like running around gunpowder storage with a lit torch, if you'll forgive my metaphor."

"Why?" Sasha asked at once. "Why?" So many questions in those "why"s. Why keep her from reenrolling? Why was she so dangerous in his eyes? Why was she here if he objected?

Why?

"Didn't anyone teach you to listen without interrupting?" For a second, he sounded just like Portnov. Sasha bit her tongue.

"I understand where your advisor is coming from," Coach continued.

"But I vehemently disagree. I can't refuse to teach you, it is my job after all. But don't expect me to babysit you as all your previous professors were wont to do. It's not my fault you've missed so much. Your informational component is rather lean, and your physiological component appears to be hypertrophied. Especially since you seem to lack control over your own bladder."

Sasha imagined duct tape sealing her mouth. It was very hard to hold back.

"I am not saying it to humiliate you." He was reading her like a store sign. "I am not your enemy, and I don't wish you ill. Then again, I don't wish you well, either, so take all that as you will. Regardless, the fourth-year program is extremely strenuous. No need for complicated examples—you've had a chance to see it today."

Coach held a pause as if trying her patience. Seemingly pleased with the achieved effect, he spoke very slowly, practically underlining every word. "I predict that without supplemental lessons, you won't make it to graduation."

The invisible tape across Sasha's mouth popped with a deafening crackle.

"Tell it to my advisor!"

"I *have* told him." He didn't seem surprised by her outburst, clearly expecting this reaction. "Our entire faculty failed to convince Farit Kozhennikov that you must be left alone." Coach stared back at her dispassionately. "We failed to convince him that he should not poke a lighter at a nuclear bomb. But who knows, perhaps you will make it? So I suggest *you* tell your advisor. Try to find common ground with him."

"With Farit?" Sasha choked on her question.

"I realize it sounds outlandish." Coach winced slightly. "But it's worth a try. Explain to him that you are not capable of mastering the program. Explain that he is asking for the impossible."

"And you?" Sasha asked softly. "Is what you are asking for—is it possible?"

Another pause followed. If Coach was thinking of something, none of his thoughts were reflected in his immobile face. His pupils spread into wide black holes, then rolled back into two tiny dots.

"Fine," he said neutrally, very businesslike. "My subject is called Analytical Specialty. In case you forgot, my name is Dmitry Dmitrievich. As a rule, I don't write reports during the semester, but at the end of the semester we'll have a differential pass-fail exam. Everything you manage to learn is your achievement. If you miss something, whether you are ill or for any other reason—remember that you've been warned."

Sasha smiled bitterly.

"Thank you. You've been abundantly clear."

"Nikolay Valerievich Sterkh is going to supervise your error correction work," he said, ignoring her comment. "Your first individual session with him is at six tonight, auditorium fourteen, as usual. Bring a notebook and a pen."

"What about Oleg Borisovich?" The thought of Portnov filled Sasha with unexpected warmth. "Will he be teaching us again?"

"Oleg Borisovich teaches Intro to Specialty," Coach said just as dispassionately. "He now has a class of new first years. Incidentally, thank you for reminding me . . ."

He got up, walked over to the familiar bookcase, and pulled out a stack of books, worn out, with ripped and taped-over spines.

"Repetition is the mother of learning, as they say, although if I were you, I wouldn't get my hopes up."

She didn't think her hopes could be any lower. "What did I do wrong? During the final exam?" Sasha whispered.

"You did everything right." Coach placed the books in front of her. "You're simply not who we thought you were, that's the problem."

"Then why am I being punished for your mistake?"

"No one is punishing you . . ."

Coach's voice sounded suddenly human. For a split second, his face became very much alive, full of pain, and almost lovely—and in a split second it turned back into a fixed mask with black holes for pupils. Sasha recoiled.

"No one is punishing you," he repeated with bitter frustration. "Rather, you are very dangerous. You are a weapon . . . a weapon of formidable power. You are an assassin of reality, Sasha, you are a destroyer of grammar, and I will do everything possible to prevent you from ever *reverberating* again. Other than that," he hesitated for a moment, "other than that, you are a wonderful girl, and I am not your enemy. However, I've already told you that."

As she was leaving auditorium 1, only a few minutes remained before the end of her lunch recess. The vestibule was deserted, but a few voices carried from the cafeteria downstairs. *I don't want to explain anything,* Sasha thought resentfully. *I don't owe anyone any explanation, I'm not a scapegoat!*

The schedule board looked totally different from two hours ago: squares and rectangles of group classes had disappeared, and only narrow ribbons of individual classes remained on the display. Sasha found her name on the list: she had an individual session with Sterkh at six tonight. *He's going to spell out everything to me,* Sasha thought, her hope as irate as her recent anger. *He'll explain this* assassin of reality *nonsense.* She wanted to think Coach had made a joke, but clowning around was not really popular in the institute, especially among the faculty.

"Excuse me!"

Sasha turned around. A portly woman in a white blouse stood by the door to the dean's office, arms akimbo.

"Are you Samokhina?"

"Yeah," Sasha mumbled. She vaguely remembered this woman. Or was it someone else, but similar? Sasha was never particularly chummy with the dean's office staff. Unlike other students, she never had to submit a change of marital-status paperwork or beg for a stipend after getting a C.

"Come in," the woman commanded. "Did you expect me to hunt you down? Who's supposed to worry about your dorm room if not you?"

A new three-story brick building had replaced the old wooden one. Wrought iron balconies stretched along the second and third stories. Here and there feeble-looking grapevines crept along the bars.

Sasha recalled the day Farit Kozhennikov brought her to the tiny apartment rented for her as a reward for her perfect grades. Those were strange and wonderful days; back then Sasha first realized how much she liked to learn, how studying made her happy, and how the world that opened up to her was beautiful and harmonious. To quote Kozhennikov, she had "tasted the honey."

It was bittersweet now.

Sasha pulled open the heavy metal door with a broken magnetic lock. There was no concierge in the vestibule of the new dorm, and no key stand. Everything was different: an overstuffed sofa and chairs, a plasma-television screen on the wall, a few succulents in enormous round planters. On the television screen, a news program was on mute, but she could see people in bizarre clothing crowding each other, screaming. Cars flipped over. The camera jerked in the operator's grip. Sasha wanted to turn off the TV or at least switch the channel, but she couldn't locate the remote and the cable was plugged in too high up behind the screen. With a slightly delayed reaction, she realized she didn't have to watch it—no one was forcing her.

Shielding her face from the screen, she noticed a round, opaque object that resembled a space helmet hiding among the succulents. A minute later she realized it was a pay phone. A diagram on the side of the phone explained how to call using one's student ID. The dean's office staff had already issued Sasha her ID card.

For a few long minutes she stared at the diagram, then at the card, then back, like a monkey trying to figure out how to wear a pair of glasses. She needed time to gather her thoughts.

Finally, she dialed the number that had been beaten into her brain and listened to the dial tone. She'd remember these digits in a coma.

"Yes, Sasha," Farit Kozhennikov said. "A bit too early for you to call me. The classes have barely started."

"I was told I am an assassin of reality and a destroyer of grammar."

"Did Dmitry Dmitrievich tell you that? He's exaggerating," Kozhennikov said airily. "Don't take it to heart."

"I'm just trying to understand." She tried to sound casual but her voice betrayed her. "He doesn't explain anything, he just tries to scare me."

"How unusual," Farit said, and she could somehow hear the hint of a smile. "None of the faculty have ever behaved this way."

Sasha acknowledged his irony. Gritting her teeth, she continued, "He said my informational component is too lean, and that I'm not going to manage. That I am not going to make it to graduation."

"Then he's contradicting himself, isn't he?" Kozhennikov said, clearly amused by the thought. "Either you are an assassin of reality, or you're not going to make it. It's not really ethical of me to discuss your professors in your presence, but in this case he's definitely wrong. You are determined, talented, you are highly motivated, and if your motivation is not enough, I will make sure to add some."

Sasha almost dropped the phone.

The new dormitory was significantly cleaner and cozier than the old barracks; it was also surprisingly quiet. Sasha cocked her ear: not a single sound. No running water, no steps, not a single voice.

"Ghost ship," Sasha said to herself. "Where is everybody?"

She walked along the seemingly endless corridor, stopped by her door, and inserted her student ID into the electronic lock. The lock buzzed, blinked green, and the door opened.

Upon entering, her suspicion that upperclassmen lived in much better conditions was once again confirmed. The place resembled a decent hotel room. A small table by the door housed a microwave and an electric teakettle. A whiteboard was hung over the desk, complete with a couple of brightly colored magnets and a set of markers. Sasha's gaze lingered on the board. It reminded her of the shock she experienced in auditorium 1 earlier that day.

On an impulse, Sasha grabbed the board and tore it off the wall. *Your informational component is rather lean . . . You've missed so much . . .* Considering Sasha's recent experience in class, Coach was right, and Farit Kozhennikov was wrong.

Sasha looked around the room. Stripping the skin off her knuckles, she stuffed the board behind the wardrobe; the markers fell off and rolled on the floor. The green one peeked from underneath the wardrobe, and Sasha kicked it back, out of her line of vision.

It would never have occurred to her before that Farit could be on the outs with the faculty, that he had the upper hand, and that they, unable to refuse, would nevertheless sabotage his ordinances. And now Sasha found herself between a rock and a hard place. Farit would surely punish the student, not the faculty.

Removing the whiteboard was the right decision. The room now looked much better and even more spacious. Of course, her old grapevine-adorned walk-up had been a hundred times better, but at least she wouldn't have to share a room with her classmates. That would have been unbearable, especially now when every look in her direction clearly read: *How are you better than Zhenya? Why did Zhenya perish after failing the exam, but you came back? Why did they forgive you when they have never forgiven anyone before?*

Sasha sucked on a skinned knuckle. She would have to prepare a universal response, something like "None of your goddamn business." Or even "Not your grammatical worry."

She opened the wardrobe and stared into the large dusty mirror. Her reflection stared back at her from the foggy glass; she looked like a frightened girl, and not at all like an informational object. She looked disheveled, worn out, her lips bitten and flaky—a real beauty.

Sasha glanced at the empty shelves and hangers in the wardrobe. The only clothes she owned were the ones she wore: a pair of jeans, a sweater, a light jacket, and a bra, panties, and a pair of socks and shoes. The dried-up spots on the knees of her jeans were from the side of the road where the mutilated body of Alexandra Samokhina was loaded up into a van, which had only been a day ago—if even that long.

Shaking off unnecessary thoughts, she struggled to lift her heavy backpack onto the chair, then pulled out the books, one after another, arranging them on the empty tabletop: *Textual Module,* volumes 6, 7, and 8. Sasha gazed at the volumes with something akin to nostalgia . . . and something akin to dread.

Did Portnov regret her fate? Did he feel guilty? It was an interesting question. Does a dictionary pine for a long-forgotten word?

She returned to her backpack and pulled out *Conceptual Activator,* two fat, unwieldy volumes. *Exercises for the Third Year, Updated and Revised Edition.* Sasha fumbled around in the backpack, like a cat pawing inside an aquarium, but caught nothing else: no more books. Everything she was given she'd seen and worked with before. It was insulting, their best student having to suffer through this all again. Yet, also necessary?

Or were the faculty trying to sabotage her after all?

She picked up *Textual Module,* volume 8, took a seat behind the desk as she'd done a million times before, and opened the book. Yellowed paper, an old library smell. Pages and pages of sheer gibberish, complex and nonsensical text that Sasha had learned to read, learned to love, the text that opened the gate into the blissful world of crystal meanings.

No meaning came now. Her eyes kept wandering off, and she had trouble focusing on the pages. Her physical body, tired and starving, refused to comply, kicking and screaming like a child facing an injection needle. The gibberish evolved into screeching and gnashing in her head, her eyes watered, and sweat rolled down her back, just like during her first year, though now it was possibly even worse. Sasha struggled to get to the end of the paragraph, then started again from the very beginning. She remembered what this text could do to a human being, but, unlike in her first year, she now couldn't wait for the text to work and to restore her previous lightness. Sasha the informational object, Sasha the Word of the Great Speech longed for the meanings inside *Textual Module* like someone dying of thirst longs for water. Sasha the human being fought back as if forced to drink acid . . .

When she finally came to, she found herself on the floor, her cheek pressed against a broken pencil. The open *Textual Module* lay a few inches away by the table, its crumpled pages facing down.

Trying not to look at the pages, Sasha picked up volume 8, closed it shut, and placed it on the table. She considered volume 7 but decided to put it aside and open volume 6.

I am not giving up.

Even with the lower module, it started all over again: screeching in her ears, chills, revolting gibberish flooding her eyes like molten lead. Sasha's tears soaked the page; she kept on reading:

"The prices—oh, the prices were simply ludicrous! In the end, Mom rented a tiny room in a five-story building twenty minutes from the shore, with windows facing west . . ."

The wheeled desk chair wobbled under her weight, and she fell backward.

"Hello, Sasha. I am glad to see you."

Sterkh's auditorium 14 hadn't changed a bit, except that it was early fall outside the window. Last time she was here it was January. Sterkh hadn't changed either; his long ash-blond hair still framed his face in two falling curtains, his wings made his jacket fold into ridges on his curved back, and his sharp chin lay on a high collar, blindingly white on the background of his perfect black suit. He still had the same manner of steepling his long slim fingers. How many years had passed for him—fifteen? Two hundred and fifty? Eight months?

The only thing that had changed was the way he looked at Sasha. Before, his eyes could be benevolent or stern, irritated or angry, but never before had he looked at her with such a painfully tense expression. Sterkh gazed at Sasha the way a judge would look at a ghost of a man wrongfully convicted.

"Hello, Nikolay Valerievich," Sasha said. "I am sorry. I was reading *Textual Module,* and I lost track of time."

"I'm glad to see you," Sterkh repeated. Sasha understood that he wasn't lying and that his joy was burdened by guilt or perhaps fear. "Look here, please."

Instead of a watch, he wore a large mother-of-pearl mirror with a leather strap on his wrist. A reflected beam of light slammed into Sasha's eyes, blinding her for a second. She remembered the sensation as never being particularly pleasant; however, the blindness and the pain in her eyes stopped almost immediately. Sasha blinked. Auditorium 14 became blurry like a soaked-through watercolor landscape, then cleared up again.

"I was convinced you'd pass your exam with flying colors," Sterkh said, a hint of surprise in his voice, as if he was shocked by his own ability to make mistakes. "I was convinced you would get the highest score. You've surprised me so many times; you've given me hope, taken it away, then surprised me again . . . I feel responsible for what happened, Sasha. Even if there was nothing I could do. I couldn't do anything for you. I thought I'd never see you again."

"But you are happy to see me," Sasha said, as if feeding him a line.

"Yes," he said, surprise in his voice growing stronger. "I am happy. But it's not as if you'd just come back from vacation. It's much more complicated than that. Sit down."

Sasha perched on the edge of her seat.

"Are you going to tell me you can't teach me because I am an 'assassin of reality'?"

"We are obligated to teach you," Sterkh said gently. "It is our mission. I'd be lying if I told you that the situation does not frighten me—I am indeed frightened to the core . . . But you are my student, and I always tell my students the truth."

"Thank you," Sasha muttered. "Nikolay Valerievich, what's a 'destroyer of grammar'? What exactly is frightening you? How can you be scared of me?"

"I am not scared of you," Sterkh said after a long pause. "What terrifies me is how easily ancient traditions are annulled these days. But as your professor, I wish you nothing but good luck. I will do everything in my power to help you."

"Thank you," Sasha said sincerely. "But you didn't answer my question. Why am I an assassin of reality?"

"You are not an assassin." He shook his head, as if regretting an unfortunate misunderstanding. "Right at this moment, you are neither an assassin nor a destroyer, but your potential—"

He cut himself short and frowned.

"I'd like to return to this conversation a bit later."

"But, Nikolay Valerievich—"

"No buts." Once again, his voice was measured and firm. "You know perfectly well that here at the institute, certain questions will remain unanswered until you complete a certain amount of work, and no one else can do it for you."

He pulled a tablet out of his desk and placed it in front of Sasha. Roughly the size of a notepad, the tablet had no company logo and only a single button on the side.

"This is your new tool. Inside is your individual schedule, which must be followed precisely, to the minute. I will send you assignments, and you will complete them and send them back. Open your notebook, the paper one, and on the first page please write 'Error Correction Assignment.'"

"Whose errors am I correcting?" Sasha asked softly.

Their eyes met, and for the next few minutes neither said a word. Eventually Sasha lowered her gaze and began to write. At first her pen scratched the paper and refused to work.

"You will write in your notebook every day," Sterkh continued calmly. "Your correction work will be finished when you describe the final exam of January thirteenth, with details: what happened, where it led to, and how to fix it. And then . . ."

He paused, then glanced sharply at Sasha, and suddenly smiled.

"And then we shall fly, Sasha," he said, and his voice was different, slightly hoarse. "We shall fly again."

Sasha felt so grateful that she nearly threw herself into his arms.

Despite its quirkiness, historical Torpa was quite a cozy and pleasant town. The boulders glowed under the streetlights, the streets snaked gracefully in all directions, the brick walls boasted mysterious alcoves. The sun was setting, and in the shaded yards, a few lights came on behind multicolored curtains, giving the buildings a festive, cheerful look.

Sasha wandered around, inhaling and exhaling the season. Almost fifteen years ago she flew above these roofs. Several lifetimes ago she roamed these streets with Kostya. Sasha walked faster, then slower, then faster again, trying to process this endless and endlessly strange day. She'd never left Torpa, but now she was back in Torpa, and the eight months' memory gap bothered her immensely, since it was almost fifteen years that had disappeared without a trace. Once again, she was facing studies that tested her limits, but that crystal-clear comprehension she had before the final exam, that sense of harmony and belonging that made her decline Farit's offer—all these things now felt dim and mangled, and Sasha found herself in the midst of uncertainty and fear. Once again, she'd have to punch above her weight, and not for the sake of the higher concepts, but just to avoid giving Farit a reason to punish her.

But what happened to her during the final exam? What was it?

She heard a set of brakes squeal by the side of the road. Sasha shuddered, expecting the worst, but there was no accident, just a silver Mazda that drove by, then stopped just ahead. The driver's door opened.

"Sasha, is that you?"

Sasha recognized him right away. If there was anything good about this long day, it was that trip from the airport into town, and that moment when the pilot had wished her luck, and she waved in return. And here he was, standing next to his car, in his white uniform jacket with black epaulets, no hat, his hair tousled, his face radiant.

"I saw you walking down the street. Torpa is such a weird place— miracles abound when you step outside . . ."

Sasha gave him a suspicious look, but his words weren't intended to make fun of her. He was simply so happy to see her that he'd inadvertently picked up on something hidden from human eyes.

"Torpa *is* a really weird place," Sasha said, pleased with his reaction. "But it's not exactly a megapolis, so it's easy to run into people when you walk around."

"You don't think I was following you, do you?" His face suddenly paled. He was clearly worried.

Sasha found it hilarious; there was such a dissonance between the macho pilot image and this reaction of a confused little boy unfairly blamed for some misdemeanor. She laughed, and this laughter worked like medicine. Alexandra Samokhina's death, Coach's threats, the upcoming discussion with her classmates; at this moment in time, all these things lost their importance, stepped back, freed her from their weight, and the fist that had been squeezing her chest let go and let her breathe for the first time in hours.

He was cautious not to touch her, not on purpose, and not by accident. He didn't allow as much as a brush of a sleeve. Not even when they passed through the narrowest streets.

"These roofs look magical when you fly above them," Sasha said, admiring the sunset over the city from a high terrace.

"Yes, on a glide slope," he said competently. "When the sun is low and the clouds are sparse. It can be stunning."

And Sasha laughed again.

It was getting dark when they landed at a tiny table on an open terrace of a downtown café. Candles and roses under the striped awning would have suited Paris in its prime more than this provincial joint.

A waitress appeared at their table, smiling at the sight of Yaroslav, then staring at Sasha as if wondering what a young, handsome pilot saw in this pale girl in a worn jacket. Pursing her lips, the waitress placed a black satin-covered menu directly in front of Yaroslav.

He leaned toward Sasha to share the menu, and they sat still, almost touching their heads together like a couple of children bending over a book of fairy tales. A flock of sparrows, confused by the streetlights making the night as bright as day, charged a rosebush, and it shook as if possessed by demons.

The menu smelled of printer ink, and of pickled mushrooms in oil, and delicate smoked salmon, and spices, and French cheese. All these scents, except for the dry smell of paper, were borne inside Sasha's throat as she read the names of the dishes. She glanced at the prices and the scents lost their luster.

"Everything is so expensive," she said with regret.

"Will you allow me to treat you?" he said, looking into her eyes.

He gazed at her with hope, almost pleading. It was a very strange gaze. For the first time during this walk, she felt awkward, constrained. Loaded with tiny birds, the rosebush chirped and twitched.

They barely knew each other. It was a lovely evening, and it was still going on, and it was still lovely. But why was Yaroslav looking at her so intently?

She couldn't deny how pleased she was to see him again. After this terrible day, she was happy to walk by his side, laugh at his jokes, breathe easily. It seemed like he wanted . . . more, though? Had she sent a wrong signal? Given him false hope?

She must have. It was wrong and she should have been ashamed. Hope was not for informational objects. Love and life were for normal people, like Alexandra Samokhina, who'd died on the highway earlier this morning.

Holding her breath, she covered his hand with hers. Touching his long fingers, she felt a pang of regret, sharp as a blade. He froze, afraid she'd let go.

"Yaroslav, forgive me," Sasha said wistfully. "I can't see you again. We can't be together. Forgive me."

"But—"

She pushed her chair back and fled while the waitress watched them with poorly concealed satisfaction.

The air felt cool and moist, a classic autumn night. The linden trees on Sacco and Vanzetti Street looked bigger and older now, more fragile, their leaves turning yellow earlier than before.

"It's all right, you'll find someone else," Sasha muttered as she ran. "Women must drape themselves over you on a regular basis. You're a grown man—what is this love at first sight nonsense? It's not like we're toddlers in a sandbox. This is ridiculous."

Who she was convincing, though, wasn't clear.

The windows of the dormitory lit up one after another; the "ghost ship" was coming to life. Sasha was prepared to deflect idle questions and random dirty looks, but the vestibule was still empty. Faint music came from somewhere inside the building.

Sasha stumbled up the stairs to the third floor. She struggled with the key card, then flipped the light switch. The lights made her room seem almost cozy.

With a sarcastic grin, she closed the curtains and pulled the tablet out of her backpack, thinking of the olden days when Torpa had no cell towers and touch screens seemed magical. Sterkh had given her a quick overview, but this device seemed easy enough to use.

Mon–Sun:
    6 am: intensive fitness.
    8 am: error correction work, self-study.
Tue:
    2 pm: Analytical Specialty, ind., auditorium 1
Fri:
    6 pm: Analytical Specialty, ind., auditorium 1
Mon–Th:
    6 pm: error correction work, ind., auditorium 14
Fri:
    4 pm: error correction work, ind., auditorium 14
Sat:
    4 pm: error correction work, ind., auditorium 14

What was implied was that, when she didn't have class, she would be studying. Such was the way of the institute.

This is my life, Sasha thought. *This resembles what I used to think of as my life.*

Someone knocked on her door, making Sasha jump. For a moment she thought that Yaroslav had followed her, that he'd found the dorm, found Sasha, he was here, and she would have to make a scene in front of everyone . . .

Carefully, as if afraid of burning herself, she peeked into the peephole and saw her classmate Denis Myaskovsky. Sasha wiped the imaginary sweat off her forehead.

"What do you want?" Sasha asked, keeping the door closed.

"Open the door," he said. "What are you afraid of?"

Sasha turned the lock but continued blocking the entrance.

"Den, I need to study. Just tell me what you want, then leave."

"Whoa," Denis said, slightly taken aback. "Just like that, huh. I forgot how bitchy you can get. Where were you all last semester?"

"Fourteen years," Sasha said grimly. "I was gone for fourteen and a half years, but thanks for asking."

Denis stepped from foot to foot, shocked and confused by Sasha's statement. For a few moments, he said nothing, then proceeded with a delicate cough.

"We collected some money for you. Like, just to cover some initial expenses."

"What?"

He pulled out an envelope.

"Let's not do it over the threshold, it's a bad omen."

Sasha took a step back. Denis stepped into her room and handed her the envelope. Sasha stared at him in confusion.

"We are not your enemy," Denis said softly.

The first floor of the new dormitory housed a gym, with treadmills, balls, and barbells, with metal monsters for every possible muscle group, and mirrors along the walls. Some sort of a buffet table was arranged behind a low partition: tables, a few chairs, a bar, an espresso maker. Sasha hesitated, afraid of taking another step: the eyes of her classmates pulled her apart, blurring her contours, turning her into a plume of smoke.

"Over here." Anna Bochkova waved to her as if nothing had happened.

Lisa Pavlenko ran steadily on a black treadmill, focusing on nothing but her breathing. The rest of the Group A fourth years, all fifteen of them, ponied up to the bar or sat at the low tables; they looked like regular café patrons, but no food or drinks were to be seen. Tablets or smartphones with large displays lay in front of each student.

Avoiding their stares, Sasha placed the envelope stuffed with cash on one of the unoccupied tables.

"Thanks, guys, but I don't need it."

"It's a loan," Andrey Korotkov said. "You can pay it back later. We get a stipend every month, and it's not like there is much to spend it on. And you've got like one pair of pants."

"Go buy yourself some new undies," Lisa said from the treadmill. Her voice sounded even, and her breathing didn't change. Sasha took a closer look: it was definitely Lisa, in her natural habitat, same as always.

Her eyes swept over the faces of her classmates: they had all changed, just a tiny bit more than would be expected of regular twenty-year-olds after a long difficult semester. But none of them looked like functions. And none of them resembled stern judges demanding answers.

"Wow," she blurted out. "I thought after the exam you'd be . . ."

She fell silent.

"That we'd become robots?" Yulia Goldman smirked. "Or mannequins?"

Denis Myaskovsky offered her a chair, and Sasha plopped herself down. She took another look around. Kostya sat by the bar, and she could see his profile. An empty cardboard coffee cup was next to his tablet.

"So tell us," Denis said.

She steepled her fingers, just like Sterkh in the auditorium.

"I don't remember anything. We went to take the exam. I opened the assignment, then started doing it—the simple part first. Then—nothing. I didn't exist. Then I existed again, but it was almost fifteen years after the exam. I was in the apartment where I grew up, right in front of the door to my own room, but inside—inside was me. Another me. So I came in and nearly pissed myself. She was also terrified. And I tried to *claim* her, I mean, it was a dumb idea, but . . . I simply couldn't help myself . . ."

"Yeah," Denis murmured. "No one could have."

"What was she like?" Yulia Goldman asked greedily. Sasha looked up.

"What do you mean?"

"The other you. I was just thinking . . . what would the other me look like? Without the institute," Yulia said wistfully, her eyes growing dim and distant.

"She had a normal life," Sasha said softly. "Not spectacular, just a regular life."

She faltered, afraid of insulting the dead woman, a stranger for whom she felt more fear than sympathy.

Lisa sped up, making the treadmill screech. Her sneakers pounded the rubber like rain falling onto a tin roof.

"And then what?" Denis asked, breaking the prolonged silence.

"Then . . . Time produced a loop, and that woman, Alexandra— she died."

She faltered, aware of saying the wrong thing. The most crucial question remained unanswered, and instead of answering it, she was entertaining them with her tangled memories.

"What about you all?" she pressed on. "What happened after the exam? Do you remember?"

Everyone exchanged glances.

"Assignments," Andrey said curtly.

"Just assignments," Yulia said. "Same as before."

Sasha thought Yulia tried to look away, hiding something unsaid. Perhaps Sasha was mistaken.

"But do you remember or not?"

They exchanged glances one more time. Denis nodded and shrugged, indicating that they remembered but had no desire to discuss it.

"We simply walked out of the assembly hall," Anna Bochkova said placatingly. "With the certificates of passing the exam in our hands, and final grades. Most people got a B. Kozhennikov and Pavlenko got an A, Denis, a C."

Denis cringed. Kostya kept staring at his tablet, as if Sasha weren't even there.

"We didn't feel anything, no particular joy or anything like that," Anna continued, as if giving an official report. "No one saw anyone taking the exam, everyone was only concentrating on themselves. The whole thing took about an hour and a half. When we came out, only Sterkh and Coach were waiting to congratulate us. They said we were now at a different base, but the hall was the same, and it was the same horse with the same rider . . . And then we noticed both you and Zhenya were gone. The grades were displayed on the bulletin board, and Zhenya had an F, and you . . ." Anna looked at the others.

"What?"

"You just had a blank."

"A blank?"

"Sterkh told us it meant you didn't pass," Denis said grimly.

Sasha swallowed a wad of bitter saliva.

"But don't think we cried for you," Lisa said, smiling. "We had things to do after the final exam: winter vacation, dancing, partying, ski resorts."

"What did Coach tell you?" Andrey asked. "Why did you get a blank, and why did they bring you back?"

Sasha bit her tongue. She debated telling them about being an "assassin of reality." It wouldn't explain anything, and instead would just create more confusion and tension. But maybe she needed to trust them.

She shrugged, trying to formulate a fair and respectful answer, and then suddenly froze with her mouth open. She choked on her breath, and a new thought emerged past her lips.

"Wait, if our exam happened many years ago, then the second years . . . Have they passed their exams yet? People from Yegor's class?"

She thought she saw Kostya flinch.

"If the exam happened in the past," Sasha said, growing more and more agitated, "then there must be some reports, some documentation. We can figure out who passed and who didn't . . ."

"I don't think so," Andrey said, scratching the tip of his nose. "I think they have one more semester to suffer through. Time is nonlinear, in case you didn't know." Having just experienced that, she ignored his condescension. "Anyway, take the money, or we'll throw it away."

Sasha sighed, picked up the envelope, and put it into the inside pocket of her jacket. She felt like a panhandler.

Lisa finally switched off the treadmill, slowed down her pace, and jumped off without taking the time to stabilize her breathing. Not a single drop of sweat rolled down her forehead, not a spot of moisture was visible on her thin long-sleeved top. Either she was indeed a mannequin, or the "intensive fitness" in her schedule had transformed Lisa into an Olympic champion.

Lisa stopped in front of Sasha, drowning her in the expensive scent of her deodorant.

"Show me your arm."

Confused, Sasha looked at her arms. Lisa held a dramatic pause, then hitched up her sleeve. Just above the crook of her elbow was a dark tattoo, the round symbol from the reverse side of Farit Kozhennikov's gold coins.

Sasha looked around; everyone was watching her, not just Lisa. Sasha swallowed and pulled up the sleeve of her thin sweater. Obviously, there was nothing on her arm. Only clean skin.

"Fascinating," Lisa said, raising her thin blond eyebrows. "You haven't been branded, and yet, you are a fourth year. An exception to the rule, as usual."

"I didn't ask for it." Sasha jerked her sleeve down.

Narrowing her eyes, Lisa stared at Sasha.

"So, it was Kozhennikov who vouched for you again, wasn't it?"

This time Kostya flinched so hard that his empty coffee cup rolled off the table. Sasha knew she'd let her guard down too easily. Her classmates were playing good cop/bad cop, Lisa being the obvious choice for the role of bad cop.

"Farit Georgievich Kozhennikov informed me that he would charge a very high rate for his services," Sasha said slowly. "He also reminded me that he had never asked for the impossible. Did he ever ask you for the impossible, Lisa?"

The blond girl's face betrayed her emotion. She raised her middle finger in an obscene gesture; suddenly, Sasha saw that finger directly in front of her own face, even though Lisa still stood a few feet away. From Lisa's impossibly long arm, her middle finger transformed into a bone hook, grabbed Sasha's sweater and sliced through the thin fabric, touching her skin. Sasha jumped back. Lisa smirked and walked out of the room without so much as a backward glance.

The coffeemaker gurgled softly in the corner. Somewhere along Sacco and Vanzetti, a car tooted its horn. Otherwise, the dorm was as quiet as a morgue.

"You shouldn't have talked to her that way," Yulia Goldman said with a hint of reproach. "You know how Lisa gets when you remind her of Farit's dealings with her . . ."

"*I* shouldn't have? Seriously?" Sasha squeezed the slashed fabric as if expecting and fearing her heart to fall out through the hole.

"All of us are very unstable right now," Denis said gently, gauging Sasha's reaction. "The stabilization will be completed before the summer finals. We need to be gentle with each other."

"Again, are you serious? Is she being gentle with *me*?" Sasha breathed heavily. "It's amazing she hasn't killed anyone yet with her antics."

"We get penalty points for aggression," Andrey Korotkov said with a sigh. "Please don't complain to anyone. Promise?"

Sasha was about to say something biting and clever, but at that moment Kostya got up from his seat. Still avoiding her eyes, he said, "I have a needle and a thread. We should patch that hole before it spreads further. Come on, let's go."

His room looked uncharacteristically clean, quite different from his old dorm, where dirty socks took up half the space. Kostya perched on the edge of a neatly made-up bed. Sasha chose the desk chair. A clean whiteboard hung above the desk, a set of color markers placed on its shelf, and Sasha had to look away as if trying to avoid looking at shiny surgical instruments.

Kostya deftly operated a needle and thread to patch the cut on her sweater. Above his elbow was a clearly visible tattoo, not dark gray like Lisa's, but dark brick red. A round sign, the symbol for "Word."

"Did it hurt?" Sasha asked pointlessly, wrapping a bath towel tighter around her shoulders. Kostya's towel.

"I didn't feel anything. We didn't even realize we had been tuned up after the final exam," Kostya said, smiling. "At first I thought it was a temporary tattoo, like henna, or just an ink drawing."

He was quite good at darning her sweater, like a seaman sewing a ripped sail, but Sasha knew the stitches would be prominent right in the middle of her chest.

"I thought you were upset with me for some reason," Sasha said. "And that you didn't want to see me."

Kostya sighed.

"Do you remember Portnov? *When you think of a word worth saying out loud . . .* That word is 'Zhenya.' One word. Do you understand?"

"I think so," Sasha said thickly.

"No one told us why she failed and what she did wrong." He continued to place one stitch after another. "But I know. Before the exam she told me I used her as a . . . as a condom. First I slept with her because I needed sex, and you valued yourself too highly for a quickie. Then I married her to make you jealous. I made Zhenya believe she and I were a family. Then I left her and started sleeping with you because you so graciously allowed me access to your body. Can you imagine—the final exam was about to get started, and here she was, throwing all this at me. Then they called us in, and she dragged all this with her, all this emotional baggage of hers. I was so freaked out that somehow I passed and got an A. And when I came out of the assembly hall after the exam, saw the bulletin board, and realized you both failed, you *and* Zhenya . . ."

He looked down and fell silent.

"Kostya," Sasha whispered. "You didn't do anything wrong, neither to me nor to Zhenya."

He didn't answer. Finding it hard to sit still, Sasha wrapped the towel tighter around her shoulders and paced around the room.

"Explain this to me, please. If you are no longer human . . . we've been warned that after the final exam, we'd be finished as humans and would begin as grammatical concepts—but then, how can you experience all these emotions?"

"These things are not mutually exclusive!" He pricked his finger, winced, and licked off the drop of blood. "Everything has a grammatical meaning. Betrayal, manipulation, envy, jealousy . . . Zhenya's failure was a result of my action. And the same thing with you. When I realized that, I—I couldn't study. I finished the second semester with all C's. Coach made me retake his exam . . ."

"What?"

"Yeah," Kostya said, taking a deep breath. "In the winter, back in

February, I found a stray puppy on the street and was dumb enough to bring it home. I'll never do that again."

"Kostya," Sasha mumbled, her lips as dry as a desert. "But it's . . ."

"Yeah." He nodded. "We thought that our transformation into a grammatical form after the exam would mean freedom from fear. From all this. The Great Speech is beautiful and harmonious," he said, his voice reaching a lofty tone. "And that's the truth. But it's not the whole truth. They hid something from us: we can progress as concepts only as long as something human is left in us. The Word itself, Word that is fully mature, does not grow. It can only serve as an instrument of Speech. That's why during the first two years, they broke us down and squeezed the *concepts* out of us. Now they are trying to cultivate and maintain our human nature. They are preserving us as humans, our human reactions, until we defend our theses, until we take the final exam. Do you understand?"

She did and she didn't, because that was the way of this place. "What happened to the puppy?" Sasha asked softly.

"It died," Kostya said sharply. "Like my grandmother. Everyone dies, if you haven't noticed. People get sick, they get run over, they break their necks . . ."

Sasha felt a chill.

"You sound like *him*."

"I will become just like *him*," Kostya said dryly. "After I graduate. Some day."

He made a knot at the end of the thread and bit it off, handing the sweater to Sasha.

"Here, I did my best."

"Thanks," Sasha said, managing a weak smile. "Listen, about your mom. Does she exist?"

He nodded. "She does. But she's a different person."

"What do you mean?"

"You know."

"I do but need to hear it anyway."

"Time is discrete," he said patiently. "It's not a line from the past to the future, as we had thought before. It's more like a system of bubbles that are either vaguely connected or are completely separate from each other. Fourteen years later, my mom is a different person, she's not the person I remember. And she still has a son—well, in theory. We even call each other on holidays. I am her son in theory, an illusion of a son. Plenty of families are like that."

She hated that she agreed so readily with that assessment. *I am going to dwell on it later,* Sasha said to herself.

"Tell me something," she said, trying to distract herself. "Dmitry Dmitrievich, Coach—he is downright evil these days, isn't he?"

"Well." Kostya winced. "He's dual, he has a doppelgänger . . . He's like a magnet with two poles. There are two sides to his essence: one is this sweet, darling man, our Coach, our Dima Dimych, everyone's pal. He teaches physical education to first and second years. But in reality he controls physiological changes in students on the verge of metamorphosis. And he has another side. I wish he didn't mix his guises. Sometimes he switches back and forth a hundred times a second, and he doesn't care that we retain our human emotions. We're used to it now, but in the beginning it was terrifying. It's just that half of him is very human, and the other—like a psychotic universe with no sense of ethics or compassion."

Sasha thought about dancing with Dima Dimych as her partner, and about telling her mom what a wonderful teacher he was . . .

"He fails people all the time," Kostya said softly. "He doesn't do it to be mean, it's just his principles. His exams are crazy difficult. No joke."

A tiny pizzeria was housed in the basement space across from the institute on Sacco and Vanzetti Street. Sasha bought the last slice two minutes before closing.

Returning to her room, she unlocked the balcony door for the first time. The balcony stretched along the entire floor. There was a touch of rust on its railings, and the balcony itself was only marginally more comfortable than a medieval chastity belt, but she enjoyed standing there, breathing in fresh air, letting the wind fan her face. The familiar trees had grown, and some had even managed to dry up and lose half of their branches.

"You must rebuild your informational component and reconstruct the exam in your memory," Sterkh had told her. "Make sure you write in your notebook every day. Do it every day, without breaks."

Sasha inhaled the cool air and thought of the seashore. Back on the wharf, many years ago, Mom smiled at Valentin, her new acquaintance, and dimples formed in her cheeks. It was a special smile; the way she smiled at Sasha was different.

That evening Mom saw a knight in shining armor. A man appeared out of the thick, viscous daily swamp, a man illuminated from inside, pulling her to him like a magnet, a man who understood her, whom she understood as well. How was it possible that two strangers would be made so perfectly for each other, and so quickly at that? Thinking of what happened next, Sasha gritted her teeth, knowing exactly how such an impossible thing was possible. Thinking of Valentin's heart seizure, his wife's arrival, Mom's dispassionate face, her dull, hopeless eyes . . .

She thought of Valentin coming back, and fighting for Mom, and begging for forgiveness, and divorcing his wife, and . . .

The puzzle pieces fit together. Sasha's mother was granted happiness, and she granted her daughter the right to leave for Torpa, and Farit Kozhennikov got what he wanted.

As always.

And now there was no man in her mother's life, and never had been. Mom probably didn't even realize her loss, or perhaps she vaguely felt it, but had no way to change anything. Her life was dedicated to her daughter, and now it would be dedicated to her granddaughter, and ahead of her was nothing but inevitable loneliness.

And the same for me, Sasha said to herself, again gritting her teeth. *And that's perfectly fine.*

By now her pizza resembled shoe leather, slightly stained by cheese and adorned with a sprig of dill. Nevertheless, beggars could not be choosers, and Sasha devoured half of her supper before freezing mid-bite, struck dumb by the most mundane thought: *Whatever happened to Valentin? Was he alive? How did his fate turn out? Was it possible that he ended up being happy?*

Sasha had never called the landline at Valentin's old apartment, but for some reason she still remembered the number from a piece of paper pinned to their refrigerator by a tiny magnet depicting the Swallow's Nest castle.

She bounced all the way downstairs, not quite believing she'd actually dial that number.

"Hello," a young-sounding male voice answered.

"Hello," Sasha said. "May I speak with Valentin?"

"Who?" the young man said.

"Your father." Sasha did not hesitate for a second.

"But," the young man was clearly confused, "he hasn't lived here for a long time."

"Would you mind giving me his new number?" Sasha asked.

"But who are you?"

I am Password, Sasha thought grimly. *I am an assassin of reality, a destroyer of grammatical structures.*

"I am with social services," she said out loud. "We have him registered at this number."

"But he hasn't lived here for sixteen years!"

Why hasn't he?

"Bureaucracy." Sasha made herself speak calmly. "We must have never updated his information. Could you please help me do that now?"

She didn't bother writing the number down; she simply memorized it and thanked her nameless interlocutor, then hung up and wiped the sweat off her forehead.

Valentin was divorced. He divorced his wife anyway, many years ago. He left his family of his own accord, regardless of his meeting Sasha's mother.

But who did he leave his family for? Did he have a new family? What if he had another son, and the new son was named Valentin after his father?

"Hello," a man's voice said on the other end of the line. The voice sounded tired and slightly muffled. Sasha hesitated, struggling to recognize it.

"Valentin . . ."

She forgot his patronymic. It was gone from her memory without a trace.

"I am your wife's colleague." She blurted out the first thing that came to mind.

"I am not married," he said slowly. "Who are you calling for?"

"I apologize, I must have the wrong number," Sasha said. She ended the call and stood there for a bit, pressing her forehead to the plastic wall of the phone booth.

He was alone, just like her mother. It was fair . . . but it made her sad.

"Leave them alone, will you?"

Sasha turned around. Somehow Lisa had managed to get extremely close without making any noise. Involuntarily, Sasha braced herself as if expecting the other girl to rip her stomach open using nothing but her bare hands.

Glancing at Sasha's face, Lisa stepped back and stretched her lips in a conciliatory smile.

"You've dialed your mother's number three times. And hung up three times. Do you think they have nothing better to do than to listen to your calls?"

Sasha looked down at the phone in her hands, realizing Lisa was absolutely correct. She hated that Lisa was spying on her, that she knew Sasha's home phone number. Of course, an informational object, a Word of the Great Speech, had no need to put any effort into spying. Lisa knew more about Sasha than Sasha cared to admit.

"It's none of your business," Sasha said wearily.

"Step aside." Lisa took a step forward, forcing Sasha to retreat toward a potted plant. Lisa picked up the phone and looked at Sasha over her shoulder.

"What's your mother's name?"

"Don't you dare," Sasha whimpered, adding two seconds later: "Olga Antonovna."

"Olga Antonovna?" Lisa said into the receiver, very gently and very confidently. "I am an old friend of Alexandra's. I'm calling to express my sympathy and ask if there is anything you need. Anything at all."

Sasha went momentarily deaf, as if a jet plane flew directly over her head. Lisa listened to the answer, nodded as if the other person sat in front of her, then kept talking, sorrowfully, guardedly. To Sasha, it seemed she was taking forever. Eventually Lisa hung up and stood silently with her back to Sasha, then turned and glanced at her again, questioning.

"Thank you," Sasha whispered.

Sasha had forgotten that stale tobacco scent of Lisa's room. Amused by Sasha's expression, Lisa folded herself into a chair and put her feet up on her desk.

"Isn't it hilarious that you ran out and married a classmate so fast your head must have spun?"

Sasha took a cautious peek at the whiteboard above Lisa's desk. A tube of toothpaste and two black markers stuck out of the magnet holder. For a few seconds, Sasha stared at the toothpaste.

Smiling, Lisa continued, "I thought you didn't care for boys in high school, like you were all about books and good grades, stuff like that."

"I didn't run out and marry him." Sasha forced herself to look away from the whiteboard and sit down on the edge of a chair. "It was a different woman."

"It was you," Lisa said categorically. "Of course it was you!"

She looked Sasha up and down as if choosing a steak at a butcher shop. Sasha cringed. Lisa blinked, instantly transforming from a discerning shopper to a very young, very unhappy girl.

"Do you think that maybe in some parallel text I lived happily ever after with my Lyosha? Until we broke up, like normal people. Or maybe we never broke up—"

Her voice caught, and she stared through Sasha, through the walls, into space. Sasha opened her mouth, trying to find some moment-appropriate words, but Lisa did not wait for consolation. Her face changed again; a grown-up Lisa looked back at Sasha with deeply sunken eyes.

"Your mother is holding up just fine. She's surrounded by people—relatives, colleagues. Everyone is there to express sympathy, all that stuff. It's terrible, of course, but not unnatural. Don't get involved, Samokhina. Don't even think about it. You don't belong there."

I don't belong here, either, she thought but didn't say. "I am not getting involved," Sasha said grimly. "I am a stranger to them. I am grammatically foreign."

"You should be happy about that," Lisa said forcefully. "Be happy you're a stranger to them. That means *he* won't eat them alive when you fail an exam."

"I am not going to fail," Sasha said quickly. Lisa gave her another look, shrugged, but decided to change the subject.

"How come you never talked about your mad high school romance during our first year?"

Who was I supposed to talk to, you? Sasha thought, but, out loud she only said, "There was no mad romance. I don't even understand what I found so appealing about him. He was a coward, a show-off, and a cheapskate."

"Was he cute?" Lisa squinted.

"Yes. He is super popular . . . " Sasha faltered. "Was super popular."

"So you were in love," Lisa mused. "People like you turn first love into a big shopping trip for a white dress and a long veil."

Sasha held her tongue. One hole in her sweater was enough for today.

. . .

A message from Sterkh arrived at 8 A.M.: "Dear Sasha, please use the attached file for today's assignment. See you tonight, N.V."

She poked her finger at the "Homework: Corrections-1" line, nearly breaking the monitor. The screen lit up in red as bright as if she had pressed her face against a working streetlight. Three dots swirled round and round in the middle of the screen, like burning birds above a global catastrophe.

The animated picture was akin to the black "fragments" Sterkh had given her before. She fastened her gaze on the swimming dots, trying to keep all three in her line of vision. She held her breath and began counting: *One. Two. Three . . .*

. . . One hundred ninety-seven. One hundred ninety-eight.

She saw herself falling from the sky, limp, head down, into the sea of red light. Below her was the city of tiled roofs and narrow streets, of weather vanes and the tower, the city straight out of fairy tales, out of a picture book, except it was all red, with no other colors to be seen. She thrashed in the air, trying to remember how to fly, but instead only sped up her desperate fall. The weather vane on top of the tower looked like a thin needle, and it was getting closer and closer, and Sasha could not look—or veer—away.

The weather vane pierced her flesh. Sasha found herself impaled on a needle at the pinnacle of the city. At a distance, she saw mountains and arched bridges, and she felt almost no pain, even though the spike of the weather vane poked out of her left collarbone, barely missing her face.

. . . And that's what it was all about. This weather vane was built for Sasha, and Sasha alone. The scenario had a few possible interpretations, but it wasn't particularly complicated: Sasha was supposed to extract a certain concept from *unexistence* and apply it to herself.

"No." She twitched like a butterfly mounted to cardboard. "I refuse, I don't accept, I will never!"

The red city blurred in front of her eyes, transforming into a symbolic image. The pain flared up and became real.

"I know it's hard," Sterkh said, pulling his sleeve over the mother-of-pearl mirror on his wrist. "But you didn't expect it to be easy, did you?"

Inside auditorium 14, Sasha pressed a tissue to her face. She had a

55

nosebleed that refused to stop. A tablet with a shattered screen lay on the desk.

Earlier in her room, when she came to, she could think of nothing better than to throw the device against the wall. She didn't even bother lying about breaking it by accident.

"Nikolay Valerievich . . . This correcting errors business—is it basically a simulation of different ways to execute me, one more exotic than the rest?"

He touched his sharp chin in a slightly nervous, awkward gesture.

"No. You got it all wrong. I have no idea how you even came up with these ideas, considering you are no longer a first-year student! It's not punishment. It's work. Work that has to be continued."

"But the tablet—" Sasha began, her voice trembling.

He wouldn't let her finish.

"The screen will be replaced. I will ask for a new protective case. Don't worry about the tablet."

Sasha stuffed the dirty tissue into her pocket and pulled another from the pack. She felt a hell of a lot worse than the tablet, but no one offered her a protective case.

"Open your notebook," Sterkh said with forced enthusiasm. "On the first page, under the title, write down . . . What was it—a simulation or a projection?"

Sasha hung her head. "A simulation. With built-in meanings."

"Describe these meanings." His voice had turned deceptively sweet.

"Correcting Errors" was written at the top of the page in chicken scratch. Sasha hesitated, and a drop of blood fell from her nose onto the lined page. It blossomed like a poppy.

"Continue," Sterkh said. His voice had no hint of mockery. Sasha looked up, and Sterkh gazed back at her solemnly.

Sasha picked up the pen and touched it to the paper. The pen didn't work. It scratched the page, but nothing came out.

"Continue," Sterkh said forcefully. "Come on."

Sasha looked at the page. Another drop of blood fell next to the first one. Her mind blank, Sasha dipped her ballpoint pen into the fresh spot.

"Completing assignment Corrections-1 . . ."

The pen glided over the page easily as if it were mass-produced to write in blood.

". . . I was given access to an informational model . . ."

She froze, staring at the crooked lines that were changing color from red to rust. A new drop fell off the tip of her nose. Sasha dipped her pen once again.

"Not comprehending the point of the assignment, I failed to . . ."

"But you *did* understand the point," Sterkh said gently.

"No, I didn't!" Sasha tossed her head.

Without responding, Sterkh opened a desk drawer, peeked in, then rummaged inside looking for something, frowning. Sasha held her breath, hoping he wouldn't find whatever he was looking for, but Sterkh fished out a folder full of papers and a large manila envelope. He stepped to the windowsill with his back to Sasha and shuffled the papers around, hiding them from view.

"Open it tomorrow at eight. Not a second earlier, not a second later," he said, placing the sealed envelope in front of her.

"Is it necessary to write in this notebook in blood?" Sasha blurted out.

"It's not required," he said solemnly. "However, blood is not only a bodily fluid, but also a catalyst for a multitude of meanings. You are an adult, Sasha. You shouldn't be so scared, like a child in a doctor's office. You will succeed as long as you work hard."

His voice did not falter, and yet Sasha knew he was lying to her. Perhaps he was lying to himself. "You will succeed": such empty words, devoid of meaning, a spell leeched of power.

"You're not going to report me, are you?" Sasha asked softly.

He shook his head, avoiding her eyes, then sighed.

"I never complain about my students to their advisors. You know that. But eventually we'll have winter exams, we'll have an official transcript, we'll have grades. And then I won't be able to help you."

Nearly all of her classmates were gathered around the bar, some with cups of coffee, some with their tablets, some staring at their smartphones. As before, Sasha stopped in the doorway for a moment. Thankfully, Kostya wasn't there, but she did spot Lisa by the far wall, weighing herself in front of a mirror. Sasha caught Lisa's eyes in the reflection.

"You look terrible," Anna Bochkova said casually.

Sasha did her best to look careless. Her patched-up sweater was now adorned with rust-colored stains, her nose was swollen, and she had no illusions regarding her looks.

"Lisa," she said awkwardly. "May I speak to you for a moment?"

Her classmates exchanged surprised glances, tinted with distrust and even confusion. *The sky is falling,* their faces said. But poker-faced Lisa followed Sasha down the corridor and into the empty hall, where the television was on with the sound turned off.

Lisa pulled out a cigarette and flicked the lighter.

"The third assignment at the final exam. What did you have for the third assignment?" Sasha asked softly.

A cigarette between her lips, Lisa held the lighter in front of her face, staring at the long bright orange flame. For a few seconds no one spoke. Sasha worried that Lisa was about to throw the lighter in her face.

Finally, Lisa inhaled and exhaled, took a deep drag of her cigarette, and put her lighter back into her pocket.

"I am not going to discuss the details with you," she said, and her voice sounded deep, calm, almost indifferent. "But in essence, they *claimed* us, just like we *claim* objects or concepts."

With her left, cigarette-free hand, she reached for the television panel, and her arm stretched out like a telescopic antenna, elongated by three extra meters. Her palm touched the screen and flattened into a thin membrane; her bones and tendons became visible, and through them Sasha could see the anchor reading the weather report. A second passed, and the anchor began to cough, pressing his hand against his throat, struggling to speak and staring at the camera with a shocked, frightened expression. Lisa pulled her hand away. Sparks flew from the wires behind the panel, and the screen went dark.

"Like we *claim* objects, concepts, or people," Lisa said, kneading the fingers of her now perfectly ordinary hand. "But after the exam, we become parts of Speech. Not in the sense of being nouns, adjectives, verbs—that, we knew a long time ago. But in the sense of becoming details of one mechanism. We belong to the Speech. None of us are whole on our own and none of us ever will be whole, we are nothing but parts, fragments . . ."

Sasha waved her hand in front of her face to drive away the smoke, then took a step back. "Speech will be using you," Oleg Borisovich Portnov had said to them once.

She walked over to the television panel, stood on tiptoes, and reached for the screen. She attempted to *claim* the plastic frame stuffed with electronics, but detected nothing aside from typical printed circuit boards, electronic chips, and interconnections.

"Have you considered using a hammer?" Lisa inquired. "Like the star student you are."

"Are you the star student now?" Sasha rubbed her hand. The skin on her palm itched as if from mosquito bites.

"An A in Coach's class is like a Nobel Prize, no less," Lisa said with a hint of complacency.

"You are going to be a very useful, very well-educated part of Speech," Sasha said.

She expected a witty retort, but Lisa simply took another drag of her cigarette. The glowing tip almost reached her fingers.

"What else could I be?" Lisa said after a long pause. "No one asked us if we wanted to matriculate at the institute. No one asked when they made us study. Do you have any idea how many times I dreamed of murdering my advisor?"

She took another drag, greedily, like someone about to be executed.

The cigarette smoke set off the fire alarm.

Lisa's hand reached all the way up to the ceiling and turned it off.

At five minutes to eight, a white letter-size envelope lay on the desk next to the stack of old textbooks and an empty Styrofoam coffee cup. The envelope was biding its time. "Corrections-2." Sasha looked away.

Wearing nothing but a T-shirt and a pair of panties, she stepped out to the balcony and took a deep breath of the autumnal air with its lingering traces of summer, the linden trees of Sacco and Vanzetti Street, and the scent of dying flowers. Thin fog slowly dissipated. Sasha stood outside, unaware of the cold.

Lisa's exercises did not include the city with the tiled roofs. There was no city in Kostya's exercises either. There were other images and other visualizations, but none of her classmates would share any details. Just like Sasha wouldn't tell anyone about the monster that lived inside the tower.

She heard footsteps on the second-floor balcony. Below, right under Sasha's feet, Andrey Korotkov leaned against the railing, lit a cigarette, and only then looked up. He almost dropped his cigarette; Sasha waved to him. After all, she wasn't naked, so why was Andrey so surprised at the sight of a girl in panties? He wasn't exactly a little schoolboy anymore.

She stepped back into her room, sat down at the desk, and focused on three red dots in the center of the page.

Outside auditorium 14 the sun was shining, and yellow leaves dropped softly off the linden trees. Intellectually, Sasha knew the leaves were yellow, the walls of the auditorium pale beige, Sterkh's hair ash-blond, and the collar of his shirt—pure white. And yet, everything in her line of vision was saturated in shades of red: scarlet, ruby, vermillion, garnet. The color was oppressive, and she wanted to shut her eyes, but under her eyelids things looked even worse: red sky. Red weather vane. A spike through her collarbone.

Sasha's notebook lay before Sterkh. Inside, crooked lines written in blood declared: "I will not do it i will not do it i refuse i refuse i refuse."

The words repeated, crawling over each other, and it looked as if Sasha had written a long, detailed essay, albeit in an awful chicken scratch.

"Your tablet is still being repaired," Sterkh said, not looking at Sasha. "You will receive your next assignment as a hard copy in an envelope again."

"Nikolay Valerievich, it's pointless." She let her eyes wander around the room, concentrating on nothing—that made things a little bit easier. "I refuse."

"Refuse what?" he asked softly. "What are you refusing? Yourself, your predestination, your future?"

Belatedly, Sasha realized that Sterkh was furious and spoke softly only to prevent himself from screaming.

"Are you refusing to fight, to change things, to eat, drink, sleep, get up in the morning? Are you refusing to work on correcting your mistakes? And what do you think is going to happen to you?"

"I'd agree a hundred times over!" Sasha burst out. "Just like all my classmates had agreed, or the ones who survived. But I can't, don't you see? I can't accept it, and he cannot make me. It's a vicious circle."

"He?" Sterkh said softly.

"I figured out whose projection is in the tower," Sasha said, looking away. "One of the infinite multitudes of *his* projections. Why did he bring me back to the institute, why is he asking for the impossible?"

"Think of how many times you felt desperate," he said, even softer. "So many things *seemed* impossible. And you always found a solution."

Yaroslav Grigoriev stood by the entrance to the pizzeria; luckily, today he was not in uniform but rather in jeans and a hoodie. Frantically, Sasha tried to figure out which day it was—he had two flights to Torpa a week, so today must have been one of them. And here he was, standing across the street from the institute, watching the windows, and looking away every now and then pretending he was there by accident, holding a pizza box as his alibi. Even if it was common knowledge that only starving students could digest the tomato paste–covered rubber sold in that restaurant.

Sasha cringed at the thought of having walked out onto the balcony wearing nothing but a tank top and a pair of panties. What if Yaroslav showed up in front of her dorm?

The tiny fourth-floor window was made of stained glass, so no matter how hard he tried, Yaroslav could not see Sasha's pale face. And yet, he stared—without hope. His gaze was not greedy or predatory, just wistful. And so tender.

What the hell, Sasha thought with a hint of desperation. *Such a handsome man, such a courageous pilot, and here he is, acting like . . .*

A young woman walked by. She must have gotten distracted by the sight of Yaroslav or perhaps she simply tripped on the dead leaves because she suddenly lost her balance and flapped her arms, trying not to fall. Her cell phone slipped out of her fingers and would have landed in a puddle if Yaroslav hadn't caught it at the last moment with his pizza-free hand.

The girl spoke to him, grateful and impressed and clearly eager to further the connection, but Yaroslav was already on his way, still holding that useless pizza box, and the girl watched his departure with obvious disappointment.

As did Sasha, surprising herself to no end.

"Hello, Samokhina."

Sasha took a second to cross the threshold, as if her feet would not cooperate. Coach gave her an appraising glance.

"You look tired. And the semester is just starting."

"I'll rest this weekend," Sasha said reluctantly.

"How are you doing with your error correction project?"

"It's proceeding according to the academic plan," Sasha mumbled. She could have sworn the hastily washed bloodstains on her patched sweater itched like nettle burns.

He smiled faintly. Then he closed his eyes and momentarily, instantly transformed. Only then did Sasha fully realize what Kostya meant by Coach "having a doppelgänger" and "mixing his guises." In front of her stood a handsome young man, who blushed easily and was only slightly older than his students, or perhaps even the same age.

"Do you prefer working while sitting down or standing?"

"Depends on what I am working on," Sasha mumbled, unpleasantly surprised by this metamorphosis. "Certain things are easier to do while lying down."

"You were never fresh with me before," he said with a slight reproach. "All right, let's look at the whiteboard. I am going to render a projection, and you're going to read it dynamically. Let's go."

He picked a marker, a black one this time, and stepped to the whiteboard. His sports jacket bulged slightly around his shoulders, not because of wings, like Sterkh's, but because of his massive, tire-like muscles. With a quick side glance at Sasha, who was still standing in the middle of the auditorium, he drew the first line, as if marking off the horizon, and began writing down signs and symbols at breakneck speed.

. . . It felt like running along a hallway lined with mirrors, circular saws, and razor blades. The information packet contained a short time loop between *today* and *now,* and a multitude of action choices, some fixed and some that allowed a million interpretations. Flickering lights and shadows, textures and meanings. Faster. Faster yet. As if a treadmill track under a runner's feet gained the speed of an airplane, and the runner rolled forward head over heels and flew off upside down.

The diagram on the whiteboard rippled under a horde of gray ants; the projection turned blurry and lost its meaning. Sasha began to fall; she was grabbed under her arms and placed back into her chair. Coach had caught her like this so many times when she'd fallen off the beam or uneven bars. She remembered his touch: always reliable, always friendly or brotherly, never creepy, without the tiniest hint of eroticism. For a second Sasha imagined she was at the gym again, and a table tennis lesson was about to begin.

In the last three days she'd passed out quite a few times, but the sensation was impossible to get used to. Sasha put her elbows on the desk, leaning forward, her eyes shut, listening to an eraser sliding over the whiteboard somewhere in the outside world, making a sound similar to a cricket's song. Coach cleaned the whiteboard silently, and Sasha chose not to speak, either.

"Don't you have money to buy new clothes?" he asked gently. Surprised, she opened her eyes. The whiteboard sparkled. Coach Dima Dimych, young and sensitive, looked like a Bengal tiger cub.

"I have money." Sasha forced the words out of her dry throat. "I don't have time for stores."

"You can order everything online." He sat down behind the teacher's desk. "Do you want me to teach you how to place an online order?"

"Am I failing because I failed the error correction assignment?" Sasha asked, staring directly into his pupils.

"You are failing because you can't succeed," he said gently, almost lovingly. "The lesson is over. There will be no makeup classes."

Her schedule merged its beginning to its end, like a Möbius strip, like flypaper. At least inside auditorium 14, in front of Sterkh, she could allow herself a meltdown.

"He is sabotaging me." Sasha rocked herself back and forth. "He refuses to explain things. I missed a whole semester, I can't understand anything, he has to go back to the basics!"

"Dmitry Dmitrievich is not capable of sabotaging anything. He is a function. Or, rather, he's a system of functions," Sterkh said sorrowfully.

"If his function is teaching, why isn't he teaching me anything?"

"His function is not teaching . . . " Sterkh faltered, as if regretting his own words. He glanced at Sasha, who waited tensely for him to continue. "A grammatical structure such as Dmitry Dmitrievich has a reserve of purposes and functions," he said slowly, carefully choosing his words. "Of missions and functions that are very hard to process for us, former human beings."

"'Us, former human beings.'" Sasha realized Sterkh had just placed both of them on the other side of the invisible barrier, as if they were allies.

She leaned forward, seizing the opportunity.

"Nikolay Valerievich. Help me. You helped me back then, during my second year . . ."

Sterkh glanced at something near the legs of his chair, bent down, and picked up a large black feather, stiff, with a metallic bluish sheen. He rolled it between his fingers as if trying to figure out how to best use it for household purposes.

"I am doing what I can, Sasha. But . . ."

Sterkh looked at the open notebook in front of him, at thick red lines: "do not be afraid do not be afraid do not . . ." With a heavy sigh, he placed the feather between the scribbled-upon pages, like a bookmark.

"So many of you have passed by—nominalized adjectives, proper nouns, pronouns, occasional verbs. But I have never met a student like you, Sasha. All I can do is shrug and admit that this is way out of my range."

Disappointed, Sasha did not respond. Sterkh handed her the notebook along with the feather bookmark, rose abruptly, and took a few steps around his office. He spent a few moments tapping the window with the tips of his fingers, then walked back to Sasha, pulling up the sleeve of his black sports coat.

"Look in here, please."

The mother-of-pearl mirror on a leather band sent a concentrated ray of light into Sasha's eyes, and she struggled not to blink.

"I will think of something," Sterkh said gently. "I will figure out how to help you. I promise."

The streets of Torpa were not as secluded as during the workweek; today Sasha saw families with children, and teenagers on bikes, and retirees with tiny dogs on leashes. All of them looked perfectly ordinary, normal, just like thousands of other passersby on the streets of small towns. The problem was that to Sasha, every passing car looked like a certain silver Mazda.

Downtown Torpa did not look like a ghost city, thrown out of history for fifteen years and then resurrected. And yet, there was nothing modern about Torpa: its narrow cobbled streets bore signs of being both two dozen and two hundred years old. Sasha paid close attention, almost sniffing the air, searching for the elusive plume of the last decade and a half that had melted into nothing.

She stopped in front of the sporting goods store where Yegor once purchased two pairs of skis. It had the same sign, by now more vintage than outdated. Sasha decided going in would be a bad idea, so she walked on until she came to a two-story shopping mall that was not there before. How convenient; now she could surprise Coach with new duds at her individual session on Tuesday. Did people still say "duds"?

Did they say that fifteen years ago?

She couldn't remember.

"Are you looking for anything in particular?"

The salesperson, a tall curvy woman of about thirty-five, watched Sasha with curiosity. Sasha suddenly realized that the woman was the same age as Alexandra Koneva, née Samokhina.

"Jeans," Sasha said curtly.

The salesperson gave her the appraising look of an experienced stylist.

"Would you consider trying on a dress? With that gorgeous figure of yours—"

"Jeans," Sasha repeated. "Blue jeans."

The woman nodded enthusiastically, demonstrating complete understanding, and stepped toward the row of hangers.

"You must be a student; what's your specialty?"

"Management information systems," Sasha said without hesitating.

"Management is good," the salesperson said, taking three pairs of jeans off the shelf. She sighed. "Back when I was in tenth grade, I fell in love with one of your kids. He was so handsome! I told my mother I wanted to apply to the institute, and she just about murdered me. She said it was a cult, full of drug addicts. Told me to stay away. She even sent me to my grandmother for six months, and when I came back, that pretty boy of mine was, umm, different, I guess? Just shuffling around, staring into space. Strangely, I never saw him again."

She gave Sasha a searching look. Stone-faced and silent, Sasha picked up a couple of cartoon character T-shirts from a pile. It sounded as if, in her youth, the salesperson may have fallen in love with Victor or Lenya, the second years. Both had been very handsome before the destruction phase had begun. Or, perhaps, the woman pined for Zakhar, who eventually failed the exam . . .

Sasha glanced at the large dressing room mirror, partly obscured by a heavy curtain, and saw a man in a dark hoodie. She turned sharply; the man stood in front of the store, his profile visible to Sasha. He seemed to be fascinated by the greeting cards display. After a moment, he left, apparently no longer interested in the cards. He never looked at Sasha.

Sasha ran out and caught up with him in the lobby of the shopping center.

"What do you want from me, Mr. Grigoriev?"

But it wasn't Yaroslav. It was a total stranger, a man of about forty, balding and very confused.

He wasn't the only one.

What am I doing, chasing his ghost?

CHAPTER THREE

The next sunny Sunday morning found Sasha in Torpa's tiny terminal. She watched passengers shuffle from the aircraft to the exit, airport staff unload luggage onto carts, and technicians walk around the aircraft.

She had a special reason to be here. This confusion grew day by day, preventing her from studying, and she needed to quash it like a rebellion—with utmost cruelty. Whatever Grigoriev the pilot thought, whatever he had fantasized, Sasha would force him to part with his illusions. She'd force herself to part with her illusions as well, because, frankly speaking, she was absolutely sick of illusions. Yes, she liked him. But she wouldn't tell him about it. On the contrary, what she was going to tell him would make him, a grown man, avoid her like a plague.

With that purpose in mind, Sasha learned the flight schedule by heart; luckily, it was quite short. She also knew the frequency of the bus trips in and out of town—every hour and a half.

Eventually, the flight crew walked down the airstair: a couple of flight attendants, a younger one and an older one, and a pilot trainee, a short skinny guy resembling Alexander Pushkin. Closing the procession was Yaroslav Grigoriev. Sasha saw him from afar . . .

. . . and her heart stopped for a moment.

She remembered how they strolled the streets of Torpa, not touching each other, only their shadows intertwined on the glossy cobblestones. Only trails of scents mingled in the autumn air.

On a glide slope . . .

And later they sat side by side, and the rosebush was bursting at the seams with sparrows. His hand with its long fingers lay still under Sasha's touch, like a delicate bird she didn't want to frighten.

"Who are you going to kill if I don't study hard enough?" she'd asked Farit Kozhennikov not so long ago.

"You've gotten cheeky," Farit replied.

Yaroslav walked, as if in slow motion: his white jacket, black epaulets, a peaked officer's cap. Sasha wished for him to keep on walking toward her, never getting closer because he was about to approach and then she'd have to say something. She'd have to make a decision . . .

Who are you going to kill?

The hurried stream of passengers had already moved across the waiting area behind Sasha's back. Yaroslav disappeared inside the building. Sasha tore herself away from the window, dashed across the room, stumbled over someone's bag, apologized, and collapsed in the closest seat, keeping her head low.

They walked by her, all those passengers and their luggage. Two flight attendants and the pilot who looked like Pushkin. Then she saw a pair of black shoes below a pair of uniform trousers and heard the voice that sent shivers up and down her spine.

"Yes, Dad," he said on the phone, wearily, patiently, and very lovingly. "What should I pick up on the way? Of course, whatever you want. But in this weather we should probably—"

The glass doors closed behind him. Sasha looked down to let her tears fall onto the dark fabric of her backpack in her lap. She didn't want her face to be wet.

I can't live without you.

She always thought this expression sounded unnatural, and such a cliché.

She waited for her tears to dry, then she raised her head.

"No, Farit, no. Nice try, but no."

She got up and left, and on her way out she saw the familiar Mazda leave the parking lot.

...

Shopping bags were strewn all over her room. She'd tossed her purchases on the floor, on the bed, on the desk, everywhere, and her room now resembled a messy warehouse. All her money, everything that Denis Myaskovsky had passed to her, and everything Farit had given her as an advance toward her stipend—she'd spent everything on clothes. At least now she knew what had made her go back to the store yesterday, grabbing two bags full of lacy lingerie in addition to everything else. "It's so feminine," the salesperson said, trying to ingratiate herself.

Sweet languor, the desire to please, attraction, longing, the proverbial butterflies in her stomach. Sasha's body knew what was happening before her oxytocin-addled brain did.

That's why Lisa, having run into Sasha in the hallway, had said suspiciously, "I am getting a man feedback from you. A normal man, a grown-up. Like if you had a crush on someone, but not like a little girl, but like an adult."

No! she thought now, ready to slam her head into the wall. *I am going to study hard on my own. I am extremely motivated, and there is no reason to add anything to my motivation! No need to add anyone, Farit! No one! I . . .*

She stopped for a moment, her eyes shut. *Forget Yaroslav. Forget his name. Stop thinking of a polar bear. Hair of the dog is the only cure.*

She glanced at herself in the mirror, brushed her hair, and left the room. Luckily, she saw no one in the hallway. Luckily, Kostya was home.

She walked in without knocking and locked the door behind her. She stepped toward Kostya and took him into her arms.

He froze at first, and then embraced her, but it felt awkward, like hugging a tree with dry, brittle branches. Sasha forced herself to remember their first year's kissing marathons in empty foyers, and how forbidden, how amazing, how joyful and sweet it was. And yet, hugging him now, she felt nothing. The thought of touching Yaroslav's hand with a tip of her finger made her feel as if she was hurled into a fire, but squeezing and caressing Kostya was just as appealing as making out with a sofa cushion. With terrible timing, she thought of Zhenya, of New Year's Eve, of Kostya's infidelity, and everything that happened after, and she was surprised by her thoughts because she had forgiven him a long time ago.

But he wasn't cold. He was nothing like a winter tree with brittle branches. Sasha felt his heart beat faster, felt his breath quicken . . .

He pulled her closer.

Simultaneously, they pulled away from each other. Sasha took a step back. He raised his hand, as if building an invisible wall between them.

"Sasha, I'm sorry. I can't. Because of Zhenya."

She was grateful to him.

Textual Module, volume 8, was in pretty bad shape, as if someone had used it for a football, its spine half torn off. Pages stuck out in different directions. Portnov used to tell second years: "Now you must apply conscious efforts to use *Textual Module* as an intermediary between you and the archive of meanings available to you at this stage. Theoretically, you may encounter just about anything, including a fragment of your most feasible future."

"My sweet, darling book," Sasha said with an idiotic smile. "You know that I always read you diligently and with a great deal of attention. Tell me about the future. Not mine. His future. Please."

The only times she used that sassy yet pleading tone was when she'd spoken to the elevator in her building when she was a child. She felt the need to appease the elevator because it had tremendous power over her and could stop between floors, and that was the stuff of Sasha's childhood nightmares. She couldn't explain why she decided to speak to *Textual Module* today of all days, as if her life depended on it.

Gingerly, she pulled the damaged cover open like pulling a piece of old silk off a pile of treasure. She began reading the first paragraph, then the second, then continued further, forbidding herself to stop, turning the pages like ripping old bandages off dried-up wounds. Gibberish tossed and turned in her brain like tank treads, and her tears saturated the paper. Sasha read, struggling through the grinding noise and the howling that filled the book, and suddenly bright light sliced her eyeballs.

. . . *A luminous spherical cloud, like a wheel hung on a silver rod. A pearly blue funnel, a soft glow: cosmic dust and clouds of gases, forming a queue. A bit longer, and the clouds would move beyond the event horizon. The point of no return.*

Sasha gulped air, as if emerging from an ocean depth. The meaning ended. All that remained was a nervous tremor and regret over the missed opportunity.

The archive of meanings available to Sasha resembled a library, where books lay in disarray, some with missing pages or torn covers. Pornographic novels, philosophical treatises, home economics tips and tricks, school textbooks. Some time ago Sasha managed to bring order to all these volumes, but whatever had happened at the final exam shook up the shelves like an earthquake, and the meanings scattered and became white noise.

A shadow passed. The light flickered, the window quivered under a gust of wind, and the balcony creaked.

Sasha opened the balcony door.

Wrapped in an old-fashioned leather trench, Sterkh stood on the balcony, his hands on the railing. The outline of his wings vanished in the semidarkness. His ash-colored tresses swayed in time with the wind.

"Good evening. I hope I didn't frighten you."

"Good evening." Sasha shook in the raw September air. "Are we going to fly?"

"Not tonight," he said curtly. "But I have something for you."

He pulled an envelope out of an inner pocket.

"Sasha, the assignment I gave you on Saturday—I need it back. Take this one instead. Open it tomorrow at eight in the morning."

"Won't you come in?" Sasha mumbled. A bit too late, she remembered her room was a mess.

"Thank you, but no." He shook his head. "Next time."

Sasha stepped back into her room, picked up the Monday assignment in its sealed envelope, and closed her eyes in a rush of wild joy: She didn't have to open this blasted envelope. Didn't have to plunge head down from the red sky onto an iron spire. Didn't have to hear the sound of the weather vane piercing her lungs and emerging between her ribs. Didn't need to feel the monster's command in her bones. Didn't need to stain the pages in her notebook with her own blood . . .

She glanced at the second envelope, which Sterkh had just given her; it was smaller and much thinner. What kind of an assignment had he brought her? Was it a new kind of execution? Was Sasha going to be burned at the stake in a public square, or cut into a thousand tiny pieces?

On the balcony, Sterkh waited, looking above the roofs. The wind touched his wings and the feathers bristled and changed colors, from steely blue to pitch black.

"I apologize for showing up without a warning," he said, taking the sealed envelope from her hand. "I happened to have an idea regarding you. I hope your tablet will be fixed by Monday, and I will no longer have to act as a pigeon post."

A second later, an enormous shadow made the lights flicker off on Sacco and Vanzetti Street; the shadow passed, and the lights went back on.

There was no doubt that Sterkh was an exceptional pedagogue. If he ever made mistakes (and in regard to Sasha, he was wrong at least twice), he had no problem admitting his errors to his students' faces. With all his ostentatious courtesy, however, he was absolutely brutal when it came to the curriculum. In this, Sasha had no illusions.

The envelope contained a sheet of paper with two handwritten lines: "*Conceptual Activator*, volume 2, page 109. Define and delineate the basic concept of the diagram as the name of the subject. Implicitly express the essence of the subject through what it is not."

Sasha felt a shiver run up and down her spine. A wave of delicious terror washed over her, the same one she felt opening a new textbook in the beginning of her third year.

The diagram on page 109 looked relatively simple, and yet Sasha felt like an ice-skater entering the rink for the first time after fracturing both her ankles. By noon she completed the first part of the assignment: "the name of the subject" turned out to be the word "freedom." Her next step would be "implicitly expressing" freedom through what it was not.

She had known how to work hard since her first year. Actually, she developed her work ethic in first grade. She knew how to concentrate so hard that even her cup of tea and a sandwich remained untouched. Her nice fat notebook lost a bunch of pages, like a linden tree in the fall. Her trash bin, on the other hand, was overflowing. Much-sharpened pencils became short and stubby. Her back straight and stiff, Sasha wrote down one meaning after another, sorting out names, building associations, using paper to create a model of the world that had everything but freedom. A world in which the concept of freedom was replaced by an oddly shaped hole.

Almost immediately she lost her way in broad daylight, in freedom and will, prison and chains, freedom as a grammatical concept and as physical reality. Random images intertwined, distracting her: a fist stopping right in front of someone's nose and, for some reason, a long line to an outhouse (an awareness of a physiological need?). Sasha tore up the paper, sharpened yet another pencil, and began again. She had to compile everything that did not constitute freedom, had nothing to do with freedom, and simultaneously expressed freedom so that it could never be confused with anything else.

By lunchtime, her notebook had lost all its pages. Sasha dug through her backpack and all the shopping bags and realized that in her mad search for clothes and lingerie she heavily miscalculated her need for office supplies. Glancing at her watch (it showed five minutes to two), Sasha went into the hall barefoot.

She knocked on the very first door, but no one answered. She knocked on the next one. Eventually she made it all the way to the stairs, losing all hope in finding anyone at home, when one of the doors opened, and her old roommate Oksana, a student in Group B, peeked out.

For a second they stared at each other with the same expression, as if they both saw a ghost. Oksana spoke first.

"Then it's true. They brought you back. Amazing."

"Oksana, lend me a notebook or some paper," Sasha said. "I really need it right now. I'll buy another one for you tomorrow."

By half past five, after a never-ending series of efforts, she discovered that there was no freedom whatsoever. It simply did not exist. A few times Sasha thought she was about to catch the elusive meaning, grab it by its tail, like a cat chasing the light of a laser pointer. Previously so harmonious and lucid, the world of ideas grew faded and distorted, like a ray of spring sunshine on rotten wallpaper. The notepad Oksana lent Sasha had been filled out with writing and doodles, and Sasha thought it smelled terrible, even though it couldn't possibly smell of anything but, faintly, cardboard.

Contrary to his custom, Sterkh was not waiting for her in auditorium 14; instead, he was pacing along the corridor, his arms behind his back, seemingly anxious. Hearing Sasha's footsteps, he turned to her quickly.

"So, how is it going?"

Sasha met his eyes. Of course, he knew it right away, but continued to look questioningly for a few more seconds, hoping for a different answer. Sasha looked away first, feeling Sterkh's disappointment like a toothache.

Once inside the auditorium, she placed the only surviving sheet of paper on his desk. The rest of the notepad had perished in her trash bin. Sterkh looked at the paper in astonishment, as if Sasha had brought him a ticket for last year's holiday show.

"That's all I could do," she mumbled, even though no explanation was necessary.

Sterkh paced around the auditorium, his folded wings quivering under his jacket. He turned on his heels and looked at Sasha with a new glimpse of hope.

"Show me what you wrote on correcting errors."

"Nothing." Sasha barely moved her lips.

"I asked you to write daily," Sterkh said very softly, with a childish hurt in his voice.

He opened a desk drawer, took out a tablet, and placed it in front of Sasha. The tablet looked different. A thick screen and a plastic protective layer disfigured the delicate device, like a pair of heavy old-fashioned glasses on a lovely young face.

"Thank you," Sasha said.

Avoiding her eyes, he picked up the sheet of paper from her notepad.

"In your second year, you were a solar prominence, a force of nature that could not contain itself. And now you are rational, competent, intelligent, strong-willed . . . You were taught well, and you studied hard. Did what happened during the final exam completely destroy you?"

"Yes," Sasha said. Impulsively, she added, "And I think Farit knew it was going to happen. He knew I couldn't do it, and he was simply playing with me. He likes having such a fascinating, rare toy."

"You are awarding him human motivation," Sterkh said heavily. "While he . . ."

He faltered and was silent for a few moments, then got up and said decisively, "Wait for me, please."

He pulled his phone out of his black jacket on the way to the door. Sasha lowered her head and listened to the sound of the wind outside, counting the minutes to herself. *One. Two . . . Ten.*

When Sterkh came back, his face, habitually pale, now looked grayish green, and it terrified Sasha.

"What happened?"

"I tried to help you . . ." Sterkh clutched the back of his chair with long elegant fingers. "But he . . ."

74

"Did you report me?" Sasha gasped for air. "Nikolay Valerievich, did you complain to my advisor?"

"I wanted to help you," Sterkh said in a dead voice. "But I think I harmed you instead."

Sasha made the distance from the institute to the dorms in a thick mental fog. She hadn't eaten anything, but she wasn't hungry. She felt as if her human shell had thinned out, worn out like an old nightgown, nearly transparent after many rounds of laundry. Someone greeted her, but she didn't react.

In the hallway of her dorm, a large screen broadcast the latest news. The sound was turned off, but the anchor's facial expression clearly indicated he was informing his audience of yet more bad news. He looked quite distressed.

And here it was. Pieces of an aircraft all over the screen. A familiar-looking wing, blackened with soot—Sasha thought she may have sat near a round window right above that very wing. She recalled watching forests and rivers float beneath her.

On a glide slope. When the sun is low and the clouds are sparse. It can be stunning.

Silence plugged Sasha's ears, like Sterkh's headphones. She thought she shrank into a dot, then blew up noiselessly, and the air blast took down everything—walls, roofs, light, darkness, time . . .

In total silence she went up to her room and unlocked the door with her entry card. The only thing she worried about was that her refurbished tablet still contained the file named "Corrections-1."

. . . Two fifty-seven. Two fifty-eight.

The wind whistled in her ears, and the vertical fall made her feel faint. Sasha saw herself in the sky above the red city, saw the tower, the spire, and the tip of the weather vane directed at her stomach.

This city was neither a model nor a projection. It was neither volatile nor stable, neither real nor imaginary. *Express the essence of the subject through what it is not.* This city could only be understood by turning it inside out.

And now Sasha understood the price of Sterkh's assignment.

The tower was neither center nor heart, neither concept nor structure nor illusion. The monster inside was neither alive nor dead. The monster was not freedom, but it could be described using the concept of freedom. It was not fear, but it could be understood by shedding fear, if only for a few seconds.

Sasha felt jerked upward like a paratrooper whose parachute has just opened. She thrashed in the air, threw her arms out, and found herself flying rather than falling.

On a glide slope.

For the first time in all her attempts to complete Sterkh's assignment, for the first time in all her flights and falls over the red city, Sasha saw her own shadow on the cobblestones. She expected it to resemble a soaring bird, but instead her shadow looked more like a dragonfly with disproportionately large, frozen wings. And yet, she flew, in circles, in spirals, leaving the weather vane to her right, then to her left, then losing sight of it entirely. The air felt spiky and hard, like set construction foam.

Sasha saw the eyes of the one who stared at her through the walls. It was a very familiar, assessing, studying gaze. Sasha felt herself smiling and that smile frightened her.

Her feet touched the cobblestones in front of the tower, and her wings shuddered and hung loose.

The tower unfurled, and the thing inside it climbed out into the square. Sasha looked into the monster's eyes and did not look away.

The red air quivered. The thing in the tower flowed forward like an oil slick. The grammatically correct comprehension that death was inevitable and painful enveloped Sasha in a cloud of stench.

"Go to fucking hell!" Sasha bellowed. "I hope you blow up, you bastard!"

The pavement under her feet softened like aspic and swallowed Sasha's feet up to her ankles. Struggling to escape, Sasha twitched, unfolded her dragonfly wings, and attempted to take off only to realize she was firmly glued to her spot.

The monster moved deliberately, slowly, spilling from point to point in space, centimeter by centimeter. It planned to devour its victim leisurely, luxuriously, and was now deliberating one of the millions of excruciatingly painful ways to make her die, or perhaps deciding on applying all of them at once. Sasha growled, staring at the creature's unmoving, sterile, merciless eyes.

Accept me.

It was said without words. The order was made outside of speech, and outside of the Great Speech—it was the essence of order, a naked idea of a command.

"Go fuck yourself," Sasha croaked.

In one huge jump, the monster negotiated the distance between them and enveloped Sasha, possessing her, making her a part of itself. The last fleck of light she saw was a flash of the tiny mirror in Sterkh's hands: fate, destiny, predetermination, necessity, compulsion, law. Sasha recognized this moment as the point in time when she could realize her freedom, expressing it through what freedom was not.

"I banish, I refuse, I deny . . . I love."

A ballpoint pen fell onto the laminated floor. The sound tapped her fading consciousness, like a doctor's reflex hammer tapping the tendon below the kneecap. The pen made a hollow plastic sound—it was a material object, sold at the office supplies store; its barrel was only half full, or perhaps even completely empty. Nearly devoured by the tower-dwelling monster, Sasha reached for the pen with her trembling hand; she grabbed and squeezed the smooth plastic, and the pen seemed to acquire its own will. The pen wrote in blood, and something between a text and a scream escaped from its tip in a jagged sinusoid of a medical monitor. It was an assembly line, a conveyor belt tossing symbols from one reality into another . . .

Sasha opened her eyes. She found herself in her dorm room; the tablet lay on the floor, but both the case and the protective glass remained intact.

The ballpoint pen looked short and stubby. Her "Corrections" notepad was filled up to its last page, in compact dense writing in red and rust brown. It was a pile of symbols, complete and utter gibberish, as if Sasha had copied the contents of *Textual Module*.

She finally got some use out of the stupid notepad. She found what she was looking for.

"You are Password—a key word that opens a new informational structure. Macrostructure. Do you understand what it means?"

They tried to stop her during the final exam. She escaped their power, to *reverberate* and open a new informational expanse, a world without fear.

Instead, she'd made a mistake. She became Password, and the Password was "Do not be afraid," and expressing it through negation distorted its meaning.

All aircrafts are capable of crashing.

She had read the contents of her notepad several times, starting with the very first entry: "Completing assignment Error Corrections-1, I was given access to the informational model . . . Due to misunderstanding the point of the assignment, I failed to . . ."

The first entry was followed by repeating words, incoherent complaints, and finally a fragment of *Textual Module* written in longhand. Reading it for the first time, Sasha went blind for a few minutes; when the fog cleared, she began again. Clanking gibberish released a fragment of text, not quite straightforward but more or less readable: "You are Password—a key word . . ."

A knock on her door made Sasha shudder.

"I am sleeping," she said, and was surprised by the sound of her own voice.

"No need to lie," someone said gravely behind the door. Sasha involuntarily recoiled and pushed her feet off the floor, making her chair roll over to the balcony door.

The lock turned without her participation. Farit Kozhennikov entered, closing the door behind him.

"You know it wasn't the same flight, don't you?"

"It was every flight, all of them," Sasha said, fighting a bout of dizziness. "All the flights in the world. All of them, every time. All aircrafts are capable of crashing."

"Enough of your tantrums, Samokhina," he said almost inaudibly. Sasha heard the sound of running water. A cold glass was placed in her numb, crooked fingers.

"Well, whose fault is it that you can't work without someone kicking you," Farit said. "But when someone does, you are like a hand grenade, ready to blow at a moment's notice."

Sasha drank the water, spilling half on her new T-shirt. Farit glanced around the room, picked up Sasha's jacket off the back of the chair, and hung it in the closet. He straddled the chair, facing Sasha.

"You need to learn how to use obscene language. Don't waste your time on euphemisms. Your pilot is doing just fine. I need him alive. And so do you."

"A different flight," she repeated like an old record. "But I couldn't do it. I failed. I didn't make it."

"Remind me—what is the price of experience?"

She did not reply.

"That's my clever girl," he said with satisfaction. "You recalled what happened during the final exam, you figured out and isolated your error, and you finally processed and accepted the most important examination requirement."

Sasha took a few minutes to absorb his words, then jerked up the sleeve of her thin sweater. Her forearm was perfectly smooth, only goose bumps, blue veins, and a familiar birthmark.

"You don't get a sign, because freedom is an inalienable quality of Password," Farit said. "However, should freedom be expressed through something else, Passwords can be caught. You retain your freedom, but it's expressed through unfreedom. Fate, destiny, predetermination, necessity, compulsion, law . . . and, of course, love."

"My freedom," Sasha echoed.

"That's right. The third assignment on the final exam is when students voluntarily transfer their freedom, sacrificing their own will in exchange for a new status."

"Voluntarily?" Sasha said, scowling at him.

"Voluntarily indeed," he said, nodding. "Students surrender their freedom with a great deal of relief, of joy. They are thrilled to give up so little in exchange for inner peace. When your professors realized that not only did you not intend to give in but had no concept of what was required . . ."

He laughed as if recalling a particularly clever joke.

"I am Password," Sasha said.

"That's right." The light of the table lamp was reflected in his glasses. "Passwords would never sacrifice their freedom, which means Passwords by definition cannot complete the third assignment. This works like a circuit breaker. Passwords are filtered out during the exam and are not allowed to graduate."

"'He should not poke a lighter at a nuclear bomb.'" Sasha glanced at her right hand. Burn marks remained in those spots where her fingers had touched the pen.

"But it's my bomb," he said happily. "It's my well-trained, well-schooled bomb. I can't take possession of you, but you have taken possession of me, and I'd like to point out that it was completely voluntary. I no longer expect you to disobey and get out of control."

"Why?" Sasha said through gritted teeth. "Why are you doing this, you bastard?"

"You can just call me Farit," Kozhennikov said sweetly. "You're old enough."

"I thought you told me to use obscenities."

"Touché. Still, 'Farit' will be fine."

"I don't want to." She squeezed her burned fingers into a fist.

"I'm sure. You and I have a lot in common, more than between either one of us and those you're used to thinking of as humans." He took off his glasses and proceeded to study them, holding the thin black frames with the tips of his fingers. "When Sterkh says, 'us, former human beings,' you think you are both in the same boat, or on the same side of a volleyball net. When your classmates hold a collection to cover your initial expenses, you feel like you're one of them. But Sasha . . . even Sterkh doesn't entirely understand what you are."

"I don't understand it, either," Sasha said, looking into his calm, perfectly human brown eyes. "Or rather, I don't want to understand it."

"You don't have to—yet." He winked at her. "It's enough that *I* understand it."

He rose and stepped toward the door, then paused to look at her.

"I'm pleased with you, but there will be no breaks or excuses. From this point on, please study Analytical Specialty seriously, thoughtfully, not just skimming the surface like you have until now."

"I—" Sasha gasped in resentment.

"You." He raised his hand as if flagging down a cab. "Find a way to excel in Dmitry Dmitrievich's class, otherwise, you will suffer consequences. And don't dump your pilot, he's feeling rather sad."

Catching her eyes, he snorted and put his dark glasses back on.

"Do love him—it's so very important for you. Love like an adult, instead of loitering in airports, waiting for flights. Remember that all aircrafts are capable of crashing."

In the morning, instead of her usual assignment, she received a curt message from Sterkh: "Sasha, please stop by auditorium fourteen as soon as possible. Bring your notebook."

From the gym downstairs, she could hear the clanging sound of barbells. A scent of coffee permeated the corridor. And yet, the dorm seemed empty, perhaps even deserted. Sasha stepped into the courtyard without running into a single other human being. The day promised to be sunny and unseasonably warm. Through the alleyway, Sasha passed onto Sacco and Vanzetti.

Subconsciously, she put off her meeting with Sterkh. She didn't really want to talk to anyone at that moment. The new reality that opened up last night was disproportionately huge, and now Sasha rejoiced in hiding inside her human self, inside the five senses, inside hunger, thirst, inside denial, anger, and bargaining. From now on, every time a wave of terror washed over her, she could remind herself that Yaroslav was alive. It was much more important. Yaroslav was alive, and the fact that Sasha was Password paled in comparison.

Tiled roofs glistened in the sun, a murder of crows circling above. The cobblestones under Sasha's feet seemed more than simply old; they looked ancient. Sasha stood still for a minute, her breath coming out in a little cloud, then went up the stone steps to the entrance of the institute. In the hall, under the equestrian statue, she saw a group of fifth years.

Sasha remained by the entrance, watching as they moved in a cluster, synchronous, as if each one was a shadow of the other. Ignoring her, the fifth years marched over to the schedule board, stopped in front of the electronic tableau, and looked up in perfect unison. Sasha could have sworn there were now six of them where a moment ago she saw only five, two girls and three young men. And now they were seven, and a moment later five again; as their own reflections, they turned and moved across the vestibule, toward the entrance to the assembly hall, merging and separating again, but never losing a single step. Sasha blinked. The fifth years disappeared, and only Kostya sat by the foot of the stone statue, a tablet in his hands.

"Did you see that?" Sasha asked.

"They are having a thesis consultation meeting in the assembly hall," Kostya said softly, not looking at her. "Dependent words are lining up into homogenous chains to save energy. They form a train with a subject noun or a verb as the engine."

"Are we going to be like them?"

"We *are* like them already." Kostya was still avoiding her eyes. "Except for you, obviously. You are special."

"Are you mad at me?" Sasha asked after a pause.

"Yes," Kostya said. "Like a total idiot, I still worry about you. Our love has gone away, and all the violets have died, but fear stuck around."

He finally tore himself away from the screen and looked up, and Sasha saw his red, inflamed, very tired eyes.

"I know *he* came to the dorms. And that *he* was in your room."

"Kostya, your father and I have known each other for a very long time," she said placatingly. "Don't worry about me. How do you know that, by the way?"

"He came to see me, too. Is that a new dress?"

Leaving for the institute that morning, Sasha had pulled the first random item from the pile on the floor—whatever didn't need to be ironed. It was a jersey knit dress, and now it hugged her body like a glove, making Sasha feel naked.

"What did he want from you?" Kostya's gaze made her nervous, and she forced a little smile. "You're doing well with the assignments, aren't you?"

"With Coach, you never really know if you're doing well or not," Kostya said grimly. "And *he* likes to play a concerned father every now and then. He comes, and he asks just like you, same words, 'You're doing well with the assignments, aren't you? There won't be any surprises during the winter exams, will there?' Fucking hypocrite . . ."

Kostya sighed. A few moments later, his face brightened a bit.

"You wouldn't be on your way to the cafeteria, by any chance?"

"I wouldn't be," Sasha said, glancing at the clock above the entrance. "Sterkh is waiting for me."

"An unscheduled meeting?"

"Do you know my schedule?"

On her way out, Sasha turned back and saw Kostya still looking at her, his face darkened with anxiety.

She walked up to the fourth floor and passed a long corridor with a squeaky parquet floor; stopping in front of the auditorium, she reached for the door . . . and froze in place. Not because she heard voices. No, not a single sound came from behind the door. And yet, whatever entity happened to be inside the auditorium exuded tension, like the ultrasonic hum of an enormous colony of hornets. Sasha sensed it, but not with her ears or skin; this buzzing could not be heard, it could only be comprehended.

She took a step back, careful not to betray her presence, but whatever was happening inside the auditorium stopped abruptly, as if someone pressed down a bass string.

"Come in," Sterkh said. He sounded different, slightly hoarse. Sasha entered.

Hunched over more than usual, Sterkh was leaning onto the desk. By the window, Coach appeared in his nonhuman hypostasis, his face resembling a gas mask. The tension between the professors burned like acid.

"Hello," Sasha said after a minute pause.

"Did someone ask you to come in?" Coach's eyes, with their diaphragm pupils, expressed nothing.

"I asked her to come in," Sterkh said dryly.

A faint draft flew through the room even though all the windows and doors were closed.

"I am expecting you in class today, Samokhina," Coach said. "Watch the schedule and don't even think of being tardy."

He left. Sasha thought Sterkh sighed with relief. His wings, folded under the sports jacket, tensed up, then relaxed again.

"Nikolay Valerievich . . . " Sasha faltered. "I am sorry for everything I said to you yesterday . . ."

He shook his head, as if saying: *No need to mention anything.*

"I am Password." Sasha rummaged through her backpack and pulled out her notebook. Every single page was covered in writing. A black feather lay between the last page and the cover, like a bookmark. "I don't entirely understand it, but I am even more afraid of it than Dmitry Dmitrievich. Although he doesn't really know what fear is."

Sterkh opened the notebook and looked through it, as if this gibberish scrawled in blood was expected and perfectly reasonable.

"Congratulations. Overall, the errors have been corrected, and you are now entering the next phase. You are standing at the threshold of many incredible discoveries . . ."

This was clearly not what he wanted to say.

"Why didn't you tell me right away?" Sasha allowed herself a hint of reproach.

"It cannot be explained, it can only be experienced," Sterkh said wearily. "And besides. No one knew if you'd make it. Dmitry Dmitrievich was convinced it wasn't even worth a try."

"Nikolay Valerievich." Sasha waited a moment, then spoke again. "Why does Dmitry Dmitrievich have an issue with you, and not Farit Georgievich?"

Sterkh picked up the feather, lifting it toward the sunlight. The feather shimmered bluish black.

"Dear Sasha, this is our own departmental internal business, and you don't need to deal with any of it. A small gear inside a large mechanism—a system—is perfectly at ease until the rules of the game change . . . and the gear, making the same rotation, suddenly flies off the axis and becomes a rock between the grindstones . . ."

Suddenly, Sasha was overcome by fear.

"Don't worry," Sterkh said, checking himself. "This is a purely theoretical discussion. I am happy you made it."

His voice expressed many different emotions, just not happiness.

"So what's going to happen to me now?" Sasha asked. "I am going to graduate and repeat the same thing I tried at the last exam, except that this time I'm going to succeed?"

"You have a long road ahead of you," he said, avoiding her eyes. "Test, term papers . . . I can only promise you that I will teach you without any breaks or exemptions. Even if I had a choice whether to teach you or not . . ."

"But you don't have a choice, because you took the same final exam," Sasha said, immediately thinking better of it.

"Well." He smiled politely. "It is in our nature to fulfill our destiny. To meet one's raison d'être. But you know, as an educator, I punched above my weight as well."

He strolled across the auditorium, placed the feather on the windowsill, and gazed above the roofs.

"Sasha, I deceived you. I lied to you, and in a way, I betrayed you."

"But, Nikolay Valerievich . . ."

"Granted, I had no choice. You had to either complete the process of correcting your errors, or you would break, fall apart inside, and turn into broth. Hence, my little ploy. You did not give up your freedom, and yet you gave it up because I taught you how to express ideas through what they were not. Perhaps this was my mission, my destiny—and once you graduate, I can leave."

"Leave—where?" With every second, this conversation plunged Sasha deeper into despair.

"Retire." Sterkh laughed, trying to lighten the mood. "While his logic may be incomprehensible, Farit Georgievich knows exactly what he's doing."

He opened a desk drawer and pulled out a small brochure bound in cardboard. Sasha recognized her own report card, with its worn-out corners and a tiny ink spot on the back cover. She's had this report card since her first year; it had all her grades for Portnov's subject, all her philosophy, English, and physical education results.

A frightened first-year student stared back at Sasha from the photo on the first page. Inside, on the "Year 3, Semester 1" page, the word "Specialty" was written in her own handwriting in the "Exam" column, followed by the name of the professor, Nikolay Valerievich Sterkh, and the grade—an A.

The A was written in red ink over a thick layer of Wite-Out, the bright white fluid used to correct typewriter-produced documents. Sasha stared at the grade, feeling neither joy nor relief. She didn't know what she was feeling.

A murder of crows occupied the linden trees outside the window and decided to raise a ruckus.

"If I am not dangerous . . ." Sasha tore her eyes away from her grade, "why does Dmitry Dmitrievich . . . "

"Who said you're not dangerous?" Sterkh said, smiling. "You are not dangerous for *Farit*. Farit can afford to play with grammatical exceptions, he knows that Speech changes, and he considers these changes very amusing. However, Dmitry Dmitrievich is a rule of grammar that binds Speech and holds it together. He does not tolerate exceptions."

Sasha turned the page of her report card. Across the blank lines, in Sterkh's ornate handwriting, was written: "Passed/promoted to the next level." Sasha turned the page: "Year 4, Semester 1." The page was empty, with space left for the subjects, faculty names, dates, grades, and signatures.

"If he doesn't tolerate exceptions," Sasha said, struggling with words, "how am I supposed to pass Analytical Specialty?"

"Assuming you master the program," Sterkh said in his familiar teacherly voice, "learn the necessary information, demonstrate your knowledge and skills . . ."

His intonation changed and his voice sounded a tiny bit hoarse.

". . . then he cannot fail you."

"Nikolay Valerievich," Sasha blurted out as if someone had pushed her in the back. "Could you tutor me a few times? I mean, help me with Analytical Specialty."

For a second, she thought he was going to agree, but he shook his head ruefully.

"In any educational process, it is crucial to maintain a systematic approach and consistency, and every teacher is responsible for their own part of the process. I wish you luck."

Kostya stood by the electronic schedule tableau, which by now looked like a quilt, large group lectures replaced with little patches of individual sessions. Watching Kostya's back, Sasha somehow knew that he'd been standing there for a while and that he had absolutely no interest in the schedule since he'd already memorized all the important stuff.

"It's all good," Sasha said to the back of his head.

Kostya took a moment before turning to face her, and Sasha realized he was watching her—studying her without using his eyes. For a second she considered reaching for him, placing a hand on his shoulder and learning what was happening inside him, but she held herself back.

"I got an A on the exam," she said, feeling rather awkward. When Kostya turned to her, he was smiling broadly, but Sasha thought she saw a hint of doubt on his face.

"An A?"

"I am a straight-A student after all," she said, unsure whether she was kidding. "And Sterkh did torture me quite a bit with all this 'error correction' work."

"What kind of errors?" He tried to act nonchalant, but Sasha could see how nervous he was. "Can you tell me?"

She wanted to tell him. She wanted him to know how she failed the third assignment, how she crushed the tower along with the monster inside it, and how she went on, and grew to unimaginable size, and was about to create a new world, but got scared of poisoning her creation with her eternal fear. And she refused, and tried to give up her fear, even though the condition of passing the exam was to accept fear as the basis of the universe. How could she explain to Kostya that there had been no errors, and that Sasha herself was a mistake, a toy for some, an unacceptable system failure for others?

What did she want from him, sympathy? Understanding? Would her classmates regret forgiving her miraculous salvation, regret collecting money for her, regret accepting her back into their pack? She longed to keep up the illusion of being human among humans, just another classmate, another student among other students . . .

"I can't," she said, avoiding his eyes. "I am a verb, and you're a pronoun, we have different conceptual devices . . ."

"Yes, of course." Kostya hesitated. Sasha was sure he was about to say something important.

"I saw Coach." Kostya lowered his voice. "I think he was mad about something, Sasha. He was practically buzzing. Don't piss him off, please. Seriously, don't piss him off."

Sasha nodded, shuddering involuntarily.

"We have a bit of time," Kostya said. "Do you want to grab a slice of pizza?"

He sounded like an awkward child, as if he and Sasha were teenagers, as if they'd just met, and he wanted to let her know how much he liked her. As if they didn't have a long history of betrayal, forgiveness, passion, and parting; Sasha felt very sorry for him.

"I wonder when third years have their exam?" she said, looking up at the schedule. "On January thirteenth?"

"Are you waiting for your Yegor?" Kostya drew back several paces.

"He's not my Yegor," Sasha said, annoyed. "And we discussed it all already. Kostya, we're not even human, so where is this ridiculous jealousy coming from?"

The electronic tableau blinked. Names, numbers, and the titles of the individual sessions began crawling from row to row, from square to square; the schedule kept changing, some classes were added, some moved to another slot. The tableau looked like an airport flight schedule, a snowstorm making the flights scatter like roaches from a sudden light.

"Dammit," Kostya nearly pressed his face against the glass trying to watch the changes. "What is all this?"

"It's because of me," Sasha said grimly.

As Sasha watched, her error correction classes disappeared, replaced with a new schedule. Applied Specialty ("individual session") crawled up the schedule and was now starting in one minute. Actually, in forty seconds.

"Sasha, hello! What a lovely new dress!"

Dima Dimych got up to greet her—a charming young coach with the widest shoulders and the widest smile. He looked so demonstratively pleasant, as if the scene in Sterkh's office had never happened.

As if he never stood by the window, so inhuman that even a solar flare would seem nicer in comparison.

"I am glad you like it." Sasha tugged on the hem of her dress. The ease with which Coach swapped his guises made it difficult for her to pick the right line of behavior. Conversing with a nonhuman, alien structure was uncomfortable and terrifying, but this Dima Dimych persona now seemed false, almost mocking.

"I am so used to seeing you in jeans." Dima Dimych chatted easily, as if in the middle of a tony cocktail party. "I am sure jeans are convenient, but this is so much more feminine. You are all grown up now, and this look is so very becoming . . ."

He very visibly blushed.

"You've never given me compliments before," Sasha said, pulling on her hem again even though she had sworn to herself she wouldn't do that. "Especially such risqué ones."

"Before you would have believed them," he winked at her, "and now you see right through me. Anyway, you've completed your work on correcting your errors and you've accomplished quite a bit, haven't you?"

His diaphragm pupils widened, pushing him out of the Dima Dimych image, then narrowed again. Sasha shuddered. He smiled, as if teasing Sasha for her silliness.

"I am Password," Sasha said.

"And what do you plan to do with this knowledge?" He stretched and massaged his massive biceps. His jacket strained at the seams.

"What do I plan to do?" Sasha was taken aback. "Nothing. What can I do? My advisor . . ."

She faltered, as if someone threw sand down her throat. Coach frowned and nodded, letting her know she didn't need to continue.

"Are you coaching first years?" Sasha asked hopelessly. "Basketball, stretching, table tennis? In this time or in the past?"

"Time is not a stream, it's a structure," he said gently, as if explaining the foundations of arithmetic to a four-year-old. "I don't exist from moment to moment. I occupy a sequence of events, now, then, always."

"Then you must know whether Yegor Dorofeev, a third year, passed his final exam." Sasha held her breath.

"A verb, conditional tense." Coach nodded, as if reminiscing about a good friend. "He is facing a multitude of possibilities, but he hasn't made his choice yet. He'll be taking his exam in a few months, but fifteen years ago."

The bell rang. Individual sessions did not adhere to the common schedule, but the bell functioned as usual, a long, demanding, rattling screech. One could tell time by the bell, without looking at the clock.

"Dmitry Dmitrievich." The words came out with difficulty, clanging like metal parts. "I must stay in the institute. It's my destiny, fate, predetermination . . . It has nothing to do with my freedom and it's not my decision."

"You have my sympathy, as much as humanly possible," he said and immediately winced. "Ugh, that sounds so hypocritical. I apologize. I realize that it's not your fault, and I don't blame you—our internal departmental squabbles should not concern you. I hope Nikolay Valerievich reminded you of it. On my end, I promise to fulfill all the conditions proposed by the program and prescribed in the methodology . . ."

Sasha felt a twinge of hope. He spoke calmly and kindly, without any subtext. Perhaps he'd already taken his anger out on Sterkh—assuming he was even capable of anger. He must have accepted the fact that Sasha passed the exam—assuming he was capable of acceptance. Or perhaps other processes, things that Sasha could not imagine, had taken place inside his structure—the same structure located and lasting in the multitude of dimensions. But now he would teach her. He was her professor, he was obligated to teach her.

Coach selected a marker from a cup and glanced at Sasha, making sure she was ready. She forced herself to express attention, diligence, and concentration, as if Coach was holding the keys to her fate rather than a plastic marker.

Coach drew a horizontal line. His hand wove a piece of graphic lace, growing blurry in the process. The diagram became whole, came to life, then shrouded Sasha in a layer of revolting sticky web: despair. No exit. Stagnation, decay, cogged millstones grinding everything in sight to powder. Sasha endured it for a few seconds, then shut her eyes, and the tears flowed, as if she were slicing a sharp onion.

An eraser was pushed across the board, wiping away the diagram with a sound of crickets singing.

"Time's up, Samokhina. Class is over."

"To live is to be vulnerable. A thin membrane of a soap bubble sepa-rates one from impenetrable hell. Ice on the road. The unlucky division of an aging cell. A child picks up a pill from the floor. Words stick to each other, line up, obedient to the great harmony of Speech . . ."

Textual Module slipped off her lap and fell on the floor. How many times did this happen—a hundred? A thousand? That explained the book's ripped cover and battered spine.

Sasha got up and made her way out to the balcony. The lights were off both in her room and outside, but it wasn't the darkness that blurred her vision. It was information that Sasha struggled to process and structuralize.

The Great Speech was beautiful and harmonious. But then why was the world it described so ugly and poisoned by fear? What could Sasha do? She couldn't stay idle any longer, couldn't refuse to act; remaining passive was no longer an option.

Three red dots glowed in the dark sky. Sasha squinted: only two, not three, a red one and a white. An aircraft flew above Torpa, high above the clouds, following its long-distance itinerary. Sasha could have reached for it to see what kind of people were on board, and who was in the pilot's seat; she could have observed its path, like two halves of a single arc, one reaching into the past, the other into the future, and the future was indeterminate—a multitude of possibilities. And yet, the past itself was indeterminate.

All aircrafts are capable of crashing. To live is to be vulnerable. Fear is love. How does one formulate the order "Do not be afraid" without the negative particle "not"?

"Be brave," Sasha whispered.

A gust of wind flew along Sacco and Vanzetti, rolling wet yellow leaves into tiny tornados.

On Sunday morning Sasha again entered the Torpa terminal. Men and women turned their heads to look, the former with interest, the latter with interest tinged with jealousy. In a cloud of expensive perfume, Sasha strolled through the building, taking careful steps in her elegant high heels and a short, well-tailored dress.

"Miss, are you celebrating a special occasion?"

An industrious young man in a business suit and tie caught up with her; one look at Sasha's face made him almost immediately lose his courage.

"Are you here to meet someone?"

"My fiancé," Sasha said, her tone as friendly as the Snow Queen's. The young man quickly fell behind.

A crowd was waiting near the arrivals. Sasha assumed she looked rather out of place, as if she wore an evening gown to a pajama party, but she didn't really care. *Be brave,* her blood pounded in her ears.

She was going to step right up to the ramp and look directly inside the cockpit. She would say hello, casually, as if nothing had ever happened.

She wore exquisite lingerie under her dress, surprised by how much they suited her, all these pieces of silk and lace, all these things she used to ridicule before, things she'd ignored, considered insignificant.

She felt a little dizzy.

Don't dump your pilot, he's feeling rather sad, Farit had said. Farit was a master of manipulation, he was the one who brought Yaroslav to Sasha. But what if that wasn't the case? What if Sasha and pilot Yaroslav Grigoriev met by pure chance, what if their meeting was a gift of fate, a miracle they both earned, or maybe it wasn't even something they deserved but rather a pure unadulterated piece of luck, a slice of true happiness?

But what does it matter whether Farit brought him or not? Sasha asked herself. Yaroslav was real. His feelings were real. Farit wasn't the one who made him who he was. All Farit did was cheat a tiny bit, shuffling a few opportunities, orchestrating a meeting . . .

Or perhaps not. Sasha suddenly felt lost as she considered the possibility of Yaroslav's feelings being grown in a test tube, *manifested* on a piece of paper, constructed out of nothing. What if Yaroslav was but a projection of Sasha's childish fantasies onto a conveniently approachable single male?

Oh no, no, no. She shook her head violently, surprising the people around her. She didn't command herself to be brave only to poison herself with rotten thoughts, stinky like old herring. When a membrane of a soap bubble is all that separates one from a blazing inferno, one cannot afford to be weak. The weak fail final exams, and Sasha could not afford to fail.

The plane was late. Ten minutes, then twenty. The crowd grumbled, quietly for now. *We're so spoiled,* Sasha thought. *This is such a good airline, no planes arriving an hour or two behind schedule . . .*

These simple thoughts did nothing to distract her from what really mattered: Coach would not teach her. Sasha would have to find a way to pass Analytical Specialty in December all on her own.

A music video was playing on the television monitor on the wall above her head; the sound was off, but the video itself looked so gaudy that Sasha wanted to reach inside, just like Lisa had done, to *claim* the studio with all the dancers and singers, and make them—make them do what? Drop on the floor and do push-ups? Scatter away in fear?

The plane was now half an hour late. Sasha felt a note of her own nervous sweat, still undetectable by a human nose, weaving itself into the cloud of her expensive perfume. Why was the plane so late?

The window where Sasha had her vantage point faced the runway, and she must have been the first one to notice a silver dot in the sky. A white spark. The aircraft was gliding along, unhurried, as if enjoying the moment. Sasha stood up straight and glanced at her reflection in the window. All the determination she came with was now gone. She regretted wearing all those ridiculous scraps of lace; she wasn't going to approach the ramp anyway, she wasn't that stupid.

But perhaps she could accidentally find herself right by his side in the crowd of people, by sheer chance; she just needed to come up with a story of why she was there at the airport in the first place.

The aircraft touched down, sending ephemeral ribbons of smoke from the chassis. Slowing down, it rolled toward the terminal. Sasha glanced at her palms, wet as if she had been washing clothes in an ice hole, and just as cold.

Several cargo platforms rolled up to the aircraft, followed by a passenger ramp. Sasha tried to see a familiar silhouette in the cabin window, but the bright sunlight blocked her view.

Passengers filed along the ramp. Suitcases flowed from the luggage compartment. A minute later the terminal became busy and loud. Newly arrived passengers looked at Sasha with peaked interest, tinged with curiosity and jealousy. Throngs of people gravitated toward her, like sharks casually moving toward a surfer, only to part around her, as if the sharks realized the surfer was actually a tiny island.

After the passengers, a group of flight attendants descended the ramp. A man in a white shirt with black epaulets came out, his uniform cap pushed low on his forehead. The second pilot followed, a different one, a portly ginger.

"Excuse me, are you meeting someone?" Another suitor appeared over Sasha's shoulder.

Yaroslav looked up, and Sasha panicked, thinking he might see her through the window. She slipped through the crowd, wobbling slightly on her high heels. She hid in the besieged fortress of a women's bathroom and waited almost an hour, until the loudspeaker announced that there would be no more flights and the airport was about to close.

A plasma monitor broadcast the news channel, with the sound turned off. War, air raids, a terror attack. Three hundred fifty casualties.

Sasha found a small stool, struggled to push it over to the wall, kicked off her heels, and climbed on top. Standing on tiptoes, she pulled the cord out of the outlet. The monitor went dark.

"Shut up, vultures," Sasha said to her reflection in the dark plasma panel and wiped the sweat off her forehead.

"Whoa," someone said behind her back. Sasha saw another reflection—Andrey Korotkov. He gazed up at her, with an unusual, surprised expression, and Sasha realized that her dress was quite short.

"Hey." She jumped off the cabinet. "Do you know where the remote control for this piece of crap may be?"

"You look stunning," Andrey murmured.

"That's what Coach said, too," she said, putting on her shoes.

At the bar near the coffee station, a handful of students were either fighting or having a heated discussion. When Sasha entered, all conversations ceased. At the far corner of the bar, Kostya choked on his drink and coughed.

"Interesting." Lisa studied her with narrowed eyes. "I smell a bitch in heat, but it's nothing but an illusion. Samokhina derives her greatest pleasure from cockteasing; she lures men over, then dumps them. Don't get caught in this trap, boys."

"Pavlenko." Denis Morozov got up, his face tense. "Any reason you're at it again?"

"Come with me," Sasha said, and for a split second Denis thought she was talking to him. He smiled anxiously, glancing in Kostya's direction, but then Sasha repeated her words, looking into Lisa's eyes.

"Pavlenko, come to my room."

"I am straight, you know." Lisa took a sip of coffee from her cup. "I don't do girls."

"Please," Sasha said.

"You are such a stupid bitch, Samokhina," Lisa muttered, bent in half trying to fish out Sasha's whiteboard from underneath her wardrobe and chasing down scattered markers. "You are such a hopeless, dismal idiot. Why didn't you just sleep with him? It's so simple—just go ahead and fuck him! But, oh no, we are the queen of all tragedies, we must rip our passion into tatters . . ."

Huffing, Lisa hung the whiteboard above the desk, and the room immediately shrank and felt colder.

"You are such a pain in my ass."

"At first I just didn't want to get him involved," Sasha said. "I figured I'd send him away, then forget him . . ."

"Did you really think you could save him by playing your silly games?" Lisa snorted derisively. "No, babe, it doesn't work that way. You are still here at the institute, you are still a student, which means you aren't in control and there is only one way you can save your pilot."

She placed the markers on the desk: black, green, blue, and red.

"Analytical Specialty is a subject like any other. If even a dumbass like Kostya managed to pass it, you are definitely going to be just fine."

Sasha decided not to comment.

"Grammatical parsing is performed mentally, and it's enough for a C," Lisa said, inspecting the white surface of the board. "And if you get a C, you pass the exam. Do you have any toothpaste? Sometimes you rub and rub and rub, but there are still traces left behind. And it's extremely important to erase every trace of your simulation. These diagrams are super toxic."

"I don't want a C," Sasha said. "I need to understand how it works."

"You cannot understand how it works, you can only do it." Lisa dragged the black marker across her palm. "Step one: you observe the diagram. Then the diagram observes you, and if you miss this moment, the diagram devours you. Let's assume you made it. Next comes conversion to a different system of symbols. Let's take your specialization into consideration—after all, you are a verb, fancy and hyped up, but if we speak plainly, you are a verb. You are going to act, not describe what you see. Did you get his phone number?"

"I didn't ask him."

"Does he use social media? Have you tried to find him?"

"No." Sasha raised her voice a tiny bit. "Please don't."

"You are making it so much more difficult for yourself." There was a hint of pity in Lisa's voice, either toward Sasha or because the black marker was nearly dry. "Do you know why I am helping you?"

"Because you're a nice, sweet girl."

Lisa actually laughed out loud at that, a disturbing sound. "Right. Obviously."

Then Lisa froze, staring into space, not moving, not even breathing or blinking for two and a half minutes. Sasha waited in silence. Finally, Lisa took a deep breath. A smirk slid off her face like a crumpled silk scarf.

"You *are* an idiot. I no longer . . . I don't feel anything. Every now and then I think of Lyosha. Where is he now? Nowhere. The person he was back then no longer exists and hasn't existed in a long time. Even if someone like him exists, a person with the same name in his passport, with the same genetic makeup . . . don't you get it?"

"Get what?"

"If I could love someone like you love your pilot, I'd never get out of bed."

Her dull eyes brightened a bit.

"I am helping you because I can monitor data streams. If anyone can annihilate this thing we still call Farit Kozhennikov, it's you, Samo-khina. Watch and learn, I am not going to repeat it."

She drew a thick horizontal line across the whiteboard.

Kostya showed up at night when it got dark. By then Sasha could see through the walls; all the voices, inside the institute and beyond its doors, simultaneously rose and fell, interwoven like brightly colored threads. Under her thin sweater, Sasha's back was covered with tiny scales: persistent practice caused her old issues with uncontrollable metamorphosis to return, but now Sasha accepted it stoically, like an unpleasant but manageable chronic ailment.

She saw Kostya before he knocked on her door. He was holding a cardboard container with something edible inside. In her current working mood, Sasha would not distinguish an eclair from herring.

"I am studying."

"I'm sure you are."

She hesitated, but then decided to unlock the door.

He glanced at the whiteboard covered in toothpaste. A nearly empty tube lay on the table.

"You haven't eaten all day." He placed the cardboard container on the shelf next to the microwave.

"I don't need to eat. I am an informational object."

"Until you pass out," Kostya said with quiet reproach. "Then you're a hungry informational object. Here."

He handed her a new tube of toothpaste. This time Sasha felt a wave of true gratitude wash over her.

"Thank you! I'm sorry, I really do need to study. I have all these gaps from last semester. And Coach . . . you know what he's like."

"I do know," Kostya said, looking a little pale. "Everyone is really surprised, by the way. What is up with you and Lisa?"

"We have a purely business relationship," Sasha said.

"Obviously." Kostya stepped from foot to foot, not in any rush to leave. "Sasha, are you seeing someone? Outside the institute? Where do you go on Sundays?"

"None of your business," Sasha said without thinking, then immediately felt ashamed. "I mean, I am not seeing anyone. Just an imaginary friend."

"People will never be able to understand us," Kostya said softly. "You know that. Even a first-year student could never understand a second year. What can you expect from those who never enrolled at the institute?"

"I know." Sasha winced. "Why are you telling me this?"

"I don't want you to suffer," Kostya said, looking into her eyes. "I made you unhappy . . . because I was stupid. Yegor . . . well. It was my own fault. He didn't make you particularly happy, either. Why do you need all this again? I don't want some stranger, some random guy—"

"Kostya," Sasha said. "When I tried to jump your bones, you told me you couldn't go through with it because of Zhenya. Just deal with it already, will you? Look at me: I have scales under my sweater, I can see through the walls and draw time loops. What would I do with a man?"

He left without a word, and two minutes later Sasha forgot all about him. To Lisa's credit, she sacrificed two hours of her own study time for Sasha. Sasha still had a whole night ahead of her, and another day, and one more night. She hoped that this time when she saw Coach she would be prepared.

"Hello, Samokhina." Coach stood by the window, watching the yellowing linden trees. "Such a gorgeous autumn this year, like a painting, and so warm. Don't you think so?"

"Hello," Sasha said thickly.

He turned to face her, as if something in her voice had caught his attention.

"Do you have a sore throat? Are you ill? Do you have a cold?"

"I'm fine," Sasha said, her voice even softer.

By the time of her Tuesday session with Coach, she'd managed to stabilize herself: no scales, no feathers, no black holes in place of her eyes, no multi-digit structures in place of her hands. The informational component of her personality came into agreement with her physiological component, but on a new level. Occasionally, the world would begin to spin, and she felt lighter than air, about to fall upward into the sky at any moment, but then she would gain control once more, only to let herself go just to see if she could do it again.

She studied on her own for hours on end. Sterkh had let her skip their Monday session.

"Very interesting." Coach continued to study her face. "Obviously, I will not be discussing my colleagues with a student, but some of our faculty are certainly intent on spoiling you rotten. Well, let's take a look."

She bristled at the idea of anyone at the institute being spoiled, particularly her, but knew he wouldn't even comprehend her anger.

He crossed the empty classroom and stopped by the whiteboard, then drew a long line, the first necessary measure of every diagram— the horizon. Sasha concentrated, switching off all outside lights, cutting off any external data, pushing her attention against the board like an atmospheric column pressing down on the surface of the global ocean.

An event simulation. A temporal loop with variations, transported onto a two-dimensional surface. Third dimension . . . Fourth. Sasha peered through intertwined cords of time, probabilities, distances, and saw a woman with a baby carriage shuffling along an icy street, navigating enormous piles of snow. In reality, there was no woman, no baby carriage, nothing but projections on a whiteboard, meanings, proportions, flickering shadows. A block of cloudy ice breaks off a ledge and flies down. It collapses on top of the baby carriage. On top of the woman. Inhale, exhale, probabilities are linked in a different formation, the web is woven into a new pattern, the acceleration of a free fall changes its definition in all physics textbooks. The woman freezes in terror, icy dust is reflected in her eyes, icicles roll like pencils, and the baby . . .

The diagram fell apart. The sound of the eraser gliding across the board no longer resembled a cricket song—it screeched instead. Sasha attempted to catch her breath and exhale the frost that was stuck in her lungs; she *was* there, in that snow-covered street. She *saw* the probabilities intertwine, she felt the icy dust and the horror that had no name through the skin of her face. Standing in the middle of the auditorium, Sasha grinned like a madwoman: for the first time ever she'd learned something in Coach's class. As horrendous as this experience was, Sasha had nearly managed something this time, and a victorious feeling spread inside her like warm honey.

Coach regarded her smile. Tossing the eraser onto his desk, he pulled out his phone.

"I need the dean's office to inform fourth years, Group A, that in thirty minutes they have to attend an unscheduled class in auditorium one."

"Group A, do any of you have a teaching certificate? Is anyone planning to teach at the institute, not after graduation, but right now?"

Only three people in the room knew what he was talking about, but the rest figured it out immediately.

Lisa froze in her seat. Kostya turned his head and glanced at Sasha in her seat in the last row by the window. Sasha struggled to smile at him even though she had no idea what to expect.

"Open your notebooks," Coach said coldly. "Write down the following."

"Back in kindergarten?" Andrey Korotkov said, venturing a joke.

"It's a penalty assignment," Coach said, without as much as a glance in his direction. "One more joke, and I will be contacting your advisor."

If they suspected things were serious before, now they knew for sure. Coach had not had to threaten sanctions before, his exam being enough of a threat. After a minute pause, the auditorium filled with the sounds of clasps on backpacks and satchels snapping open, the rustling of turning pages, and the clicking of ballpoint pens.

Coach stood with his back to the whiteboard, crossing his enormous arms and staring at the window above their heads. His face became unnaturally detached, and his eyes . . . empty, like a marble statue's.

"Singularity," he said in a mentoring tone, and Sasha shuddered. She felt as if Coach's empty gaze was directed at her, and her alone.

"Singularity," he repeated louder. "In philosophy, singularity means the state of being singular as it relates to an entity, event, or a phenomenon. Mathematical singularity is a point in which a function takes an infinite value."

Laura Onishhenko raised an unsteady hand.

"I can't keep up with my notes."

"I will repeat it later," Coach said, and that perfectly neutral phrase sounded ominous. "Particularly for those who have forgotten how to write at a normal pace." He continued, and it took a moment for Sasha to realize he was lecturing once more. "Technological singularity is a hypothetical point in time at the onset of which technological progress becomes incomprehensible to human beings. Cosmological singularity . . . Samokhina, are you writing it down?"

Sasha stared dully at the empty page in front of her, realizing she never bought Oksana a new notebook. She bought so many for herself—and completely forgot about Oksana.

" . . . the state of the universe at the start of the Big Bang, characterized by all matter compacted into a small ball with infinite density and intense heat," Coach continued evenly. "I am going to repeat everything one more time; whoever fails to get it this time will have to have a chat with their advisor."

Pens scratched faster, ballpoints pushing down on the rustling paper. Coach repeated the entire passage verbatim, and this time Sasha managed to write it all down.

"Pavlenko," Coach said softly. "Get up."

Lisa got up. From her place in the last row Sasha saw the back of Lisa's head and her rigid shoulders. Lisa's posture had never before been less than perfect.

"You have committed a serious offense," Coach said. "Which I reported to your advisor."

Lisa inhaled sharply. Sasha jumped up, having no idea what she was going to do.

"This concerns the entire Group A," Coach said, looking directly at Sasha. "And the entire Group B. Any contacts, conversations, and/or written communication with Alexandra Samokhina are strictly forbidden. The violators will be severely punished."

"Pavlenko didn't do anything wrong," Sasha said loudly, and her voice sounded unusually high. "We've always helped each other. Since the first year. No one ever punished us for that. It's unfair—you're saying we broke the rules, but you just made them up now!"

"Group A, you're free to go," Coach announced as if Sasha didn't exist.

"Lisa, I am going to call Farit." Sasha could not believe she was actually saying these words. "And *he* is going to listen to me, not to Dmitry Dmitrievich!"

No one was brave enough to look at her. Only Coach was still facing her, looking as emotional as a cement wall topped with barbwire.

The long beeps continued, but the voicemail never came on. Dumbfounded, Sasha stood by the phone booth, realizing that she had actually believed his words: *You and I have a lot in common . . .* She'd believed that she could have something in common with Farit, that she could simply call him and protect someone from execution, someone like Lisa . . .

Lisa left the auditorium right after Coach told them they were free to go. The trite remark had come across as mockery, because the only free person in that auditorium was Coach, and nominally at best. No one chased after Lisa, no one stopped her or expressed their support; it was abundantly clear Lisa did not want anyone to follow her. She simply vanished from the vestibule.

Sasha didn't want to think about where Lisa actually went, what her advisor was going to make her do, and how she was going to pay for her offense. Sasha didn't even try to speak to any of her classmates to avoid getting them into trouble. There was no point anyway. She had one goal, an idée fixe: to get hold of Farit and, for the first time in her life, to get him to reach a compromise, to make him change his mind.

But Farit never picked up his phone. After her sixth attempt, Sasha learned that silence did not necessarily mean refusal to answer. Silence itself could be the answer.

Who was the woman Sasha saw in Coach's diagram, the one standing under the block of ice? Who was the baby in the carriage? Did that block of ice actually fall, or was it an educational model, a projection bowdlerized by a thousand filters?

Had I known in advance how much trouble Lisa would be in, would I still have asked her for help? Yes, the correct answer is yes. If I knew that Lisa would be punished, I'd have still used her. Would still use her.

And if I knew that I would be the one punished, what then?

Back in her room, she spread some paper on the desk and sharpened her pencil to a point. Two hours remained until her session with Sterkh, and Sasha intended to spend that time working. As she was about to touch the pencil to the paper, someone knocked on the door.

The ability to see through the walls disappeared along with her spontaneous metamorphosis, yet she knew exactly who was behind the door, and how dangerous it was for him. She held her breath waiting for the visitor to leave, but he refused to give up.

"Sasha, open the door."

"Go away," Sasha whispered. "He is not just threatening you. He will report you. Lisa was enough. Where is she? Is she at the dorm? Where did she go?"

"She left," Kostya said heavily from behind the door. "Did you call *him*?"

"Go away!" Sasha shouted this time. "I couldn't do anything for her, and I won't be able to do anything for you! It's like I'm a leper! I am untouchable! I bring misery to everyone, and I will keep making everyone miserable! Go!"

"Nonsense," he said, and Sasha knew that only the thin wooden panel separated their faces. "You will make it, Sasha. Just hang in there."

"You've absorbed an entire semester's curriculum in a few days," Sterkh mused, inspecting the page ripped out of Sasha's notepad.

In his fingers, the page twitched and the penciled lines grew three-dimensional, reminding Sasha of a fly struggling to break out of a spider's web. Sterkh crumpled it up, reached for his lighter, switched it on, and touched the flame to the paper.

"Please make sure to dispose of any physical manifestation of your work as soon as possible."

He placed the smoldering scrap into a clean ashtray. The notion of *guilt* shrank and blackened against the bright porcelain, expressed in graphical symbols of what it was not.

"Nikolay Valerievich, how is the concept of cosmological singularity expressed in the Great Speech?" Sasha asked.

Sterkh looked at her sharply and yet wearily, as if wondering whether his student was mocking him.

"Password is the First Word. That much should be obvious. Singularity is a projection of Password onto the physical world. It is a starting point, a kickoff of the universe. I assume the question was rhetorical. Unless you would like to talk about it."

"I don't have any more humans to talk to," Sasha said. "Except for you."

Sterkh steepled his long pale fingers in a familiar gesture.

"First, I haven't been human in a very long time. Second, I'm used to working with simple, concrete things—projections of ideas, titles of names, grammar and matter . . . I can't discuss topics outside of my expertise."

"Then why did you offer?"

"I didn't."

The dorm greeted Sasha with a widely cast net of sounds and scents, disjointed and yet harmonious, as if a large orchestra were tuning up before starting an overture. Steps, voices, the sound of running water, music both loud and soft, slamming of doors, the howling of wind in the windows that were cracked open, drafts, the gurgling and humming of kitchen appliances, the aroma of freshly brewed coffee, vague trails of somebody's perfume . . . Sasha stopped in the middle of the vestibule, listening and sniffing the air. The sense of theatricality had yet to leave her; she felt as if the dorm, suddenly sentient, were putting on a performance for her, Sasha, perhaps wishing to console, or encourage, or welcome her. Or perhaps the exhausted Sasha was simply hallucinating. The dorm now sounded like a real, densely populated home, and as much as Sasha loved silence, she had to admit she liked it better this way. Among other things, silence meant indifference, and Sasha already had gotten enough silence calling Farit.

Sasha glanced up at the plasma screen; again, with the sound on mute, it displayed a line of ambulances crawling toward an unknown destination. She moved her eyes toward the phone hidden among the potted plants, then looked away and walked toward the first-floor hallway. The smell of coffee grew stronger, but the voices trailed off.

Her classmates huddled together like a gaggle of birds. Neither Lisa nor Kostya were there. No one raised their head when she walked in.

Of course they didn't—they were forbidden to speak to her. Or even look at her. The fourth-year students at the Institute of Special Technologies knew that this was not given as a choice; they were going to ignore Sasha, and she couldn't risk getting them in trouble.

The overhead lights came on, reflecting in the dark autumn windows. Someone's ringtone grew louder—a cartoon-like voice singing in Japanese. Sasha suddenly realized that her classmates weren't simply sitting side by side, they were all parts of a whole; they weren't merely a group of students, a group of human beings, but rather something large and fundamentally different. Something terrifying. A cluster, a fragment of a larger system. A grammatical structure.

Sasha approached the bar counter and pulled out a stack of bills secured with a rubber band.

"Thanks. I got my stipend."

She spoke to the coffee machine. No one would be able to blame her for provoking her classmates and making them break the rules.

"Andrey, do you need any money?" Denis asked, keeping his eyes on his tablet, demonstratively ignoring Sasha as per instructions. It was a perfectly neutral question, about nothing in particular.

"Money is a universal equivalent, any item or verifiable record that is generally accepted as payment for goods and services and repayment of debts," Andrey Korotkov said, regurgitating the general definition to no one's benefit. No restriction had ever been issued against sharing reference materials. Having finished, Andrey looked at Anna Bochkova pensively.

"There are no goods or services that would be required by the name of an object," Anna muttered, as if thinking out loud. "That would be needed. Will become needed. No."

"I am very sorry about what happened," Sasha said to the electric teakettle. She should have said nothing, but the conversation that came out of nowhere put her in a trance, like meditation music. She really wanted to apologize. She wanted to be a part of the whole, at least for a split second. She wanted to hear their voices and not be alone.

"The Great Speech is beautiful and harmonious," Andrey began again, and Sasha detected a note of sarcasm in his voice.

"No one wants penalty assignments." Yulia Goldman looked at Igor Kovtun, then added sotto voce, "Or calls placed to our advisors."

Sasha bit her lip. Coming here was a bitchy move.

"However, no one regrets anything," Igor said, glancing at Dmitry Biryukov over his shoulder.

"No regrets whatsoever," Biryukov confirmed. He sighed heavily. "Grammatical structure is beyond freedom. But we're also beyond regrets. Beyond accusations."

"A universal equivalent," Andrey reiterated authoritatively. "A universal one!"

Sasha hesitated, looking from one person to another. Obeying her intuition, she picked up the stack of bills from the counter and dropped it into an open backpack. As she reached the door on her way out, she stopped for a moment, keeping her back to the room.

Behind her, the room began to move. The sound of chairs scraping the floor, loud yawns, someone's phone conversation, laughter, coughing, questions, answers, requests to make more tea . . . She would have thought her classmates were performing in a show called *Ordinary Student Life*, if she didn't know that they had simply switched their mode of existence.

Today they rebelled against Coach's will, even though they could not afford to rebel. They violated an order they could not violate, finding workarounds, employing tricks. They supported Sasha, armed with the knowledge and understanding of who she was. *What* she was. The remainders of people—fragments, shards of human beings still left in them—challenged the Great Speech.

I hope they don't get into trouble for this, Sasha thought. She gritted her teeth and walked toward the stairs.

"Lisa?"

Lisa Pavlenko's room was empty. Sasha knew that without trying to *claim* Lisa's space. She knew that behind the door Lisa's clothes, textbooks, and shoes were scattered all over the floor, that her whiteboard showed traces of a diagram Lisa had not erased completely, and that the remaining nodes of that diagram still twitched on the white surface like stunned fish in a net. Lisa wasn't there, and it did not look as if she'd be back any time soon.

Beyond accusations, the grammatical structure that was the sum of her classmates had said earlier.

Sasha went back to her room, grabbed a new notepad from her stack, and dropped it off by Oksana's door.

Next Sunday morning found Sasha in the tiny Torpa airport. The weather report was broadcast on a large monitor; a cheerful young woman pointed and waved against the background of a meteorological chart. A sunny day, the young woman said, and the chart confirmed her words. Expect bright sunshine in the morning, yielding to a few clouds in the afternoon.

Outside it was getting dark very quickly, as if the sun were turned off by a dimmer switch. On the pavement under panoramic windows several freight transporters, a fuel tanker, and a fire engine lined up in a row. There was only one line on the flight schedule board: DELAYED ARRIVAL. Expected in fifteen minutes.

Aside from Sasha, only a dozen people lingered in the waiting area. Everyone spoke too loudly, and nearly everyone held a phone to their ear.

"It's landing in fifteen minutes!" a freckle-faced girl with closely cropped hair shouted. "It's delayed! How's your weather? There is something really weird going on here . . ."

Sasha stepped toward the window and pressed her palms against the glass. The sky looked alive and terrifying. A bluish-gray impenetrable wall crept over the city, swallowing the airport. Sasha thought she could hear a soft approaching rustling. Gusts of wind made the glass twitch like the skin of a drum.

"That's quite a storm," a man muttered behind Sasha's back. "They promised us sunshine, and nothing warned us about this . . ."

Thunder came almost simultaneously with a flash. White lightning slammed into the weather service mast on the other side of the field. Everyone went very quiet, then spoke all at once.

"Call the air traffic controller! How long until they land?"

"It'll be over soon, it's a quick thunderstorm . . ."

The glass shuddered under Sasha's palms.

"There is no way it would land at the alternate airport under these conditions!"

In the outlines of the swirling clouds Sasha saw lines drawn with a marker on a whiteboard. She imagined a crude diagram—one that existed and matured in all five dimensions. She leaned forward, searching for meaning, terrified that someone's hand would push an eraser over it and make it disappear.

The plane did not move toward the alternate field. Sasha shut her eyes and tried to figure out why it couldn't do it, and why it kept circling, caged in by the storm front like a fly in a glass jar. Starting at the *now* point, this fragment of reality developed into thousands of variants and disintegrated into probabilities. Sasha could see them but couldn't change anything. Lisa was right, Sasha was a verb, fancy and hyped up, but a verb in the imperative mood: Reach for it. Do it. Give.

Change. Be brave.

The waiting area was saturated with fear, like a sponge with soapy water. They didn't know what Sasha was feeling, but they could read, and the next moment the schedule board went dark and the single line of data disappeared, replaced by a sequence of letters announcing: Updated information coming soon.

A dark silhouette appeared from beneath the heaviest cloud. It dangled in the air above the runway like a child's toy on a string. It flew across the runway, not along it, the lights on its rounded front end highlighting the almost ninety-degree angle. It looked so surreal that everyone in the waiting area went very quiet. Then everyone screamed.

This is not happening, Sasha thought. *This doesn't make any sense, that's not what we talked about. What if he's not flying today? What if his schedule changed, or he's sick, or on vacation?*

She realized she could see inside the cockpit. She saw a peaked uniform cap against the chair, white fingers gripping the yoke, and fiercely focused, tormented eyes with unnaturally wide pupils.

She twitched, trying to break into this reality, grab the imaginary lines with both hands, shift the knots, and rearrange everything, but to no avail, as if she were trying to chop up a swamp with an axe. The diagram did not actively resist, but neither would it let her in; the diagram existed outside of Sasha and her efforts. Around her people were screaming: Every one of them had someone they loved on board that plane. Someone they were waiting for.

A fire engine howled and took off, almost immediately slowing down, unsure of the location of the approaching climax.

The aircraft descended, staggering across the runway like a drunk. Aiming to finish it off, the lightning struck it from above, and all the lights went out. Only the shadow of the aircraft remained visible, wrapped in residual discharges.

Barely touching its wheels to the runway, the shadow performed a pirouette, turning ninety degrees against the wind along the runway. As plumes of smoke poured from the tires, the rain came down, flooding the glass and concealing the plane from its audience. Lost in a throng of screaming people, Sasha ran along the corridor, past the security checkpoint, past the confused airport staff, outside, into the rain.

The aircraft was slowly turning toward the terminal. Not a single light was on.

"Lisa!" Sasha blurted out before she had a chance to reconsider.

On a bench on Sacco and Vanzetti Street, under balding lindens, a glassy-eyed Lisa Pavlenko sat in a cloud of cigarette smoke. Sasha didn't think of the boycott, or of her own role in Lisa's situation; she was simply happy to see Lisa alive and well and to know that no matter how harsh Farit's punishment was, it was now all over.

"Oh, it's you."

By the time Lisa focused her eyes and responded, Sasha regretted her outburst at least three times. She was ready to see Lisa shake her head and leave, but instead the blonde patted a spot on the bench next to her.

"Want one?"

Sasha stepped closer and pulled a cigarette out of the offered pack, unsure of her own actions.

. . . She ran out of the airport as soon as it became clear that the emergency landing did not cause any casualties. Outside it was pouring rain, an ambulance stood nearby, its lights flashing, and passengers disembarked dragging their carry-ons. They didn't look nearly as shell-shocked as the people who waited for them on the ground. The captain in his white uniform stood on top of the ramp, supervising the unloading, speaking on the phone, and looking completely still among the general hustle and bustle, at least from a distance.

The thunderstorm was moving west. The shuttle bus driver was delaying his departure, waiting for other passengers. Under the receding rain, Sasha walked toward the highway and hopped onto a passing bus.

"You need to inhale the smoke," Lisa said. "If you hold it in your mouth, you'll end up with throat cancer."

Sasha choked in surprise.

"Do you know what *he* did to me?" Lisa said, slowly and lifelessly, like a sleepwalker. "*He* brought over Lyosha. The man my Lyosha had become. And then *he* said, 'I am taking it easy on you.' Samokhina, study hard. Do something to *him*. You are the only one who can."

Lisa got up and staggered toward the alley.

As soon as Sasha collapsed on the bed, her tablet began to ring. It was an old-fashioned sound, just like the rattling bell of the telephone that stood on a shelf in Sasha's mom's apartment. Sasha jumped up and pressed Answer before realizing that she'd just got played. The very ringtone served as a hook, an instrument of emotional blackmail.

"You called me," Farit Kozhennikov said.

Recalling Lisa's eyes staring through the smoke, Sasha failed to respond.

"And I was busy," Farit continued serenely. "What did you want to tell me?"

"You must have been busy watering your flowers," Sasha muttered with poorly concealed hatred.

"Flowers?" He sounded surprised. "I suppose it could be flowers, why not? Go ahead, ask your questions, you can't help yourself anyway."

"I am working on your assignment," Sasha said through gritted teeth. "I am doing my absolute best to succeed in the Analytical Specialty class. I found one person, the only one who could help me. And what have you done to her—as a reward?"

"There is no reward involved," he said, demonstratively patient. "You know the rules. If a professor alerts me, I must respond. How else would you ever succeed in this program?"

Silently, Sasha suppressed a surge of rage and despair. If she'd learned anything at the institute, it was the art of self-restraint.

"As far as I am aware," she said, monitoring her own breathing, "you received no alerts regarding me. Then what exactly happened at the airport?"

"Two individuals can help you," he said dispassionately. "One of them is me, and I am helping you as much as I can. I spur your imagination. I hint at possible directions. I have been helping you since the first moment we met, if you care to remember."

Sasha bit her lip, nearly drawing blood.

"But the other, and the more important one, is you," Farit said. "Help yourself, Sasha."

For a split second Sasha stopped at the entrance of auditorium 1, mentally marking time measures. *Then. Now.* She smiled beatifically at Coach, as if she were a first year meeting the young gym teacher on the dance floor.

"Whoa," he said softly. "Are you sure about this?"

"There are no rules against it," Sasha said.

"No rules?"

In the next instant, the Dima Dimych facade had disappeared even though his facial features remained unchanged. A nonhuman guise looked back at Sasha. A lid from a cooking pot had more expression than this thing did. Pushing back her fear, she jerked up her chin.

"I'm ready."

"Give up this idea, and I will pretend this never happened," he said with mechanical precision.

"Dmitry Dmitrievich," Sasha said, gazing into his empty, expressionless eyes. "You didn't leave me any choice. You don't want to teach me, you don't allow anyone to teach me—well, I'm going to find a way to learn on my own."

A tiny pause seemed as long as a doorbell's ring. Sasha found herself in a time loop, where every moment was particularly valuable; she would reach the final anchor of *now*, then step back in time into *then*. And the lesson would repeat itself. This would continue until Sasha was comfortable with the material.

"Fine, he said. "Let's begin." He stepped toward the whiteboard. "Read and convert this dynamic projection. Three. Two. One."

Sasha put her right foot forward and bent her knees slightly, as if readying for a sprint. She swayed back and forth, checking her coordination and balance, then focused her eyes on the very center of the whiteboard so she could see the entire surface.

The marker touched the white plane. The marker was green.

A process. A sum, no, a network of processes, all intertwined. So much destruction, only a faint trace of creation. The diagram spilled into the third dimension, acquired three dimensions, entered the fourth, spun into a spiral directed at the past and future simultaneously. It was complex, much more convoluted than the story of the baby carriage and a block of ice, familiar to Sasha from the last session. More complex than the story of an aircraft flying in a thunderstorm, which Sasha witnessed in person at the airport. This diagram existed on a different level and in a different system of symbols, and Sasha recalled Lisa's words: "You observe the diagram. Then the diagram observes you, and if you miss this moment, the diagram devours you."

The thing drawn on the board sensed Sasha's presence. The system she could neither control nor comprehend broke into her mind and began to tear it apart, gagging and slurping, forcing it to decompose.

Sasha could not shut her eyes. She could not turn away or even pass out. The diagram on the whiteboard devoured her, digested her alive. As she realized what it meant to experience a "fate worse than death," she remembered Oleg Borisovich Portnov, his narrow glasses on the tip of his nose, his long blond ponytail: You will not be distracted or taken out of your trance by an alarm clock, or a scream, or anything else. Only the sharp sensation of pain. A quick one!"

She found a solution.

The diagram hummed like a wasp's nest. Sasha stood with her back to Coach, facing the window. Her mouth was full of blood, and the index finger on her right hand felt numb. Blood dripped onto the wooden floor. Sasha didn't care to see where her teeth had clamped shut and what had happened to her hand; the important thing was that she was still there, she was herself, she felt better.

"Blood is not only a kind of physiological fluid," Sterkh had told her once. "It is also a catalyst of an array of meanings . . ."

"Did I warn you?" Coach said softly behind her back.

Sasha did not respond.

"*Then*," he said calmly.

. . . There are no rules against it.

Sasha stopped at the entrance of auditorium 1. The whiteboard was as pure as a dress of a yet sober bride. Sasha glanced at her right hand; it was still intact. So far. She was back in the time loop, but at least now she knew what to do. She had a solution.

"No rules?" He stared at her, his expressionless face resembling a gas mask.

"I am ready to work," she said hoarsely.

He approached the whiteboard and picked up a marker. Sasha leaned forward and bent her knees as if readying for a jump. *Three. Two. One.*

A process. A network of processes. Third, fourth, fifth dimension, layer upon layer. A split second later Sasha realized that he wasn't re-creating the previous diagram; he was creating a new one. This time the marker was blue, not green. Sasha had counted on working with the same diagram because practice makes perfect, but she had miscalculated. Coach handed her a different, more complicated assignment, one she didn't know how to handle.

Sasha could not shut her eyes or look away. She tried to bite her hand, but her teeth closed on nothing. She rushed to the beginning of the measure, to the initial anchor of the time loop, trying to reset it from the start.

"Then!"

That's when she knew she was locked in someone else's loop rather than her own. He'd switched up her anchors, replacing them with his. She hadn't orchestrated additional sessions for herself; instead, Coach had trapped her like a rat in a kitchen bucket. She was now fully in his power.

Terrified, she managed to clamp her teeth on her index finger. She heard a crunch.

She stood with her back to Coach, facing the window. Blood dripped onto the wooden floor. She didn't think she still had an index finger. Behind her, the diagram hummed like a wasp's nest.

"Then," Coach said.

"There are no rules against it."

"No rules?"

Sasha was silent.

"I am waiting for you to cry uncle," he said after a long pause. "I assume you now understand your mistake and how to fix it. Just say 'enough,' and I will stop."

"I am ready to work."

"There are no rules against . . ."

She lost count of the repetitions and no longer attempted to read and understand the new writing on the whiteboard. She couldn't grasp a single layer.

"Enough."

"Louder."

"Enough!"

"I'm so tired of you," he said, sounding like Dima Dimych. "Class is over, you're free to go, get some rest."

At ten past six her tablet chirped with a message from Sterkh: "Sasha, where are you? I am waiting for you in the auditorium."

Sasha was lying on her bed, the tablet on the floor nearby. She needed to respond. She closed her eyes instead.

Coach's diagram, the one she'd never managed to analyze, was analyzing her, dissecting her without anesthesia, methodically making its way farther and farther into Sasha's head. Realities commingled. As if through a fog, Sasha saw her room, the tablet on the floor, three messages from Sterkh on its screen—and simultaneously the diagram on the whiteboard, blue and green lines changing to black and red.

Sterkh wouldn't help her. No one would help her. Either she would help herself or turn into broth.

Outside, rain came down in sheets, drops banging on the glass. Sasha struggled to get up, pulled on her new jacket with the tag still attached, laced up her brand-new sneakers, and unlocked the balcony door.

The highway circled Torpa just like fifteen years ago, but now the number of road signs and lanes had grown. In the headlights, side barriers glowed white and yellow. The rain came down hard, each drop plopping onto the ground, shattering, and popping back up. Watery dust hung over the street.

By the time she reached Sacco and Vanzetti, Sasha was already soaked to the bone, and still had a forty-minute walk to the highway. She stopped by the bridge, where most cars decelerated, and raised her hand.

She'd never hitchhiked before but wasn't the least bit surprised when the very first truck slowed down by the roadside. Sasha took a step back, intimidated by the enormous beast with a sharp metallic odor.

A few moments later she was installed in the cabin high above the ground, the truck's headlights piercing the rain. Road signs flashed by. *Reflected light,* Sasha thought. *These symbols are enormously meaningful: they regulate traffic.*

The truck driver spoke to her; she saw audio waves emanating from his mouth and vibrating near his neck. Soft music came from the speakers, making the air tremble and float around the cabin. Affected by these meaningless physical phenomena, the diagram imprinted on Sasha's retina was gradually dissolving. It was letting Sasha go.

She closed her eyes and opened them immediately, a second later, when the morning came, the rain stopped, and everything looked bright. The truck was parked by the side of the road. A gas station a hundred meters away was reflected in its side mirrors. The driver was talking, smiling with thin unshaven lips. He was about thirty years old, but already carrying a bit of extra weight. One of his incisors was chipped.

He wanted something from her. He was someone's projection, a shadow of high hopes or defective contraception, yet he was a human being, alive and natural, and Sasha felt very sentimental and almost cried. This driver had freed her from Coach's diagram. He misinterpreted her expression. Still smiling, he unzipped his fly, placed a hand on the back of Sasha's neck, and pushed down lightly . . .

She *claimed* him by connecting a new information packet to her system. The driver shuddered, unable to remove his hand, like someone grabbing a high-voltage wire. His eyes dimmed and rolled back.

Information ran out almost immediately: either the packet was on the smaller side, or Sasha crushed him too fast. Nevertheless, he was still human, a half-erased projection of a Word uttered some time ago. Sasha sighed, brushed off his limp hand, opened the door, and jumped down onto the slushy road.

The air was fresh and cool, saturated with thick concentrated autumn. Sasha tried to remember the driver's name—she was sure he'd told her, but she hadn't listened. His name was an empty sound—he was a driver, a long-haul trucker, a function. Nothing more. But she was also a function for him. The difference was that she could *claim* him, and he couldn't do the same to her, no matter how much he tried.

She took one last look at the truck by the side of the road and began walking toward the familiar bus station. A store tag, once soaked and now dry again, dangled off the hem of her jacket, bumping against her knee.

The yard in front of her childhood home looked exactly the same. The trees grew taller, the facades became darker, and the bench near the entrance was wet from the rain, just like that time when Sasha spoke with Farit Kozhennikov. The kitchen window was exactly the same, and so was the balcony, and Sasha walked down the same path she'd taken millions of times on her way home from school, and only when she reached the door did she slow her steps.

Behind her back, very close to the path, a car stopped with an unpleasant fussy screeching sound. She heard two voices, a man and a girl's, arguing behind the locked doors. Facing away, Sasha pulled her hood lower and sat down on the wet bench.

"You are behaving like . . . " The car door opened, and the man's voice filled the yard. "And you should be! Why do I have to . . . You are thirteen years old! Don't you get it? Your grandmother . . ."

"Because it's your fault! Everything is your fault! It's your fault that Mom died! You need to know it's your fault!"

A teenage girl in a dark red jacket leapt out of the car and dashed to the front door. Sasha caught a quick look at her face, enough to see that she had nothing in common with the young Sasha: gray eyes, light eyelashes, thin stubborn lips, and an inflamed pimple on her chin. She was so young. Poor kid.

She did look a lot like Konev. But she looked like someone else, too—perhaps like the old photos of Sasha's mother? Sasha felt a touch of bizarre discomfort, as if the girl was her own vague projection. Was she hers? Wasn't she?

The girl ran inside, and the door slammed shut like a guillotine blade. Sasha waited for Konev to follow her, but minutes went by and nothing happened.

Sasha looked at the car. It was a Volkswagen, a newer model, unfamiliar to Sasha. It looked expensive, even luxurious. It was always obvious that Konev would do well for himself.

Konev sat with his hands on the steering wheel, staring ahead and seeing absolutely nothing. He looked fit, youthful, husky. He hadn't slept well; he had been drinking. He hadn't shaved in a few days; stubble covered his strong chin. Back when she knew him, he was quite proud of his curly blond beard . . .

He flinched as if someone had called his name, sat up straight, and caught Sasha's gaze in the mirror. His red-rimmed eyes opened wide. Too late, Sasha realized she'd let her guard down and was too close to the car. Konev recognized her immediately. His reaction was clear; Sasha felt a chill, expecting him to say, "I want it to be a dream," but he was silent.

"Easy-peasy," Sasha murmured placatingly. "Roll down your window."

He couldn't disobey her. Sasha came closer and placed her hand on Konev's shoulder, feeling his muscles contract under his dark mourning shirt. She *claimed* him, gently unfolding the essence of his being in time, like a children's accordion book.

It was clear that the other Alexandra Samokhina had not treated this man as fairly as he deserved. Konev was neither empty nor worthless; he wasn't even vindictive. He loved his wife still, and some time ago, he had loved her deeply and passionately, and had a chance to make her happy. If only Alexandra had managed to see what Sasha saw in him now. But that woman had missed her chance, and the mistake was made. And now he was overwhelmed with real grief and genuine guilt. His daughter's words didn't just hurt him—they destroyed him.

Sasha reminded herself that time never stood still. She was standing right next to someone's car, having *claimed* another person, all of him, lock, stock, and barrel, and this person was still in shock.

"Easy," she whispered, barely moving her lips. "Don't flinch, Kon. I'm nearly there."

She pulled out his sense of guilt, sick and toxic, and brightened up his grief, like a cup of tea is lightened by a slice of lemon. She chose the most virtuous, wholesome, and honorable facets of his personality and placed them in the center of her composition. Then she removed the memory of the last few minutes since he'd spotted Sasha. Finally, she let go of his shoulder, turned, and walked away, stopping only when she reached the wall of dense yellowing bushes.

The car door opened and closed. Through the thick branches, Sasha watched Konev walk toward the front entrance, his gait quick but firm.

The elevator opened. Standing by the edge of the courtyard, Sasha could see Konev approach the familiar door. She watched him raise his hand to press the doorbell, then hesitate and reach into his pocket. Of course, he still had the key . . .

Sasha watched Konev enter the apartment. Mom appeared by the door to her room; she looked older, haggard, but alive. Konev spoke to her, saying the very words that had to be said in that moment, with the intonation that was necessary, and Mom's eyes began to change, soften, and the bedroom door opened slightly, and a pale face of a teenage girl peeked out.

From a distance, Sasha touched the girl, very lightly, just enough to interpret the most crucial, most painful signals. Trauma and grief, that was expected, but there was something else. Loneliness. A father-daughter conflict, some misunderstanding at school, bitterness, abandonment. Even in the most difficult years of her childhood, Sasha had never experienced anything like that.

You are not an orphan, Sasha thought furiously. *You have someone who can stand up for you. I may not know you, but I am your mother—I am a projection of motherhood as a concept, and there is no reason for Farit to lie about us being grammatically unrelated. Your father and your grandmother will always take care of you, but you should know that you also have me, and you can rely on me.*

The girl accepted Sasha's thought as a mirror accepts a ray of light, without processing or interpreting it, but rather simply reflecting it. Her face lit up. She stepped forward, and wrapped her arms around her father's neck, and cried; watching her mom's face, Sasha knew that this hadn't happened in a long while. For a few seconds Konev did not move, but eventually he held his daughter in his arms. His hands shook.

They will survive this, Sasha thought in surprise. *They will support each other, console each other, and may perhaps even be happy. I did it. That's all I could do for them, but it's not insignificant, is it? That's what I came for, to help, to support—and to let go.*

And something else, she thought, euphoria rising inside her. *It's time to correct some other errors.*

That night she wandered the streets, turning on burned-out lightbulbs, draining puddles, correcting botched, shoddy graffiti. At some point she saw a homeless kitten hiding under a parked car. Sasha leaned against a tree trunk and inhaled deeply, *claiming* the street, the courtyards, the buildings on both sides; she touched them gently, like rosary beads, until a light came on in one of the second-floor windows. A woman dressed in boots on bare feet and a jacket over a bathrobe came out, confused but determined. She walked past Sasha without noticing her, pulling her phone out of her pocket. A bright beam rummaged under the car. The woman spoke to someone; Sasha lowered her eyelids and saw two round green eyes in the light of the phone. She saw the woman switch from human tongue to gentle cooing and reach underneath the car with her hand . . .

The feeling of omnipotence that she first experienced in her childhood courtyard swept over Sasha, suspending her in the center of the world, devoid of gravity. The woman carried away the kitten, changing its fate right there and then, and Sasha watched her, not thinking or feeling anything at all. The human language had no words for the state she was in. And yet, she had to pull that world out of a puddle, the world that was drowning in fear, the world trembling on its thin wet striped paws, and she had to pull it out and change it forever.

"Nikolay Valerievich, I am sorry—I've been playing hooky."

Finding a pay phone in the modern world was not a trivial task.

"I noticed," Sterkh said expressionlessly on the other line. His voice did not bode well.

"Can you please tell me . . . that truck driver, the one I . . . did he survive?"

He was silent for a very long time. Sasha began to shake again.

"Yes," he said finally.

"Thank you. You see . . . I must be growing as a concept again. I know I have to attend classes, but I need to work on correcting my errors."

"You *must* attend your classes." His voice was as dry as a well in a desert. "You are still a student here."

"I will make up all the missed classes. I promise. You know I will."

"Yes, I know," he said slowly. "Sasha, you must be careful. Please."

"Nikolay Valerievich," Sasha said. "This world is going to change, it will renew—and it will be better. Please have faith in me."

"It's not a question of faith," he said thickly. "Some errors you cannot correct, you can only learn from them. Do come back."

...

Two hours on a train reminded her of her childhood, even though the train car was a newer model, nothing like the old boxes Sasha remembered from her trips with Mom. It was a bright sunny day, thick forest stood sentinel along the tracks, and each tiny detail seemed like a good omen: brightly colored toylike cars waiting at the railroad crossing. A heron on a wet field, looking quite picturesque at a distance. Children on bikes. A trace left by a plane in a porcelain blue sky.

She was on her way to bring love back to two people who deserved it, years later. Valentin and Sasha's mom were made for each other, and the very fact that they were still single only proved their right to happiness. Of course, Valentin had aged, he was completely alone and nearly estranged from his adult sons, he could be depressed or have a drinking problem. She may have to pull him out of poverty, restore his faith in himself. But all that needed to be done was to allow these two people to meet once, and their happiness would become irreversible.

She arrived at a gated community. A guard at the entrance. Sasha hesitated a bit: the Valentin she imagined lived in a decrepit five-story building. However, he was a renowned expert in the field of medical equipment, so why wouldn't he be well-off?

"Hello, Valentin Petrovich. I was the one who called you."

"Hello. I must admit I don't quite understand how I can help you."

He stood at his doorstep, a well-groomed, successful man, an absolute stranger. Sasha didn't even recognize him right away. He'd aged quite a bit less than Sasha's mom, and she found it unexpected and rather unpleasant.

Not to worry, she said to herself. *Mom will blossom as soon as she falls in love. She'll start looking younger. Valentin will definitely appreciate it.*

"I am here on behalf of Olga Antonovna Samokhina," she said out loud. "You met her many years ago at a summer resort."

He gazed at her without irritation but with some degree of weariness, unclear on why he'd agreed to speak with her in the first place. Preparing for their meeting, Sasha was convinced her name would unlock his memory. And if it didn't, she'd push it along just a tiny bit.

"You suffered a heart attack," Sasha continued gently, looking into his eyes. "She helped you. Visited you at the hospital. Do you remember?"

She showed him a photo on her tablet: Mom laughing at the surf's edge, looking young and joyful.

"I don't remember," he said sincerely. "You are confusing me with someone else. I don't remember the faces of everyone I've met."

His confusion was taking up the last seconds of this awkward conversation. He was about to apologize, say good-bye, and lock his door.

All three surveillance cameras recorded the girl taking a step toward the man in the doorway, stumbling, and instinctively grabbing his elbow to steady herself. The man didn't pull away; on the contrary, he tried to hold her up . . .

Sasha entered his memory. She saw him from the inside, saw what he was like and what he had become. She saw a harmonious but perfectly insular world that did not allow for other people or attachments. There was no welcoming lighthouse; this man was perfectly self-sufficient. Sasha unrolled his timeline, unspooling his worn-out memories . . .

It was early evening. Mom was leaning against the balustrade, and Valentin stood by her side, towheaded and pale, having just arrived that morning. Mom smiled, and dimples appeared in her cheeks. It was a special smile.

A few steps away, Sasha sat at a bench underneath an acacia tree, sullen like a wet sparrow. She was alone on that bench, completely alone. "Look at the dolphins," Mom shouted, and Valentin laughed joyfully.

And then everything changed. Mom frowned, her smile was now strained. That's what it was: on their very first evening together, he let it slip that he was married. And Mom said no that very second, refusing to even try, closing the door to any opportunity. That's just who she was.

It wasn't Sasha on the bench under the acacia tree. It was the young Alexandra Samokhina, a year away from high school graduation, four years away from her wedding to Konev, nineteen years away from her death on the highway.

"Miss, are you ill?"

But it was he who was ill: he couldn't comprehend what was happening, why everything suddenly went dark; he didn't know if he'd suddenly lost consciousness and why Sasha was still hanging on his arm like an umbrella. He was still holding up. He was a tough guy. He exercised, had annual checkups, lived in a gated community with no particular attachments and no pets of his own.

"I stepped on something," Sasha mumbled. "I am sorry, this is so awkward, I'm gonna go."

Security cameras watched her nod stiffly and walk away along the bike path past the impressive facades, flowerbeds, and tennis courts. The cameras did not detect her shock, did not record her failure, and certainly did not recognize her earlier omnipotence that now sloughed off like leaves from an autumn tree.

"Some errors you cannot correct, you can only learn from them."

The world without love that she had just glimpsed terrified her more than she had expected. Mom had made a conscious decision to decline happiness, and she'd had a really good reason. But Valentin—he'd declined happiness as well, and perhaps he had made a mistake. If these two people had met earlier, nothing would have been amiss. There would have been nothing to fix. And instead of Sasha, a completely different person would have been born.

She stopped, pressing her palms to her forehead. The titillating power was replaced with uncertainty. Again, Sasha saw a thin membrane separating existence from *unexistence*. She, Sasha, was an eventuality, a lucky chance for someone, a tragic accident for someone else. It took her a minute to regain her balance and return to reality: these two had declined their chance at love. Their love was neither in the past nor in the future; it did not exist. But Sasha existed, and she had a chance, she could . . . could she?

"Be brave," Sasha whispered to herself. Her omnipotence, found and lost, came back to her for a second, like a premonition.

"Dear passengers, this is your captain speaking. In a few minutes our aircraft will be landing in Torpa."

The sound of his voice, woven into the low buzz of the aircraft, made Sasha's heart beat even faster than when he'd announced the takeoff.

"Please fasten your seatbelts and remain in your seats until the aircraft makes a complete stop. Thank you."

Tiled roofs stretched underneath the wing. From above, the ancient Torpa looked so much like the city with the tower from her textbook that Sasha flinched.

"Ladies and gentlemen, we have landed. Our crew wishes you a wonderful day."

The last one to disembark, she had no luggage, not even a carry-on. She passed the working crew by the cargo door and stopped on the airstrip, a hundred steps from the rest of the passengers filing into the building like ants.

When everyone else was gone, he finally descended the airstair, rolling a small suitcase with a long handle behind him.

"Hey," Sasha said, unsmiling.

He didn't hesitate. "Come on," he said, taking her hand as if she were a child.

Sitting in his silver Mazda, Sasha felt a belated pang of fear. Did she dare? Did she risk everything, go all in? Bravely apply for a bit of happiness? Swallow the bait Farit had foisted on her? Or was she simply about to jump into the arms of a stranger who, for all she knew, had several women in his life?

He never even asked why she'd left on that first night and why she'd fallen out of a clear blue sky now, without warning. He didn't say that he had tried to find her, and now she had found him. He was silent, as if their meeting was par for the course. And yet, when people meet, they talk, even if their meetings are normal, routine, ordinary. People talk about the weather, or their plans for that evening, or any number of mundane but pleasant things. Yet Yaroslav said absolutely nothing, as if they'd just had a fight.

The car flew along the highway past the new housing developments, and ancient Torpa floated toward them, showing off its tiled roofs, this time from below. Glancing at Yaroslav's profile, Sasha was suddenly scared that he was taking her back to the institute. Like the last time. She was terrified that he misunderstood her, that he was simply driving her home because he thought that she needed a ride again.

The scent of his cologne inside the car drove Sasha crazy. Yaroslav was still quiet, seemingly deep in his thoughts. Sasha shut her eyes for a moment. The shock she'd experienced during her latest Analytical Specialty lesson reshuffled the fragments of the puzzle that was the essence of Sasha, and now projections of different ideas tumbled inside her like pieces of glass inside a child's kaleidoscope.

She had taken a risk, and he hadn't even noticed. He was busy with his own thoughts, and all he was doing was giving her a ride, and he was about to let her out at the corner of Sacco and Vanzetti, and here he was, driving past the new developments, and into the old Torpa, and he was about to turn right . . .

He turned left.

Inside Sasha, a newly sprung bitterness gave way to panic.

"I knew you were on this flight," Yaroslav said softly. "Or rather, on every flight to Torpa, I imagined you sitting behind me, in the cabin."

Sasha looked at him closer. Yes, he was focused and slightly detached, but not because he had more important things to worry about than their meeting.

On the contrary.

The silver Mazda drove into the heart of the old town, an area Sasha rarely visited. The streets here were steep, going sharply up and down, and the houses were quite rustic, hidden behind rural-looking carved fences. The car would fly up the hill, and Sasha's heart would jump into her throat, like a tiny fish escaping a predatory pike. The network of streets and roofs would split open, and the car would roll back down the cobblestones, making Sasha's heart plunge back into her stomach.

"Where are we going?"

"Right here."

Yaroslav parked the car in front of a carved gate, dark from rain. He stepped out and unlocked the gate. A wooden house, at least a century old, stood inside.

"Don't be so surprised," Yaroslav said, watching her face. "This is where I grew up."

"Right," Sasha said hoarsely, and immediately caught herself. "What about your father, isn't he waiting for you?"

"He's not home." Yaroslav drove the car inside the gate. "He has a standing chess date with his buddies. When the weather is nice, they play outside, when it isn't—at the library."

"But he knows you flew in today!" Sasha suddenly longed for an old man to open the door and cheerfully invite them in for tea. Or perhaps not cheerfully, but more like cautiously; she desperately wanted him to show up and break the tension of this moment because Sasha simply could not decide if she was making a choice, committing a crime, or doing something stupid.

"I already called him." Yaroslav unlocked the door. "And told him not to rush. Don't worry, you will get a chance to meet him. Later."

She hesitated one last time, followed him to the squeaky threshold, and touched the doorframe gingerly. The house was calm and content, as smooth as a forest lake on a windless day. No one had ever been hurt in there, and even arguments had been few and far between. And yet, loneliness darkened the windows like black curtains, and the distant sense of guilt filled the air with bitterness. Everyone who had ever lived there left behind a multitude of shadows, old ones, nearly colorless, and new ones, cherished and carefully guarded; the keeper of the common memory was one man, the same man who wasn't home right now.

Sasha jerked her hand away; she'd gone too far, it wasn't polite— worse than going through someone's locked drawers.

"Come in." Yaroslav showed her into the living room. "Have a seat."

What kind of silly talk was that? "Have a seat," as if they were in class or at a meeting! Where and why was she expected to sit down?

Stepping over the threshold, Sasha looked around the living room. Old furniture and a grandfather clock with a large pendulum keeping time she knew was an illusion, books and photographs on the walls that appeared semitransparent to her, like decorations made from cloudy glass. Through them, Sasha saw silhouettes and meanings, flashing like a high-motion video.

It was akin to an exercise Portnov had once assigned to her: immaterial entities that were measured by numbers and expressed by symbols but could not be written down or imagined. The sequences of meanings stretched and intertwined, imprinting onto each other, reimagining and stretching even further. *I am trying to escape,* Sasha realized, breaking out in a cold sweat. *I am about to dive into the informational component, shrug off my human form like an empty skin, and fly off . . .*

"Who are you?" Yaroslav asked softly. His question worked like a tiny flame of a birthday candle placed between her fingers. Sasha blinked and became instantly aware of the light, the sounds, the scents of the old house with its light notes of valerian root and heart medication. Yaroslav stood by the opposite wall, his white uniform cap lying on top of the clock.

"Who am I?" Repeating the question was an annoying habit, but it gave her time to think. Although Sasha hadn't quite decided what she would think about.

Why was he asking that question? He'd taken her hand, brought her into this house . . . Normal people would kiss as soon as they stepped over the threshold. But this third-degree interrogation was decidedly unusual.

Then again, nothing about this was normal.

And yet, back in his car, she wanted him to ask something, anything.

"If I don't answer," she said helplessly, "what will you do?"

He seemed to have expected a different answer. Perhaps he wanted her to laugh and turn everything into a joke. Or perhaps he expected her to explain everything, simply and clearly.

"Because, you see . . . " He paused for a moment. "I don't believe in love potions or hypnosis in the middle of the street . . . I don't believe in fate or love at first sight. But since we met, I can't think of anything but you. It's not normal, Sasha. It resembles . . . what does it resemble?"

"Since we met, I have loved you very much," Sasha said. "That's the truth. There is nothing else I can tell you."

And it was the truth, even though she wasn't sure how she knew it was the truth. It felt wrong to say, yet she also knew she couldn't deny it. Since the moment they'd met, he'd been on her mind, and as much as she'd tried to avoid those thoughts—and him—here she was.

She waited for his reaction, terrified and hopeful. Would he believe her, would he think she was lying, did he know in advance, did he have no idea, was he expecting this answer, or was it a complete surprise for him, and how long would this silence last?

"Last question," he said, looking at her earnestly. "Do I get any choice in loving you?"

Once again, the walls were becoming transparent, and through them Torpa appeared in silhouette—or perhaps it wasn't Torpa, but rather the red city from Sasha's error correction assignment. A tower topped with a weather vane stood in its center.

"I need a pen and some paper," Sasha said.

He looked surprised and somewhat hopeful. Perhaps he imagined Sasha writing down her terrible secret she couldn't articulate. At this point, though, she couldn't imagine what he was thinking, and refused to reach out, to invade him even just a bit. It was the least she could do.

Without any comment, he went into another room and came back immediately with the supplies. Sasha waited by the massive table made of solid wood, a table that remembered joyful dinners, abundant delicacies, guests, champagne, and occasional coffins laid out for viewing—

Yaroslav placed a sheet of lined paper and a ballpoint pen in front of her.

"Sasha, what's wrong?"

"Nothing." She stared into space.

"I didn't want to upset you," he said tensely. "If you tell me that you're a witch, or a mermaid, or a fallen angel, I will believe it. I am ready for it. It's just that I have this sense of being manipulated. I would love to just be low-maintenance and ignore it, but I can't pretend like nothing is going on . . ."

Sasha fiddled with the pen.

"Actually," he said, making a decision, "forgive me. I'm an idiot. Forget what I said. Come here."

He stepped closer, his scent enveloping her, intoxicating her and taking away her will. Sasha gritted her teeth.

The symbol of *affection*, and above it, without taking the pen off paper, the symbol of *creation*. Portnov had taught her to recognize and reproduce symbols, and she taught herself to *manifest* them. Sterkh had taught her to express ideas through what they were not.

This particular three-dimensional symbol, developing in time, splitting in half, then splitting again, like a fertilized egg—this symbol was "love." And if she did something like this—Sasha's pen nearly tore through the paper—it would no longer be *love*. It wasn't *hatred, indifference, resentment,* or *estrangement,* but it wasn't *love* either.

Perhaps it was *freedom*.

Sasha's gaze wandered toward the wide windowsill, where under a slightly opened window she noticed a half-melted candle and a cheap red lighter. Sasha clicked the tiny wheel, and a miniature flame devoured the symbol on the piece of paper, making the drawn lines twitch and convulse for the last time.

"Please make sure to dispose of any physical manifestation of your work," Sterkh had told her.

The ashes fell onto the windowsill. *I am making such a mess in this beautiful home,* Sasha thought. Yaroslav stood by the table, pale, his eyes enormous and dark, beads of sweat on his forehead.

"Sasha . . ."

"You have a choice," she said with a wry smile. "You are free. Don't love."

Kostya intercepted her in front of the institute.

"Where were you?"

"Don't push it," Sasha hissed. "Did you forget the boycott?"

"Fuck this boycott! Where were you, Samokhina? Coach is marking you down for absences!"

Sasha shuddered. The mere thought of attending Coach's classes made her nauseated.

She morphed her fear into anger.

"Why do you care? Get out of my way, you are nobody to me!"

Kostya paled and took a step back. Walking up to the fourth floor, Sasha cursed herself: She had become quite a shrew. A malicious asshole, ready to gnaw a helpful hand. Even the sincerest sympathy, the strongest friendship couldn't possibly survive it. Out of the goodness of her generous heart, Sasha was about to scorch the earth around her, making the Coach-imposed boycott a natural attitude toward that bitch Samokhina.

She knocked on the door of auditorium 14, waited for the invitation, then entered. Nine and a half minutes had passed since the start of the session.

"Hello. I am late."

Sterkh motioned for her to sit down, steepled his fingers, and looked at her distantly.

"Nikolay Valerievich," Sasha said. "You can hit me. I won't resist."

"If I thought it would help, I wouldn't care about your resistance," Sterkh said pensively.

He placed his chin on his steepled fingers and gazed at her across the desk. His pupils were tiny, like poppy seeds.

"So? Did you make the world better?"

Sasha managed a crooked smile. He didn't have to hit her when she was down.

"Sorry," he said curtly. "We'll count your antics as a practical lesson. But what are you going to do about Analytical Specialty?"

The dorm greeted her with aseptic, cosmic silence. Sasha went up to her room and spent an hour in the shower, watching the stream of water hit the plastic curtain, like rain on a windshield of a truck.

Eventually she turned off the water, and it drained noisily, and then the soft padded silence of the evening returned. Sasha's tablet chirped: she had a new message.

Wrapped in a towel, she plodded back into her room and pulled the tablet from underneath the bed. It looked a little dusty. The message was sent anonymously, no name, no return address. Sasha had never seen anything like that before. A hint of mild curiosity poked through her apathy.

She opened the message, even though common sense reminded her not to take candy from strangers. The body of the message was also empty, but there was an attachment, a large graphic file.

She wanted to ask someone for advice, to put the tablet aside until at least her next session with Sterkh. But she couldn't stop. *One claw is snagged, the whole bird is bagged.* Sasha poked her finger at the screen, and a file preview opened, a puzzle of tiny fragments.

The pictures were numbered one through one hundred. In preview format, she couldn't see the details, just vague outlines.

"Must be porn," Sasha said out loud and giggled. "Porn sent to a work device. I wonder who's responsible."

Her finger touched the screen, opening Image 1.

A sound flooded her ears.

It was the sound of a marker on a whiteboard.

CHAPTER FOUR

Snow came in the middle of December. Her Applied Specialty exam was scheduled for December 16, Analytical Specialty for December 20.

Without a single word, Sterkh wrote "A" in her report card, and they simply sat in silence. Sasha was the last one on the list, and there was no one from Group A waiting. Outside it had been dark for a while. In her head, Sasha gave a couple of hundred appreciation speeches in honor of the man sitting across the desk but did not dare to say anything out loud.

The file she'd received from the anonymous user contained a hundred images, from simple to complex. There was a system in the order of these images, just like there was a system to Portnov's exercises during their first year. They made her sweat but didn't rip her apart or dissolve her in acid, like Coach's diagrams during their memorable last meeting.

The entire institute knew she was blowing off Analytical Specialty. In her presence her classmates exchanged demonstrative looks. *Have you given up?* they asked silently. *You, Samokhina, you dropped everything and gave up?* Lisa kept frowning, more and more often taking her frustration out on her classmates. Kostya was restless. Sasha wanted to approach him and ask for forgiveness, but every time she stopped herself from doing so, afraid of incurring Coach's wrath. Of Kostya incurring Coach's wrath, she corrected herself. But that didn't stop her completely. Once she went as far as buying a cute card and slipping it under his door.

He was so pleased by her attention that he couldn't quite hide his excitement. Sasha realized that Kostya would forgive her anything: insult, disdain, indifference. It made her feel terrified rather than happy.

She still attended Sterkh's classes and always showed up on time. Sterkh handled himself formally, with a bit of restraint. He never commented on her absences in Coach's class, and Sasha never admitted how much she valued the sent file and how she learned to work with the images. Sasha preferred not to think about how dangerous this was for him and what Coach would do if he found out about his colleague's insurrection. She didn't want to ponder the consequences and yet, she couldn't help imagining them—and wonder if her imagination went far enough.

Every morning she would open a new audio file, a routine assignment from Sterkh. She'd put on her headphones and hold her breath, listening to the silence, letting it in and using her willpower to regenerate it. From the dead silence of a snow-covered cemetery, she would sculpt the noiselessness of a deserted space station, the hush of a public square a second before the execution, the emptiness of destroyed auditory nerves. Turning the *unsound* inside out, she used it to express things that were not silent: the breathing of a sleeping child. The rustling of snake scales in the sand. A whoosh of a turned page. The whistling of air coming out of a punctured tire. The longer she shuffled through the meanings, the more transparent they would become, and Sasha struggled to choose human definitions. She simply existed in someone else's silence, allowing it to penetrate her through to the last cell.

And when the silence dissolved her completely, Sasha, still wearing her headphones, would step toward the whiteboard and pick up a marker.

The first move—a line, the horizon, a skewer onto which probabilities would impale themselves later. The aroma of marinated meat. Summer, childhood, a picnic, a riverbank, a firepit in the sand. A panicked scream amid all the fun: a boy, drowning. A stranger, about nine years old. His parents are not at the beach, and his teenage brother thrashes around, knee-deep in water, until the adults pull the body out of the river. This appeared to be a fragment of a memory, but Sasha was sure the memory could not have been hers.

She erased the diagram from the whiteboard and reproduced it again and again. Here it was, a short time loop placed onto the whiteboard as if onto an autopsy slab. The boy sinks underwater—disintegration, decay; must switch the symbols in the structure and redirect the time vector. Step back two measures. The boy is sputtering. Step back three more measures: the boy frantically waves his arms, the sun glitters on the water surface, the glare forming a grid . . .

. . . and the lines drawn with a marker on the whiteboard would disintegrate. Every time Sasha thought that with just a little bit more effort, she would turn this diagram inside out, and the boy would survive. But, like a rubber ball slipping from fingers into the water, the only possible death-less and fear-less version slipped from her grasp. Sasha told herself that this would warrant a C, and a C would be enough to pass the exam this time.

Under Exercise 20 Sasha discovered the assignment Coach gave her back in the auditorium: a woman with a carriage walking across the yard, a block of ice falling off the roof. Now, with a deeper knowledge base, Sasha could study the diagram in more detail: the ice collapsed on either the woman, or the carriage, or both, but neither the woman nor the baby happened to be real people. Both were variants representing any mother or any child. And again, Sasha sensed the existence of a death-less option, but still could not reproduce it, and so she gritted her teeth and forced herself to move to Exercise 21.

The exercises consumed all her energy, and it was spectacular: by the end of the day Sasha would feel absolutely drained, unable to think of the house that smelled of Valerian root, or the grandfather clock with the massive pendulum, or the ashes scattered on the wide windowsill. *You are free. Don't love.* She would go straight to bed and fall asleep only to wake up at six, go for a run, eat breakfast at the cafeteria, and be ready to receive a new audio file from Sterkh at eight o'clock sharp.

December 16 found her in auditorium 14, with the first A of this semester in her report card.

"I'm going to make it," Sasha said, breaking a prolonged silence. "I am going to pass Dmitry Dmitrievich's exam."

Sterkh shook his head; clearly, he did not share her optimism.

"May I offer you some advice?"

"Of course," she said, and added quickly, "Thank you."

"You need this man, the pilot," Sterkh said softly. "You need a complex, powerful, emotional package. Fuel. Energy. Information. And the fear of loss, too! And not just fear, and not so much the fear itself."

"This man," Sasha said, shocked at the change in her own voice. "This man is not *fuel*."

Sterkh's jaw tightened.

"You misunderstood me. I am not asking you to jump into his arms . . . or his bed. But to pass Dmitry Dmitrievich's exam—"

"I am very grateful to you for your support and all the help you've given me," Sasha said quickly, her tone suggesting Sterkh should shut up immediately.

"He's tied to you grammatically," Sterkh said, raising his voice slightly. "He's attached to you. If you fail the exam—"

"I will pass," Sasha said.

All these months, up to her ears in studying, she pushed away the memory of her last session with Coach and of the diagram that devoured her consciousness. On December 19, when twenty-four hours remained until the exam, her memory returned in full, and Sasha was seized by anxiety.

All these months, she had hated Sundays. On Sundays she took her earliest, longest runs, and then piled on the most unpleasant assignments, clearing her mind of planes and airports. On December 19, having not slept all night, Sasha walked out of her dorm into the darkness of the winter morning.

It was snowing. Every streetlight had a yellow halo, like an actor on the dark stage. Here and there festive colorful lights blinked on the facades. When Sasha arrived at the airport, the sun was rising, slowly and grudgingly.

No, she wasn't going to meet up with Yaroslav. Since she gave him back his freedom, he never attempted to see her, which was quite understandable. He made his choice. And while she was glad for it, Sasha also hated herself for the pitiful hope she occasionally experienced, especially on Sunday.

Today, the day before her exam, she wanted to see him, but from a distance. Perhaps tomorrow, when she entered auditorium 1, this memory would support her. *Fuel. Energy. Information. And the fear of loss, too!*

Right on schedule, an aircraft dove from underneath the low cloud onto the end of the runway. It landed somewhat awkwardly, with a little hop at the touchdown. Sasha was unpleasantly surprised: she was used to thinking of Yaroslav as the master of his craft, the best pilot in the world.

Pulling on their hats and wrapping thick scarves around their necks, their breath curling in tiny clouds, passengers came out and trotted toward the terminal. Flight attendants descended the airstair. The second pilot, the one Sasha had seen before, the Pushkin look-alike, walked by.

Next a middle-aged man came out, wearing a black coat over his summer uniform. Unhurriedly, as if without a care in the world, he strolled along the recently shoveled wet pavement. Perplexed, Sasha moved her eyes toward the aircraft door; several women in yellow light-reflecting vests over winter jackets ran up the airstair, carrying brooms and plastic bags. The door closed behind them.

Like a queen at a gown fitting, the aircraft was surrounded by ground staff—a water cistern; cargo and sewer trucks; luggage handlers tossing suitcases onto the loading platform; an electrician grounding the plane before refueling. Passengers left the terminal. Sasha sat by the window, trying to understand what had just happened.

Flight attendants walked past her, chattering away. The second pilot ran by, pressing his cell phone to his ear, clearly in a rush. The middle-aged man in a black coat did not leave the terminal, but instead headed toward the restricted part of the building.

Sasha came to. Breathing out clouds of steam, she ran to catch up to the flight attendants.

"Excuse me, please. Where is Grigoriev?"

"He doesn't work this route anymore," the younger flight attendant said, while the older one considered whether or not to respond to a stranger.

"But why? What happened?"

"He doesn't report to us." The flight attendant shrugged. "Maybe he was promoted. Or disqualified . . ."

The older woman glanced at her colleague with obvious disapproval, gave Sasha a once-over, and walked briskly toward the parking lot.

Sasha had nearly given up hope when the door finally opened. The steps creaked.

"Who's there?"

Sasha was taken aback: The voice did not seem old. It sounded just like his son's, but deeper.

"My name is Alexandra," Sasha said, taking a step backward from the gate. "I am an acquaintance of Yaroslav's."

The gate opened, and Sasha saw him for the first time: a tall man, poised and graceful, yet visibly tired. He wore thick Coke-bottle glasses and his hair was completely white. His plaid shirt was well ironed and possibly even starched, and perfect pleats on his trousers looked slightly odd above his house slippers. There was a subtle yet undeniable resemblance to Yaroslav. Or, rather, it was Yaroslav who resembled his father.

"Do you need a place to stay while you're in Torpa?" he asked, in turn studying Sasha through his thick lenses.

"Oh no," she said, embarrassed. "I live here, at the dorm. I am a student."

"I see," he said, with an unreadable expression. "Come in."

The yard hadn't been shoveled in a while, and only the narrow path to the house had been partially cleared. A silver Mazda was parked under a canopy.

"Is Yaroslav . . . is he here?" Sasha stopped.

"No, he isn't here," the old man said, his slippers crunching the snow, occasionally missing the path.

"Then where is he?" Sasha couldn't help herself. "He should have been working this route today. It was his flight."

"His schedule has changed."

Reaching the porch, the old man stomped his feet to shake off the snow. Sasha opened her mouth then closed it again like a fish.

"Come in," he said, opening the door for her.

"I couldn't possibly," Sasha mumbled. "You already practically walked barefoot through the snow for me. I am only here for a moment, I just wanted to ask . . ."

"Come in," he said gently.

Quickly, Sasha raised her head as if asking permission to enter once more, this time addressing the house itself. Icicles hung below the roof, tiny, harmless, like lollipops from her childhood. The attic window was nearly concealed by the snow. The house seemed to be watching her, its gaze benign, amiable, with not a hint of bitterness.

"I wanted to ask," she stepped over the threshold, "just wanted to ask if anything had happened to him."

"He's healthy." The old man walked to the middle of the living room, where a chessboard was set up on the dining room table next to a large magnifying glass. "But I assume you have parted ways . . ."

"Actually," Sasha said quickly, "nothing really happened between us. We didn't have a fight. It's just that . . . there are all sorts of circumstances. I can't really explain."

Nodding in understanding—or indifferent lack thereof—he felt for the back of a chair and sat down cautiously, as someone who did not rely on excellent vision.

"How could he leave you all alone?" Sasha said without thinking. "Doesn't he ever come to Torpa anymore?"

"He does." The old man smiled. "And I am not alone here, I hired a very nice lady to help me with the household chores. Yaroslav is quite busy—he's starting a new life."

Sasha felt a chill. *A woman?*

The grandfather clock with a massive pendulum, where Yaroslav's white uniform cap had rested recently, was counting the fractions of the prolonged silence.

"New routes," the old man spoke again. "Transatlantic. He's always wanted to work those."

He was watching her, not like a stranger or an idle observer: without curiosity, but rather with sympathy. Sasha made an effort to smile, without joy, but rather with certain relief.

The old man nodded, seemingly satisfied.

"I must admit, I am happy for him. His mother would have been pleased, too."

He leaned over the table and Sasha watched as he became a part of the house, and the house became an extension of the old man. Behind his back, long-lost meanings appeared in the air: a beautiful woman in a sundress, an elderly couple, a baby in the arms of a young man, and even a large shaggy dog, and some other people forming a single grammatical whole like intertwined symbols from *Conceptual Activator*, full of harmony, living at a point in time and flowing farther and farther back into the past . . .

The pendulum swung, the shadows disintegrated, carrying away their meaning and leaving behind the scent of Valerian.

"My name is Anton Pavlovich," Yaroslav's father said. "It's easy to remember. Like Chekhov."

He suddenly laughed.

"I used to say it to all my new young friends in the chess club. One girl kept calling me Alexander Sergeyevich, like Pushkin.

"And you are Alexandra."

Sasha used a large shovel to clear the yard. By the time she could see the bare ground, her muscles ached, and she could barely stand up straight.

She placed her palms onto the icy hood of the silver Mazda and waited for a few moments, but the car did not respond; it only beckoned her with the old scent locked inside.

"What should I tell him if he calls?" Anton Pavlovich asked.

"I'd like to stop by again, if you don't mind," Sasha said softly. "The day after tomorrow. And then I will let you know what to tell him."

Once again, the dorm felt deserted like a ghost ship. All the living and breathing creatures who resided here were holed up in their rooms, studying, memorizing, practicing before tomorrow's test. Sasha reproduced the entire set of the diagrams on the whiteboard, first odd, then even, then in no particular order. She wiped the sweat off her forehead and felt marginally better—she was definitely ready. As he flew over the ocean, Yaroslav could relax, even if he knew nothing of Sasha's war against herself and against Coach and would never know about Farit Kozhennikov. Yaroslav thought that the world was predictable and occasionally even fair. Instinctively, he believed that relying on everyday existence and doing one's job was enough for things to turn out well. Millions of people were alive and well, and nothing terrible ever happened to them. So why shouldn't he be the same?

Because of me, Sasha thought, and then shook the gloom away.

She took a deep breath and opened *Textual Module,* volume 8, the shabbiest, most worn-out textbook she'd ever seen.

"Darling book, sweet book," she murmured, laughing but not feeling any mirth, "show me a fragment of a probable future . . ."

The paragraphs of volume 8 did not rumble like tank treads; instead, they howled, emitting infrasound, like an earthquake turning mountains to dust. Sasha read one page, another, then another:

"Everything that existed on the outside turned hostile. Everything that existed on the inside became redundant. Sasha felt her essence dissolve, disintegrate, spread into a puddle of broth—the essence of who she thought she was, a girl, a daughter, a human being, a person . . ."

Sasha screamed and tossed the textbook aside. It fell faceup, spread out like a flying bird. Sasha pinned it with her foot, as if afraid the book would struggle, and began to rip out its pages. She didn't stop until the entire floor was covered with shreds of paper.

"Greetings, Samokhina. I was beginning to forget what you looked like."

Sasha placed her report card on the table next to the group transcript. All of Sasha's classmates had already been there, and a grade was marked next to each last name.

The last one on the list, she intentionally showed up a bit later to avoid waiting by the door, absorbing everyone's tension. In the coatroom packed with wet jackets, she ran into Kostya, who suddenly took her arm just above the elbow to stop her.

"Listen . . ."

"It's fine," Sasha said, struggling to smile. She looked at his hand lying on her sleeve. Embarrassed, Kostya let go of her arm.

"He's nicer than usual today. He hasn't failed anyone yet. Good luck, all right?"

And here she was, stepping across the threshold of the auditorium she hadn't seen in a few months. Outside was dark, and snowflakes pecked at the window like Hitchcock's birds.

"So, Samokhina," Coach continued, leaning back in his chair and crossing his massive arms. "Do you really think you can skip the entire semester's worth of my classes and still pass my exam?"

A thick green marker lay on the edge of the desk. Sasha had a hard time looking away from it. Two days ago she thought she was going to succeed, that her devotion to hard work would save her hide like it always had. But any minute now Coach would pick up that green marker and annihilate her efforts. Making the marker screech across the board, he would draw the diagram that could penetrate her consciousness and putrefy it.

"Please let me at least try," Sasha forced out. "I studied independently."

"So then go ahead and grade yourself." He smirked. "Independently!"

At this moment, Coach didn't even bother pretending to be human.

However, he didn't look fully detached either: a gas mask could not be expected to act sneering or acrimonious.

"If I complete the assignment, you can't fail me," Sasha said, as if climbing a sheer cliff. "You are also determined. In your own way."

"Freedom-shmeedom," he muttered, as if to himself. "A single idea and so many intricate reflections . . . Un-debt, un-coercion, and—incidentally—un-love. Who sent you the instructional materials, Samokhina?"

"W-what instructional materials?" Sasha stopped in her tracks.

"The very same instructional materials that have been downloaded to your tablet that is currently inside your backpack . . . 'that rat that ate the malt that lay in the house that Jack built.'" He watched her like a cat watching a mouse, with pitiless curiosity.

A couple of days ago Sasha had made a mental note to delete the file before the exam, to destroy the evidence. Dealing with her anxiety, shoveling the snow in front of Anton Pavlovich's house, and then analyzing *Textual Module,* volume 8 for different versions of the future, she completely forgot to destroy the incriminating evidence.

And yet, her own stupidity be damned, he had no right to search her belongings. Her tablet was her property. Well, no, it belonged to the institute. It was a study aid, and she could be ordered to give it back at any moment. There was no sender's name . . . but Coach obviously knew everything by now. And he would find out anyway, now that Sasha had shown up to take the test after missing three months' worth of classes.

"Well?" Perhaps he was studying her reaction, or simply entertaining himself, assuming such a complex grammatical function had any need of entertainment.

Sasha said nothing. She had nothing to say. Shifting the blame from Sterkh meant making things worse.

"I see you didn't understand anything at all," he continued with a hint of regret. "About what I said regarding singularity."

"I understood everything," Sasha said softly.

"And you're still planning to *reverberate?*"

"I don't have a choice." Sasha looked into his diaphragm pupils, and they contracted instantly, as if concealing something from her.

"You have a choice," Coach shared leisurely. "Unlike your classmates, you are capable of saying no, a skill you have already demonstrated before."

"The Great Speech is beautiful and harmonious," Sasha said haltingly. "But it's full of errors. I must . . . no, I *want* to correct them."

"It was me who sent you the instructional materials," he said in the same tone of voice.

"What?" Sasha immediately bit her tongue. The word came out more like "What the fucking hell?"

"My responsibility is to teach you"—her insubordination did not seem to faze him—"so all the formalities have been met, and I fulfilled my obligations as faculty. I could have reported you every time you missed a class, but I chose the path of least resistance."

Snowflakes beat against the glass as if demanding to be part of the exam. Sasha felt as if the life preserver she'd been clutching the entire semester had turned out to be a bear trap.

Sterkh wasn't the person who helped her. And all these months she'd believed in his support. She thought she wasn't alone, but it turned out she was lying to herself. She thought someone gave her a hand, but instead a hole was dug for her. Sterkh didn't support her, he simply watched her move toward failure.

"And now you bravely showed up for the exam." Coach gazed at her, not blinking, and behind his diaphragm pupils was absolute, impenetrable darkness. "Well, then."

He picked up the green marker, just like in her nightmares, and Sasha knew it was all in vain. All the formalities had been met, but as soon as he approached the whiteboard, she'd say: "Enough." She'd give up immediately, but he wouldn't stop.

"What is grammatical analysis of a standard diagram?" he asked, holding the marker with the tips of his fingers.

"It defines connections between names and actions in a closed time loop . . . with many variations," Sasha mumbled.

"What's the general principle of building diagrams?"

"They are models of catastrophes," Sasha said. "Each diagram is a model of something terrible that may happen . . . or that may be avoided."

"Bloody kindergarten," he said, playing with the marker.

"What did I say wrong?"

"You said *everything* wrong, your discourse is that of a human being."

"That's because I *am* a human being!" Sasha shouted.

"Good for you, you get a gold star," Coach said without as much as a hint of emotion, sounding not only devoid of sarcasm but downright chilling. Sasha couldn't take her eyes away from the green marker.

"All right," he said after a long pause. "Here, take the marker. Here is the whiteboard. Reproduce the simplest diagram you can analyze. Let's be fair: you build probabilities, conduct the analysis, and I give you a C, a passing grade. Or are you looking for an A, for your straight-A report card?'"

She understood his words and felt firm ground under her feet. She felt the space outside the window, the snow falling sideways, and the blurry glow of streetlights along Sacco and Vanzetti.

It was when the green marker was passed from Coach to Sasha that the balance of power shifted in the auditorium: she believed she would pass, and not just pass, but earn an A.

He sensed a change in her mood and narrowed his eyes slightly, but Sasha no longer feared him—she was free of that fear. A vertical stream carried her from absolute despair into euphoric omnipotence: she didn't just "show up" for the exam. She'd learned her lesson from everything that had happened to her. And now she knew, really knew, what she had to do.

Sasha inhaled, exhaled, and drew a horizontal line on the whiteboard. And there you had it, it began, and there was no way back: a suburban road, a streamlined green highway. A small dark blue Škoda, a woman behind the wheel. A sleepless, difficult night. White lines marking the pavement. Eyelids getting heavy, consciousness floating away, and with it away floats the steering wheel . . .

Sasha entered an additional meaning into the network of lines, making the marker squeak; the phone in the dashboard holder rings loudly, as shrill as a fire engine. The woman wakes up and manages to maneuver the car back into its lane. The phone continues to ring. The woman sees her ex-husband's name on the screen, or, perhaps, not quite ex, but already estranged. She hesitates, then puts him on speaker. Her ex-husband shouts—no, he speaks in a barely audible whisper—that he's deeply sorry, that he knows he behaved like an asshole, that they must think of their daughter, and they haven't finished their conversation. He begs her to come back.

The woman is distracted. Her car crosses into the oncoming traffic, the woman slams on the brakes, the car skids on the wet pavement, a suburban bus is approaching . . .

Becoming one with the whiteboard, a part of the diagram, Sasha scowled. Five measures back: the highway, the woman falls asleep behind the wheel, the phone rings, ex-husband screams that she's a selfish bitch, that she doesn't care about their daughter, he tells her to burn in hell . . .

A turn of the steering wheel. The car flies into the incoming traffic . . .

The lines on the whiteboard were changing colors, from green to black and red. Sasha no longer felt euphoric; she rushed to the finish line, afraid of looking back or thinking about her actions. If she didn't finish in the next few seconds, her marker would fully dry up, and the whiteboard would have no more clean space . . .

Five measures back. The morning highway, the woman behind the wheel. A frantic attempt, Sasha's hand holding the marker cramps up, and . . . the phone rings a second before the woman falls asleep.

The ringing sound wakes her up. A bus is coming at her, its head-lights glowing like a theater stage. Blinded by the lights, Alexandra turns the steering wheel to the right, then to the left, avoiding the collision. The car skids to the side of the road, slides down to the river, and freezes half a meter away from the concrete base of the bridge. The phone is still ringing, but Alexandra ignores it. She's just avoided a sure death.

Sasha took a deep breath. Here it was, the happy ending, the first one ever! This was the only possible variant. Alexandra Samokhina would now take a cab home, where her mother stayed awake, looking out of the window where the sun was just beginning to rise, and . . .

Behind the wheel of the blue Škoda Sasha saw herself. She'd never driven a car before. She saw the name on the telephone screen even though she'd never had a smartphone like this. She felt the burden of a sleepless night in the back of her head, the scent of unfamiliar perfume, someone else's memory, someone else's years gone by. She recognized that she was falling into Alexandra as if into a deep well, merging with her, and this invasion was about to tear Alexandra apart, and reality could not handle that.

The lines disintegrated. The phone screen with the missed call, the mirror above the windshield—everything turned into a dull murky projection on a crumpled sheet, and below a network of meanings, impossible to imagine and impossible to describe.

Sasha would have screamed had she still existed.

. . .

"You were quite close to getting away with it, Samokhina."

The eraser slid across the whiteboard with a delicate sound resembling a cricket's song. Sasha experienced the instant joy of existing in space, functioning, acting, continuing. She lived, she was. *Unbeing* had been canceled.

"But you managed to drown yourself." Coach tossed the eraser into the corner and sat behind the desk, reaching for the class transcript.

"You are used to being special, aren't you? The best student, who can do no wrong? Not with me, Samokhina, not in my class. You were told to demonstrate that you have mastered working with diagrams. But you decided to show off. Well, congratulations. You have distinguished yourself."

He plucked the plastic top off his old-fashioned fountain pen with a gold nib.

"You failed. You have two more tries."

"No," Sasha stammered. "Listen, I need to understand . . ."

He raised the pen over the transcript.

"What did I do wrong?" She was about to lunge at him just to stop his hand. "Just tell me. What happened?"

"When you come back to retake this exam, you can tell me exactly what you did wrong." He wrote an F next to her name. "Come back on the twenty-third. Study hard."

Fourth years from Group A gathered in the hallway by the entrance to auditorium 1; walking through their formation felt like running a gauntlet. Everyone watched her, silently, questioningly, and everyone immediately knew what had happened.

Kostya went pale, his tense face turning to stone. The girls exchanged sympathetic glances. Lisa said, addressing no one in particular, "Turns out no one is more equal than others. Everyone gets their ass handed over to them, and the best students are no exception."

There was no sarcasm in her voice, only exhaustion and anger.

The small crowd parted before Sasha. As she moved through, she noticed a few people from group B, and even some fifth years. She was convinced she was simply having a bad dream, a common nightmare of any student during finals, and that she would wake up soon, in time for her exam.

Kostya stepped in front of her.

"Don't panic. You have two more tries! You need to get your shit together and pass! You can do it!"

By talking to her, he had directly violated Coach's orders. Or perhaps now, after her failure, the boycott no longer had any power. As Kostya kept talking, Sasha perceived his words as colorful soap bubbles, floating in front of her face and melting into the air.

She frowned, trying to understand. Kostya was clearly shocked. He forgave her for being rude and for being wrong. He was worried about her, he sympathized with her, but another feeling, just as strong and perfectly human, balanced out the scales. That feeling was joy. Jealous, Kostya was happy when the object of his jealousy was in trouble.

Sasha glanced at her classmates, at Andrey, Denis, then Anna, Yulia, Oksana from Group B . . . Her classmates knew everything about her life, they knew every detail, and so did Kostya. They knew that Yaroslav would have to pay for Sasha's failure.

"You have two more tries," Kostya repeated like an incantation, and Sasha suddenly knew she hated him. She took a blind step forward.

"Hold it!"

Someone clutched her shoulders and jerked her backward. Sasha turned and found herself staring into Lisa's cold, furious eyes. Lisa shook Sasha by the shoulders, breaking Coach's orders, despite how much she'd already had to endure.

"Don't you dare get hysterical!"

Compassion wasn't Lisa's strong suit. However, she was an expert at expressing anger and contempt toward Sasha for failing to meet Lisa's expectations. Lisa wanted to spur Sasha, provide her with additional motivation.

And if it embarrassed Sasha, all the better.

"We've had it worse than you! All of us have! Suck it up!"

But Sasha had never considered giving up. On the contrary. The hatred she felt toward Kostya multiplied exponentially and was about to spill over the entire class. They passed the exam, didn't they? Then they should have been celebrating. They should have been gloating behind her back. Samokhina, the same Samokhina who'd always gotten away with everything, this time Samokhina got her ass handed to her, and wasn't it a wonderful reason to celebrate?

In front of her, their faces went blurry. Through the haze, over their shoulders, she saw another face. Farit Kozhennikov stood by the entrance, near the concierge's booth, looking at his phone as if none of it was any of his concern.

Outside, her rage vanished in a split second, as if Sasha suddenly sobered up. She observed herself from a distance and realized how unfair she was being toward her classmates. None of them deserved hatred—they did not deserve even a hint of reproach. Not even Kostya. Particularly not Kostya.

A black SUV was parked by the entrance to the pizzeria. To get to the car, she needed to cross Sacco and Vanzetti Street. Such a short distance, and Sasha needed time to prepare. She had to strategize. Yaroslav was somewhere between the continents, many kilometers above the ground, the cold ocean beneath him . . .

"Farit, I have to talk to you." She cut out all the formalities, attempting to remind him of that time in her room when he told her: "You and I have a lot in common, more than either one of us and those you're used to thinking of as humans."

He held open the door of his SUV and motioned for her to get in.

"That's a lucky coincidence because I have to talk to you."

With one sentence and his breathy intonation, he reminded her who was whose advisor. She winced, but held her ground, forcing herself to relax and speak after a pause.

"Both of us want me to pass this exam. And graduate."

She intentionally used "both of us," and he got the hint. Getting into the driver's seat, he smirked.

"Both of us, Sasha. Both of us want you to pass, to succeed, to make it. We are allies, you know that."

"Then we can speak openly." Sasha held on to the conquered territory. "If anything happens to Yaroslav . . . if he as much as breaks his finger, I will join forces with Dmitry Dmitrievich, who doesn't want me to graduate. Together with my new ally, I will make every effort to ensure that I don't survive . . . that I don't make it to graduation. This wouldn't please you, would it?"

She struggled to push out these words, but she had to indicate this change of status, the new phase in their relationship.

Farit took his time getting comfortable in the driver's seat, buckling himself in, and turning the key. Eventually, he glanced at Sasha, but the dark glasses obscured his eyes, and Sasha could not interpret his expression.

"What exactly did you do during today's exam, Sasha?"

Sasha raised her chin.

"I met the requirements of the program. Completely. I put in a lot of effort, and—by the way—I succeeded. And I will continue working, working hard, punching above my weight, if—if you continue being my ally."

"We'll let your professor judge whether or not you met the requirements," Farit said less than enthusiastically, and Sasha felt her determination melt away. "What exactly did you do?"

"Reproduced one of the training diagrams." Sasha gazed at her own double expression in his dark lenses.

"I assume something went wrong?"

"I don't know," for the first time, Sasha's voice cracked, "Dmitry Dmitrievich didn't explain."

"Then I will explain, as someone older and wiser." He turned on the heat, seemingly not in a rush to drive anywhere. "You decided to arrange the fate of Alexandra Koneva. You did not take into account that if Alexandra is alive, you don't exist. Even inside a training module. But you didn't think of that. Obviously, you failed the exam—it was a rather crude error."

Outside the snow was falling, swirling around the streetlights like clouds of disturbed ashes. Sasha felt like someone who was shown an elephant in the room they thought was empty.

"You had a perfectly legitimate option," Farit said pensively. "I handed you a turnkey solution. Sterkh gave you a hint: information, energy, fuel."

Sasha blinked at the instant memory of an aircraft popping out of the murky thunderstorm, just aboveground, across the runway. It would have been so easy to re-create this short fragment of reality and work out a handful of variations: oily black smoke, and fire reaching the sky, and the fuselage engulfed in flames, and broken wings . . .

"No," Sasha said in horror. "Not even within a training module. No."

"Or any other variation." He didn't bother arguing. "Just not the one where Alexandra is alive. May I ask—how did you come up with this in the first place?"

"I wanted to diagram a normal world," Sasha said heavily. "A good world, even within a single projection. Without all *this*," she said, waving her hand toward the institute.

"The world where *I don't exist*?" He smiled benevolently.

Sasha hung on the edge of the precipice. She had a lot to say to him; instead, she clamped her jaws together, imprisoning her tongue.

"It's a challenge," he mused. "It's quite good, actually, quite gutsy. You are afraid, you throw a challenge, your fear ramps up, and you openly rebel . . . and at some point you realize you are about to be absolutely terrified. Utterly horror-stricken. Right?"

Sasha clutched her own knees with her clawed fingers, hurting herself.

"No, Farit. Please don't."

She realized she was repeating the same thing multitudes of students had said before her. Nothing had changed. She couldn't threaten or blackmail him, she couldn't bargain with him, she couldn't plead because she knew it was pointless. Sasha was still the same young girl sitting on the bench, sobbing over her letter of admission to the Institute of Special Technologies.

"When you go back to retake the exam, stay away from omnipotence," he said coolly. "Stick to completing the program requirements as *we* tell you rather than what you want them to be. And don't argue with your professor."

"Farit . . . Georgievich," Sasha whispered.

He gestured for her to step out of the car.

The winter Torpa resembled a gingerbread house from a holiday card. Tiny lights flickered and winked behind every window. Ski tracks followed along the road, the falling snow diminishing their athletic icy glitter with a softer one, full of clear blue sparks.

As Sasha ran, she thought of Yegor and his plans to buy a pair of skis and ski along the river. On January 13 the doors of the assembly hall would open, and the third years would come out—those lucky enough to have passed the exam. Those who entered these doors fifteen years ago; perhaps Yegor would be among them. Sasha ran up the hill, slipping on snow-covered cobblestones, then down the hill, struggling to maintain her balance. It was slippery and dangerous, and she was terrified of breaking her leg.

The retake was scheduled for Thursday.

She hadn't yet figured out what she was going to tell Anton Pavlovich, how she was going to prepare him and what she needed to warn him about. And if Yaroslav was out of pocket, if he was in flight, she couldn't reach him.

Sasha ran down one of the hills and slowed down, trying to catch her breath and pressing her hand to her burning side. *Don't panic,* she ordered herself. *He—Farit—needs Yaroslav alive. There will be some kind of nuisance, an accident or an illness, or perhaps he will not be allowed to fly. He may be discharged, but all of this could be reversed. Why am I running, why would I want to upset an elderly man ahead of time? What is the point of frightening him? And—again—if I do manage to get hold of Yaroslav, what am I going to say to him?*

Or perhaps—this was a brand-new thought—*what if Farit arranges for Yaroslav to find happiness with another woman, just to punish me? Arrange for things like lust, bed, children, family . . . And I will be forced to watch it. Wouldn't his happiness be a bigger blow for me than any of his troubles?*

She shook her head, making the drops fly off her wet knit cap. Of course not, Farit wasn't that stupid. Sasha's jealousy meant nothing next to all the daily catastrophes. And yet, today Yaroslav wasn't going to die. He wouldn't die today.

She had to wait for the news. She had to be patient.

Sasha ran her palm along the back of a bench under a streetlight, gathering a handful of clean snow. She began to eat it, cautiously, like a precocious toddler. Her mouth was dry. She'd had enough of running, she was tired, she needed to get back to her dorm room, grit her teeth, and read *Textual Module;* it always helped her to get distracted.

From the silence of a snowy night came a distant sound. Sasha pricked her ears: in Torpa, the sound of an ambulance's siren was not a common occurrence. But neither was it rare. Sasha despised the sound and would have preferred the howling of a pack of wolves.

A gust of wind caused the snow to drift and brought in a strange smell that Sasha could not identify right away: her nose had lost some of its sensitivity after her run in the freezing cold. The siren was approaching with great speed, and now it sounded like there was more than one. Several ambulances were getting closer, all of them sounding hysterical.

The wind smelled of smoke. As Sasha jumped back onto the sidewalk, the snow lit up in red and blue flames, and an enormous fire engine rushed up the hill, flying past Sasha. Another one followed, its siren blaring.

Sasha watched them hurtle by.

Then she ran after the sirens, and at some point she'd almost caught up with them.

Her mind had almost caught up with what Farit had done.

The icicles had melted a while ago, the attic window had burst, and fire was pouring out as if from a rocket nozzle. Firemen fiddled with water hoses; someone was running around in search of a hydrant. People hopped around on neighboring roofs; some of them were carrying pails or even garden watering cans, and none wore coats. Ducking away from the sparks, they poured water over the roof tiles, trying to save whatever could still be salvaged.

"Get out of here! This is not a circus!" a fireman screamed at Sasha in a hoarse, strained voice. Sasha heard every word, clear as a bell, even though all around her, the sirens howled, and the fire roared, and people sobbed, called for each other, and swore.

"Fell asleep with a lit cigarette?"

"He didn't watch the stove!"

"Didn't have a chance to pull him out!" a portly woman in a ski jacket shouted into a phone. "Why bring an ambulance, we have a fully functioning crematorium here."

Sasha heard her voice as absolute silence. As if by opening her mouth and tensing her vocal cords, the woman sucked the sounds out of the universe, further and further diminishing their supply.

In the silence the planet explodes. And in absolute silence, the star collapses to a single point without density, without time, without mass.

Singularity.

The heat from the house made it impossible for her to approach the blackening fence. The silver Mazda under the canopy looked charred. Sasha knelt down and placed her palms onto the fence. It felt like a red-hot iron. She did not pull back.

The Great Speech was beautiful and harmonious, and Sasha was its favorite weapon, a verb. Fire was a grammatical structure, a noun, a verb, an adjective. It was a combination of meanings. Sasha felt a set of nonexistent headphones grip her head.

Putting together the pain of her burned hands and the silence in her ears like puzzle pieces, Sasha *claimed* this grammatical structure and became the burning house.

The pain disappeared as if switched off, replaced by an unpleasant sensation of regret, a discomfort caused by the burned-out first floor. The trembling attic, the tense load-bearing beams that were about to collapse. And, strangely enough, the awkward, almost shameful realization that the first spark of this fire was caused by a faulty wire, over there, by the melted electric meter.

Sasha moved to the fourth dimension and perceived time as an odor. She smelled the exact moment when the wires began to spark. The temporal point reeked, not of smoke but of dead flesh. If a burning house could vomit, Sasha would have spewed her guts out.

She entered the fifth dimension: probability.

Scattered cracks of the blackened concrete formed a pattern. The house froze, its disintegration had ceased. The flames froze up, the beams stopped cracking. Sniffing the air, Sasha gingerly began to move backward in time.

The fire pulled back under the roof. It settled on the curtain like an enormous butterfly. It clung to the floor. Dropped the sofa, losing grasp on the supine body of a man on its cushions. A bookcase appeared by the wall, then a grandfather clock with a large pendulum, and the pendulum swung . . .

The familiar movement wrestled the power over time away from Sasha, transforming pure energy into a human count of seconds. The time restarted itself, and the house trembled. The fire shot up, taking over its previous positions, and the beams began to sag.

The stars explode in silence.

Sasha tasted time on her tongue, like a spoonful of honey with a pinch of pepper. This time rolling back to the beginning of the fire was much more difficult. She didn't look at the pendulum to avoid losing count. Probabilities got tangled up into a ball, and she had a hundred fingers on each hand.

Then she found one probability.

A power line surge. She was too far from the transformer substation; she couldn't reach it. A spark goes out. Another one; it goes out again. Then a whole cascade of sparks rushes forth, tiny lights dance on the hardwood floor, the rug begins to smolder, the smoke fills the room, the man on the sofa stops breathing.

Back. Jerking herself backward, Sasha ceased being the house; she no longer had an outline and was now amorphous like smoke. A spark falls, the first one. The man on the sofa wakes up. He jumps up, detects the short circuit . . . he tries to pull the heater's cable out of the socket . . .

. . . He is electrocuted. His sharply ironed shirt begins to smolder.

Hundreds of possibilities, and like her exam—like every practice she'd done—this diagram had no happy ending. Sasha wasn't thinking, she had nothing to think with, but she still existed—she was present—she continued. *I can't change . . . I am a chance factor, a third party; I see the diagram, but I need the diagram to see me.*

She didn't move yet she took a step back somehow. *What am I in this grammatical fragment? I am not a guest, not a firefighter . . . not an object, not a name, not an attribute . . . not even an observer! How can I express myself if I don't exist here?*

Her mind whirled, and then it stopped.

The old man was back on the sofa, he was alive, and he was asleep. A spark, then another, the old man woke up . . .

Somewhere else, the universe exploded soundlessly—again. The old man's shaking hand grabbed a fire extinguisher, shot white foam all over the smoldering floor, and only then pressed a button on the electric meter, turning off the lights . . .

Darkness.

Sasha came to in that darkness, in zero gravity, with neither top nor bottom. She was woken up by her body gaining its shape back, getting an outline. Yet, she found no firm footing; she was suspended in the freezing air, immobile, gliding above the wind. The direction of gravity was in the same direction as her gaze, which meant she was looking down at the snowy forest. Which also meant that the faint glow above the horizon was Torpa.

A faint glow?

Her body seemed enormous and rock-hard as if forged from steel, with multiple joints. Curiously, the most natural part of her body were the wings. Sasha felt each individual feather, all of them so stiff and light. She managed to move her wings and eventually, with tremendous effort, she regained sensitivity in her arms and legs and managed to wipe off her frozen tears.

The icy air burned her nostrils. Her wings broke through the snowfall, an unfamiliar sensation. Sasha had never flown in a snowstorm before.

Here stood the buildings of Torpa. The new buildings, the deepest night, decorated trees on the square. A sparse stream of headlights on the highway. Here was the old town; Sasha held her breath, immediately sinking into the cold air current. Ashes? Smoldering ruins? Coals?

The house stood under the cover of snow; a thick layer of white powder concealed the attic window. Not a single light was on; the December night was dark. The snow had a smooth, untouched surface. The yard she so diligently shoveled three days ago was once again as white as a wedding cloth.

As Sterkh used to say, "Bare footprints on white roofs are aesthetically displeasing."

Sasha touched the tiles with her lug sole boots, not putting her weight down, but rather suspending herself in the air like a gargoyle, her tense wings spread far and wide. The silver car stood under the awning, dreaming of the airport. Through the beams Sasha saw a candle burning in the living room and an elderly man in a thick sweater. The man sighed and wrapped himself tighter in a warm blanket, a cup of tea steaming in front of him.

Yesterday's page was torn neatly off the wall calendar: it was December 21.

"Hello, Anton Pavlovich!"

He was happy to see her—absolutely, sincerely overjoyed.

"I have been waiting for you, you promised to come back, Alexandra. It's cold in here, but I'm expecting the electrician to fix the wiring later today. Yesterday I nearly . . . but why speak of such nonsense. I was thinking of going to the library, it's warm there, but decided to wait for you."

Sasha stopped at the threshold. She felt uneasy, suddenly terrified that the time would once again stop being a sequence of seconds and instead become a smell or a taste, and that Sasha would lose her outline, crumble into dust, or vanish in clouds of smoke. To hold on to her body, she pressed her palms to the wall. To an outsider, it would seem as if she lurched to the side, losing her balance.

Here it was, the house. A foundation. A roof. Mass. Temperature. Time: the swinging pendulum. Sasha felt reassured.

All night Sasha roamed among the snow piles like a stray dog. In the early morning, Anton Pavlovich finally dozed off, wrapped in three blankets, making sure to blow out the candle and leaving the fireplace cold. Carefully, gently, Sasha reunited with the house and confirmed that the beams stayed strong, the gas tank was secure, and there was no immediate danger, unless a plane fell from the sky . . .

A plane! She ran through the center of Torpa back to the dorm, where no one slept. Her classmates met her with a multitude of wary eyes: they expected to see her in despair and were surprised to see her frantic excitement.

Sasha stopped in the vestibule, in front of the television panel. As usual, the screen displayed the latest news channel with the sound turned off, and as usual, the news channel reported multiple disasters. Sasha stood on tiptoes, touched the screen, and tasted the news on her tongue.

Rot and fumes. War and epidemic, but not a single plane crash. Her classmates wandered around, trying to figure out what was going on; the more Sasha gagged on information, the more nauseated she became, and the lighter she felt. All aircrafts were capable of crashing. But not this time. This time she won.

And now, having made the return trip through the town of Torpa, out of breath and sore from falling on an icy patch, she stood in front of Anton Pavlovich, stepping from foot to foot.

"I wanted to ask if there had been any news from Yaroslav."

"He's doing well." The old man looked saddened. "So well that he doesn't share any details."

He glanced at the fire extinguisher in the corner of the room.

"You know what this is? Such an excellent device, first-rate. You must buy one, or order one on the Internet. Yaroslav brought three of those in the beginning of winter and told me to place them in different strategic points throughout the house. Particularly near the stove. It was a terrific idea, and I am so grateful to him."

"Anton Pavlovich." Sasha took a deep breath. "You shouldn't be living alone."

He looked up at her, and his eyes behind the thick lenses were enormous and quite surprised.

"That's why I'm going to move in with you," Sasha continued. "My winter break is about to begin. Actually, it's already started, I just need to pass one tiny exam. You won't object, will you?"

...

On December 23, at ten in the morning sharp, she knocked on the door of auditorium 1, waited for the invitation, and entered. His face immobile like a mannequin, Coach mounted the teacher's chair. Across from him, Sterkh sat in the first row, clad in a black suit, his ash-blond hair reaching to his shoulders. Compared to Coach, Sterkh looked irritated and caustic, and perfectly human. Farit Kozhennikov settled in the last row by the window, where Sasha herself usually sat. Judging by the expression on his face behind his dark glasses, he was dying of boredom.

Sasha stopped, wondering what she was supposed to do next. She'd been waiting for this meeting, she prepared for it, she even rehearsed, and still she was caught unawares.

"You see, Samokhina, we had to assemble a committee, just for you." There was no indignation, no reproach, no ridicule in Coach's voice. He spoke evenly like others would count from one to ten, count not the steps to one's goal, not sheep at bedtime, and not blows—but simply naming numbers, one after another.

Sasha looked at Farit. For a moment she felt herself turn into a burning house. *You are afraid, you throw a challenge, your fear ramps up, and you openly rebel . . . and at some point you realize you are about to be absolutely terrified. Utterly horror-stricken.*

She placed her report card on the table in front of Coach, as if showing a trump card, then looked directly into his diaphragm pupils.

"I am ready for the retake."

"Now," Coach said. He picked up a green marker and stepped toward the whiteboard. Sasha watched him move as if in slow motion.

She wanted to scream for him to stop. Wanted to hold on to his massive shoulders, thwart him, make him stop. Yet again, her victory was turning into a trap. He had planned ahead, he had calculated every move, he saw the future in all its variants, and he knew all of Sasha's decisions in advance. He could've destroyed her during her first try, but he chose to do it now, in front of witnesses, and this would become the end of his secret conflict with Farit and his public conflict with Sterkh. The marker was about to touch the whiteboard . . .

"Just a moment," a voice said from the back row.

Sasha jumped as if poked with a needle. Farit Kozhennikov sat sideways, his legs stretched into the aisle, as no student was allowed to sit. Making sure everyone was watching him, he took off his glasses and placed them on the desk.

"As Alexandra Samokhina's advisor, I'd like to say a few words."

Coach may have foreseen this turn of events, he may have not: his face remained perfectly indifferent, like an alabaster mask. Sterkh, on the other hand, reacted by squeezing his lips into a thin line. Sasha glanced at the window behind Farit: the softly falling snow made a beautiful holiday picture.

"If I am not mistaken, the girl completed her second semester assignment ahead of schedule, is that correct?" Kozhennikov said calmly. "Event correction in the current grammatical tense, wasn't it?"

Sasha froze, pretending none of it had anything to do with her. Even in such danger—or perhaps because of it—she longed to soar high above, unfold her wings, feel snowflakes on her flight feathers . . .

Ignoring Farit, Sterkh stared directly at Coach; the tension thickened quickly and inevitably, filling the room with a barely audible hum, a gut-chilling infrasound. It was very stuffy in this room. So very difficult to breathe.

"Farit Georgievich," Coach spoke after a pause. His voice reminded Sasha of a well-running engine. "Academic success of the girl in question is a credit to her faculty. Her failure is all her own. I counted on you as her academic advisor to ensure that she follows the institute's strict guidelines."

"Of course, Dmitry Dmitrievich," Farit said politely. "This student in particular has demonstrated an excellent work ethic and strong motivation."

Keeping her eyes on the window, Sasha recalled the firemen rushing around, the fire busting out of the round attic window, the snow melting everywhere. She sneered; oh yes, she had an excellent work ethic. Sneering made her lips ache.

"Good for her," Coach said with a heavy dose of sarcasm. "Especially considering how many absences I marked her down for."

"But you never reported any," Farit said softly. "And since there was no report—one of those strict guidelines, as you put it—I'd like you to stay within the limits of the curriculum."

He glanced at Sasha; freed of the dark glasses, his eyes looked ordinary, dark brown, with normal human pupils. "Please stick to the curriculum defined for year four, semester one."

Sasha lost her nerve and looked down. The lack of air in the room remained, but something had shifted, for better or for worse, she couldn't tell.

"Fine," Coach said after a pause. Sasha thought she detected a hint of a threat in his voice. "For the sake of pedagogy, I'd make her retake the exam one more time. But since we're only nominally following the rules here . . . Let's see whether she can use her chance. Samokhina!"

She looked at him, instinctively, like someone jerking her hand away from a flame. Like an antelope taking flight, spooked by the slightest movement. Behind his black diaphragm pupils, she imagined a winter night and a deep, pitch-dark silence of a distant snow-covered forest. Then time ended. *Then* and *now* merged into a single abstract notion without outlines, mass, or density.

She didn't realize she had taken the marker. She only knew it when she drew a horizontal line on the board. It was a straight line, without a beginning or an end, and the tip of the marker touched every point simultaneously. Sasha recognized her infinitude and nearly scattered into dust particles, but the informational skeleton, developed by many months of training, took the blow and withstood the pressure. Sasha pulled her own self from infinity and brought it back within the limits of reality, as if mercifully throwing a caught fish back into the river.

The drowning boy was almost at the bottom when someone's hand grabbed his hair, too long and in need of a summer haircut, and jerked him upward. There, in the sand, among rows of tanned legs, the child began to breathe again, and the sun glittered on the water, and the women scolded him, because they were used to scolding children and because they were relieved that things turned out all right.

"*Then,*" Coach said.

His face immobile like a mannequin's, Coach mounted the teacher's chair. No one else was in the auditorium. Sasha looked around trying to get her bearings. According to the clock, it was December 23. Ten in the morning. She was on time.

"Your report card, please," Coach said without emotion.

In front of him was a green marker with a dry, completely used up tip. Sasha stared at the marker for a few seconds before she gathered her wits and placed her report card on the table.

Coach took a gold-tipped pen from his chest pocket and wrote "B" in the Analytical Specialty row. He reached for a new transcript with a single name on it, and smoothed out the paper with his hand, even though the paper was already perfectly smooth.

"Why a B?" Sasha asked, barely moving her dry lips.

"Because it's a retake," he said coldly. "I never give A's at retakes."

"And you no longer . . . you changed your mind to . . ."

She couldn't quite come up with the correct word. "Kill"? "Destroy"? He'd just tell her she was using human expressions.

"Have you changed your mind about failing me?" Sasha pressed her report card to her chest. "And now I can graduate?"

"Sit down," he said, pointing to a chair across from him. Sasha remained standing. Coach shrugged and signed the transcript.

"Thank your advisor. Your work has been counted toward the next term paper, so you're only responsible for the theoretical coursework. But tell me, Samokhina—do you really believe that you've rebelled and won?"

For a few seconds, Sasha stood silently in the middle of the auditorium. Eventually she moved to the chair to the first row, the same one Sterkh was sitting in before. She sat down, her back ramrod straight, and put her hands on top of the report card. She would listen to whatever he would say to her next. However, she wasn't obligated to believe him.

"This semester, Farit Grigorievich Kozhennikov did more for your academic success than any other faculty."

"Not just this semester," Sasha muttered.

"The burning house was not a punishment, it was his gift to you," Coach said, pretending not to hear her. "Your advisor took your rebellious energy and presented you with the term paper on a silver platter. Truth be told, you've done things like that before, but on a minor scale, on the surface . . . Remember? 'The Great Speech is beautiful and harmonious, but full of errors. I *want* to correct them.'"

Sasha recognized something she said in this very auditorium three days ago.

"These are not errors, Samokhina," he said, putting the transcript away into a large cardboard folder. "These are control points of reality, its syntactic markup. Your classmates are going to defend their theses and graduate, they will get their places within the grammatical structure, become part of it, and will enjoy their relevancy and compliance with the general structure. They will know absolute harmony. But not you. Not you."

"Fuck your harmony," Sasha said.

He rolled his eyes. She expected him to shift into his Dima Dimych

guise, but his facial expression went back to its habitual state of ostentatious detachment.

"Do you think that by saving kittens, you are changing the world?"

"I am growing as a concept." Sasha stared over his shoulder at the
clean whiteboard. "If it weren't for me, this world would have one more
burned-down house and one more dead human being."

"Nicely put." He shook his head with regret. "How many burned-
down houses do we have in this world?"

"That is irrelevant," she countered. "*This* one did not burn down."
Sasha lifted her chin. "And I will save as many kittens as I want to."

"Really?" He swayed back and forth in his chair, threatening to break
it into pieces. "My dear girl, do you realize that when singularity creates
a new system, it utterly rejects—destroys!—the previous one? Along
with all those kittens, old men, pilots . . . everyone you're ready to rescue,
everyone for whom you are ready to burn and shatter into pieces?"

The room suddenly seemed brighter. It wasn't because of the per-
spective he opened to her just now. It was because at this moment, she
thought she could talk to him, and that she could convince him.

"No, no!" She shook her head as vehemently as if someone had
asked her to take off her clothes and walk around the institute naked.
"You are operating with archaic concepts! 'Destruction,' 'decay'—
these are properties of *today's* Speech, but I am not going to drag them
to the new reality! We don't need this trash. No one is going to burn or
shatter because Password . . ."

He was gazing at her with his diaphragm pupils, and Sasha faltered.
The illusion had dissipated. Everything Sasha was trying to say sounded
"human." Sasha did not participate in dialogue with Coach, she simply
made sounds in his presence. For him, her words were nothing but a
monotonous noise. Like the babbling of someone's baby. Speaking
further was pointless, but to stop mid-sentence was to appear spineless.

". . . Password opens a new reality and thus changes the rules of the
game," she said stubbornly.

The bell rang, utterly meaningless, but loud and commanding.

"And what sort of rules will you offer in exchange?" It was hard
to detect sarcasm in Coach's monotonous voice, and Sasha had no idea
whether he was making fun of her or asking in earnest.

"I will create a new system," she said, refusing to give up. "A system
that will not require a choice between bigger and smaller evil."

"Will not require a choice," he said doubtfully, as if tasting some suspicious new food. "Are you going to create a harshly regulated, deterministic world? One that exists outside of freedom?"

He looked into her eyes. Afraid to fall into the space behind his glasses, she forgot her manners and turned away. Outside, the sun was shining, and the snow was beginning to melt around tree roots.

"You will never be able to understand me," she said, her own audacity making her tremble. "Because you are not Password."

"Don't lie to yourself." His voice changed, suddenly becoming so human that Sasha felt a chill. "Do you know how many Passwords actually managed to *reverberate*? How many new realities, entirely new ones, did they create? And where is this world without fear and without death, the one you're painting for yourself, like a toddler drawing a house, the sun, a Christmas tree?"

The silence within the auditorium became as palpable as in Sterkh's exercises. It felt thick and dense, like butter.

"You know the answer," Coach said with unexpected gentleness. "Here at the institute, everyone who teaches you, motivates you, invests their time, makes you believe that you absolutely must actualize—all of them are your worst enemies, Sasha."

"And are you my friend?" she said, her eyes drawn to the spent green marker.

"I detect a note of sarcasm." He smiled, and his smile resembled a death mask. "But I will give you a straight answer. I want to protect the Great Speech from you, the Great Speech you've seen once, albeit briefly. You can't truly appreciate it because you are human. As a matter of fact, you are much more human now than you were during your third year. Once you *reverberate,* you will find yourself in the vacuum, in the midst of ruins of all harmonies and meanings, and the most interesting thing is that you will be able to comprehend it. Do you wish this fate upon yourself?"

Sasha recalled the "possible future" she read about in *Textual Module;* she could see the torn-up pages coalescing so that it was whole once more. Again, she shuddered.

"I assumed that this issue would be resolved between you and your advisor—I would give you three F's in a row and let him deal with you. But you are constantly breaking plans made by others." He paused. "During our sessions, I gave you advanced assignments. It was all part of the learning process. Albeit somewhat extreme."

"Holy shit," Sasha muttered.

"Well, we're not here to twiddle our thumbs," he said dispassionately. Uttered by an emotionally detached nonhuman entity, this idiom from Dima Dimych's repertoire sounded ominous. "I don't kill students during class. But I can erase any Word, whether it has *reverberated* or not, and I do it on a regular basis. I cleanse the Great Speech from failed constructions, from archaic lexical units . . . from redundant informational fragments."

"That makes *you* the assassin of reality," Sasha whispered. "Not me."

"Metaphors are not my strong suit," he said with a slight shrug. "Metaphors are entertaining, sure, but I have to admit, sometimes they dilute the meaning. No, I am not a killer. How can I be? I make it so something never existed, and if it didn't exist, it couldn't have died.

"You, however, potentially, are one."

"That's why you tried to annihilate me," Sasha said.

"I don't 'try.'" He winced as if she had said something vulgar. "But it never ceases to amaze me what a silly little child you are."

Sasha got up, tilting the light student desk. She thought the floor underneath her feet was tilted as well. He grinned easily, recapped his pen, and put it in his pocket.

"You will never be rid of his power. You can *reverberate* into perpetuity, like a mad cuckoo inside a clock. Ever and ever, you will reproduce *him,* or the idea he embodies. At the end, only you and he will be left, outside matter, outside form, mass, density, temperature, and other baubles. And it will be your free choice." Coach's voice was dripping with sarcasm now, no question. "Because Password and freedom are inseparable.

"Have a good winter break, Samokhina."

Kostya caught up with her in the hallway. He ran over and was about to hug her, but at the last moment he changed his mind and put his hands behind his back.

"Congratulations."

"Thanks," Sasha said. She coughed a few times to clear her throat. "I am sorry for acting like a bitch."

"No problem." He stepped from foot to foot, still trying to figure out whether a friendly hug was an option or not even close. "What did . . ."

He stopped. No one ever asked questions like that directly. Of course, when Kostya's grandmother died after he failed his first-year exams, everyone knew about it right away.

"Nothing," Sasha said, then corrected herself immediately. "Nothing terrible. I don't even have . . ."

She was just about to say, "I don't even have a puppy," but thankfully, bit her tongue. *Am I horrible enough to make jokes like that?* she thought with disgust.

"I don't have any illusions regarding Farit," she said slowly. "If I mess up again, he will make me pay in full."

"Is everything all right with your pilot?" Kostya asked, adding quickly: "I hope."

"You shouldn't listen to Lisa's gossip," Sasha said, then immediately changed the subject. "Did Coach allow you to talk to me?"

"Fuck his boycott." Kostya gritted his teeth, his face tense and manly, then added: "Yeah, he did. He messaged everyone that the boycott was a temporary disciplinary measure and was now rescinded."

"Asshole." Sasha shuddered. "He gave me a B."

"Were you looking for an A?" Kostya glanced at her with a mixture of surprise and sacred fear. "Listen, Samokhina. We should celebrate." He caught her eyes and immediately corrected himself. "I mean with the whole class. With everyone. Everyone was rooting for you. Honest to god."

"I'm sorry, I don't have any time," Sasha said. "Tell everyone I said hello. Tell them I am very grateful, thankful, indebted . . . Honest to god.

"But I have somewhere I need to be."

For the first time this semester, she went down to the administrative floor in the basement, below the cafeteria. A long corridor, a row of doors. Sasha remembered the upholstery as brown, and now it was new, bright black. The doors no longer had signs, and Sasha stopped in confusion. She'd been in Sterkh's office a few times, but it was a very long time ago. In her previous life. Was it this door or the other one?

She knocked on the faux leather but got no answer. Eventually she pushed the door ajar and gathered enough courage to stick her head inside. Nothing had changed in the reception area, except that a laptop had replaced the executive assistant's typewriter, and the assistant herself wasn't knitting but instead was staring into her phone.

"Excuse me," Sasha said. "Is Nikolay Valerievich . . ."

"Nikolay Valerievich," the assistant said calmly, as if she'd been expecting Sasha. "Samokhina from the fourth year is here to see you."

The office door opened.

"Nikolay Valerievich, I won't take up your time. I just wanted to warn you that starting today, I will not be complying with the institute's rules. I am going to skip classes. I will come and go as I please. I will not be living in the dorm. Please don't take it personally. I very much value you as my professor."

"You want to prove to yourself that you no longer fear anything." Sterkh intertwined his slim fingers in the familiar gesture. "This is a toddler's rebellion, Sasha. Like when a child first realizes herself as a person separate from the adults. I know my words hurt, but someone needs to say them to you."

"Thank you for caring about me," Sasha said in a voice sweet enough to sound belligerent.

"What did you get on Dmitry Dmitrievich's exam?" Sterkh asked. He spoke with exaggerated lenience, as if addressing an actual toddler.

"A B." Sasha smirked. "I've never had B's in Specialty before. I got a B in second-year legal studies . . ."

"As long as you believe in your own omnipotence, you are in danger," Sterkh said gently. "And everyone around you is in danger. And I don't know how to get through to you, how to explain . . . how to save you, really."

"I cannot be saved." Sasha scowled mirthlessly. "I am not a kitten drowning in a puddle. I refuse to be afraid. And I have reasons for it."

"Perhaps," Sterkh said heavily. "You know, Sasha—I very much value you as a student. Don't forget what I taught you."

Something in his voice made her stiffen, but she ignored it, seized by euphoria and a healthy dose of fury.

"I thought you were kidding," Anton Pavlovich said.

In the hallway of the old house, Sasha faced him, snow on her heavy boots, a duffel bag in her hands, and a small backpack over her shoulder. With one free elbow, she was holding on to a real tree in a flowerpot.

"Do you have any ornaments? Anything would do—even beads or candy. I can cut up some paper into snowflakes, like I did in preschool."

"Sasha." He hesitated. "You must have your own friends, young people, dancing into the wee hours of the morning . . . I would hate for you to sacrifice any of this for me."

Sasha thought of the flames shooting out of the attic window.

"Trust me, Anton Pavlovich. Not only am I not sacrificing anything, on the contrary—I am very happy about this opportunity. You shouldn't be greeting the new year by yourself, and neither should I. And Yaroslav is working, just as you said."

"Yes." The old man smiled guiltily, as if embarrassed by something. "He will greet the new year several times, flying over the ocean. I can only imagine the merrymaking on board his plane."

"Merrymaking," Sasha repeated, placing her little tree onto the dining room table and looking at it critically. She pulled on a few branches to straighten them. "I've never celebrated New Year's Eve on a plane."

She imagined a phantasmagorical event inside an aircraft, garlands and confetti everywhere, passengers in carnival masks dancing in the aisles, tiny decorated trees nestled into luggage racks, and Farit Kozhennikov in the last row stretching his legs into the aisle, sipping a fancy cocktail and watching the festivities, while sparklers reflected in his dark glasses.

"We will have some merrymaking ourselves." Sasha shook her head, chasing away her vision. "I bought some food and a bottle of champagne; do you have any glasses? Let's see what we're missing, and I'll run to the store."

"What about your parents?" he asked, still standing by the door, like a guest in his own house. "How are they celebrating the new year?"

"I grew up with just my mom, never even saw my dad." Sasha gave him a particularly happy smile to avoid any notion of drama. "But she has her own life. Lots of loving family members. They are with her, she's not alone."

Sasha faltered. In the last three days, she'd called Mom six times, using a different cover every time, like a spy. Twice she spoke with Konev, once with Anya, twice she remained silent, and only once had she gathered enough courage to wish Mom a happy and healthy new year, pretending to be an employee of the housing association.

Mom hadn't recognized her voice. Sasha thought she sounded

lively, a tad cynical, but overall content and even happy. Ending the call, Sasha felt a shadow of resentment. She should have been pleased—the whole reason for calling was to make sure things turned out exactly how Sasha willed them to be.

Maybe the problem was that it wasn't *exactly* what she wanted.

"We've got sparklers," Sasha said, unloading the contents of her backpack onto the kitchen counter. "And fairy lights. We'll have ourselves a real holiday."

"Thank you," Anton Pavlovich said quickly. "Unfortunately, I must admit I'm strictly against any kind of pyrotechnics. I didn't want to tell you, but my house almost burned down a week ago."

"Do not be afraid," Sasha said, surprised by the parental notes in her voice. She sounded as if a small child happened to stand by her side. "You are completely safe with me, nothing will ever happen again, ever."

She caught his eyes and immediately corrected herself.

"But if you don't like it, we don't have to light the sparklers, or we can simply do it outside, in the snow."

"You sound like Father Frost," he said, smiling tentatively.

"To a degree, I am him." Without an invitation, Sasha opened the refrigerator and put a few wrapped packages onto the empty shelf. "Is there anything special you'd like for dinner? Some favorite holiday dish? I was raised on the Russian staples—Olivier salad and herring under a fur coat—but maybe that's not to your liking?"

"If Yaroslav calls, should I be hiding the fact that you're here?" he said softly. "Or may I tell him the truth?"

Sasha closed the refrigerator door, making sure it properly shut. Her hands were suddenly very cold, and she stuck them under her arms.

"If he calls, just tell him everything is well. He'll know you're telling the truth by the sound of your voice."

"I used to go down to the river," he said, picking up a jar of pickles and gazing at it as if its contents were exotic fish rather than marinated vegetables. "I used to walk all the way down Sacco and Vanzetti, passing your institute. And all the time I would see the students. They had something in common with you. Something I can't quite put my finger on. But to me, they all seemed closed up. Encapsulated. Focused on each other and no one else. When these kids spoke, smoked, kissed in dark corners as I was passing by, it was as if I did not exist. As if they were inside their own closed world. Behind a sheet of glass."

"You think I'm strange," Sasha said, feeling rattled.

"Why won't you talk to Yaroslav?" he said, looking into her eyes. "What happened between you two?"

"Are you asking me to leave?"

She suddenly saw herself from a distance. Everything that only a moment ago seemed logical and reasonable now felt arrogant, eccentric, almost rude. He wasn't a child. And Sasha wasn't Father Frost.

"No," he said, taking a step toward her and looking at her with something akin to fear. "Not at all. I am so glad you are here. Let me show you your room."

On December 31 she stopped by the dorm to pick up some textbooks. A brightly decorated fake tree stood in the first-floor vestibule. Sasha's classmates, both groups A and B, sat at the bar and near the coffee machine, staring at their phones and tablets. They weren't talking, but something connected them, something barely discernible, like a set of multicolored lights threaded together by green wires.

Something that she wasn't a part of.

"Isn't anyone going home during the break?" Sasha asked.

"What's the point?" Igor Kovtun said lazily. He was perched on a tall stool, swinging a foot clad in a summer sandal over a thick woolen sock. His T-shirt revealed the muscular arms of an athlete. Just below the elbow a round blue tattoo-like symbol marked his servitude to the Great Speech.

None of us are going anywhere, Sasha thought. *We belong to the institute.*

They *belong to the institute,* she thought with sudden rage. *They exist in the closed world, as if behind a sheet of glass. But not me. I am not a frog in a jar.*

"How's your pilot doing?" Anna Bochkova asked carefully.

"He's doing great." Sasha picked up a cardboard cup from a common stack. "Can someone show me how to use the coffeemaker?"

They stared at her as if she'd just stepped into the spotlight, center stage.

"And all his relatives are just fine!" Sasha raised her voice. "And that's how it'll be from now on. No one at this institute will ever punish me again!"

"Can you please elaborate?" Lisa said, her voice dull and hollow.

Lisa sat on the other side of the bar; Sasha had not seen her when she first came in. Now Lisa stood up, white as a sheet.

"Details, now. Did you spread your legs for Farit Georgievich to earn immunity?"

Sasha recoiled. "Watch it."

Keeping Lisa in her line of view, she backed up slowly. Everyone watched her. Even a drop of oil in a glass of water wouldn't be as foreign and as rejected. She couldn't explain anything to them. Nothing at all. They sacrificed themselves, and Sasha didn't, but it wasn't to her credit, and it wasn't their fault.

Coffee forgotten, she slowly turned to face the door, her back to Lisa and the rest of her classmates. One step, then another one; the door was so close.

Kostya walked in briskly, confidently, aware that Sasha was there, a huge smile on his face.

"You're here to celebrate!"

"No," Sasha said, watching his expression change. "You can celebrate without me. Happy New Year."

A vintage plywood postal box stood on the table next to the small tree. Christmas toys were arranged in neat rows on the dark polished surface. Anton Pavlovich stood by the table, wiping his glasses and squinting. Sasha slid her feet into a pair of slippers.

"I didn't realize you had the ornaments, so I bought some walnuts and foil to wrap them in . . ."

"Of course I have ornaments," Anton Pavlovich said, straightening the collar of his meticulously ironed shirt. "We used to decorate two trees, plus one more outside, but the one outside eventually dried up, and we ended up having to take it down."

Sasha looked closer. The ornaments were pedantically sorted out by types: antique figurines, snowmen, skaters, clowns, at least seventy years old. Lanterns and icicles, half a century old. Old-fashioned and modern, fancy and simple; Sasha saw her own reflection in every glass sphere.

"A whole collection," she said, afraid to touch them.

"I have more of these tiny ones." Anton Pavlovich bent over the nearly empty box. "Here."

From the cotton, wool-covered bottom of the box, he pulled out a handful of multicolored glass baubles, each the size of a cherry.

"I am so glad you came, Sasha. My vision is not what it used to be, and this requires some skill. But don't worry about your walnuts and foil, we'll find some use for them, too."

With the tips of her fingers, Sasha picked up a large red Christmas ball and raised it up to the light. Grammatical parsing for a C. Verification for a B. Visualization for an A; inside the ball, she saw a reflection of a blond woman in a cocktail dress, a boy of ten by her side, behind them the branches of an enormous tree adorned with a string of lights. The people inside the ball moved and spoke, and Sasha could have read their lips, but her hand twitched, and Sasha placed the ball back on the table, afraid of breaking it.

"What's wrong?" Anton Pavlovich asked softly.

"Yaroslav's mother," Sasha said. "What happened to her?"

"She got sick," Anton Pavlovich said, his shoulders drooping a bit. "It was a long time ago. My son had just turned twelve. But I remember it like it was yesterday."

Sasha estimated the temporal distance. No, she couldn't reach that far. Plus, time was discrete, and if she saved that woman, Yaroslav would be different, and Anton Pavlovich would be different, perhaps happier, but different.

"The world will soon change," Sasha said. "No one is going to die anymore."

"That's impossible." He smiled, slightly disturbed by her reaction. "But if that's what you want, then let it be. Let everyone live forever."

There was no television set in the house. The grandfather clock with a large pendulum lagged two minutes behind. Thankfully, Sasha remembered she had a tablet, and the tablet had a timer with a second hand. At half past eleven she started the countdown, catching a glimpse of files in her email. At the very top of the list was a new, unopened file. This time it was definitely sent by Coach, from his official email address.

I don't kill students during class. During our sessions, I gave you advanced assignments. It was all part of the learning process.

She neither thought about it nor wavered briefly. A tap of a fingertip, and there was no file, and quite possibly, there was no Coach any longer. She had a right to do this—she was on vacation.

The doorbell cooed. Sasha wondered who would possibly show up at the gate twenty minutes to the new year. She felt uneasy. "Let me," she said to Anton Pavlovich, who also visibly tensed up.

Sasha slipped her feet into her unlaced boots, threw a jacket over her shoulders, and stepped out into the dark wintery yard. Motion-activated light came on under the roof.

It was a perfect New Year's Eve's night, with nothing left to wish for: no wind, light snow, and just chilly enough to keep things clean and dry. Sasha made her way to the gate through the snow sparkling in the glow of a streetlight and realized she was too short to peek over the fence. The gate did not have a peephole.

"Who's there?" she asked authoritatively, letting the guest know they weren't wanted.

A long pause followed. Then the key turned in the lock, and it was like a nightmare, when you don't want to let the monster in and it's pushing through anyway.

The gate opened. Sasha saw Yaroslav Grigoriev, dressed in a black coat, snow on his shoulders, carrying a bouquet of pine branches in one hand and pulling a wheeled suitcase by its long handle. Sasha stared at him; it was snowing, and the long pause was growing awkward.

"Is this the earliest you could make it?" she asked, her voice unnaturally thin.

It was six minutes to the new year. Then five. In front of the festively set table, Anton Pavlovich sat by himself, gazing at the decorated tree and waiting patiently.

In the kitchen, Yaroslav faced the window, his hands planted on the windowsill. Sasha sorted through the food scraps laid out on the counter: a couple of lonely potatoes, boiled carrots, beet tails left over from salads.

"Sasha, it's just too much," he said softly. "I don't want to spoil anyone's New Year's Eve. Let's have a quiet celebration tonight, and then we'll make it so you can live your own life, happily, and I will take care of my own father."

"I have to tell you something," Sasha mumbled.

"You don't owe me anything. Let's not play these games, all this chopping off a dog's tail in pieces."

"I am not human," Sasha said desperately. "I am an assassin of reality and a destroyer of grammar. I am singularity. I am Password. Forgive me, I cannot change it. And I cannot hide it from you. That's it."

"You are a witch."

"If that makes it easier."

With three minutes left before the new year, Yaroslav tuned the grandfather clock with a huge pendulum, and the new year was chimed in just after midnight, in an old-fashioned and sentimental manner. The three of them drank some champagne. Yaroslav insisted that Anton Pavlovich sit at the head of the table. Sasha kept circling the table, refilling plates, switching dishes, and generally pretending to be quite busy. Calmly, as if nothing were out of the ordinary, Yaroslav talked to his father about his new job, and his speech brimmed with professional terminology and expressions that the old man must have been familiar with, because he nodded frequently, did not ask any clarifying questions, and listened with obvious interest. Sasha wasn't listening. Yaroslav was just fine, that's what he was trying to tell both his father and Sasha, and it was enough for both of them. The clock was ticking happily, encouraged by everyone's attention. Fireworks boomed on the next street over, a massive fork clanged on Sasha's plate. Yaroslav spoke, smiling. He undoubtedly had decided Sasha was insane after what she told him, and that probably explained all her quirks to him fully. He would probably want to do something about it, but not just now. He wanted his father to have a happy and peaceful New Year's Eve . . .

Yaroslav fell silent and looked at Sasha sitting across the table. With a quick smile, she handed him a bowl of salad, as if it was the last thing she could offer.

He took the bowl from her hands, but only to place it back on the table. He got up, circled the table, sat down next to Sasha, and put his arm around her shoulders.

She froze.

He spoke again, addressing his father, who watched them through his thick lenses as if through a heavy rain. Sasha couldn't hear a single word, but now she could feel Yaroslav's warm side move under a light-colored shirt, and his heavy, hot arm, like a bear's paw. Now he was talking about a city by the ocean, tall white buildings by the beach, and the long time when he circled the city waiting for permission to land.

Very slowly, thread by thread, Sasha relaxed her muscles, leaning against him and putting her head on his shoulder. The only thing she regretted was not setting up a temporal anchor; now she couldn't relive this minute, like her favorite recording.

But it was probably for the best. If she'd had a chance to set up an anchor, she may not have had the courage to move farther in time.

At one in the morning, Anton Pavlovich wiped his glasses with a hand-kerchief, thanked Sasha and Yaroslav for a lovely evening, complained about being sleepy, and went into his room. A heavy door made of a solid piece of wood closed softly behind him. Paralyzed with fear, Sasha held her breath. Her shoulders ached, but she was too anxious to move.

Gently, Yaroslav took his hand off her shoulder and leaned over to look into Sasha's face. He pulled her closer again, and she realized she wasn't ready for this turn of events. Fussing around the house, chatting with the old man, encasing him in the intricate lace of daily holiday activities, sleeping curled up on his sofa, returning to her studies, shuffling to classes . . . Punching above her weight, flying over Torpa . . . Stopping catastrophes and canceling other people's deaths . . .

Yes to all that.

But seeing Yaroslav, sensing his touch, inhaling his scent—Sasha was afraid of this, like a child who'd climbed up on top of a tower and was now afraid to look down.

"I should clean up." She slipped out of his embrace. "Put the leftovers back in the fridge."

She couldn't even remember what kind of lingerie she was wearing tonight. How vulgar. What did it matter if she simply wasn't ready. She felt awkward, terrified, ashamed: after all, he was a stranger, she barely knew him.

He caught her and took a dirty plate out of her hands, then held her hands in his.

"You're shaking."

"You must think I'm crazy," she said, aware of shaking like a wet mouse, chilly with anxiety.

"Come with me."

Sasha felt the floor shift under her feet. Yaroslav picked her up easily, and she felt his warm hand on her ribs. He carried her into the semidarkness, and she held on to everything they passed on the way—the back of the chair, the doorframe, clothes on a hanger, the edge of the curtain—she held on, not trying to stop, but to slow down the movement. She was ready to explode like a balloon in the stratosphere.

Fireworks crackled and jumped in the dark windows. When they reached his bedroom, he closed the curtains, and the sounds of the night's festivities grew distant. Sasha made a feeble attempt to escape, and he stopped her by the door and covered her shoulders with his hands, like large epaulettes.

"Do not be afraid."

"What did you say?"

"Do not be afraid." He gazed at her from the semidarkness, and the fireworks were reflected in his eyes, even though the curtains were drawn.

"You need to say 'Be brave,'" Sasha told him. "Without the negative particle."

For the first few minutes she had to control herself, otherwise she'd jump out of her human skin, stretch up to the clouds, and *possess* the house, the city, the fireworks and the sparklers, and the trees decorated in the squares, and all the people celebrating the new year, and all the planes in the black sky. Eventually, she felt so good in her human body that there was no longer any need to guard herself, to set up limits, and to track her own reactions.

They were two teenagers who played hooky and locked themselves in an empty apartment, the first time for both, both frightened and in love. And at the same time, they were a married couple, who knew each other well, whose children were sleeping in the next room. And again, they were old and gentle, they were grandparents, and Sasha saw the names of their grandchildren in the distant glow of fireworks. She may have unlocked the time and built a multitude of models, unaware of her actions. Or perhaps, everything she felt was so rich and so dense that it led to the creation of new meanings, like a point of unbearably concentrated space that eventually gives itself free rein and forms matter, energy, and the laws of physics.

Yaroslav was by her side, closer than any human being before him, and Sasha luxuriated in his closeness without *possessing* him. It was a dance on the thinnest of ice, at the edge of the abyss that takes one's breath away. They existed side by side, merging together, but respecting each other's boundaries. Sasha suspected he felt the same way; perhaps he did not understand it, but he sensed it and was not afraid and, now, neither was she.

The fireworks died down in the wee hours of the morning.

She woke up four times to make sure he was still there, wrapped her arms and legs around him, then fell asleep. When she woke up for the fifth time, the sun was peeking through the drawn curtains, and she was alone in bed.

In the living room, separated from her by a thick wall, Yaroslav and his father were speaking softly. Sasha could eavesdrop, but the mere idea terrified her. Judging by their intonation, their chat was light and pleasant, just the way a family conversation should be on the morning of the new year. Sasha raised herself on her elbow and recalled everything that happened the night before, up to the tiniest movement, up to the brightest spark.

She exhaled, fell back into the pillows, and closed her eyes.

The first morning of the new year is a dangerous time; miracles melt into the thin air before actually occurring. Looking around the room, probing into her own mind, Sasha attempted to understand: Was there space for a miracle in here? After everything that had happened to her, things had to change. And yet, Sasha was the same, and the room and the light outside the window were the same, but the future . . .

Sasha concentrated, trying to figure out whether the future had changed, and was horrified to know that it hadn't. Yaroslav wasn't about to walk in and tell her he was staying in Torpa forever.

She shared her fate with Kostya. And with Yegor, even with a difference of one academic year. Yaroslav was fuel, energy, information, the fear of loss. He was Farit, or at least he was Farit's creation, and she hated that . . . but also wasn't sure she cared.

Sasha pulled the blanket over her head, on the verge of tears, and at that moment, the door opened, and someone tiptoed in.

Sasha peeked out from under the blanket like a hare from behind a bush. An aroma of freshly brewed coffee filled the room. Dressed in a pair of shorts and a light shirt and carrying a tray in one hand, Yaroslav looked like he'd come straight from a bright summer day.

"Our crew welcomes you on board this aircraft . . . Sasha, what happened?"

"Nothing." She crawled out from underneath the blanket, blissfully undisturbed by her own nakedness. Hiding her eyes and wiping away tears, she took the tray with a cup of coffee and a slice of apple cake from his hand and placed it on the windowsill. She turned to Yaroslav and held him tight, sure that he was about to gently free himself from her arms and tell her he needed to get to work.

Instead he picked her up, gently, and held her.

The coffee was now cold, but neither one of them cared much. They lay in each other's arms; the room smelled of pine needles and apple cake, and a man's shirt was draped over the back of a chair.

"Forget what I told you last night in the kitchen," Sasha muttered, nuzzling his warm ear, tickling him with her lips. "I was kidding. I won't do it anymore."

He shifted slightly to see her face and smiled, his eyes brilliantly green.

"My father was so very grateful for the fire extinguishers, the ones I got for him."

"It was such a smart idea," Sasha said, squeezing his hand.

"But I never brought him any fire extinguishers," Yaroslav said softly. "I never even thought of it."

He fell silent. Sasha's fingers went cold in his warm hand. Yaroslav gazed at her tenderly, and if there was a question in his eyes, it was deeply hidden.

"You probably just don't remember doing it," Sasha whispered.

"I probably don't," he agreed too easily. "Sasha, what year are you at school? I never even asked you."

"Fourth." Sasha freed herself from his arms, worried she was going to make him cold.

"Then it must be easy to switch to remote learning, isn't it?"

"No," Sasha said quickly, feeling as if she were falling into a bottomless well. She recalled the endless arguments with Mom, about transferring from Torpa after the first year, then after the second . . .

"Everything is fine," he said, caressing her arms from elbows to wrists. "We'll think of something. What did you say last night, 'Be brave'?"

"I can't switch to remote learning," Sasha whispered.

"I'm not talking about that," he said, his eyes darkening like leaves in a thunderstorm. "You were brave. And I am ready, too. Ready to accept you for who you are, and not ask any questions."

"Yes." Sasha choked in gratitude.

"When I am with you," he continued, carefully choosing his words, "sometimes it seems that the world is just a film shown on a white sheet, and I see a rip in the fabric and peek behind it . . ."

Sasha sat up in bed and stared up at him.

"It's all right." He smiled at her as if she were a five-year-old who just scraped her knee.

"Last night . . . no, that's not right. You see . . . I know for sure that you are not crazy, you are not a con artist, and that you are very honest with me. You are always honest, even when you suffer from it. But I am deathly afraid of losing you. I am begging you: do not leave me, no matter what price I have to pay."

Yaroslav left on January 2. He had a long-term contract with a large airline that could not be canceled.

They had a day and a half and two nights together. They used some of that time to hang up a large map on the living room wall—for Sasha to mark his itineraries with pins, week after week. She could always use her tablet, but the old map smelled of time and serenity, and the tiny flag pins were so pleasing to stick in and pull out. "Everything that is valuable is beyond matter," Sterkh said to her once, but now Sasha thought it was the other way around: the map. Snow. Yaroslav. Everything that had true value could be touched.

On January 12, Anton Pavlovich departed for a winter resort in the company of his close friends from the chess circles. Sasha helped him pack and escorted him to the shuttle bus.

On January 13, at 2 p.m., the assembly hall doors opened, and the third years walked out into the hall with the equestrian statue. Twenty people who had passed the exam. Twenty people, out of nearly forty students selected three years ago.

Sasha saw her former roommates, Vika and Lena. Saw a few guys and girls whom she didn't really know well but saw every day at the institute. She kept searching, looking from face to face, and again from face to face, and was about to howl in terror, but then Yegor came out. Last one to emerge, he lingered by the door, as if waiting for someone, as if hoping that all his classmates were about to pile out, and they would laugh, and hug, and squeeze each other's hands like they did after the previous test.

Coach appeared in the doorway, clad in a black suit with a black shirt, looking funereal, and Sterkh followed immediately, hunched over a bit more than usual. Standing in the distance, Sasha could not and did not want to hear what these two were saying to the shaken students.

"A slaughterhouse," Lisa said, clicking her lighter and taking a drag right next to the concierge's booth.

"Excuse me!" the speaker barked. "Smoking is forbidden! Looking for a penalty?"

Lisa put the cigarette out on her wrist. Sasha grabbed her hand.

"Are you nuts?"

"A slaughterhouse," Lisa repeated, staring ahead with glassy eyes. "They eliminated half. Leave me alone, whore."

The third years slowly shifted over to the scheduling board; dark only a few moments ago, it suddenly lit up, displaying a list of names followed by scores: B. F. F. C. A. F. F. Swallowing a gob of bitter saliva, Sasha took a few steps over to where Yegor was standing, apart from everyone, visibly confused by his surroundings.

"Listen, Yegor . . . " She couldn't bring herself to touch him, so she simply stopped two feet away.

He turned around and stared at her for a moment without recognition, and then his eyes got as big as saucers.

"Samokhina?"

As if immediately forgetting about her, he turned to his classmates.

"Guys, girls, Samokhina is here! They told us she failed! They lied to us, they are constantly lying to us!"

He looked like someone who'd just scored the winning goal at the World Cup.

"Our classmates will come back! They were just trying to scare us, everyone who got an F will come back!"

"No," said someone behind Sasha's back. She turned to look.

Kostya stood by the base of the equestrian statue, hands in the pockets of his hoodie.

"No," he said louder. "Those who got an F will never come back. Don't even dream about it."

Yegor raised his upper lip, baring his teeth like a rabid dog ready to attack. He walked across the hall toward Kostya and, without any warning, slammed his fist into Kostya's jaw in a brilliantly executed uppercut.

Caught off guard, Kostya lost his balance, stumbled, and fell backward. Yegor stood over him, as if he was suddenly blind, as if he'd missed a goal that was perfectly within his reach.

"Put some ice on it. Here are some fresh ice cubes."

"I don't need any." Kostya turned his head. "Nothing material has any value. Although I'd miss my teeth."

With Sasha's help, Kostya made it to his dorm room. She brought him a plastic container full of ice from the first-floor ice machine.

"I shouldn't have picked on him," Kostya said wistfully. "Did you see what happened to their class?"

"A slaughterhouse," Sasha whispered, unintentionally quoting Lisa.

"When I came out of the assembly hall and saw that Zhenya got an F and you got a blank, I did not respond with aggression." Wincing, Kostya pressed the ice pack to his swollen jaw. "I fell into this dreary, depressing swamp. Your boy has healthy young responses."

"He's not my boy. And he's older than us."

"Did you notice that he wasn't even happy to see you? Or he was happy, but not to see you personally. He clutched on to you because he thought you were a precedent." Kostya tried to smile and winced in pain.

"Listen, I don't know what you all think of me, but I don't have an agreement with Farit," Sasha said. "I have a strategic balance of sorts."

"And now you're not afraid of anything anymore," Kostya muttered, and she wasn't sure whether it was a question or a doubt spoken out loud.

"Well." Sasha hesitated. "I am working on it."

"And your pilot." Kostya was still avoiding her eyes. "Isn't he afraid of you?"

"He's fearless," Sasha said after a pause.

"I am in Singapore, flying out in an hour and a half."

Even stretched over many thousands of miles, his voice put a spell on her. Sasha couldn't help but smile when she listened to him. As she gazed at the old map on the wall, the old phone receiver, a plastic tube on a twisty cord, warmed up in her hand, heating up but not burning.

It seemed the house was listening to their conversation, delicately and unobtrusively.

"I miss you," Sasha said. "I keep thinking of every word you've ever said to me."

"I am closer already. With each hundred kilometers. I am flying, imagining you sitting behind me in the cabin."

"Tell me something else. Anything at all. I just want to hear your voice."

"We're having a tropical rainstorm right now. You can't see farther than your own fingers. But when we taxi on the runway, it will stop. I will be home in March."

Sasha closed her eyes. Gentle warmth filled her from the inside. Spring would come in March, the snow would yield, the icicles would melt, and tomcats would go insane . . .

"Are you laughing? Sasha, you have such a great laugh, please laugh again."

"Meow," she said, laughing so hard she couldn't breathe and feeling a hot wave wash over her.

At night, wandering around Torpa, she disassembled herself into pieces, put herself back together again, and realized her immortality.

Perhaps it was Yaroslav and not Sasha herself who defined the fate of the Great Speech when he dared to accept her, when—fearless—he did not push her away. Yaroslav freed her from fear and made her who she was. Sasha ventured into the darkest areas of the city where the stars shined brighter among the roofs, and gazed at Orion with its promises of early spring.

The utter annihilation Yegor's class went through. Her classmates' rejection, Lisa's hatred, Kostya's doomed devotion—Sasha had not forgotten any of it, she discarded nothing. All these things were necessary pieces of the puzzle; without them the picture would not have been complete, and the errors would not have been fully corrected. But in the new macrostructure Sasha was about to create there would be no place for either doom or death.

Once again she felt omnipotent.

And for the first time in her life she wanted to have a child.

CHAPTER FIVE

G reetings, Group A, today we have an orientation session. We are starting a new semester with Analytical Specialty. At the beginning of the winter break I sent out materials for individual work. You are going to take turns reproducing informational objects on the whiteboard. Let's go down the list. Goldman."

Sasha sat by the window in the last row, feeling a cold draft on the back of her neck. Yulia Goldman stepped up to the whiteboard, picked up a marker with shaking fingers, and stood still, her back to the auditorium. Sasha noticed her elegant short haircut with uneven tresses dyed several different hues and tried to figure out the last time she'd been to a hair salon.

Yulia began to draw a complex fine ligature, starting from the center and weaving the ornament in a circle like a basket. The ornament became audible, babbling, whispering to itself, echoing its own words: "Which, when, why, what . . ." The tip of the black marker sank into the whiteboard as if into a thick fog; Yulia stumbled, began from the beginning, and stumbled again . . .

"Stop," Coach said. "What year are you?"

"Fourth," Yulia stammered. Her forehead was shiny with sweat, and the fashionable haircut stuck out like after a rainstorm.

"Not first? Not second, are you sure? Fascinating," Coach said, stretching his lips into a smile. "A year and a half left before graduation, who would have thought."

"I tried my best," Yulia mumbled.

"Attention, Group A!" Coach got up. Yulia seemed tiny next to him. "I am going to repeat for those who have forgotten: by the time you get to defending your theses, no one is going to be saved by 'I tried my best.' All of you, every single one, will be finalized as informational objects, and you are solely responsible for how the Great Speech will use you, as a golden platter or a chamber pot. This is a metaphor."

Sasha could not hold back her laughter. Her classmates stared at her in horror, and Kostya jumped in his seat as if someone had put a pushpin on his chair. Sasha choked back her mirth, pressing her hands against her mouth, but Coach nodded to Yulia as if nothing had happened.

"Sit down, Goldman, we're going to have a serious conversation during your next individual session. Bochkova."

Sasha's classmates stepped up to the board, one by one. Never before had Sasha witnessed them complete their assignments in such proximity and such detail. Sweating, huffing, biting their lips, they reproduced informational mirages, unimaginable by the human mind, and this duality of human weakness and universal perfection pulled her in like a glance into the abyss.

They were living projections of colossal ideas. They were reflected in each other, refracted each other, forming a unified crystal lattice. It was impossible to believe that several years ago these complex, nearly complete instruments of the Great Speech were just a handful of terrified teenagers. Except it also made total sense. That's what this school was, a series of contradictions that added up to the whole.

Sasha thought the same could be said of the Great Speech.

Lisa Pavlenko got up. Red splotches burned on her white cheeks, creating an impression of another pair of eyes, bright scarlet ones. Lisa threw herself toward the whiteboard like someone dying of thirst running toward a spring and began to weave an intricate lace with a blue marker. Her movements looked feverish as if the lines burned her from the inside and she had to get rid of them immediately. It was a frenzied, animalistic, not particularly attractive but mesmerizing spectacle.

Under the tip of Lisa's marker, dissonance replaced harmony, morphing into decay, and within the decay, harmony arose anew. Sasha allowed herself to follow the rhythm, realizing that there was sweetness in the decay, that she was seeing satisfaction in failure, and Lisa was about to surprise them all someday . . .

"Samokhina!"

At first Sasha got up, then returned to the visible reality, and only then remembered that over the winter break she'd deleted Coach's file from her email, and so had nothing to report on.

"Come here, Samokhina, step to the whiteboard," Coach said, motioning for her to come closer. "Group A, what we have here is a miraculous transformation. From an outsider, this girl has once again become a leader. She even passed her spring semester coursework in advance. Samokhina, reproduce the diagram of correction in real grammatical tense—the one you attempted on December twentieth."

Everyone understood his words, and no one needed any additional explanation. Sasha gathered their glances like a weaver's loom gathering threads from multiple spools; only Lisa Pavlenko was not looking at her. Lisa was cleaning the whiteboard, already perfectly white, but she kept scrubbing it with toothpaste. Her hands were stained with chalky residue, and so was the sponge she was scrubbing with. Lisa was trying to eliminate her diagram, up to the last molecule, ensuring that not even a shadow remained on the board.

"I won't," Sasha said.

Lisa turned to look at Sasha. Her face appeared to be sculpted out of the very first snow.

"I will not!" Sasha said again, louder this time.

The very notion of returning to—or recalling—the house going up in flames and Anton Pavlovich lying on the burned sofa made her feel terrified and nauseated. She didn't want to make anyone witness to this scene. But more than anything, she wanted to confirm and prove that there was no more fear inside her, that she was no longer subject to someone else's power.

The silence dragged on. Lisa froze by the whiteboard, as if afraid of moving without permission. Sasha's classmates stared at her, and everyone was clearly thinking of her words: No one at this institute will ever punish me again!" Kostya's eyelid twitched.

"Why?" Coach asked softly. His question seemed to surprise her classmates more than Sasha's démarche.

"I don't want to," Sasha replied.

"Freedom," Coach said, and his eyes remained glassy, even though his voice was brimming with thick human bile. "You wanted to learn something new about yourself and about fear? You will."

The black SUV was parked at the corner of two narrow, snowed-in streets. In the morning a snowplow cleared the intersection as much as was possible, digging out two crisscross grooves. Tall white snow piles had already been marked by the neighborhood dogs.

Sasha wondered whether urinating dogs knew they were leaving a unique imprint on the snow. It could be a diagram of someone's farcical death or a miraculous escape, or a detailed plan for the creation of a new universe. There was enough information, one simply had to know how to work with it.

The black SUV did not care about the snowplow's efforts. It made a way for itself, leaving tread marks behind, and Sasha spent a few seconds trying to read the third and fourth dimensions in the pattern.

From the intersection, she could see Anton Pavlovich's house with its carved fence and dark tiled roof. A grayish wisp of smoke and heat burst out of the SUV's tailpipe. Sasha approached.

"Get in," Farit said, opening the door from the inside.

He wore gray glasses, massive like a skier's goggles. Sasha climbed into the passenger seat, forcing herself to take deep, slow breaths, preparing for what could be the final battle. She existed outside of fear. She was free.

"You have a small debt," Farit said. "A retake for the winter exam. And yet, during the very first class of the new semester, you're written up. Samokhina, who do you think you are?"

"I forgot to thank you, Farit," Sasha said cautiously. "For your help during the retake. For your very timely praise of me as a highly disciplined student."

"Highly disciplined students don't say 'I don't want to' during class." His previously casual voice turned icy in an instant. "I had given you a chance, and you missed it."

Don't you dare be afraid, Sasha told herself.

"I *am* still a highly disciplined student," she said, refusing to lower her eyes. "I am motivated, and I do not need any coercion. I cannot be punished, and I will not allow . . ."

The last sentence was a mistake. Sasha understood it too late.

"I thought we had an agreement," she said, a little softer. "I—"

"I. Cannot. Be. Negotiated with." Two burning dots, two still stars in the dark sky, reflected in his opaque lenses. "Have you asked your pilot about his family?"

"What family . . ." Sasha began. She froze. Farit sneered.

"He's married—officially. He has two daughters. Twins, three years old. In Moscow. Do you know anything about it?"

Sasha felt as if the roof of the black SUV had caved in and pressed down on her head, as if the vehicle stood on the conveyor belt moving under a press.

"Go fix it," Farit said softly. "You know how. You can put out fires."

"No," Sasha said. "No, that's impossible. There was no wife, no kids just a moment ago. It was a different world, a different text."

"Impossible?" Farit's voice was silky and sweet. "But why? Would anything in your relationship contradict this turn of events?"

"He contradicts it," she said softly. "Who he is. He's different. He wouldn't. I saw—"

"You were too scared to *possess* him, avoiding any forbidden knowledge. If you did, you'd know that he was hiding something, or maybe not, depending on your luck. You were honest with him." Farit smirked again. "And he didn't share this very important thing about himself with you. To be fair, you didn't ask."

Sasha did not respond. She was in shock.

Her perception of the world as a material space, governed by physical laws, had collapsed a long time ago, after the very first meeting with Farit Kozhennikov. And now her perception of people and of herself had collapsed as well. The only question more important than her life was whether she was wrong about Yaroslav from the very beginning, or whether Farit had replaced reality.

Was Yaroslav married when they wandered the streets of Torpa, when he first opened the door of his house to her? When he held Sasha in his arms on the eve of the new year, did he know that his two tiny daughters gazed at a different Christmas tree somewhere? And why, if that's what fate had to offer, why hadn't he said a single word about his family? Could she trust him at all?

At sixteen, more than anything in the world, Sasha had been afraid of losing Mom, and that fear led her to Torpa and forced her to study harder than she'd ever imagined. When Sasha distanced herself from

Mom, they became "grammatical strangers," and then Mom was safe, or as safe as possible. Then Yaroslav appeared and filled Sasha's thoughts. And now he was at risk of sudden death: a flock of birds flying into the engine, or a fatal disease, or a terrorist bomb in a faraway airport. Once again, Sasha had had to study harder than she'd ever imagined. She'd become a burning house, changed Anton Pavlovich's fate, and believed that she'd escaped the power of everlasting fear.

Sasha had prepared herself for something even bigger. She'd been convinced that by the time Farit wanted to kill Yaroslav, she'd have learned how to catch aircrafts in midair, cancel cell mutations, and defuse bombs. And yet, Farit had managed to kill Yaroslav by changing his past, and there was nothing Sasha could do about it. Farit replaced pilot Grigoriev just like evil spirits replaced babies with changelings in old fairy tales, and instead of the man Sasha loved there now was a stranger.

But what if Farit never replaced anyone? What if this was always Yaroslav's free will, his actions, his choice, and Farit simply provided the missing information?

"Go fix it," Farit had said, knowing full well this was irreparable. Any catastrophe could be reversed, unless it was caused by deliberate human action. Freedom was the everlasting source of evil.

"Yaroslav existed, and now he doesn't," Sasha muttered, shuffling through the snowy streets of Torpa. "But he did exist . . . I am not stupid, I'd recognize a lie . . ."

Would she though? Out of the blue Sasha thought of the New Year's Eve of her first year, when she'd stumbled upon Kostya and Zhenya learning the joys of teenage sex under the counter of the coatroom. After that incident, she'd developed trust issues, yet she'd forced herself to believe people, with a perseverance worthy of a higher cause.

She stopped in someone's yard, knee-deep in snow. *Let's assume Yaroslav had a reason not to tell me about his marriage and his kids,* she thought. But what about Anton Pavlovich? Did he not have a daughter-in-law and granddaughters in that reality? Or was he convinced that Sasha didn't need to know these minor details?

She recalled the old man's words, and the pauses in conversations, and the look in his eyes, finding more and more proof that Anton Pavlovich knew everything. He knew Sasha had no idea about this. He kept silent, considering the situation perfectly normal. Sasha wasn't just losing Yaroslav, she was losing her family, again. Even though everyone was still alive.

In the wee hours of the morning, her boots full of snow, Sasha slipped on the side of the road and fell, hard enough to cause her to cry out. She got up, rubbing her knee; the pain was as bright as a projector, and in the light of her pain she saw clearly as day: Yaroslav had lied to her from the very beginning. Sasha had made him up to be perfect and allowed herself to be tricked.

The snow fell softly. Wisps of smoke curled above the tiled roofs. The streetlights burned brightly, the windows glowed, and behind every window everyday life, painstaking and ordinary, went on. In the darkness, shadows of words uttered in the past, worn out without ever having *reverberated,* began a new day, meaningless and circuitous. Loose, spongy time resembled frog eggs. Sasha stood in the middle of a snow pile, absorbing her new knowledge of the world.

Now now, is it really worth all this trouble, said the building doors, slamming themselves shut. *How can you compare terrifying things, such as fires or car accidents, with a tiny lie? Not even a lie, more like insufficient information sharing.*

But I told him I was Password, Sasha thought. *I even told him that! And he said nothing.*

She jumped up onto a bench, from there hopped onto its wooden back, and spread her arms to keep her balance. Three steps, that's how long her runway was, and then the bench moved away from under her feet, becoming tiny, like a toy, far below. In two convulsive strokes, Sasha flew up to the roof level, broke into open space without antennas or wires, unfurled her wings, and entered the sky vertically, like an arrow. Wet clumps of snow fell off her boots, immediately freezing like icicles, and the soles became spiky, like instruments of torture.

The icy wind took away her breath. At the zenith, Sasha spread her wings and looked down.

Torpa's outline floated in the network of clouds, morphing into a page of an enormous *Conceptual Activator.* Sasha realized that this city was nothing but a phrase, a compound sentence, and it was really easy to move the comma.

Had Kostya known that his affair with Zhenya would result in her failure at the exam, he would have been terrified and would have acted differently. Had Yaroslav known that his deception would be revealed and that Sasha would not forgive him, he would have been terrified and would not have lied. Farit was absolutely, inhumanely right: he and Sasha had much more in common than Sasha and Kostya, or Sasha and Lisa, or Sasha and Sterkh. Sasha understood Farit, but she could never understand Yaroslav.

Farit told her this a long time ago, and then repeated it again and again, and she did not understand. Was not *ready* to understand. Words traveled like the light of a distant star to reach her consciousness only now: fear shapes reality.

Sasha froze in the sky above the central square, right where the tower weather vane would be if Torpa had such a tower. She looked down. A yellow cab appeared from around the corner, cowardly tapping the brakes on the slippery road. From above, Sasha saw its trajectory, as if the cab simultaneously existed in all points of its itinerary. She wondered why, when working on Coach's diagrams, she always tried to prevent a catastrophe. The effort was akin to pouring sand into wondrous wells that brimmed with a revitalizing, invigorating, omnificent nightmare.

An all-season tire skidded on the ice. The steering wheel turned too sharply, and reality wove into a different knot, a brighter, more beautiful, more prominent one. The tin shell creaked as if crumpled, windows and headlights shattered, but the yellow cab was only starting its path. It hurtled down the steep street, breaking everything on its way, tangling up other probabilities, changing multitudes of other lives.

Down below, things began to move as the information started to flow. Minor projections of meanings lined up in queues like metal shavings around a magnet. Small crystals of fear melted into symbols and wove themselves into the fabric of reality around Sasha, and once again she felt herself changing from the inside.

Snow twirled above Torpa, windows shattered and sang, and a huge tree crashed into a power line. Lights went out and sparks flew.

Trees collapsed one after another, groaning as the roots pulled out of the icy soil. Snowbanks grew like waves in split seconds. At the central square, an ambulance whined, stuck in the snow as if inside an anteater's trap. Red and blue lights blinked in the blizzard, and the wind howled louder than all the fire engines of Torpa.

Sasha circled above Torpa, feasting her eyes on the two processes simultaneously happening in multiple dimensions. Torpa plunged into chaos, and out of this chaos grew the order of the highest standard, the order of the consummate fear. Amorphous life took on well-defined contours. Never before had Sasha experienced such a free, authoritative euphoria.

To live is to be vulnerable. A thin membrane of a soap bubble separates one from impenetrable hell. I am bestowing life upon you, go and live. You are vulnerable, and I will remind you of it. Ice on the road. The unlucky division of an aging cell. A child picks up a pill from the floor. Words stick to each other, line up, obedient to the great harmony of Speech . . .

. . . A patient suffering from a heart attack does not last until the ambulance arrives. But what if it weren't for the blizzard? Or if the elevator never got stuck between the floors? What if . . .

Whatever filled her inside grew stronger than her human shell. Sasha was spun, thrown in a tailspin, tossed into the world of multiple dimensions, cold and dry like a discarded snakeskin. Everything that existed outside had become hostile. Everything that existed inside had become superfluous. Everything Sasha used to think of as herself—a girl, a daughter, a person—everything melted, dissolved into a puddle of broth.

"Fix it," Farit had said.

She was.

A dark silhouette, barely distinguishable in the blizzard, flickered above her head. A sharp tip of a wing slashed across her cheek, drawing blood.

"Implicitly express yourself through what you are not. Now."

She was not a name, not a feature, not a pronoun, not a conjunction. Not Alexandra Samokhina, who died on the highway. Not a leaf from a linden tree. Not a function who'd never been human. Not a milquetoast tool of the Great Speech.

Sasha felt herself plunging, rolling, smashing her wings, falling up. There, up in the sky, a gap in the celestial fabric gaped like an enormous maw, as if a trail left by a jet had created a jagged rip. Inside something burned, a wondrous source of light or perhaps a crackling fireplace, but Sasha could not choose, she was simply falling into the zenith.

But she was not a mirror reflecting her advisor. Neither a sack for absolute fear nor a container for inevitable death. She was not Farit Kozhennikov.

A whirlwind caught her, and she tumbled, dropping feathers. She vomited, and gold coins flew off her lips, sparkling joyfully, flipping around like stars in a cartoon sky, like confetti. The winged silhouette flew underneath her, touched her, pushed her up, caught and released her immediately, and the gravitational pull changed direction.

The nausea disappeared, leaving behind a thick rubbery silence. Falling down from the sky, Sasha rotated in the air, and when her face was turned up, she saw a shadow with enormous wings, circling above, escorting her fall. Then she was turned facedown, and she saw a forest and a slim railroad with a wormlike overnight train. The semaphore signal burned green, and the rails glittered from underneath the snow and pulled her over like flames pull moths.

She was caught and pushed again, and she veered to the side. Her trajectory changed, changing her fate. For a split second, Sasha saw the face of the engineer behind the glass of the locomotive; it was a pale face with eyes as big as saucers. Then she was swallowed by the snow.

The train rumbled by. Sasha lay still in the snow, hoping no one would see a half-dead girl with giant wings; but even if someone saw her, they would simply write her off as a drunken illusion. The bad part was that she saw the train as a sequence of symbols and variations, and the wheels beat in the rhythm of "de-cay, de-cay." She imagined rusty carcasses tossed into a transport plant's dump and a series of accidents, twisted rails, carriages piled up on top of each other like mating dogs . . .

Sasha pushed her head deeper into the snow, letting the ice and cold inside, freezing out signs and symbols and turning them back into human thoughts. The wheels quieted down, and the ground stopped trembling.

The semaphore signal switched. Sasha struggled to get up, feeling the wind sneak under her jacket, ripped in the back. She looked around, as if searching for someone among the trees, but aside from her and a couple of bullfinches, the forest was empty.

Finding a pay phone was extremely difficult, especially considering she had to walk away from the forest along the rails.

"Sasha? Sasha . . . are you all right? Where are you? I've been sending tons of messages, and calling, and you weren't answering . . ."

His voice sounded hollow, as if he spoke through a layer of cotton wool. It wasn't surprising; after all, he was tens of thousands of kilometers away. Almost as far as the moon. She was surprised she could reach that far. He must have really wanted to hear her voice.

"Did something happen?" He tried to speak calmly, the same way he spoke to his passengers. "I'm flying out in half an hour. Just tell me— what happened?"

The sound of his voice made her knees go weak. She couldn't be silent, she couldn't mumble, but what was she going to say? He was flying out in half an hour; it was too late to cancel the flight, he likely had hundreds of people on board his aircraft. And what if today, after their conversation, somewhere above the ocean his hand would flinch?

Inside an old pay phone at an empty snowed-in whistlestop, she watched a handful of steel-gray feathers whirl around her wet boots.

"I broke my tablet," she said, hoping the distance would muffle the deceit in her voice. "Took me a while to find a pay phone. Forgive me, and don't worry. Safe travels. We'll talk later."

"Are you feeling well?"

"Of course," she said, pressing her hand against frosted glass adorned with snowflake stars. "Come home."

She made it back to the institute in the evening, utterly exhausted; the only thing that propelled her forward was her worry about Sterkh. She couldn't reach him by phone, which was not surprising, but she had an individual session scheduled with him that evening, and Sterkh never canceled their sessions of his own accord.

That meant she'd have to go up to auditorium 14. She'd have to hear everything he would have to say to her. He probably had a lot to say; he'd find words that would make her cry from pain and resentment. But Sasha was not afraid of an argument, because Sterkh would never report her. He had a right to scold and shame her: she owed him more than just her life.

Where would Sasha be now if it weren't for Sterkh? In *Untime*, with Zakhar and all the others? In the place worse than death, in the closed loop where Sasha hovered over the destroyed Torpa like a comic villain, reproducing a singular concept—fear.

In the dorm vestibule, a television screen broadcast news with the sound off: an ambulance stuck in the snow, a burning tree on top of a power line, cops, doctors, cars flipped upside down. Sasha stopped in the doorway, remembering all the frames she'd seen here before: "Shut up, vultures . . ."

Up on the screen, a girl with a microphone screamed soundlessly at the camera. Behind her a house was engulfed by flames, and her eyes shone with unhealthy excitement: for a brief moment her life had meaning. Fear is followed by euphoria; Sasha touched the screen, scooping up the slim informational stream. She needed to know how many people had died in Torpa. How many casualties, exactly. But the girl did not reply. Instead, she choked in the middle of her speech and coughed, almost dropping the microphone. Sasha stepped back. Statistics did not matter. So she'd know the exact number of casualties, and then what? Some time ago Sterkh had said, "As long as you believe in your own omnipotence, you are in danger. And everyone around you is in danger."

She thought of Sterkh, grabbing on to that thought as if a lifeline. *He's going to help me*, Sasha thought, her teeth chattering. All he needed to do was to rewind a short time loop. Errors had to be corrected. And then he could yell at her, beat her; let him do what he wanted. Five minutes remained until their session. Three minutes. Two. One.

"Sorry I am late, Nikolay Vale—"

The windows were dark like flat black mirrors. Sasha stood at the entrance to auditorium 14. In Sterkh's seat behind the teacher's desk, Coach looked as massive as an early diving suit, rather inappropriate in this setting.

"Where is . . ." Sasha faltered, still hoping that this misunderstanding was about to be cleared up.

"Nikolay Valerievich Sterkh will no longer teach your class, Samokhina," Coach said impassively.

Sasha thought herself a cricket nailed to a piece of cardboard with a collector's pin. She felt the weather vane above the tower pierce her ribs. She couldn't talk, couldn't scream, she could only gasp for breath, for the thinning, vanishing air.

She wanted to say: "no," "I don't believe you," "this doesn't make any sense." She wanted to shout: "Where is he?" She was ready to step out, count to five, and enter properly, and see Sterkh in his usual spot.

"I hope to never hear 'I will not' during class time from you again," Coach continued impassively. "If I ask you to clean the bathroom after class, you have a right to say, 'I don't want to.' If I ask you during class, you go and clean it. Is that clear?"

"You don't have any power over me," Sasha whispered. "You are not a living entity. You are not even protein-based. You have no personality. No memory."

"Stop. Talking. Back," he said slowly and deliberately. "You are not in a position to assert yourself. You violated academic discipline, were penalized for it, and threw a pagan carnival in the town of Torpa. You were nearly turned inside out and almost pushed yourself into an irrational pocket. I can't say I'd be crushed if that happened, but rules are rules."

Sasha was silent. Auditorium 14 swam in front of her eyes.

"Are you done saving kittens?" Coach inquired sardonically. "Do you finally understand who you are and what kind of world you'd create?"

She counted to ten. After a pause, in a completely different tone of voice, like a dutiful schoolgirl, she said, "Dmitry Dmitrievich. I understand everything. I am sorry. I am asking you to please let me return to *then,* to the first class after vacation, when I said, 'I will not.' I will correct my mistake."

"It's not a mistake," he said, shaking his head with regret. "It's a realization of your freedom. Manifestation of the fundamental property of Password cannot be corrected. You really need to learn to accept the consequences of your actions."

Sacco and Vanzetti Street was perfectly dark, not a single streetlight was on. Auditorium 14 resembled a fishbowl filled with cloudy water.

"I am not here to scold you. I am not your enemy," Coach said wearily. "You're drowning in a puddle of emotions; you operate in human categories. God forbid you decide that your professor sacrificed himself to save you. Or make up some cockamamie story of the conflicts among faculty that led to a respected professor being terminated. That's not true. Nikolay Valerievich was neither human nor even a material object."

"Was," Sasha whispered.

She wanted to say that Coach had no idea what it meant to "be human," but grammar did its thing. The word "was" implied nothing about Sterkh, aside from the fact that he forever stayed in the past.

"As an informational object, your professor had exhausted his relevance," Coach continued calmly.

"And was it you who *purged* him?" Sasha asked. "Who deleted him like outdated information?"

"No," he said evenly. "But everything that has a beginning, has an end."

Sasha could barely make out his silhouette, seeing him as if through a sandstorm: a vague, indistinct shadow. For a second she thought it was Sterkh sitting across from her. "I don't know how to get through to you," Sterkh said to her once. "How to explain . . . how to save you, really."

She recalled their first meeting in Sterkh's office, and how he took her, a first year, to a restaurant and asked her about her parents. She thought of their flights over Torpa, his error correction assignments, and their very last meeting, a dark silhouette in the sky above the town.

A wave of grief and rage washed over her. The wings she'd never before unfurled inside escaped from underneath her sweater with a loud crackling noise, filling up the space behind her back and almost touching the ceiling. Coach did not move. On the contrary, his visible shell became so still that it seemingly stopped rotating along with the globe. However, the actual structure he embodied expanded and presented itself to Sasha in full—and then immediately hid behind his diaphragm pupils.

He represented gravity for all words, existing, forgotten, and made up. He became a prison that resisted chaos. He was a system of grammatical rules, a force that forbade flying and yet would not let you fall. Sasha could not catch her breath; she could not comprehend fully what she just saw—her working memory was not large enough.

Coach swapped his guises. Instead of an alabaster statue, a young, charming, and very sad Dima Dimych was now facing Sasha.

"Take a piece of paper, *manifest* the concept of loss, then destroy it. *Manifest* the idea of guilt, then add a negative particle. All these things are signs and symbols, shadows of great meanings, projections progressive and regressive, distorted to varying degrees. And not at all what you're feeling."

"You have no idea what I'm feeling," Sasha said.

He shook his head wearily.

"Not only do I have an idea, I know exactly what you're feeling, and can simulate it on paper. You tend to assign uniqueness and value to human emotions, Samokhina. Human emotions are not unique or valuable."

Sasha felt weak, tired, barely alive. Her wings were no longer there, and a cold draft made its way under her sweater though the jagged holes. Sasha was reminded of a river on the outskirts of town, and its wide black ice holes made by the current.

Outside, far into the depths of Torpa, an ambulance howled in distress. The sound burrowed into Sasha's brain like an outdated dental drill. "Casssualtiessss," the ambulance hissed. "Cassssssssualties . . ."

"There are almost eight billion people on Earth," Coach said softly but firmly. "Projecting onto time, even onto the next hundred years, they are all dead. But projecting onto your predestination, Sasha . . . Singularity is a point that encompasses matter, information, gravity, inflation, the taste of honey, multiplication tables—in other words, everything—all in one place, time, and possibility. When you *reverberate,* you will condense the universe—not even into a pea, but into a mathematical abstract notion. Are you still mourning the residents of Torpa?"

Again, he swapped guises, changing from Dima Dimych to Coach, but the bright red spots on his cheeks remained. Either he was playing at emotion or had allowed himself to succumb to one.

"I sound like a hypocrite," he said, reading her mind. "But not entirely. You feel sorry for them? I feel sorry for you. Your advisor doesn't. I can annul you as Word. You will cease to exist, cease to be conscious of yourself, cease to suffer. But you must make this choice on your own."

As the ambulance howled in the distance, Sasha stared at the floor and the tips of her shoes. She thought she was standing at the edge of an ice hole, black water flowing under her feet and putting her into a trance.

Sasha looked up.

"Can you guarantee that I will cease to be conscious of myself? Cease to remember. Cease to be, reside, continue. Exist."

His diaphragm pupils dilated.

"What do you mean, 'can you guarantee'? What do you think I am, a repair shop?"

The lights along Sacco and Vanzetti came on, blinked, then went out again. The entire town of Torpa was trying to restore electricity.

"I can guarantee it," Coach said in a different tone. "You're not going to die because you'd never have been born. You will cease to exist in the present, past, and future. Alexandra Samokhina will be your own projection, a coherent, completed story line, albeit a short one. And no one will mourn you. Your disappearance will not make anyone sad. *Unbeing* as opposed to being is the only freedom, Samokhina. An absolute kind of freedom."

Sasha frowned as if his words were a departing train she needed to run after, to grab its handrail. To catch up to, seize it. To comprehend its meaning.

"And all the mistakes I've made?"

"Not to be means not to make mistakes," he said, nodding. "All your efforts, all this punching above your weight, struggle, denial and acceptance, motivation, discipline . . . It's a burden, Sasha. Cast it off."

"Why didn't you tell me about all this before?"

"I did tell you, but you didn't hear me," he said with a hint of regret. "Because you weren't ready."

The lights on Sacco and Vanzetti came on once more; impenetrable flat windows gained depth resembling a dark stage background. Linden trees waved their bare branches over the resurrected lights. It suddenly hit Sasha that everything happening was real, that Coach was right, and Farit—strangely enough—had made a mistake. The road that led Sasha to the Institute of Special Technologies had come to a logical conclusion.

"That's fine," she said softly.

"Come here." He pulled something from the inner pocket of his jacket. It was a sports stopwatch, the kind used by referees, and Sasha thought she recognized it from first-year gym class. Coach opened it like a medallion and motioned for Sasha to approach.

She froze on the spot, but not because she'd made the last-minute decision to fight back. No, her decision was already made, but her feet stuck to the floor.

"I am just going to take a look," he said, like a pediatrician hiding a syringe in his sleeve.

Sasha moved toward him, skirting the table where she'd spent so much time studying or talking to or sharing silence with Sterkh. Coach got up, towering over her like a mountain.

"Lift your chin."

A ray of light slashed across her eyes, blinding her. Sasha exhaled with relief, hoping that this ray was about to dissolve her and wash her away, and she wouldn't have to worry about anything. However, her vision returned a few seconds later, and Sasha still stood in the middle of auditorium 14, and Coach was still looming large at the desk, leaning over a big duffel bag. Sasha's eyes watered, making it hard for her to see what was inside that bag.

"What's wrong?" she mumbled when the silence became unbearable.

"I need the will of a verb," he said, his voice deliberately calm. "And you present a human reaction with a hint of hysterics."

"No!" Sasha recoiled.

"It's not a reprimand," he said, rummaging inside the bag. "It's a fact. And we'll have to do something about it."

He pulled out a book and placed it on the desk. The book was thick and heavy, with a blank hardcover and a library stamp.

"I have never given it to anyone until the fifth year, but it looks like we don't have a choice. Open it."

Clenching her jaws, Sasha opened the first page. In the middle of the yellowish sheet was a single column of raised symbols, as small as a ladybug's droppings.

"You read it with your fingers." Coach looked at her searchingly. "Like Braille. Just not left to right, go top to bottom. And your eyes must be closed, ideally using a blindfold."

Sasha shut her eyes, then opened them again. For some reason she found it extremely difficult to touch the page for the first time.

"You will experience an unpleasant physical sensation," Coach said softly. "But you need it right now. This will drown out the human inside you, like a butterfly in a killing jar. And then you will realize your freedom, Password."

Sasha placed her index finger onto the top symbol in the column.

Immediately, she wanted to jerk her hand away.

She remembered Yaroslav's face, clenched her jaws, pressed her finger harder, and moved it down along the line of symbols.

She was expected at the dorm. The entire first floor was illuminated, with many burned-out candles placed on the tables and next to the floorboards. A large container of ice cream was swaying outside the window in a bird feeder, covered with a thin layer of snow. Anna Bochkova was wiping down the inside of the freezer.

"Hello," Sasha said.

"Hello," Andrey Korotkov said, waving to her. "Quite the beginning of the semester we're having. Almost twenty-four hours without electricity, and everything in the fridge has defrosted to hell."

"Our ancestors survived without refrigerators," Yulia Goldman said melancholically. "You don't need refrigerators in the winter."

Facing the mirror, Lisa was working out with dumbbells. Her athletic top showcased her shoulders and arms, muscles shifting under white skin marked with a forearm tattoo. Sasha caught Lisa's eyes in the mirror, tenacious, hard, impenetrable eyes.

"Sasha!"

She turned her head. Haggard, with red, inflamed eyes, Kostya looked older than he was.

"What have they done to you?"

She could have said: Just be patient. Soon everything will change, but not the way I dreamed about. A world without fear and death will not exist, but neither will Sasha Samokhina.

"Sasha," Kostya said, gazing into her face. "How can I. . . . how can we help you?"

"Everything is fine," Sasha said, watching the snow fall onto the ice cream container outside the window. "You should take the ice cream out of the bird feeder and fill it with sunflower seeds."

Lisa placed the dumbbells on the counter with a clanging noise.

"You shouldn't have shown off. You provoked them. 'I won't do it, I don't want to'—in preschool, we got into serious trouble for something like that."

She is full of empathy for me, Sasha thought. *Even though she's also gloating. But there is more empathy than anything.* Sasha looked at the faces of her classmates, as if mentally compiling a graduation album.

None of them would remember her.

"You're right," she said to Lisa. "I was showing off. But the issue is more or less resolved."

She went up to the third floor, her backpack with Coach's book inside pulling back her shoulders like a bag of stones.

The convex symbols were cold, hot, icy, searing. They pricked her like pins and twitched like insects. Two or three times her finger got stuck to the page, and she had to scrape it off with a knife and start again.

Sasha mastered the first several columns of text by sheer stubbornness, only because she was used to impossible exercises. The scarf she tied over her eyes was now soaked, as if she'd stepped into the rain. Intuitively she knew that Coach's book would help her, and she wasn't mistaken.

Yaroslav's treason. Sterkh's fate. The blizzard in Torpa, all the casualties on Sasha's conscience, everything that weighed upon her and prevented her from breathing—all this was slowly losing its significance. All the ordeals and catastrophes were becoming shadows, vague and foreign. Sasha thought she was moving away, farther and farther, along the path of convex symbols, leaving behind the extraneous, the empty, the meaningless.

She left behind Yaroslav, Yegor, and Kostya. She forgot Lisa as if she'd never even met her before. She recalled her mother, but only for a second and only in order to forget her entirely. Everyone at the institute, everyone who tortured and rescued her, turned into a chorus line on the back of the stage, by the dusty decorations, their faces and voices undistinguishable.

And only Farit was still there. He did not wish to fall behind, his shadow following Sasha's footsteps. Sasha could not see him, but she felt his presence, and she rushed to complete her assignment. Today she would run away from Farit. This was the only way of escaping him.

In the wee hours of the morning, she saw light seeping through her blindfold. She stopped thinking in words and images. For the first time in many hours, she sensed harmony, like silence a split second before divine melody.

She reached up, mentally breaking through the attic overlays and the dorm roof. She gazed at Torpa, scattered around like an anthill: the projection town, the ghost town, the phrase town. She stood still, drawing in and absorbing additional meanings, listening to the changes within her, and at that moment something happened, and the process stopped. New information ceased to flow.

She was forced to stop and return. Sasha saw her hands and realized her physical body had betrayed her: the tips of her fingers looked dark, as if a door had slammed on her hands; she remembered this unpleasant experience from her childhood. Her pricked, burned, and frostbitten fingers had stopped transmitting information.

"Fuck," Sasha said softly.

The clock showed six. The lights went on in the first-floor windows, throwing shadows on the snow around the dorm, and the treadmills creaked and groaned. It was time for a run. A little bit more, and she would have made it; a few more hours, and she would have shown up at Coach's office not as a young girl overtaken by grief and distress, but as a verb in an imperative mood. She would have been the one who defined fates, starting with her own.

She wasn't even frustrated. When one's physical body protested, one had to repress it, preferably by a physical effort, an exercise.

Sasha walked out into a frosty morning, made her way onto a barely cleared pavement strip, and ran, like a ball along a chute.

Torpa lived, moved, crawled out onto the streets. Sasha heard distant voices and possibly even random thoughts. Hysterical rumors filled the town. Someone could not reach their relatives, because the landlines had collapsed along with the cell service. Someone said the stores had terribly long lines and empty shelves, and all of them were out of pasta and toilet paper. Sasha heard this distant panic like the noise of the night train, moving from point A to point B.

Another thin sound joined the fray like the rattling of a spoon in a tea glass. Sasha realized it was pain. Her hands froze, then warmed, her fingers regained their feeling, and that meant she could finish her work.

Only when she returned to the dorm, she discovered that she'd gone for her run in a T-shirt and a pair of thin pants, and—ever curiouser—barefoot. Frowning, she assessed a chain of wet footprints along the corridor, then immediately got distracted by the textbook on her desk. The book called for her, tugging some invisible string. Sasha looked around in search of a scarf or something she could use as a blindfold.

She saw a pair of thick woolen mittens on the windowsill. Sasha stared at the mittens, trying to figure out where they came from and why they were there. A scarlet design on light gray wool: cross-stitched leaves and deer. Sasha remembered she needed the mittens to shovel snow. Today, Sunday, was the day Anton Pavlovich was coming back from the resort.

The thought hit her like the sound of a bell very close to her face in the empty room. Sasha recoiled; she looked at the mittens, then at her hands. Her fingers ached and groaned.

Sasha went into the bathroom and stuck her hands under running water. In the mirror above the sink she saw her face, a scarf still tied over her eyes. She must have gone for a run while blindfolded.

Holding her swollen fingers under the stream of cold water, Sasha struggled to remember: Why did she think that Anton Pavlovich knew everything and chose to deceive her? If she was to think logically, or, more precisely, if she wanted to come up with justification, Anton Pavlovich could have theoretically assumed that Yaroslav and Sasha had a chance to discuss everything. That Sasha did not mind Yaroslav being married. After all, plenty of people thought nothing of situations like this.

Sasha shook her head, forcing herself to regain her courage. To stop remembering. The sharp movement made her scarf slip down like a collar, and Sasha saw her pupils in the mirror. They were faceted like a dragonfly's. She leaned over the sink and splashed some water on her face, and when she straightened up, her pupils went back to normal.

She dried her hands, ripped the small linen towel in half, and used it to cover her eyes. She opened Coach's book to page twenty-five. The pages were thick and unyielding, as if made of tin. She touched the column of symbols with the tips of her fingers and knew that her sensory nerve endings were no longer necessary: she could now read the symbols at a distance, and they no longer pricked or burned her. Instead, they played with the shades of meanings, weaving and loosening up logical chains. Sasha laughed out loud: things were about to get easier, everything would be very easy . . .

Through her blindfold, she could clearly see her mittens on the windowsill. A scarlet design on light gray wool.

A strange thought glimmered in her muddled mind, wandering around like a lost child. A child wielding matches at a gas station.

Here was the familiar key chain, on a hook in a corner. The old man would be surprised if Sasha didn't show up today. He'd be sad and confused.

So what? She was trying to dissolve, yes? His sadness and confusion would be wiped away if she . . .

Just one more time, the last one. She wouldn't ask any questions. She'd just look at him. Give him back the keys. Achieve crystal-clear understanding—and only then manifest the will of the verb.

Sasha held the keys in her palm like a captured bird. She shut her eyes. A tiny projection lay in her hand, a reflection, not of a single idea, but a complex, stunning structure: trust. Protection, home. Admission. Permission to enter. Password.

Her fingers unclenched. The key chain fell on the floor.

At noon, a minibus rolled up to the gate. Carrying a suitcase and a duffel bag, Anton Pavlovich took his time saying good-bye to a couple of senior pals, shaking everyone's hands, and waving farewell; only after the bus departed did he enter the yard and notice it had been shoveled.

"Sasha, honey, thank you so much." He smiled, but tensely and joylessly. "I didn't mean to exploit you. To tell you the truth, I am quite embarrassed. When I left you the key, all I meant for you to do was to stop by a couple of times to make sure the house didn't burn down."

He laughed at his own joke, knowing full well that it wasn't very funny.

Sasha stood at the threshold, studying his face, this old man's face with its reddening nose. She mentally marked the individual logic of his character, the multilayered projection of his long life, the painful commotion of the last few days.

"It's the end of the world," he said, shrugging in response to her silent gaze. "So many areas in town are still without electricity. Such a formidable blizzard! So many accidents. Trees, wires . . . And literally nothing just a few kilometers away, nothing but a dusting of snow . . ."

Sasha opened the door, letting him in. He wouldn't let her help him with his luggage, grabbing the handle with a practiced gesture and pulling it onto the porch.

"When I heard what happened here, I was so worried about you. Everything is so fragile, you know. People exist without any idea of what could happen to them in a split second. A car skids on the ice— and that's it, or a child climbs up onto the windowsill . . . It's frightening, Sasha dear. So terrifying."

"Fear shapes reality," Sasha said softly.

"Oh?" He turned to her, and his glasses became blue from his wide-open eyes. "What a strange reflection."

"I've been picking up your mail," Sasha said. "It's over there on the table."

The old man lowered the suitcase on the floor, almost dropping it.

"Thank you. You look as if you want to ask me something. Has something happened?"

Sasha smiled sardonically: What was she supposed to do now, make a scene? The human inside her managed to trick the will of the verb, as if a possum in a trap pretended to be dead, waiting until the lid opened, then made a mad dash for freedom . . .

"Nothing happened, aside from a blizzard destruction, and a few casualties," Sasha said, surprised at how indifferent and dry her voice sounded even to herself. "And you . . . have you had a nice time away?"

He looked embarrassed, as if he heard some reproach in her tone.

"Overall, sure. The resort was lovely. But there was a television set in the main lobby. And the news was on, every day, and the news was so difficult, so unsettling. And the latest report was from Torpa, right after the blizzard . . ."

He paused, shrugging helplessly.

"I have a feeling the world is shrinking, like a piece of leather in a firepit. Like a majestic palace that developed a few cracks and is now collapsing. Or a piece of an old computer software that has accumulated so many errors that it simply cannot function any longer. To be honest, I couldn't wait to come home."

He went to his room, still wearing his shoes, leaving wet footprints on the wooden floor, while his words remained suspended in front of Sasha's face: "*So many errors that it simply cannot function any longer.*"

If he told me that a month ago, Sasha thought, *not even a month, a week ago, I would have smiled and thought that things would soon change for the better. That I would change them for the better. And now I'm departing and leaving behind the world that has developed a few cracks and is now collapsing. Because, as it turned out, I can't fix anything.*

The grandfather clock with a large pendulum tick-tocked away, and different faces stared from the photographs on the walls. A loaf of bread lay on the table: Sasha had bought it out of habit; she just couldn't help but worry about what he was going to eat, since there was no food in the house, and it would be a while before Yaroslav came back.

"Anton Pavlovich," Sasha said loudly. "I bought some groceries and put everything in the fridge. I had bad reception, and I did warn Yaroslav, but he's still nervous. When he calls, please tell him everything is fine."

The old man appeared in the doorway, holding his glasses as if they were a lizard, carefully and away from his body.

"Sasha, I keep thinking something has happened between you and Yaroslav. But I can't quite comprehend . . . You didn't even speak on the phone the last few days. He's very upset."

Sasha bit her lip. The old man wasn't lying. There were no traces of lies in his words, his intonation, or his facial muscles. Did he really not understand? Or was he convinced that Sasha didn't know about Yaroslav's family, and so there was no reason for trouble?

She wanted to touch him, turn his personality inside out, and learn the truth, down to the minute detail. She held back with a tremendous effort, but the will of the verb she was growing inside like a crystal the night before—this harmonious but fragile structure wavered.

The old man caught her eyes. He pulled back, hunched over, and stepped to the window. He leaned forward, resting his hands on the windowsill, just like Yaroslav.

"You know," he spoke softly and slowly, choosing his words, "on the way back to Torpa we had to take a few detours. The roads were closed. People said it was Armageddon. Fallen trees, flipped cars, a few roofs torn off by the wind . . . it was a natural disaster. But this didn't feel natural."

He turned to face her, rubbing his palms together and shivering.

"Fear does not shape anything, Sasha. Fear destroys everything. I lived in fear for many years, afraid to lose some people, and the more I feared, the more I lost. And now all I have is Yaroslav. And you."

The clock was ticking, not ominously like a metronome, but steadily and peacefully like an old dog snoring in her sleep.

The house watched Sasha; it remembered more than its master; it remembered the roof collapsing and flames bursting out of the attic window.

"When I was sitting here alone in the dark, I was thinking of many things." Anton Pavlovich spoke quickly, almost rushing. "I was thinking it was just a thread, a fine thread, a mere chance. That night I woke up and put out the fire, but what if I didn't? Yaroslav would have arrived to smoldering ruins. And then you showed up, Sasha, such a strange, straightforward girl, and told me you're moving in. And I believed that I'd never be alone. Never again would I be alone."

He took a deep breath as if something had gotten stuck in his throat, preventing him from speaking.

"You see, Sasha. Sometimes the end of the world is just a word. Or a couple of words. But if no words are spoken, nothing else matters. Please, wait for Yaroslav. Talk to him."

All the work she'd done the night before—everything that was supposed to help her hone the will of the verb—went bust the moment she closed the gate behind her. Anton Pavlovich may have been insulted by how quickly Sasha scurried out of his house, but she had no choice—she couldn't stay there.

More, she couldn't wait for Yaroslav. Yaroslav would never come back. The one who would return would be a different person, someone who'd made a different choice, preferred a different course of action. Sasha paid her debt to the old house when she gave Anton Pavlovich back his keys. To Yaroslav she owed nothing.

She made it back to the institute at sunset, just as the evening rays broke through the clouds, and all the snow—piled on the roofs, cornices, tree branches, parked and abandoned cars—all this snow suddenly turned pink with amber undertones, and Sasha involuntarily slowed down her steps. Observed by human beings in the spectrum available to them, the world is beautiful. To her, it was just data. Sasha pulled off her mittens and dipped her hands in the snow, reading it like Coach's textbook.

Almost immediately she felt nauseated: the snow remembered her flight above Torpa, the howling of the wind and the rattling of misplaced roofs. Precipitation had a vindictive streak.

Eventually she remembered that the textbook was waiting for her, and she was supposed to finish what she had started. She ran down the street toward the new dorm, dashed past the always-on television screen, past the public phone, past the entrance to the first-floor hallway, toward the staircase, toward her goal.

Only when she took the first two steps up, she realized that the absence of noise on the first floor of the dorm was different from the usual silence, just as the absence of noise at a cemetery is different from the silence of a nursery.

Never before had she seen so many people gathered in the first-floor common area. Third years, the new residents of the dorm, along with fourth years, both groups A and B, occupied all the seats by the bar and at the tables, and those who didn't get a chair sat on the floor and perched on windowsills. Everyone wore the same facial expression, immobile and flat. Farit Kozhennikov strolled from one wall to another, his arms folded across his chest. He wore impenetrable black glasses with a slight mirroring effect, which made it look as if he had miniature screens where his eyes should have been.

"Here's Samokhina," he said when Sasha came in. "Showing up when the train has left the station, as usual. I just finished informing the students about the changes in the Specialty department."

Everyone was now staring at Sasha. Again, like the very first time, she felt as if their stares made her transform into a crowd of semitransparent shadows, reflections in the eyes of all the others. Kostya gazed at her with horror, Lisa with an unkind question. Only Yegor, perched at the edge of a windowsill with his back to the dying sunset, looked at the floor.

"I have something to discuss with you, Samokhina. In private," Farit said, giving her an official nod. "Come with me."

As she walked along the hallway, their stares stretched after her like rubber bands. They broke off one after another, but Kostya's lasted the longest.

"Are you falling apart on me?" Farit asked softly.

"No," Sasha said, attempting to keep her hatred under control.

Against her will, she thought that *he,* the one walking by her side, *could* rewind reality to that moment where Yaroslav was single and never lied to anyone, and where Sterkh was still sitting in his office, leaning over his desk, his chin resting on his steepled fingers. Her thought was like a glass of water in a desert. Water poured into the sand in front of a man dying of thirst.

"You are falling apart," Farit stated with a hint of pity. "Let's go to your room."

"I don't have office hours today," Sasha said.

"Samokhina." He shook his head in reproach, or perhaps in surprise. "And to think of it, I even brought you a gift."

He stopped in the hall, near the plants, right underneath the plasma TV.

"Did you see the statistics on the Torpa casualties?"

"Yes," Sasha said, pressing a cold wet mitten to her eyes.

"You are lying to me," he said reproachfully. "Aren't you ashamed of yourself?"

She shrugged.

"Three people dead," he said nonchalantly. "A cabdriver, an old man with a heart condition, and a woman who died when a block of ice fell on top of her. She was pushing a carriage, and the baby inside almost froze before someone saved them."

Sasha said nothing. She saw nothing, her face hidden behind the wet wool.

"A lucky combination of probabilities," he continued, his voice even more careless than before. "So many got very lucky last night. You, for instance."

"You can't do anything to me," Sasha said, staring directly into his face. "Because freedom is an inalienable quality of Password, and if I choose not to exist, you cannot stop me."

"Do you think that's what Nikolay Valerievich would want?" he said silkily. "What was he teaching you for—so you could discard all his lessons?"

Sasha wanted to, but couldn't tear her eyes away from her own reflection in his mirrored glasses.

Instead she moved toward her room and opened the door.

Her room, not surprisingly, was a mess, stuff thrown around everywhere, and only the whiteboard above her desk was perfectly clean, wiped down and polished with toothpaste. Sasha stood by the window, pressing her forehead against the cool glass. Her shoes melted like candles, dripping wet snow. Her mittens felt warm like a heat pack.

"I always treat you fairly, have you noticed?"

Behind her, the chair squeaked as Farit sat at her desk.

Sasha did not respond.

"Do I treat you fairly or unfairly?"

Sasha saw his reflection in the glass. She herself was reflected twice, once in the window, once in his glasses—a dark silhouette with her back to Farit.

"Yes," Sasha managed once she realized that Farit was demanding an answer.

"I take care of you," he said with a great deal of significance. "I know you would be uncomfortable having a bunch of dead bodies on your conscience. I had to become the good fairy for one night, since you decided to debut as the demon of destruction."

"You think three is lucky?" she said, turning to him so abruptly that she nearly broke the window with her elbow.

"It's enough," he said, taking off his glasses. "For you. Let's say we're now even, considering your failed exam. You should appreciate my generosity: there could be thirty of them, or even three hundred."

"The Good Fairy," Sasha spat out, feeling as if her mouth were full of bile. "You never lied to me before."

He laughed at that, one short, barking—yet seemingly genuine—laugh. "You are too valuable for pity," he said solemnly. "But I do not ask for the impossible, we've determined that a while ago."

Sasha was silent. Farit's face without sunglasses looked very strange: as if something was missing. *I got used to seeing my own reflection in him,* Sasha thought, and suddenly felt very cold.

"You've been taught extremely well," he said pensively. "Express yourself through what you are not. You should change out of your wet clothes; you're going to catch a cold."

Slowly, Sasha removed her mittens, one after the other. She dropped them on the floor and refocused her eyes: a scarlet design on light gray wool, cross-stitched leaves and reindeer.

"Sterkh didn't warn you he was fully extended?" Kozhennikov asked softly.

Sasha closed her eyes for a brief moment. She recalled her last visit to Sterkh's office. *Don't forget what I taught you.* Something in his voice had made her tense up, but back then she was so full of courage, she was strong, and she did not notice anything.

"He did," Sasha said, barely moving her lips. "But I didn't understand."

"Knowing you, he should have spoken more clearly," Farit said, putting his glasses back on. "But since you are going through all the appropriate stages—denial, anger, and all that—it might be useful for you to learn that he had foreseen his own end, just as a declarative sentence knows it ends with a period. But a period is not a gravestone. When you came in today, I was just telling your classmates that you had nothing to do with the end of Nikolay Valerievich's academic career."

Sasha looked up and saw her own double reflection in his dark lenses.

"They didn't believe you."

"That is on them. As you just said, I do not lie. But if anyone tries to blame you, I will be the one explaining they are wrong, not you," he said silkily.

Without looking, he reached for something on her desk. It turned out to be Coach's textbook, bookmarked on page twenty-five. Sasha took a step forward as if trying to take the book away from him.

"Sit down," he said, weighing the heavy book in his hand. "The will of the verb is a will of action, Sasha. Action, not refusal. Action is to move, to do, not to stop. What happened to your plans of creating a 'normal world'? Are you going to at least give it a chance?"

"You don't need a normal world," Sasha said, lowering herself onto the edge of the bed, still wearing her wet shoes.

"Ignoring that for a second, tell me what exactly is 'normal,'" he said. "And by the way, what is it you think I need?"

"I don't know," Sasha said helplessly. "Power over me? Over something that doesn't belong to you?"

"Close," he said solemnly, not trying to deny it. "You're very close, Sasha."

He tossed the book on the desk like something perfectly insignificant.

"For now, what I need is for you to maintain your human essence—until graduation. Feed it with your emotions. Love the human in you."

"You have everything already," Sasha said softly. "Since I was sixteen years old. I am fully in your power."

He was silent for a few minutes, gazing at her from behind his dark lenses.

"If you were fully in my power, we wouldn't be speaking right now."

It took a very long minute to understand the meaning of his words. The entire dorm was very quiet. She suspected that all the third and fourth years were still sitting together downstairs, as cheerful and boisterous as oysters on ice.

"Listen," he said with a faint smile. "I am only bothering with you because you are fighting back. As long as you keep fighting, I will find you interesting. Everything I know about you contradicts any notion of you giving up. Aren't you at least going to speak with your pilot? Are you simply going to toss him out like a Christmas tree after the holidays? Are you going to push him away like a stranger? No? What if he finds the right words, what if you believe him again?"

"What if, what if, what if . . ."

"It's too much to just give up, isn't it?"

Sasha felt dizzy, as if Farit's voice was alcohol of the highest proof, or a warm poison flooding her ears.

Coach waited by the entrance to the assembly hall. Sasha's classmates passed him one by one.

"I am not rushing you," he said softly when Sasha approached. "But time is not only a system of symbols, it is also a resource. And resources can get exhausted."

"I had a conversation with my advisor." Sasha stared directly into his diaphragm pupils. "Dmitry Dmitrievich, if you exist in the future, it's easier for you to see what happens."

"Events of the future are the projection of your will." He glanced inside the assembly hall, where fourth years spoke quietly and chairs squeaked. "All I see right now is that you haven't made up your mind. You must decide. And soon."

"If possible, not now," Sasha managed.

CHAPTER SIX

Fourth years, groups A and B. You are starting this new semester with a new faculty member teaching the most important subject, Applied Specialty."

The same wooden chairs, the same dusty velvet curtains, the same flat stage that hosted annual holiday roasts and, a few weeks later, accommodated a long table for the examining committee. Here they listened to "Gaudeamus Igitur" during their student initiation ceremony, but now instead of Portnov, Coach stood on the stage, and by his side was a young dark-haired woman in a bespoke business suit.

"Please welcome Adele Victorovna."

The woman fixed her hair in a slightly awkward, nervous gesture. She was human until very recently. Perhaps she was a recent graduate, only a few years older than her students.

Lisa raised her hand, acting deliberately polite, like a proper schoolgirl.

"Dmitry Dmitrievich, may I ask a question? Would Nikolay Valerievich Sterkh say a few words—as a farewell gesture?"

Sasha felt several pairs of eyes on her at once. She lowered her head, ignoring all of them.

"Everything Nikolay Valerievich could—and wanted to—tell you, he told you during his classes," Coach informed her coldly. "Any other questions?"

The creaking and sighing stopped.

"No questions," Coach stated. "Adele Victorovna, why don't you say a few words."

She had a deep, pleasant voice, a contralto. If she were to cut off the sleeve of her elegant jacket, a round symbol would be found on the crook of her elbow, like a reverse side of a gold coin, Sasha thought. Adele was talking about high expectations and hard work ahead, approaching graduation exams. She spoke of the students' dedication and its effect on their future in the bosom of the Great Speech. She said that the current fourth years were a very strong class, cleverly composed of Nouns, Pronouns, Verbs, and Grammatical Properties, and during the next semester they would practice their exercises in groups, using syntactic dependencies.

Silent aside from an occasional creak of a chair, the fourth years listened, hating her, mostly for nothing. No, they never loved Sterkh; the faculty of the Institute of Special Technologies did not expect to be loved. And yet, Sterkh's disappearance was a personal loss for each one of them, and now they thought of Adele Victorovna as an impostor.

Sasha couldn't quite care about the teacher prattling on before her. She thought instead that, by now, Yaroslav knew she was avoiding him. The broken phone explanation had an expiration date.

Sasha turned her head and looked at her classmates in the third row. She caught a view of Lisa's pale chiseled profile. Her Lyosha had survived for some reason. He didn't die in prison, didn't perish in a knife fight, did not overdose, did not get run over by a train while drunk. He lived all these years (and time was a grammatical concept) only so that Farit could bring him to Lisa and show her the object of her eternal young love.

Her thoughts bounced back to Yaroslav.

Farit didn't need to bring Yaroslav to her. Yaroslav would get over here on his own, and very soon. Yaroslav did not fear turbulence; he routinely landed his plane through a storm front, and nothing, no power in the world, could stop him from coming to Torpa and seeing Sasha.

Adele Victorovna was reading the group assignments. Some names were repeated several times. Adele never called Sasha's name; however, Sasha was the last one on the list.

"Lisa Pavlenko and Konstantin Kozhennikov, you are to attend your session together and your homework is also to be completed as a group assignment."

Sasha looked up in surprise and saw Kostya's tense eyes looking back at her. Lisa did not move, and only her mouth turned into a thin line. Everyone but Sasha now had a partner or two. Up on the stage, Adele hesitated, sorting through her papers, and everyone in the assembly hall waited patiently under the watchful eyes of Coach.

"Alexandra Samokhina," Adele announced as if asking Sasha to come up to the stage and receive a prestigious award. "You . . . you and I have things to discuss. Auditorium fourteen, tonight at eighteen hundred hours sharp."

The fourth-floor hallway brought back unpleasant memories. Sasha knocked on the door and entered without waiting for an invitation, even though she didn't have to be rude.

Adele sat in Sterkh's chair, facing a stack of papers and a tablet, similar to Sasha's. Adele was wiping her hands with a wet napkin, Lady Macbeth style, as if trying to wash off her past misdeeds.

"Next time please wait to be invited, Samokhina."

Silently, Sasha took her backpack off her shoulder and sat down.

"You are obviously one of the best students in your class, perhaps even in the entire institute. But you are very prone to misconduct. Do you think your talent gives you the right to do anything you want?"

Adele Victorovna perched on the edge of her seat, her back straight. She smelled strongly of an unfamiliar perfume and her eyes were sharp and dark. She was either very direct and unceremonious, or intent on establishing a chain of command from day one.

"You are a pronoun," Sasha said, studying Adele pensively. "A demonstrative pronoun, if I am not mistaken. And I assume you know whose place you are now occupying?"

Adele fixed her collar as if not having enough air to breathe, then tugged on her sleeves. She took her glasses out of their case and put them on; the thin delicate lenses seemed to be plain, without any diopters. Adele adjusted the glasses on the bridge of her nose, took them off, wiped them with a napkin, and placed them right back into their case.

"Nikolay Valerievich was my academic advisor in graduate school. I am a personal pronoun, not demonstrative."

"Are you going to replace Nikolay Valerievich?" Sasha said, allowing a sharper bite of sarcasm than she should have done.

"Functions are replaceable," Adele said softly.

Sasha felt a wave of intense hatred the likes of which she'd never experienced even in relation to Farit.

Adele Victorovna leaned back in Sterkh's chair. Once again, she fixed her hair, this time with both hands, visibly tense. Sasha suddenly understood how uncomfortable this woman was in her human body, as if in a stiff new suit, only a thousand times worse. She must have felt blind, deaf, imprisoned in a tiny cell—she, a manifested Word, forced to pretend to be human?

Sasha's hatred collapsed like dust over ruins. Adele Victorovna did not choose her path, she never wanted to matriculate at the Institute of Special Technologies, and she never classified herself as a pronoun. She could only be a pronoun, or she could be no one.

Sasha's facial expression must have changed, because Adele Victorovna spoke again.

"Alexandra . . ."

"Please don't call me Alexandra," Sasha said. "Alexandra is . . . she's a very different person."

"Fine, Samokhina." Adele rubbed her hands together. "I want to discuss your individual academic program. Considering that you are a lexical unit outside of traditional grammatical relations . . ."

She faltered, as if afraid that Sasha would be insulted, like a schoolgirl who wasn't invited on a field trip. Sasha waited patiently.

"In Applied Specialty, the end of the fourth year and the beginning of the fifth is pure syntax," Adele continued, sounding apologetic. "And you exist outside syntax. You are Password."

She said the last word with fear and reverence.

"Thanks for the news," Sasha said. She couldn't help herself.

"Actually, the news is that I am going to release you from both winter and summer exams, and you're going to use this time to work on your thesis," Adele said, pursing her lips. "The department has approved your topic; let me tell you what it is."

She chose a blank sheet of paper, picked up a pencil with her left hand, and drew a sequence of symbols without taking the lead tip off the paper. The drawing began to develop in time, dividing and multiplying.

"What do you think this is?" Adele asked casually.

"'Love,'" Sasha muttered.

"Correct," Adele said, lifting the drawing above the desk and turning the sheet upside down, as if tossing the crumbs from a napkin onto the countertop. The symbols spilled down in fine threads and hung in space, forming a three-dimensional figure, like a Christmas tree garland cut by an artisan from a single piece of paper.

"Dynamic construction," Adele continued, and her voice no longer had any hints of pressure or mentorship. "An idea existing in the system of projections is refracted through a multitude of filters and mirrors, reproducing a generic iterative fragment of information."

Above the desk, the multifaceted crystal twitched and grew more complex, gradually becoming opaque. Sasha felt dizzy.

"A topic that certainly allows room for imagination," Adele said. She turned the sheet over again, went over the drawing with an ornate doodle, clicked the tiny cog of her lighter and proceeded to set the paper on fire. The drawing melted into thin air, leaving no particles of ashes or dust behind. "There is nothing complicated in *manifesting* 'love,' except perhaps the volume of work. But now you have plenty of time."

"Adele Victorovna, tell me . . ."

Sasha hesitated. Her ears were ringing, and her tongue seemed stuffed with cotton wool.

"Adele Victorovna, have you had any sexual experiences before matriculating?"

"No," Adele said, showing no sign of surprise. "Why do you ask?"

Sasha could tell that Adele wasn't embarrassed or angry; she didn't seem to be offended by Sasha's audacity. Adele simply wanted to figure out what kind of information her student was asking for, and why this information was needed.

"I am trying to understand your opinion of this . . . this idea," Sasha said. "When you say 'love,' what exactly do you mean?"

Adele gazed at her from across the desk, seemingly waving goodbye to her authority. Sasha could have just as easily asked a trout about its bank loans. Adele could simulate the most complex concept on a piece of paper, but connecting love and sexual experience was an overwhelming task, even though she used to be human.

Sasha was silent, not because she enjoyed seeing Adele helpless. Sasha simply didn't know what to say.

"You see, Alexan—" Adele began, then stopped herself. "I mean, Samokhina. One thing is students' hormonal context during their second year, when the destructive phase of development is replaced by the constructive phase. Word and its place in the Great Speech is a completely different matter. We are talking about serious issues here, about your thesis, your graduation . . ."

"I understand," Sasha said. "Thank you."

He waited at the end of the dim hallway, by the window. Sasha didn't even see him right away. She was lost in her thoughts, and when she suddenly saw a human silhouette, she flinched. She thought it was Yaroslav, that he'd come early, that he was back. Why he was in the dorm, she didn't contemplate. Then it didn't matter, because a second later the man took a step forward and Sasha recognized him.

"Hey," Yegor said, attempting a smile. A weak lightbulb threw some light onto his face. "This weather though . . . Might be time to buy skis."

"Are you waiting for me?" Sasha was taken aback. Since January 13, the day of that dramatic scene in the lobby, Yegor had avoided any conversation or even eye contact.

"Will you send me away?" He tried to sound casual, even jovial. Sasha's heart throbbed. Some time ago she really cared for this guy. Some time ago she hurt him terribly.

Unhurriedly, casually, she unlocked her door.

"Come in. Want some tea?"

"Linden blossom tea?" This time he managed a smile, albeit a strained one. "Do you remember us drinking linden blossom tea?"

"I remember everything," Sasha said, mentally swearing at herself for such a pompous statement.

Yegor stepped inside and stopped in the middle of the room, unsure of what to do next. He gave the whiteboard an uneasy glance.

She followed his eyes. "Have you had any classes with Coach yet?"

"Yeah," he said, sighing with resignation. "I never thought I'd miss any of the faculty from before."

"Analytical Specialty is just another subject, same as the others." Sasha flipped up the switch, and the glass teakettle lit up from the inside. "Coach fails people all the time, his exams are crazy difficult, so . . ."

Yegor flinched, or perhaps Sasha imagined it.

"Black or green?" she asked, pulling out two boxes of tea bags.

"Forgive me, Sasha," Yegor said.

"You are silly." She smiled sadly. "You didn't do anything bad. Or rather, you did more good for me than bad. So black or green?"

He jabbed his finger at one of the boxes: "This one. Tell me something. When you were there, did you see anyone who didn't pass? Zakhar, for example? You were friends, weren't you? When you were there, in that place, after you failed the final exam? Is there anything there, anything at all?"

"You are not the first one to ask me that," Sasha said wearily. "But I don't know. Because, you see, I am an exception to the rule, and I always get lots of crap for it, from both sides."

She smiled, trying to soften her words. Yegor still stood in the middle of the room, seemingly afraid of moving from his spot.

"For a whole year I lived with the knowledge that you failed your exam. I thought of us . . . and of how you saved me. But when I saw you here, at this new campus, I lost it, lost it completely. Please forgive me."

Sasha watched tiny bubbles rise along the glass walls of the teakettle.

"When Words *reverberate,* they are brought back to their human shells to fit into the Great Speech. It's quite a shock, Yegor, I know. I get it."

"They told us that after the final exam we would cease being human," he said with childish resentment. "We were supposed to lose our fear, we'd no longer have any regrets. We'd know harmony. They praised me and told me how hard I was working. They told me a verb in the subjunctive mood was a very rare and valuable lexical unit. Then why . . . ?"

He faltered; everything he wanted to say at this moment would sound like complaining or even whining. Even in the grip of deepest despair, Yegor wanted to maintain his dignity.

Carefully, Sasha picked up the kettle and poured boiling water over the cheap tea bags.

"They lied to us. I mean, it depends on the point of view. In a way, they were telling the truth. We must develop, work, push ourselves, punch above our weight . . . And always understand just a little less than we want to. Like a donkey chasing a carrot: you think you're about to get it, and you grab it, but something new, something incomprehensible, opens up . . . Do you want sugar?"

"Do you have honey?" he asked hopelessly.

"The cheap kind," Sasha said. "But any local Torpa honey is good, it's one of their specialties. Yegor, when you say 'love,' what do you mean?"

"Me?" he said, clearly confused.

"Not right this minute." Sasha opened the nightstand and took out a jar of honey from a row of bottles and boxes. "But at some point you say the word 'love,' or at least you think about it. What is it for you?"

"It's a big idea," Yegor said uncertainly. "Kind of like the sun in the sky. It reflects in every mirror, every puddle, even the muddiest one . . ."

"When you talk about 'love,' you think of the sun?" Squinting, Sasha watched drops of honey slowly resist the forces of surface tension.

"I think of you," Yegor said.

Sasha's hand shook, and honey dripped from the spoon onto the table.

"That's right." He looked solemn, even bitter. "When you were trying to save me back during my second year. Do you remember? When you looked inside me, teaching me, altering me . . . I thought you could do anything. And that *anything* was love. Feral love, kind of scary. So many people are afraid of you, do you know that? There is this humming around you, like a transformer box. Or a swarm of hornets."

"Love as a swarm of hornets," Sasha muttered. "I should include it in the summary."

"It's not funny," Yegor said reproachfully. "Do you remember how you saved me? Do you remember?"

Of course she did.

She remembered everything.

He was a second-year student, and he was failing his exams. Sasha, a third year, broke into Yegor's memory, helped him change from the inside, and thus saved him from failure.

Yegor was the last one to come out of the exam. Sasha was waiting for him by the entrance to the auditorium. When she saw him, she screamed, "Tell me!" He stepped forward and embraced her. He staggered, holding on to Sasha like a drunk holding on to a tree.

"How did you do it? How did you manage? How?" Tears rolled down his unshaven hollow cheeks. He knew the price of academic failure. He had a mother, a father, a younger brother. Three failed attempts meant three untimely deaths.

Sasha's thoughts made a leap to two years prior to that fateful day. Two years earlier, Kostya, then a first year, failed a test and buried his grandmother. He lay in bed with his face to the wall. Everyone was sure he was going to fail the rest of his finals. Sasha came into his room

214

and made him study, made him work, and even slapped him on the face. She saved Kostya, even Farit admitted it back then.

And if she had never been born, never come to Torpa, never studied at the institute, then no one would have been there to save Yegor and Kostya. Both failed their exams, both lost their minds from their unbearable losses, and both disappeared and were forgotten like hundreds of other losers, hundreds of other Words that never *reverberated*. Why didn't Sasha think of that before?

Yegor left. Two cups with tea dregs remained on the table, two soggy tea bags lay on a saucer like dead aliens. Sasha walked around the room, from the door to the window and back. Yegor, a verb in the subjunctive mood, expressing wishes, considering hypothetical situations. The one who comes to Sasha when she particularly needs him. The one who tells her what she absolutely needs to hear at that very moment.

Farit had no absolute power over her. He'd even admitted it himself.

"I can," Sasha said out loud. "It's just an assignment for Analytical Specialty. I can do it."

Fuel. Energy. Information. She needed to stop lying to herself, stop justifying something for which there was no excuse, and instead cancel all lies and pull her love out of shit and filth. And if she could find, locate, create, project a probability in which Yaroslav did not betray anyone—not Sasha, not his wife or kids or his father—if this probability was even possible, Sasha would *manifest* it and erase Farit's presence in her life, and that meant she could erase him altogether, and that meant . . .

She stopped herself from thinking any further. She stepped up to the whiteboard and picked up a new marker.

First line is the horizon. A silver spark appears over the horizon. The aircraft hovers on the glide slope, then touches the runway, rather clumsily, because Yaroslav is not the one piloting the plane, and only Yaroslav can land so gently and so smoothly that his passengers miss the moment of contact with the ground. He disembarks along with the passengers and sees Sasha; he's caught off guard. Sasha leaves the airport by his side. Where are they going? It would be almost April, the sun would be shining, and the birch grove would show its first green leaves.

When I was only a few months old, my father left my mom and disappeared without a trace, Sasha tells him.

He tries to look neutral. He says, *How sad.* Or, *I'm sorry.* He looks guilty, and his voice sounds bitter. He says, *We need to talk, that's why*

I'm here. And Sasha says, *What about earlier? Why couldn't you talk to me before?*

He starts making excuses. He bleats pitifully, in this deep, velvety voice of his, the voice that Sasha remembers as full of gentle power and vital, lifesaving authority. This familiar voice sounds different, and she wants to plug her ears, escape the false notes that scratch her like rusty nails.

Sasha gritted her teeth and went back two measures. Here is Yaroslav walking toward her, a few faint lines etched on his forehead, his green eyes sparkling. He takes her into his arms. His touch is unpleasant to her, and she recoils. He asks questions and worries, and then, when she's done speaking, he smiles: *Nonsense, what wife and kids? I have no wife and kids.*

Sasha froze, convinced for a second that a miracle had occurred. Almost immediately, she saw that he was now lying to her face, not simply hiding the truth. Yaroslav was ready to lie before Sasha was ready to believe him.

"It's not him," Sasha muttered, scrubbing the whiteboard so furiously that sponge fragments flew into the air. "It's definitely not him, I don't even recognize him . . . I made a simulation model of a total freak. Why?"

Three measures back. A new simulation model, a new round of probabilities.

And what about earlier? But couldn't you talk to me before?

I was afraid of losing you. I thought I've lost you so many times. I was so sure I would lose you. I am a coward, yes, but I'm not a villain. I will get a divorce, I promise!

He tries to take her into his arms. His hands are revoltingly sticky and moist. Why does he think he can hold her now? He's sure she would forgive anything and believe anything . . .

Crawling along the whiteboard, the dry sponge screeched. *There has to be a way for this diagram to have a happy ending,* Sasha thought. *Even though the diagrams never have before.* But love is stronger than betrayal. And yet, Sasha cannot love this man.

A dead end. Decay. Misguided path. *Love* is a tremendous universal concept, but whatever it is that Sasha thinks of as her love is nothing but a minor distorted projection. A reflection of the sun in a mirror stained with fly specks.

She slammed her fist into the whiteboard, making the wall shudder. She could *manifest* love on a piece of paper, making the projection unfold in multiple dimensions, splitting in two, then four, like a fertilized cell. Such an image made her pause.

What was she thinking when she wanted to have Yaroslav's child?

She dropped the worn-out black marker on the floor and picked up a new blue one. She had to remember Yaroslav as he was, recall New Year's Eve, design the model from memory, add it to the diagram, and re-create love—any version of it, even the most imperfect one. *I will get a divorce, I promise. She's playing games, refusing to sign the papers, I have to take her to court. If you only knew what this woman is like . . . I wanted to settle this business first, and then tell you all about it . . .*

Streams of platitudes and clichés will pour out of his mouth, but his face, his voice, and his scent will remain the same.

Sasha fell on her knees and vomited. Gold coins with a rounded symbol on the reverse rolled all over the laminate. This happens when one is changing from the inside, overcoming an invisible obstacle. This happens to prospective students right before they get the official letter confirming their enrollment in the Institute of Special Technologies.

I am not giving up.

Sasha made herself get up from the floor. She picked up a red marker and stepped to the whiteboard.

A sunny February morning found Sasha at the Torpa airport. The heat barely worked, and a cloud of fog hung in front of her face. There were only a few people waiting at arrivals. On the electronic schedule, a single line announced the next flight was on time. Sasha stared at the panoramic window. In the last few months she'd learned where the glide slope began. She knew the point in the sky where the aircraft was supposed to appear.

And it did appear. Another man was behind the steering wheel. Sasha could make out his white shirt and black tie, his uniform epaulettes, a round aging face. He spoke into the microphone. Behind him, separated by a bulkhead and a door, was a half-empty business class. Yaroslav sat on the left. He looked very sad, lost in his thoughts. The plastic shade covered the window next to him. The flight attendant— someone Yaroslav clearly knew—said something, pointing at the window, and Yaroslav smiled crookedly and raised the shade to prepare for the landing.

The aircraft descended, hovering between the sky and the ground. Visibility was excellent. The wind—moderate. The landing strip—clear of any debris.

Sasha blinked. She mentally deconstructed the image into separate processes, pulled the invisible elements out onto the surface, and connected the evidence with the probabilities. *You don't owe me an explanation. I trust you. Love is stronger.*

A sheet of glass cracked, a flaw missed during the technical inspection. An airstream pulled the chubby-faced pilot out of the cockpit. The headwind caught and carried him along the row of windows, and the passengers may even have had a chance to be surprised. A split second, and the body of the pilot was sucked into the engine. The engine blew up, the wing broke. Concealed by a thick cloud of smoke, the aircraft dove into the landing strip and instantly went up in flames. It had plenty of fuel on board, all ready for a round trip.

The lines drawn on the whiteboard fused into the surface slowly, settling down along with the melting painted tin. The room stunk of burned aircraft fuel, flakes of soot floated around the room. Someone kicked the door and possibly even slammed a chair into it.

"Samokhina, are you nuts? Have you totally lost your mind? Open up, now!"

Shadows flickered on the balcony; someone's hand reached inside the window, then unlocked the balcony door. Lisa jumped into the room, snow on her sneakers and an unlit cigarette in her mouth.

Lisa observed the room, inspecting what was left of the whiteboard. The cigarette still clamped between her teeth, she called Sasha an idiot, then tore off the whiteboard, hissing as if from a painful burn. She dragged the whiteboard over to the door and unlocked it, letting in a bunch of her classmates.

Sasha sat under the desk leaning against the wall, like a child playing forts.

"Take it away," Lisa shouted to someone in the hallway. "Take it and burn it behind the building. Pour some gasoline over it. Third years, get the fuck out of here!"

Kostya kneeled down and peeked under the desk. Sasha looked back at him.

"How can I help you? Do you want a cup of tea? Coffee? Do you want me to call my father?"

"Don't," Sasha said, barely moving her lips.

Lisa appeared by Kostya's side.

"What the hell was that, Samokhina? Are you crazy?"

"Probably," Sasha muttered. "Tell me something—if you could decide whether your Lyosha dies or becomes a real loser and an asshole, what would you choose?"

"Stupid question," Lisa barked. "Dead people are easier to love."

Both the balcony door and the door to her room were wide open; an icy draft crawled along the floor.

"What the fuck was that?" Lisa asked curtly.

"Love," Sasha said.

"You are a whack job," Lisa said, clicking her lighter. "Come out, stupid bitch. You'll freeze your ass off under there."

"Don't smoke in my room," Sasha said, scowling. Lisa wanted to argue, but took one look at Sasha and demonstratively put out her cigarette.

Unsteady on her feet, Sasha climbed from underneath the desk and took a look around the room. Yegor was standing by the balcony, silent and ghostlike. The rest of her classmates crowded the doorway.

"Close the door!" Lisa barked. "From the other side!"

Yegor took a step back, his slippers treading the snow.

"You can stay," Sasha said. "Just close the balcony door. It's chilly."

Anna and Yulia politely disappeared. The only people in the room, which still smelled of burned aviation fuel, were Sasha, Lisa, Kostya, and Yegor, a shadow by the balcony door.

"Lisa, I promised you something," Sasha said. "And I can't do it. I am sorry."

"Fuck," Lisa muttered. "But you can't get off that easily, baby girl."

"Are you trying to monitor my data streams?" Sasha asked, smiling sadly. "Here, catch this."

She placed her hand on Lisa's shoulder, over the thin fabric of her black hoodie. She felt the close presence of Lisa's informational system, as aggressive as sulfuric acid. A split second later she took her hand away and sat down on her bed, dizzy and drained. Lisa remained standing, looking inward, as pale as a new bandage.

"There is nothing I can do to him," Sasha said hopelessly. "He's everywhere."

"Fuck," Lisa said again, trying to process the information Sasha shared with her.

"A cemetery is his projection," Sasha continued, her eyes focused on something beyond her and yet unseeing. "A hospital is his shadow. A maternity clinic is also his projection. A scratch with a bead of blood. Endorphins produced during sex. All properties of matter, all laws of the Great Speech. I can't erase him."

"Are you hallucinating?" Yegor took a step toward her, then stopped, peering into her face, his eyes full of professional compassion. He must have done this during his pre-Torpa medical school phase, trying to establish doctor-patient contact. "You talked about love . . ."

"And you talked about the sun." Sasha nodded. "The concept of love as the sun reflected in clean mirrors and muddy puddles. You see, Yegor: There is no sun. A multitude of puddles try to build a sun, to create an idea, to reach the sky with its feeble rays. Farit wants me to believe in love as an idea and to light up the sun."

"So do it." Yegor took another step forward, his eyes now full of hope. "Do it, because no one else can. It's yours—"

"If I *reverberate*, trying to counteract fear with my love, this pompous act will turn into a circus," Sasha spoke, measuring her words. "The big L-word concept died inside me like a hamster in a jar of bleach. My fear is toxic; all I can broadcast is the absence of will, depression, and the inevitability of death. I will endlessly reproduce Farit, for all eternity, and that's exactly what he wants. Coach knew it from the very beginning. Sterkh knew it in advance. And only I kept hoping for something, dreaming. And he owns the dreams, too."

Kostya stood by the desk, inspecting a faceted glass half filled with gold coins. His face looked painfully strained.

"You fucked it up." Lisa spoke in a sonorous, aloof voice that reminded Sasha of timpani played at a funeral. "You are so much stronger than the rest of us put together. Stronger than everyone who's ever studied in this institute! And you allowed Farit to turn you into a wet rag . . . a piece of shit! You are refusing to even try just because all men are jerks!"

"Not all of them," Sasha said wearily. "But I don't need all men. I needed that one."

With a quick pained glance at Sasha, Kostya carefully placed the heavy glass back on the table.

"Bullshit," Lisa said curtly. "The whole 'he's the only one for me,' 'my half,' 'my soul mate'—it's nothing but a manipulative trick, a souvenir from the patriarchal antiquity, something that should have been discarded a long time ago. What does it have to do with love?"

"What about your Lyosha?" Sasha asked.

"Never heard of him," Lisa said, scowling. She took two leaping steps over to Kostya, grabbed his head, and kissed him on the lips. At first he couldn't get free, and then went limp, submitting to her. Sasha watched them kiss, realizing that a grammatical link was developing between these two. There was a reason Adele paired them up. At some point the Great Speech would use them as a single unit to link fear and hope, give shape, create meanings, grow ideas like crystals in an oversaturated solution, build projections, weave together DNA strands . . .

"Sasha," Yegor said softly, and she remembered he was still there. He licked his lips nervously.

"Do you want me to . . ."

She thought he was going to offer to have sex with her right there and then while Lisa and Kostya were getting busy. Yegor continued after a tiny pause.

"Do you want me to speak to Yaroslav when he comes back? Lisa is right, it's at least worth a try."

It surprised her, and that somehow made her feel better. "No, but thank you for the offer." Sasha gave him a crooked smile.

She checked the hallway, where her classmates were still waiting. Sasha came back, stepped around Lisa and Kostya, still gripping each other, ruffled Yegor's hair as if he were a little boy, and opened the balcony door, letting in the raw March night. She climbed onto the railing and dove as if into a pool, but not down—up, into the sky.

"Dmitry Dmitrievich. I declare the Will of the Verb: I want to annul myself, the original idea of me, and all possible projections."

She knew that at this moment she would not think of the burning house and of the crashed aircraft. She would think of the night flight over Torpa. Of all the roofs that Sterkh had shown her a while ago, all her usual routes above turrets and weather vanes. Not the stone city where a monster sat in the tower, but the ribbon of the river seen from above, and the stars reflected in the water, and the light feathers fluttering in the wind.

Coach gazed at her through his expanding diaphragm pupils. Sasha thought that something in the future was being altered at that very moment. He pulled out his stopwatch, froze for a second, changed his mind, and got up from his desk in auditorium 1.

"Come with me."

Sasha followed him into the corridor. Since yesterday, she had known that the road would seem long, but she would not think of the wrecked car in the middle of the highway next to Alexandra Samokhina's dead body. She would recall New Year's Eve, the dark bedroom, and the fireworks—inside and out.

With every step she took, she brought back a little more of Yaroslav, the man he used to be. The man she believed him to be.

Coach was in a rush. The vestibule seemed as enormous as a city square. Sasha smiled faintly, saying good-bye to the walls, the windows, and the concierge booth. She reached the steps leading to the cafeteria and farther down to the administration office in the basement. Sasha hesitated, falling half a step behind.

"Sasha! Sasha dear!"

This voice did not belong here. It sounded wrong within these walls. Sasha turned: clad in a winter coat and a ridiculous woolen hat, Anton Pavlovich was crossing the vestibule. He didn't seem to notice either the equestrian statue or the suddenly alert concierge.

"Sasha, I need to talk to you, it's urgent. I've been looking for you."

"Let's go," Coach said tensely. "Hurry up."

"I beg your pardon." As Anton Pavlovich approached, he must have just noticed Coach towering over Sasha. "This must be a bad time . . . I just need to tell Sasha something very important. A message."

Coach squeezed Sasha's arm above the elbow, making her wince. She tensed up, and he immediately released his grip.

"I can't force you, but—"

"Just a minute," the old man said, fumbling inside his inner pocket. "Oh, here it is. You see, Sasha . . ."

It was a crumpled sheet of paper with three handwritten lines, the words large and uneven: "Sasha, you are not responding to me. My dad will give you this letter. I will be back on Sunday. Bringing my daughters. Please wait for me."

Anton Pavlovich gazed at Sasha, seeing nothing around them, and his lenses looked milky blue, like fine porcelain.

Sasha looked up. Coach watched her, his face impassive and his eyes empty.

The plane rolled up nearly to the very entrance of the airport. A chubby-faced middle-aged pilot remained in the cockpit, shuffling through some papers. His partner spoke softly into his phone; his smile was so predatory that Sasha wondered if he wanted to devour the woman he was speaking to rather than simply sleep with her. The sun poked through the clouds, reflecting in the windshield. The glass was new, replaced after the most recent technical inspection had suspected a hidden defect.

The passengers descended in a single file. Yaroslav came out last, holding the hands of two tiny girls. The girls were identical and looked quite focused. Sasha studied their faces from a distance. Jealous, she wanted to see Yaroslav's projections in the children's faces but found none—all they reflected were the recent excitement over the flight, a little tension, a hint of exhaustion. The luggage carousel began to move, offering the passengers the first few suitcases.

"I checked our luggage," Yaroslav said instead of a greeting. "We have a lot of stuff."

"Hello," Sasha said to the girls. "What are your names?"

The girls frowned and hid behind Yaroslav's back.

"Katya and Dasha," Yaroslav said distractedly. "I see our suitcase. We have presents for Grandpa in there."

In the middle of the room, two children sat on the wooden floor, rummaging through a pile of old toys the likes of which they had never seen. Perfectly identical, the sisters had very different personalities: Katya was sharp and decisive, Dasha thoughtful and phlegmatic. They were a little bit spoiled, good-natured, and inquisitive. As soon as Anton Pavlovich brought a box of old toys from the attic, the sisters forgot their initial mistrust of the new place, regained their confidence, and openly expressed their delight.

Sitting cross-legged next to them, Anton Pavlovich demonstrated how to make a train move and a bunny to play a kettledrum. Some of the toys were the same age as the house. It had been several decades since they were last touched by a child's hand.

Never having seen him before, Katya and Dasha now treated Anton Pavlovich as their best friend. Waiting for his guests only an hour ago, Anton Pavlovich had nervously wiped his glasses over and over again: "I am so afraid of not being able to connect to them, Sasha, my dear. Children don't normally enjoy the company of strange old men, especially if they have never seen them before . . ."

Katya and Dasha were not his granddaughters. They weren't Yaroslav's kids. Reading the informational streams from the other room, Sasha was torn by the contradictions. Yaroslav sat a few feet away from her. All she needed to do was to reach for him and touch him, and then she would understand everything, but that would mean a breach of trust . . .

. . . which he'd already ruined, seemingly beyond repair.

"When you are next to me," Yaroslav said softly, "I realize that the world does not work the way we think it works."

"It doesn't," Sasha agreed. She recalled the airplane in a cloud of smoke on the dark runway.

Yaroslav sighed.

"We are only here for three days. I wanted to make sure Dad met the girls at least once. Who knows what will happen later."

"No one knows," Sasha agreed.

"They are moving to another country," Yaroslav said heavily. "With their mother. And a new father."

"You are being secretive again," Sasha said. "You are not telling me the whole story. The last time I paid quite a steep price for your silent games. And so did other people."

"I am sorry," he said, clenching his jaws. "I don't know how to say it. I am not afraid of anything. Just this. I can't talk about this."

"When did you find out the girls are not yours?" Sasha asked.

He jumped up as if she'd slapped him.

"What's the difference? They are mine! How dare you ask me something like that?"

"I'm sorry." Sasha bit her lip. "It's someone else's power over you. As if someone cut off your arms. It doesn't matter who has whose chromosomes, it's just someone else's power over you. When did you find out?"

Yaroslav turned to the window and placed his palms on the windowsill.

"When they were one year old," Anton Pavlovich said softly. He stood in the doorway, leaning against the frame. Cartoon music was playing in the living room. "Things went wrong much earlier. They were so close, and then they were strangers. But they still wanted to save the marriage, for the sake of the children."

"And for the sake of the children, you are now letting them go," Sasha said.

"Dad." Yaroslav was still facing the window. "Please, watch the kids. Be there with them. There are outlets, scissors, wires, all that stuff."

"Oh." Anton Pavlovich checked the living room and sighed with relief. "Of course. Here I go. They are so sweet. They remind me of you when you were little."

He left, closing the door behind him.

"I am sorry," Yaroslav said, staring out the window. "This is very difficult for him. He was so happy when I got married, and married for love. And so happy when the girls were born. He didn't get a chance to see them—at first he was sick . . ."

He fell silent, but Sasha caught his unsaid words like smoke rings in the air: . . . *and then the kids' biological father laid claim to the woman and her daughters. And you, you refused to admit your loss and fought for what you considered yours. And the woman was torn between the two of you. It was a tragedy, not a farce, but you won't tell me anything about it. And I won't try to get into your head and learn all the details, which means this will still be hanging between us.*

"My dad doesn't care about chromosomes either," Yaroslav said softly. "These children are mine. Because I love them. Sasha, if you tell me you don't want to ever see me again, I will understand. Just like I understood why you weren't responding to me."

Sasha laughed. He turned sharply, as if bitten by a wasp.

"Is that funny to you?"

"I love you," Sasha said. "I think the sun is up."

In the middle of the night they opened a jar of last year's preserves and split a loaf of bread, spreading soft raspberry jam on thick slices with a huge knife.

The girls slept in the other bedroom, and Anton Pavlovich stayed with them, stretched out on a narrow cot.

Sasha felt like someone who woke after a long nap and remembered their name. Everything she thought of as significant took a step back into the shadows. Everything that seemed impossible became the only truth: the scent of a man, a potted geranium on the windowsill, the handle of a kitchen knife. The future. That night Sasha felt the future just as mundanely and accurately as the bread in her hand and the raspberry jam on her tongue.

Yaroslav said that his contract expired in the summer, and he would take a long vacation and come to Torpa and live here until Sasha's graduation. Cautiously, Sasha objected, saying that a long vacation might cause some issues with Yaroslav's future contracts. She used simple words, but still, chills went up her spine and along her arms. She'd been living without a future for far too long. She'd walked toward total darkness for so long that when she finally saw the light ahead, she didn't even recognize it right away.

Yaroslav assured her that even after a long vacation, a specialist of his level would have no problems getting another job in his industry. "And if they don't want me back, I'll become a cabdriver here, in Torpa," he said carelessly. Sasha listened, her pupils widening, and the dim kitchen grew bigger and brighter, even though the only source of light was a tiny lightbulb above the table.

The girls woke up and shuffled to the bathroom, still half asleep. Anton Pavlovich fussed over them, showed them the way, switched the lights on and off, turned on the water, and handed them a towel. Yaroslav listened to the noises, apologized to Sasha, and went to help his father. He whispered something, brought over glasses of water, an apple, a pack of tissues, an old stuffed bunny.

Sasha didn't mind the pauses in their conversation; on the contrary, she watched the activity with a great deal of sympathy. The old man must have felt that night that time was discrete. Two more days would pass, and the girls would disappear from his life, possibly for good. But these two days and two nights were indefeasible and irrevocable.

It was both easier and harder for Yaroslav. Some time ago, he'd held these girls in his arms and thought of the future. The future that eventually was replaced by a catastrophe. But unlike his father, Yaroslav was going to live for many years, and somewhere along his path (and obviously, he perceived time as linear), he was hoping to restore his fatherhood.

Eventually, the girls fell asleep, and Anton Pavlovich snored softly next to them. Yaroslav picked Sasha up, just like he did on New Year's Eve, and carried her into his room.

Only one more year left, Sasha thought, listening to his breathing, wrapping her arms around his smooth bare shoulders, caressing him when he began breathing faster and shivering as if from a chill. *Time is a grammatical concept, but I still have a year and two weeks left.*

Yaroslav began to talk in his sleep, quickly and anxiously. Sasha held him tighter, and he relaxed and hugged her in return without waking up. Sasha ran her hand along his back, tracing the line of his hips, trying to memorize every centimeter of his warm skin, every birthmark, and every hair. Yaroslav opened his eyes. Sasha saw his irises that resembled a moon passing over the green sun disk, or a deep pond lightly veiled in sleepy fog.

"Go back to sleep," Sasha said, smiling and stroking his head.

The fifth years take their final exam in April, on the fifteenth. They defend their theses, followed by graduation. Only one year left.

I am using him, Sasha thought, gently rocking Yaroslav in her arms like a wave rocking a ship. *Fuel, energy, information. I needed him to support me, so that the Word desecrated by fear could lean onto a new idea and resurrect itself, to reverberate, to erase Farit, and actualize as Password.*

She lay in bed, holding a man in her arms, and she also burst out like a cloud of steam from a cauldron, and flew up above the house. She saw Torpa's lights below and the forest on the horizon. She spun like a spinning top from Anton's attic: *I don't want to!*

I don't want to use anyone. Don't want to complete my mission. I don't want to change the world. Enough—I just want to live!

Yaroslav stirred with a deep heavy sigh. He turned and moved on top of Sasha, enveloping her with his body. Sasha returned into her physical body like a djinn coming back into the lamp. At that moment, her future felt as tangible as the mattress under her shoulders and his warm hands on her skin.

"Everything will be fine until May. I will look after Anton Pavlovich, you go ahead and do what you need to do."

"I really don't want to," he said, staring wearily above the potted geranium at the yard where the snow continued to melt. "Two months, almost three, being cut out of life with rusty scissors."

"But the rest of our life belongs to us," Sasha said. "I am not going into space, and you are not going to war. Imagine how much squealing and shrieking there will be when we finally see each other?"

"And who's going to be doing all the shrieking?" he asked cautiously.

"Me, of course," she said, laughing. "I will be shrieking and jumping onto your shoulders, and it's not something I can do in everyday life. But since we're going to be meeting at the airport, people will understand."

"Then I plan on doing some growling," he said after a moment of consideration. "But very softly. And later. Not at the airport. If that's all right with you."

"I'm fine with growling," Sasha allowed graciously.

On June 1, when he returned, she'd place a temporary anchor *then* and create a time loop. She and Yaroslav would live peacefully until August 31, and Sasha would replace the anchor with a new one, *now*. Out of everything she'd been taught at the institute, only one skill would be useful, the ability to make time loops.

Yaroslav would never know anything. For him, every summer would be like new and start from the very beginning. It was such a nefarious and yet beguiling thought. *Will I be able to resist, or will I go for it after all?*

"What are you thinking about?" Yaroslav asked as he opened the window and filled the birdfeeder with fresh seeds, possibly for the last time this season.

"I'm thinking about summer," Sasha said sincerely.

She thought: *All these fantasies are nothing but a tribute to my cowardice. I am ready to do anything just to be able to steal a few years of normal happy human life. To have a future is a luxury for which I must pay.*

I will find a solution, of course. But it will be much later.

"To the attention of Alexandra Samokhina."

For one insane moment Sasha thought she'd gotten a letter from Sterkh. He was infallibly punctual, and they arrived always at eight in the morning.

It was eight in the morning. A dorm room. Sasha had just gotten back from a run and taken a shower. Anton Pavlovich had checked into a clinic for his annual physical. The sun was shining, it was April, young grass was poking through the earth, and sparrows chirped happily. "What are the sparrows singing on this last day of chill? We live, we breathe, we made it, and we are living still!"

"The department of Specialty of the Institute of Special Technologies has reached an agreement on allowing Alexandra Samokhina to defend her senior thesis in advance, prior to the previously scheduled date. The event will take place in the assembly hall on April 15 at twelve o'clock."

"The department made the decision," Farit said on the phone. "You're ready, Sasha. You're in perfect form right now."

"What did Dmitry Dmitrievich say?" Sasha asked. She pressed her forehead to the cold plastic wall of the first-floor phone booth.

"He expressed a different opinion," Farit said, and she somehow knew the smug, feral look on his face. "But the majority of the faculty decided you were ready."

"I . . . " Sasha faltered like a child trying to make up a taunting rhyme. "I . . . I, as Password, will actualize my freedom. I will express my will to continue my studies for another year!" She heard her voice fill with confidence, followed by triumph. "And no one can force me to graduate. Not even you!"

"All right," he said after a pause. "In that case, you need to go to the dean's office, right now, and fill out a form. Rules are rules."

For a few seconds Sasha stood still, listening to the silence in the receiver. She didn't think he'd give up that easily.

By the entrance to the dorm, she ran into Kostya. He ran out of the alley leading to Sacco and Vanzetti Street. He looked stricken.

"Sasha, have you seen Lisa?"

"What happened?" Sasha asked.

"She got reported . . . " Kostya struggled to speak. "Adele reported her. That bitch."

Offering no more information, he sped across the courtyard toward the institute. Sasha ran after him, not quite sure why.

Farit Kozhennikov stood by the scheduling board, studying it like a diligent student. Sasha and Kostya ran into the vestibule from a side door while Lisa entered the building through the main entrance. Farit turned as if Lisa had called his name, even though Lisa never uttered a sound.

She took her hand out of the pocket of her light-colored trench. The tiny handgun looked like a toy, but the shot rang out unexpectedly loud. Lisa Pavlenko had finally gathered enough courage to do what she'd been dreaming of doing since her first year at the institute. Since she was chosen as a prospective student, to be precise.

Lisa walked across the vestibule, pulling the trigger over and over. She had six rounds in that gun. A few times her wrist was jerked forward by the recoil, but overall she did well: Two bullets went into the scheduling board, and the board flickered like a broken advertisement. Two bullets went into Farit's chest, one into his neck, and one into the right lens of his dark glasses, and the lens shattered into tiny pieces.

Farit didn't move. Lisa stood three paces away from him, squeezing the emptied gun in her hand. Farit took off his broken glasses. Both of his eyes were perfectly whole. He glanced at Lisa, then turned his gaze on Sasha, who stood frozen on the spot by the side entrance.

"No," Sasha whispered.

Kostya threw himself across the vestibule, placing himself in front of Farit and hiding Lisa behind his back.

"You have to understand that it's just a nervous breakdown . . ."

The vestibule was empty. Kostya's voice echoed, bouncing off the walls. Farit turned away from Sasha and looked at his son.

"You were put together to study, not to fuck," Farit said with regret. "Your faculty warned you from the very beginning that you must work hard, and that not everyone would make it to graduation."

Lisa dropped the gun, and it made a hollow sound on the polished stone. The gun was a projection, a nicely cleaned and oiled one, but a projection nevertheless, a distorted shadow that stood no chance in the battle of ideas.

Sasha took a step forward; Lisa turned her head, and their eyes met. Lisa stretched her lips in a contemptuous and yet beseeching smile.

"Samokhina . . ."

Kostya backed away, staring at something beyond the scheduling board. Sasha saw him from the periphery of her vision, but didn't check what he was looking at—she couldn't take her eyes off Lisa.

Samokhina, Lisa said again, moving her lips without a sound.

She turned away from Sasha and walked toward the assembly hall, rushing as if she were late for class. Something was happening there, in the dim cavern of the vestibule. From the corner of her eye, Sasha saw the stallion step from foot to foot under the stone rider.

Kostya hung on Lisa's shoulders. She shook him off, took a few more steps, fell on her knees, and held her hand out to someone, probably a product of her hallucination. Stumbling, as if she'd just learned how to walk, Sasha ran across the vestibule, and at that moment the bell rang, sharp, prissy, and authoritative.

Sasha fell and went blind for a moment. The bell shut up. The vestibule was empty, Farit had disappeared, and the wounded scheduling board flickered irregularly. Kostya stared at the entrance to the assembly hall. Sasha came closer, saw his face, and recoiled.

"I saw them," Kostya said softly. "Zakhar . . . all our guys . . . all of them. All the ones who failed, who didn't pass. Those who couldn't pass the retakes. It's worse than death, Sasha. Zhenya is there, too. I saw her. And Lisa . . . she's there, too, now."

Kostya sobbed.

"Miss, are you going to fill out that form or not? Are we adding you to the list or aren't we? Can you make up your mind already?"

The computer keys clicked and clacked just like the typewriter's keys years ago. A portly assistant with a string of coral beads around her neck stared at Sasha with the inimitable expression of *There is just one of me and a whole lot of you.*

"Go ahead and file the departmental decision," Sasha said. "I will take the exam ahead of schedule as per faculty's suggestion."

"I don't like it at all," he said. His anxiety traveled tens of thousands of kilometers. "How can you take that exam now if you were preparing to take it next year?"

"Because the delay was just that—to delay," Sasha said. "But I've passed all the other tests ahead of schedule, and my thesis is ready. It's an awesome thesis. The committee will be tickled pink."

Her dorm room was clean and strangely empty. The tablet lay in front of her on the desk, under the perfectly scrubbed, dazzlingly new whiteboard. The headphones cord was worn out, and at first Sasha was worried until she had a fleeting thought: she wouldn't have to fix it or buy a new one.

"Sasha," Yaroslav said after a pause. "I promised not to ask any questions. But now . . . please tell me."

"I will, I promise." Sasha pulled aside one of the headphones and rubbed her ear, reddening from her lies.

"Sasha," he said heavily. "I feel like . . . Please, don't be silent. I want to understand what's going on."

Sasha shut her eyes, holding the headphones with both hands.

"Yaroslav . . . remind me, where are you right now?"

"Vancouver."

"It's so far," Sasha said softly. "When I told you I was Password—I told you the truth. I am the Word that begins the new reality. During my exam I am supposed to create a new world, a world free of fear. I am going to try . . . but if I make a mistake, the world will end tomorrow."

Silence fell.

She opened her mouth to say something else, and in that moment, she knew he believed her. He knew exactly what she was saying. No one outside the institute had even been capable of that—she had no doubt there were some inside the institute who couldn't quite grasp it. If Sasha's mom was in Yaroslav's place, she would have fussed, asked questions, inquired about drugs, called the doctor . . .

I will try to avoid making mistakes. I have everything I need to succeed, I studied for so long. And now I think I can make it.

No—I am sure I can.

He said nothing. The silence was thicker than in Sterkh's headphones, a special kind of silence. The kind of silence that showed that Yaroslav knew how the world worked and Sasha's role in it.

"Our world is full of evil, it's been corrupted from the very beginning. I will create a new macrostructure, free of informational trash. Free of errors. Are you still there? Yaroslav?"

"Yes." She could tell by his voice how much effort this short word required of him.

Sasha felt dizzy.

"Sasha, I never bought fire extinguishers for my dad," Yaroslav said softly.

"No, you didn't."

"And that means, his house burned down and my father is dead."

"But he's alive," Sasha said.

A long pause followed. Tens of thousands of kilometers crackled on the communication line.

"I don't know what to say," Yaroslav said.

"Say something to help me not be scared tomorrow," Sasha said, her voice unexpectedly thin and reedy, like a child's.

"Do not be afraid," he said, struggling to breathe.

"No." Sasha shut her eyes. "You cannot express it through negation. It's not going to work."

"Don't go anywhere without me! Wait for me!"

"No, not like that. Talk to me. Talk to me as if I'm your passenger, and we're encountering turbulence . . ."

A pause. Sasha stood still, pressing her headphones to her ears with both hands.

"Dear passengers," he said, his voice calm, deep, and quite imperative. "We are encountering turbulence, it is perfectly normal . . . I mean, no, it's not normal, but you have me! I will be with you soon! I have to be with you. I am on my way!"

Sasha felt thousands of kilometers between them turning into hundreds of thousands of parsecs.

On April 15, she stepped over the threshold of the Institute of Special Technologies for the last time.

Sasha walked across the dimly lit vestibule; for a moment she thought she could see the same people Kostya had seen earlier—those who had failed the exam. Those who didn't make it to graduation. Distorted shadows that ceased to be human and never became Words. Sasha slowed down her steps, feeling her hair stand on end, but when she reached the equestrian statue, she was met by her classmates and dorm neighbors, familiar and still very much alive.

They formed a mob and an array simultaneously, as if implanted into an invisible crystal lattice. The third years stood apart from the others. Yegor stared above everyone's heads as if he'd forgotten what he showed up for.

Kostya stood still a few feet away. Entering the space between those two, Sasha swayed a little and felt light-headed. Ten steps remained to the entrance to the assembly hall, its doors wide-open in a welcoming gesture. Five steps.

"Samokhina!"

Sasha blinked. She thought Lisa was calling her name. But no: Dima Dimych stood in the doorway, empty just a second ago. He was dressed in a tracksuit, and around his neck he wore a whistle and a stopwatch on a wide ribbon.

Sasha stopped.

"You are doing exactly what *he* wants you to do," said the one who stood in her way. "You are a powerful fighter who was raised specifically to be smashed into pieces during the final competition. You were cultivated to demonstrate the superiority of the reigning champion. Forgive me this metaphor—or don't. But heed what it means."

He spoke the truth, and his words made the straw on the exhausted camel's back turn into a rock even as Sasha felt her knees buckle.

"There are battles that can be won only by abstaining," Coach said softly.

"No," Sasha said.

He could not help but retreat from her path.

The windows were tightly shut: no one in this hall needed a stream of photons to see. The assembly hall, and the stage, and the creaky chairs, and the table in front of the dusty curtain, looked like an old, ripped shell of a place, forgotten set pieces that should have been tossed out a long time ago, but no one cared enough to do it. A ramp loomed over the stage, its dark projectors and a long, handwritten poster hailing back to time immemorial: GAUDEAMUS IGITUR, the poster said. JUVENES DUM SUMUS!

"Samokhina, a verb in the imperative mood. Password."

"Password," another voice said. It sounded distant, as if two hundred years passed between Sasha and the voice's origin. "The department's decision regarding the defense of your thesis ahead of the academic deadline has been reversed. Your thesis is annulled. Please sign here."

Sasha smiled. She no longer needed anyone's permission.

Then and *now* merged into a single point.

This city was given to her by Sterkh. It was a concept of a city, and Torpa was one of its projections. The memory of Sterkh had given her strength.

Tiled roofs, high walls, narrow windows. The shutters creaked, the wind breathed lightly, and the air was scented with smoke and fireplaces. Sasha walked, feeling the warm stones under her bare feet, and every step got her closer to the central square, to her final effort, to the climax.

Farit Kozhennikov stood beneath the tower, by its arched entrance, leaning on the stones. He held his dark glasses with one broken lens in his left hand. He gazed at Sasha, just like he had gazed at her many times before: pensively, as if trying to figure out how to use her properly.

"This is the end," Sasha said. "You are not feasible. None of you are feasible."

He put his glasses back on. One eye became black and mirrored, the other remained brown, mocking and utterly ruthless.

Sasha slipped out of all set limits, conventions, and boundaries, *possessed* time and turned it inside out like a woolen sock.

A noun is a part of speech that identifies the object in a sentence. A verb is a part of speech that identifies action.

The cat sits on the mat.

Protons and electrons recombine to form monatomic hydrogen. Creation of new atomic nuclei has been completed. Creation of atomic nuclei has begun. Protons are formed.

The cat is big.

Gravitational waves. Fire burns in the middle of the cave. Distorted shadows dance on the walls. A single point devoid of mass or temperature. Time does not exist. This is it.

"This is it," Farit Kozhennikov said.

There was no moan, no squeak in response, there was nothing to waver, no one to hear.

Nothing was tossing and turning in the irrational pocket. Sasha's presence ruined its status and swallowed its meanings. *Nothing* was attempting to dissolve Sasha in the primordial soup of yet *unexisting* ideas, concepts that would become energy and matter once time started up again.

If time started up again.

Sasha strained, trying to locate the fulcrum.

Freedom is an inalienable quality of Password, but freedom is only possible in the presence of evil. Password creates macrostructure eternally burdened by fear and death. A trap.

Those who love are not free. Those who are not free do not love. I love, and that means I am afraid.

"Do not be afraid!"

Wrong statement. Command through negation.

"I refuse to be afraid!"

Wrong statement. Password is always the verb in the imperative mood.

"Love!"

Wrong statement. Love means giving up freedom. Password is free by definition.

The point of *untime*. The original black hole. Not a single star . . .

Except two. Two cold glimmering dots stared at her from above. She recognized that stare: She always recognized it in any projections or reflections. All shades of fear, from chills running down her spine to anxiety-induced diarrhea—everything revolting, humiliating, reeking of sweat and shit. Sasha was locked in the initial point, her consciousness the only thing that existed in the universe—her consciousness and the approaching terror.

"You asked why I needed you," Farit Kozhennikov said. "I needed you for this."

Sasha would have thrashed around like a drowning man in a quagmire, but there was no quagmire, not even atomic nuclei.

"Now do what you are required to do: Use your will, settle down, exist. Release the energy, let matter form, let ideas actualize. Create me all over again, because without me nothing exists. The world cannot exist without fear and death, but without love it would be just fine. Go ahead, Sasha.

"*Reverberate.*"

That's it, Sasha thought. *I am revolting, I am poisoned by fear. I don't want to stare at his dark glasses again, I can no longer put out fires, I am a fire myself.*

"Come on, Sasha," Farit said. "You can't hide from me. Go ahead, create."

Projection of the concept of *impossibility*—like a hole made by an eraser, when you try to erase your mistake, and instead you create a hole, a black hole.

"You are free, but you're not going anywhere; that's quite a paradox. Don't prolong the agony. Create the world, create me . . ."

Password is a part of speech that creates a new reality. A spoiled, burdened-by-evil, corrupted reality where good cannot be separated from evil and life is impossible without death.

"Create atomic nuclei. Separate light from dark. Create gravity, octane number, the wing's airfoil. Go ahead, create your pilot."

He fell silent, likely recognizing his error. The first one. And the last one. *Thank you, Farit,* Sasha said. *You were so close to getting away with it.*

It is not necessary to blow up the future matter with a single word. It is possible to create a single place, time, and space, like a new foothold. A location where the cavity made for fear can be filled with trust.

And only then, using it as fulcrum, synthesize neutral hydrogen.

Soar.

A spark appeared in the dark devoid of light and shadow.

Sasha saw herself in the window seat. She blinked; she had eyes. She pressed her hands to her face—she had hands. Darkness reigned beyond the round windows. A shadow of a white wing outside, a juice box in the pocket of a seat in front of her. Not a single person in sight, just empty rows and luggage compartments. Silence.

"Dear passengers," a voice came from the speakers.

"Fly safely," Sasha said softly. "Don't stop. I will explain everything later."

Spiral galaxies are unbearably beautiful. The milky-white soft spiral arms fold so intricately.

Violet, purple, crimson, turquoise. Deep colors on the background of absolute darkness. That's how the universe unfolds—in silence. A luminous spherical cloud like a wheel set on a silver rod. A pearly blue funnel, glowing softly; cosmic dust and accumulating gases are waiting for their turn. Just a bit longer, and the clouds will move beyond the event horizon. The point of no return.

"Push the thrust level to the max, now," Sasha said to no one and to everyone and to Yaroslav and to herself. "As if you were flying against strong winds in a storm front. Go."

She felt a stream of particles like warm wind on her face. Like someone's hot breath.

"You can't get away from me," Farit said. "You are poisoned by fear, you are going to be terrified."

Not on board his plane, Sasha said silently, looking out the window. You *gave me this.*

She had nothing to look with. She was suspended above the event horizon, and the black hole's pull was becoming unbearable. Time did not exist. She was Password, ready to *reverberate;* she was a girl in the empty cabin of a transcontinental aircraft, despite the fact that continents or even stars did not exist within singularity. She was something else, and she was desperately trying to formulate . . .

"Do not be afraid," his voice came from the speakers.

He pushed the thrust level to the max. Internal combustion engines are useless within singularity, but at that moment Sasha knew what true freedom was. There is no fear in the atomic nucleus. There is no fear in cosmic dust. Photons are not afraid of anything, and gravity is free of fear.

She felt a colossal pull, removing her from the category of *the impossible,* as if being pulled from the sucking mud of a swamp. It led her away from the *Nothing* that filled up the empty space. A stream of photons: glimmering bottom of a clear lake, a school of fish, two soft spiral arms of a milky, pearly nebula.

The network within the nebula transformed into alveoli, a fragment of pulmonary tissue. Pitch-black darkness became dark red. Sasha saw a heart in a net of arteries, tracheal rings, and the tiniest blood vessels of the brain. She saw a human face, so very close to hers, and a desperate eye with a bright iris resembling a passage of the moon over the green disk of the sun.

She *reverberated* and, for the first time, knew she was heard.

ACKNOWLEDGMENTS

I would like to thank Sergey Dyachenko, my husband, friend, and coauthor, for giving me twenty-nine years of love and the joy of creativity. A few days before Sergey passed away, when the sequel to *Vita Nostra* was being prepared for its English-language publication, we were discussing the final book of the trilogy. I made a promise to Sergey that the trilogy will be completed, our plans will be realized, and Sergey's life will continue in the next book.

I would like to thank our daughter, Anastasia, for being in our lives.

I couldn't survive without my family's strength and their empathy. Even though they live so far from me, in New Zealand, I feel their presence every day.

Julia Meitov Hersey, my friend and colleague, is a constant source of warmth and moral support. Her translation of *Vita Nostra* brought us the gift of readership from all over the world. She is family to me.

My dear friend Iva Stromilova was by my side during my darkest days.

Our agent, Josh Getzler, made this publication possible. Jon Cobb, Soumeya Roberts, Ellen Goff, and everyone else at HG Literary—I am so thankful for everything you do.

David Pomerico is a wonderful editor who put a part of his soul into this book. Mireya Chiriboga shines on the editorial side. Many thanks to Robin Barletta and Stephanie Vallejo for production, Allison Bloomer for interior design, Owen Corrigan for the cover design, Amanda Lara for publicity efforts, Michelle Lecumberry for marketing, Karen Richardson for copy editing, and everyone else on the Harper Voyager team.

—*Marina Shyrshova-Dyachenko*

Writing may be solitary business, but translation rarely is. There are so many people—from editors to fellow translators to enthusiastic readers—whose opinions and advice made this English-language translation of Marina and Sergey's brilliant novel possible.

Bilingual readers will notice that *Assassin of Reality* is somewhat different from the original novel. There are new scenes, slightly adjusted storylines, and of course, a different title. Every creative decision was a team effort, the result of many discussions and email threads. Marina was kind enough to consider every suggestion. David Pomerico and Mireya Chiriboga—you are my heroes.

Josh Getzler is the best agent in the world, and I will never tire of saying this. Jon Cobb is my lifeline.

There are so many other people who played different roles in the process that I couldn't possibly name them all. But I do want to mention a few: my fellow translators Anatoly Belilovsky, Lisa C. Hayden, Max Hrabrov, and Alex Shvartsman are all brilliant wordsmiths—the cleverest wordplay and the most creative solutions in *Assassin of Reality* belong to them. Rachel Cordasco included the Dyachenkos' books in her brilliant reference guide to science fiction and fantasy in English translation, *Out of This World*. Gadi Evron let us run amok with a fantastic translation slam on his web show, *Essence of Wonder*. Boris Varshavsky meticulously checked the first draft for technical errors. Frank Kovacs provided his expertise on piloting aircrafts. Sherif Moussa and Tom Sima ensured that my mind stayed active during the COVID-19 isolation months, letting me feed on their encyclopedic knowledge of just about everything; our Linguistic and Pugilistic group chat is still going strong!

My family and friends continue to be paragons of infinite patience, and they make me feel loved and supported every day.

We lost Sergey Dyachenko just a few weeks before the final draft of *Assassin of Reality* was submitted to the publisher. I watched Marina finish the book in accordance with Sergey's wishes; I have never seen anything so beautiful or so inspiring. Sergey wanted to see the sequel to *Vita Nostra* more than anyone in the world. He was convinced that every story has a sequel, and nothing is ever finite. I know somewhere not too far from here, he is happily planning the next book.

—*Julia Meitov Hersey*

ABOUT THE AUTHORS

Marina and Sergey Dyachenko, a former actress and a former psychiatrist, are coauthors of more than thirty novels and numerous short stories and screenplays. They were born in Ukraine, lived in Russia, and eventually settled in California. Their books have been translated into several foreign languages and awarded multiple literary and film prizes. Marina and Sergey are recipients of the Award for Best Authors (Eurocon 2005) and of the Science Fiction and Fantasy Rosetta Awards (2021).

ABOUT THE TRANSLATOR

Born in Moscow, Julia Meitov Hersey moved to Boston at the age of nineteen and has been straddling the two cultures ever since. She spends her days juggling a full-time job and her beloved translation projects. Julia is a recipient of the Science Fiction and Fantasy Rosetta Award for Best Translated Work, Long form (2021).